Arnulfo L. Oliveira Memorial Library

save me, joe louis

save me,

joe louis

madison smartt bell

harcourt
brace &
company

new york
san diego
london

Requests for permission to make copies of any part of
the work should be mailed to: Permissions Department,
Harcourt Brace & Company, 8th Floor, Orlando, Florida 32887.

The first chapter of this novel appeared in *Story*
(spring 1991) under the title "Cash Machine."

"The White Egret" by Kenneth Rosen used by permission.

"Down in the Valley to Pray," trad., arranged and adapted by
Doc Watson, copyright © 1967 Hillgreen Music (BMI).

"Soldier's Joy" by Jimmy Driftwood, copyright Warden
Music Co., Inc. 1957, renewed 1985. Used by permission.

Library of Congress Cataloging-in-Publication Data
Bell, Madison Smartt.
Save me, Joe Louis/Madison Smartt Bell. — 1st ed.
p.   cm.
ISBN 0-15-179432-4
1. Criminals — United States — Fiction.   I. Title.
PS3552.E517S28   1993
813'.54 — dc20   93-233

Designed by Camilla Filancia
Printed in the United States of America
First edition   A B C D E

For Cork and Jane

with love and thanks

The White Egret

In a marsh lake
a white egret
stares sideways

until a little fish
excites the swift dip
of its bitter lips

its beak. Its beak
breaks the lake
into a glitter now

less a mere morsel
of breath. Like flight
to make a word clear

a hand pauses
on a breast of air
and the egret rises

flies to blue pines
across the grave gold
marsh grass

to another lake.
Oh little white bird,
little fish

in every beginning
a sliver of silver,
a death and a hunger.

—Kenneth Rosen

save me, joe louis

She found the roll of film cleaning out the freezer, crooked behind a mound of ice trays frosted together, jumbled in with all the Unidentified Frozen Objects of the year so far. Like an archaeological expedition; *Christ, and I thought I was hungry*, she said to herself. She threw the foil-wrapped lumps away without bothering to discover what they had once been, and took another look at the roll. No label, no date to show when or where she'd shot it. Why she'd ever stuck it in the freezer, she had no better idea. She dropped it in her jacket pocket on her way to the door.

The school darkroom was empty, flushed out by midterm break. How she best liked it. The roll was still good, too. She didn't bother with contact prints, but made a rough selection squinting at the negatives as they dried, and printed them carefully, on eight-by-ten paper. The adjacent room, where the mats and mounting equipment were kept, had been given a thorough cleaning. The walls were high and as frosty white as the inside of the freezer itself. She paced nervously while the prints were drying and then stuck them on top of some others in a photo-paper box and went out with the whole thing under her arm.

It was gray and spluttering a dirty rain down the Philadelphia streets, though not especially cold. She walked to the car with her head ducked down, rain speckling the cord of her dark blond hair, which she'd gathered in a band at the nape of her neck for the darkroom. The car hacked and trembled a few times before it would catch and run. She handled the gear stick with a delicate fingertip's touch, negotiating the invisible mangled teeth of the transmission.

It was crowded in the section that was too small to really call a Chinatown. She had to overshoot the restaurant by three blocks before she found a parking place. The car shuddered and bucked as she backed it in; needed a clutch. She climbed out, clicked her key in the door lock, and stalked off, sheltering the box under her jacket from the rain, blinking as the wind whipped droplets into her eyes. Facing her one doorway from the corner was a huge striped neon sign that said BAR—nothing more than the one blunt word. It was the roll of film, she knew, that made her want to go in.

The interior was close and narrow, warm and smoky, flickering with the lights of the video games. She swung onto a stool near the door and ordered vodka on the rocks. On her empty stomach the first flush was instantaneous. In the haze of its afterglow she sat and sipped slowly, watching the rain drooling down the outside of the window glass. When she had emptied her glass she ordered another, and though she hadn't smoked in months she took change to buy a pack from the machine.

The depth of the bar was full of black men and whores, a few of these latter white. She felt eyes tracking as she walked back toward her stool, striking the end of the pack against the butt of her palm. In the dim of the mirror she saw one of them had fixed her with a gimlet stare; her hair was chemical silver, cakey holes of blue shadow for her eyes, but beyond all that she saw that the prostitute was probably even younger than she was herself. She lit a cigarette and focused the stream of smoke on her reflection in the mirror. Her own hair was a damp lump, she wore no makeup, her canvas jacket was rucked up shapelessly around her skinny shoulders. *No competition.* But the reflected stare hardened its hostility. She turned to meet the other girl direct, staring into those deep bruises she'd painted on her face. Nicotine raced in her blood like anger. She fixed the girl with her two-colored eye, whose iris streamed from green to brown. *Watch yourself,* she thought, *I'll hex*

2

you. The girl's stare broke, and Lacy turned back to the mirror, tipped her ash, and finished her vodka at a speed that suited her.

She'd been late even by the time she parked the car, so of course Marvin was already at the restaurant, wedged into one of the cramped two-person booths, screwing his fuzzy head around in circles, like an owl.

"Lacy," he called, loud enough to turn heads around the room. "You're late."

She picked her way through the tables toward him, wondering why she'd come at all. He was a small man, but hairy to make up for it. His belly had pushed the table forward, so she had to wedge her way into the booth. She laid the photo box on the cushion between the partition and her thigh. "Traffic was bad," she said. "Not that it isn't always."

Marvin looked at her, lips slightly parted, his mouth a wet, red opening in the beard. "Drink?" he said.

"Just tea," she said demurely, sucking the taste of vodka and smoke back across her tongue. A pot was already on the table; Marvin poured. She reached to the back of her head and undid the red rubber band and spread her damp hair across her shoulders. His eyes tightened on these movements. She remembered she had come for that. However slimy he might be in general, his eye was just. She looked down, flexing the rubber band around her fingers. A waiter rolled up a dim sum cart. Marvin took several of the little plates and ordered himself a beer.

"Here's to your trip," he said. A shrimp ball pinched in chopsticks hovered short of his lips, as if for a toast. "Bon voyage and all that. If you're really set on going."

Lacy found her chopsticks and got herself a dumpling. She drank some tea. "It's all for art," she said, purposely flip. "Don't you know?"

"*Ars longa, vita brevis est*." Marvin stopped eating and gave her another slow, wet look. "I think your accent's coming back."

3

"Anticipation," Lacy said, and laid the chopsticks on the edge of her plate.

Marvin leaned forward toward the chrome yellow corner of the box that showed on the seat beside her. He dropped his wistful tone. "So what have you got?" he said.

She lifted the box and set it on the table in the space he was just clearing. He cleaned his hands carefully on a red cloth napkin. With a fingernail Lacy caught the edges of the prints she'd made that morning and drew them away concealed in the box lid. Up-turned toward him was her most recent work, from a trip she'd made through Amish farmland and the depressed old mill towns up the Susquehanna River.

Handling each print by its outermost edges, Marvin looked and made his observations. Lacy pushed the rubber band into different looping shapes on the tabletop. When he had looked at all the prints he straightened the edges of the stack with his thumb and shifted to more general commentary. Like a blind spider, his other hand was creeping over her forearm. When the dim sum cart rolled back around she disengaged, reaching for a plate without quite looking at it: two deep-fried chicken feet in a viscous pool of soy.

"So what are you holding out?" Marvin's beard jutted toward the box top. She barely hesitated before handing it over; she wouldn't be trapped into playing coy. There was a school of student opinion that it was easiest to just sleep with Marvin a time or two and get it over with, though she didn't intend to take it quite so far.

He clucked, voice lifting with slight surprise. "Different camera."

"It's an old Agfa two-by-two," she said. "I picked it up in a junk shop. I haven't used it in a while, have to keep taping up the bellows."

Marvin kept turning over the prints. The images were square, faintly fuzzy at the edges, within the wide white borders of the glossy sheets. Most were different angles or shots of different sections of a rock-wall fence that bordered a hillside field and ran jumbling into trees and underbrush on the other side.

"Down home?" Marvin said in a "Hee Haw" accent.

"It's an old roll I found today," Lacy said, wondering how he would know. "Those walls are hand-laid fieldstone. People that put them there've been dead for a couple of hundred years . . ." She was prattling to distract him, she realized, and shut up. Marvin had already come to the pictures of the young man walking alongside the wall, sitting on the stones where a fallen tree had scattered them, twisting into the wind to light a cigarette. He was in civvies but his head had been recently shaved, a dark stubble just beginning to fur over the bony ridges and defiles of his pale skull. Hairless, he looked flop eared, but it wasn't a comic effect, even with his smile. The close-ups showed his jaw was long and his eyes set deep under brows like limestone ledges. His teeth were long and spaced a little apart like a dog's or a crocodile's.

"How about this guy," Marvin muttered, squinting at the last print in the set. "Who is it, anyway?"

"Macrae," Lacy said, and stretched the rubber band tight across her thumb and forefinger. "Just a cousin."

"Kissing cousins?" Marvin said. Malice shimmered in the accent he put on.

"A *distant* cousin." Lacy bit off the end of the phrase. She picked up the prints and returned them to the box and snapped the rubber band around it. Marvin was looking away from her now; perhaps he had flinched, but when his head swiveled back he laid the hand on her arm with open deliberation and spoke with a bogus avuncular sincerity.

"They've got stone walls around here too, you know," he said. "What makes you think this trip is such a good idea?"

"What makes you think it's not?" She lifted the band away from the box top, watching the rubber pale as it stretched, then let it twang back down.

"A false move," Marvin said mellifluously. His thumb stroked the soft skin of her inner forearm. "You'll regress. You're trying to go against the natural course of your development. You'll be losing time in the program, of course"—his tone shifting to piety. "And not to mention . . ."

He looked at her meltingly. Lacy held the gaze. By touch she found one of the chicken feet and hooked it into the mat of hair on his forward arm. At the light scrape of the claw he glanced down and then jerked back as if it was a tarantula. The chicken foot lifted and went corkscrewing across the room. Someone let out a terse grunt where it must have landed. Marvin exhaled a whistling breath.

"You tricked me," he said.

"It's a tricky situation," Lacy said primly. "Thanks for the lunch. And the advice, of course." She shifted to the edge of her seat and pulled the photo box toward her. After all, she hadn't eaten much, so the vodka was still alive in her belly, and the top of the box felt slightly warm too, like Macrae's eyes were burning through the cardboard.

hell's kitchen

Macrae and Charlie met each other in Battery Park by
finding out neither one of them had spare change. "Hey there,
friend," Charlie called out sharply, when he was still about ten
steps away, and Macrae chimed in with "Got a quarter . . . ?" like
he meant to join in the singing of some familiar tune. But they
both stopped there and circled each other like two strange dogs.
It was late, after ten at least, and turning cold, turning into the first
cold days of fall. The wind was blowing in off the bay in fits and starts;
the fits had a whiplash sting to them. There was nobody in the
park except for Charlie and Macrae and, thirty or forty yards from
them, a boy and girl standing against the pipe railing, twined around
each other like they thought they might be posing for a postcard.

Charlie stepped around Macrae, turning to put his back to the
wind, which reached over his shoulder and knocked Macrae's hair
up off his forehead. Thick, black, tangled hair, uncombed and uncut
for a long time. His big bony face was not bad looking, even with
his nose running slightly from the cold. He held the collar of his
raincoat shut with a blue-knuckled hand, stooping, letting the wind
bow the middle of his body backward. When the gust subsided, he
straightened back up. Charlie saw that he was young, youngish
anyway, probably not over thirty. His other hand held the raincoat
closed around his navel, where another button was missing. The
raincoat was pale and grubby and fell almost to his ankles and
Charlie thought he didn't have much on under it. Not that he was
a twirler or anything like that, he just appeared not to have enough
clothes for the weather.

"What about a dime, then?" Charlie said. "A nickel? Hell, you look like you hadn't got anything in your pocket but a hole."

"That's about the size of it," Macrae said. Not so long ago he himself had had a military sweater like the one Charlie was wearing, heavy olive drab wool with green cloth patches on the shoulders. Over it he wore one of those trick silvery jackets, no thicker than a sheet of paper, that were supposed to be magic for holding the heat. Macrae was wondering if the jacket worked as well as it was cracked up to.

"Yeah, I'm in about the same shape," Charlie said. "The question is, what are we planning to do about this situation?"

Macrae lifted his shoulders and let them fall. Charlie laid one finger on the side of his nose and looked over at the couple that was standing beside the rail. The boy's hand held the girl's hair flattened into the curve of the nape of her neck. She drew herself up inside his jacket, which he'd opened to let her in.

"They aren't going to give you anything," Macrae said.

"Look at that jacket," Charlie said. "That's two, three hundred dollars right there, a nice leather jacket like that. You can't tell me he don't have a quarter."

The girl's arms were snugged away up under the skirts of the jacket; Macrae saw her turn her head to the side and lay her cheek flat against the boy's breastbone. The wind flared and Macrae's eyes began to tear. He ducked away, flipping up his collar, feeling the thread of another loose button twist over his thumb.

"He's not thinking about giving it to you."

"He's not thinking at all," Charlie said. "Did, he wouldn't be out here at this time of night. This park gets dangerous, this late." He started moving toward the couple, feet slapping down loudly, shoulders square, nothing like a panhandler's usual apologetic shuffle. Of course there were some who traded on boldness, but Macrae had never mastered this method because the whole process of panhandling left him rigid and miserable with shame.

"Hurry up," Charlie said over his shoulder. "Don't want to get left, do you?"

Macrae's knees bent under him and he was following, not really meaning to. He had no real interest in seeing the other man fail. Charlie put his hand on the railing and sidled toward the couple, the pipe just grazing the web of skin between his thumb and forefinger. His right hand was in the pocket of the silver jacket.

"Excuse me," Charlie said. "We're in need of a little money, me and my friend."

The boy's head came languidly up. His hair was moussed and teased forward into a little flip over his brow. Macrae would have taken him for almost his own age except that the self-satisfied blankness of his expression made him look younger.

"Sorry," he said. "I don't have it tonight."

"You don't understand," Charlie said.

"Hey, look, man, I already told you—" The boy lifted his hands, palms wide, and the girl rolled out from under his arm and stood a space away from him, still connected by one finger hooked in the waistband of his jeans.

"I'm not asking you," Charlie said, and reached across and grabbed the boy's wrist with his left hand and yanked him sharply around and crowded him over with his belly against the railing. The girl's finger came loose from his jeans and she stood holding her arm extended, like there was still something to support it, while Charlie's right hand, through his jacket pocket, gouged into the boy's kidney.

"I'm telling you," Charlie said. He pushed harder, and the boy doubled over the railing, the flip of moussed hair reaching down toward the muted gleam of water below the embankment.

"Feel that?" Charlie said. "Do you? I'd blow a hole in you." With a quick turn and jerk, he pointed the mound in his pocket toward the girl. Light flickered off the silver crinkles in the fabric.

"Don't *you* move," he said. "And shut that mouth, why don't you?"

Macrae watched the girl. Gradually her arm settled to her side from the position in the air where it had been left. Her mouth was very small and cherry red and the lips were slightly parted. She was tipped forward onto the balls of her feet, quick frozen there. *You look like I feel,* Macrae thought. Charlie was thumbing the boy's wallet open.

"Twenty bucks?" he said. He held the wallet up by one corner, like a rotten dead thing, and a plastic card carrier unfolded from it and hung.

"Keep those legs apart," Charlie said. "Put your weight on that rail, son." He twisted to turn the dangle of cards under the streetlight. "New Jersey license," he said. "Don't you bring more money when you come to Manhattan?"

The boy didn't answer. He kept his face turned away from the light.

"Cheap date, huh?" Charlie said. "Going Dutch, maybe? Better have a look at that purse. And you, let's see you turn out your pockets."

A key ring fell on the pavement by the boy's left foot. Macrae was looking at his shoe, two-tone suede with a crepe sole. A handful of coins came jangling down and Charlie swept them over the edge with the side of his foot. A couple of *plunks* returned from the water.

"I want that folding money," Charlie said. "Come on now, where's that purse?"

Charlie was talking to him, Macrae realized. The wind hit him hard when he moved nearer the girl, but he didn't really feel it; the cold spot was spreading inside him now, from the root of his backbone all through his stomach. The girl wore a tiny fringed disco purse on a strap of rolled leather passed over her shoulder and neck. The strap hung on something when Macrae tried to lift it off, and the girl helped him, stooping to disengage. He passed the purse to Charlie and remained standing with one leg behind the girl, covering her unconsciously, like a guard in a basketball game.

Charlie shook the purse out into his palm: a Chapstick, breath mints, a couple of tissues, a tightly folded ten-dollar bill he tucked into his pocket.

"You all can barely afford the tolls," Charlie said. He detached the card carrier from the wallet and began running it through his hands like a scroll. "Oh, I get it. New York University . . . You didn't get your license changed over. Are you a scofflaw, kid?"

"You don't have to if you're a student," the boy said.

"What?" said Charlie, pulling a card loose from the plastic and letting the folder fall.

"If you're a student you don't have to," the boy repeated. It was the first thing he had said since Charlie'd grabbed him. "I don't drive in the city anyway."

"I'm sure that's very wise of you," Charlie said. "Wise and prudent. Keep doing that way and you'll live a long time." He held up the card he had selected, the blue-and-white arrow of Citibank.

"And now we're going to go to the cash machine," Charlie said. "Listen."

The importance of his tone made Macrae lean forward. The wind blew in his face, and he thought he could smell the girl—not perfume, but a warm, clean smell. Something like talcum powder.

"You probably think I'm a real bad guy," Charlie said. "I'm a teddy bear next to my friend here." Over the girl's shoulder he winked at Macrae. "Not that it's his fault or anything, he's just not right in the head. I try my best to take care of him, you know. I have to pretty well keep him away from the women, especially. He's got unnatural tastes that way. Not the same as the rest of us are. I don't even think about that part if I can help it. If I do I get bad dreams."

The girl made a startled movement and brushed against Macrae. His hand slipped down the sleeve of her sweater and closed on her wrist, the touch of her skin striking him with the force of an electric shock. He heard her smother a gasp, and he loosened his grip, curving his fingers over her rigid arm like a bracelet.

"I know we don't want to get into that." Charlie's voice was almost singsong. "No, we don't want to go that road . . . Let's us just go to the bank and take out a little bit of money. And let's make sure nothing happens to bother my friend or get him excited. Come on, now . . ."

The boy turned tentatively away from the railing and looked at Macrae, and then looked at Charlie.

"It'll be all right," Charlie said gently. "You can go on and pick up your stuff."

The boy hunkered down. His hands crawled over the pavement, groping after the wallet and cards and keys. Bits of glass embedded in the asphalt sparkled between his fingers as they moved. He wasn't watching what he was doing. His eyes cut back and forth between Macrae and Charlie, but apart from that, his face had the same vacant pout as before.

"We're set," Charlie said. He climbed a wide set of steps and headed across the grass, away from the water and back toward the street, guiding the boy a half pace ahead of him. Macrae followed and the girl came easily along with him. He left her wrist loose in the ring of his thumb and forefinger. Each small accidental touch of her jolted him. They passed a mound of cannonballs and a flagpole and a squat, low monument on which an Indian and a Dutchman were sculpted in relief. When they reached the edge of the park, Charlie turned back.

"Let her have the purse back, you look silly with it," Charlie said. "And don't hold her that way. Be nice, hold her hand."

That reminded Macrae of something, he couldn't think what. The Wall Street area was deserted, though brighter than the park had been, and quiet except for the gasping and murmuring of machinery inside the buildings. Macrae could hear the buildings breathing like big iron lungs. The girl's hand was cool and small in his and in the glow of the gated shop windows he could see her more plainly, though he didn't like to look at her straight on. A couple of body lengths ahead, Charlie was walking a half step behind the boy, his hand in the silver pocket floating at the small of his back.

"Where's the closest branch?" Charlie said.

"I don't know," the boy said.

"Don't give me that," Charlie said, gouging the boy in the kidney with whatever he held in his pocketed hand.

"I *don't* know," the boy said, as he sucked in a sharp breath. "We came down on the subway. You think I hang out down here?"

"I don't think about where you hang out," Charlie said. "Which way?" They had come to a corner, and Charlie turned left without waiting to be told. In tiny sidelong glances Macrae examined the girl. She kept her face aimed straight ahead, so he saw her profile against the display windows. It was a natural prettiness; she wore no makeup, or almost none. Her hair was blond with darker currents streaking it, thick and straight, falling just to the join of her neck and shoulders and turning under there. She wore a V-neck sweater of very soft wool and under it a white blouse with a little round collar. Every so often she caught her lower lip in her top teeth and then let it plump free. A nervous habit. Her pleated pants fit her loosely around the hips and nipped in at the waist and at her ankles, above the little white socks, turned over, and the black high-heel shoes. It impressed Macrae how easily she knew how to walk on shoes like that. She was a head and half shorter than he was but she matched his pace without difficulty.

"There it is," Charlie said. They had reached another corner, and off to the left was the blue-and-white awning of Citibank. Macrae could see the silhouettes of all four of them on the glass as they waited for the door to buzz open after Charlie stuck in the card. Inside, he waited with the girl several paces back from the machine, as though they were standing in line. She raised her head and smoothed back her bangs with her free hand and then looked down at the floor where she had been looking before.

Charlie dipped the card into the machine and stood aside so the boy could reach the keypad. "I don't want to see it say it don't recognize your number," he said. "Or there'll be some atrocities take place. Right here and now, do you understand?"

The boy punched on the keypad and waited and punched

another button and waited some more. Macrae raised his eyes and met the winking red light of a video camera high in the corner of the cubicle. His hands clenched involuntarily and he felt the girl flinch in response. Twisting away from the camera, he saw her eyes for a second, pale green, but she didn't hold the look. He stood with his head lowered, as hers was. Charlie slapped the boy once across the face, not hard; it was a gesture. Macrae peered up through a lacing of his fingers and saw the light on the camera blink a time or two more and then go out.

"Don't give me that," Charlie said. "Are you trying to pull some trick?"

"It's out of cash," the boy said sullenly. "*I* can't help it. Sometimes they run out. Weekends especially."

"We'll find another one," Charlie said.

At the door he turned back and grabbed a brochure that told the locations of the different bank machines. He walked along behind the boy, frowning down at the paper, then folded it and tucked it into his hip pocket. At the next corner he turned right and Macrae went after him, leading the girl. Two doors down a Blimpy was open and Macrae saw a car pull to the curb in front of it and saw the driver open the door and hoist a leg onto the sidewalk. It was a police car. Macrae's heart stopped with a slam, and he stopped breathing, but he kept on walking at the same rate. It was like an experiment with a dead frog and a battery . . . and there again he was reminded of he-couldn't-think-what. The cop heaved himself out of the car, kicked the door to, and gave them an incurious glance, hitching up his belt with a grunt as they passed. From behind him, Macrae heard the cop's belt radio cough and sputter: "Bank Street and *cszk-cszk-cszk* . . ." Unable to stop himself from looking back once, he saw the cop going into the Blimpy.

"We'll take a cab," Charlie said. They had come out of a narrow street onto Broadway, where there was a steady stream of traffic in both directions, though still nobody on the sidewalk. "Taxi!" Charlie called, throwing up his arm. A Checker cab swung to the curb immediately. Charlie and Macrae sandwiched the boy and girl into the middle of the bench seat.

Macrae was embarrassed because his palms were sweating after the cop. He pulled his hand loose from the girl's and rubbed it dry on the knee of his pants. Charlie said an address on Franklin Street and the cab turned to the left. The driver was black and wore a peculiar colored hat and was listening to a foreign-language station Macrae didn't recognize—not Spanish, anyway. He took the girl by the hand again and then realized he didn't need to—neither one of them could go anywhere, squeezed in like they were. Her leg was pressed against him and he could feel her temperature through the two layers of cloth. The veins at his temples were thumping hard enough to start a headache, and he slipped his hand up to her wrist, touching the soft cuff of the sweater again and then turning the ball of his thumb into the warm declivity beside her tendons to find her pulse, which seemed as fast and hard as his. When he concentrated on slowing the beat he thought he could feel her pulse slow also. Then it occurred to him that he was forcing her by touching her this way, and he let go.

The cab made another turn and stopped. Charlie got out and leaned in the driver's window.

"We won't be a minute," he said.

Macrae watched him and the boy mount steps on the far side of the street. From between two swollen concrete columns another blue-and-white awning thrust out.

A song ended on the radio and when some talk began the driver reached to lower the volume and then lit a cigarette. The smoke mixed poorly with a cloying deodorant stench that came from a cardboard cutout in the shape of a pine tree, hanging amid a cluster of wooden beads from the rearview mirror. Macrae lowered his window for air, then snapped his fingers loudly.

"I've got it," he said, turning to the girl. "There was this girl in grade school—the teacher used to make us hold hands together. Because we always used to fight, see? I mean, knock down, drag out, right down there on the floor . . . Then the teacher would make us sit together and hold hands for I don't know how long, an hour. It seemed like forever. I bet she didn't like it any better than I did." He laughed. "She was a hair puller. I remember her but I can't call her name."

The girl shifted slightly on the seat, taking her leg away from his. She was squeezing both her hands tight between her legs.

"Please," she said, with a catch in her breath. "Please." She didn't say more.

My lord, Macrae thought, *was that the kind of stuff that a sex maniac would say?* He didn't know. Probably she didn't know either, he thought.

"It's all right," he said.

The girl breathed in little halting gasps.

"What's your name?" he said. It was a dumb thing to say in front of the cabbie, but Macrae didn't think the cabbie was listening anyway. The girl wouldn't answer or look at him. Macrae felt as foolishly exposed as if he had told her his own real name. He lifted her hand out of her lap and stroked the back of it with a gentle rhythm he might have used to soothe a frightened animal, understanding that this wasn't right either and that there was nothing he could do that would be right.

Charlie came out of the bank with the boy's leather jacket folded over his arm and bent down to Macrae's open window.

"Okay if we just drop you all off right here?" he said, and then, when Macrae kept looking blankly up at him, "Come on, give her a hand out."

Macrae opened the door and got out of the cab, drawing the girl along the seat after him. She put some weight on his arm, lifting herself. Macrae couldn't have said just why that pleased him. He let go her hand and Charlie gave the leather jacket to him.

"Here, try this on for size."

Macrae looked at the jacket's fake fur collar, then up at the boy, who was standing on the curb with girl beside him now, but not near enough to touch. There was heavy stitching on the shoulders of the jacket where he held it and the leather was smooth and unbending under his fingers.

"I wouldn't want to take your coat," Macrae said. "You have it." He pushed the jacket against the boy's chest and held it there until the boy folded his forearm over it. Then he stepped off the sidewalk and got back into the cab. Charlie was leaning forward across the front seat.

"Canal Street," he said. "Canal and West Broadway, around there." He leaned back against the seat cushion. "You jackass," he said.

Macrae untwisted himself from where he'd screwed himself around to look through the back glass at the boy and girl, who still were standing a little apart on the sidewalk where they'd been left. He thought they might have got the license number, but then it was only a couple of minutes to Canal Street.

"Who're you calling jackass?" he said.

Charlie flipped his hand over, glancing at the cab driver. "It'll keep," he said.

"He don't speak English good," Macrae said.

Charlie shrugged. "You never know." Both his hands were folded over his knees. The silver jacket hung flaccidly against his side, and Macrae let his arm drop, brushing along the near pocket. Charlie grunted and moved a little away to make room. Macrae fidgeted at his raincoat collar and the loose button came off in his hand.

"I was wondering . . . ," he said.

"Wondering what?"

Macrae took a pinch of Charlie's jacket pocket, feeling the two layers of fabric slip against each other between his thumb and forefinger. The plastic zipper touched the edge of his palm.

"If these jackets keep a body warm like they claim."

"They do all right," Charlie said. "I wouldn't say they quite lived up to the advertising." He snorted. "You had your hand on a whole lot better one back yonder."

The cab driver stopped at a red light and looked back at the two of them over his shoulder.

"Yeah, this'll do," Charlie said. He got out and paid through the window and the cab made a right turn onto the empty street. All the storefronts were dark except for Three Roses, where music spilled out the door with the light and a couple of black men were shoving each other on the sidewalk in front of the beer sign. Macrae saw that Charlie was looking that way too.

"We better not stay in this area," Macrae said.

"I think not," Charlie said. He led the way across Canal Street to the green balls of the subway. Down the hole, he bought ten tokens and passed a handful to Macrae, who followed him through the turnstile. It was warmer in the tunnel than it had been on the street but the change of temperature somehow made him shiver. He wiped his nose with the back of his hand.

"Cold, are you?" Charlie leaned out and spat toward the third rail.

"I wouldn't have taken his jacket off of him," Macrae said, and paused. "I don't much care for you calling me a jackass either."

Charlie looked at him, and now Macrae noticed that he had to look up. He had faded red hair cut close to his head and white eyebrows and pale, strange eyes. Though he might have weighed the same as Macrae he wasn't much taller than the girl had been.

"I take it back," Charlie said. "You don't want to get sentimental about a thing like that, though . . ."

Macrae turned the tokens over in his pocket. There was a disk of a different feel and he pulled it out and looked at it: the button, cream-colored plastic with a brown swirl, like fudge-ripple ice cream. He put it back in another pocket.

Charlie spat in a high arc and hit the third rail with a sizzle. He said something Macrae didn't catch over the roar of the train pulling in. They got on and stood holding the poles, though the car was empty except for one wino stretched out on a bench.

"Well, but you cleaned out his bank account, didn't you?" Macrae said.

"Is that what you think?" Charlie said. "Machines don't let you take but four hundred dollars in one day."

"That's what we got?"

"We who, paleface?"

Macrae looked at him.

"Easy," Charlie said. "I was just funning you." He sat down on a bench under the subway map. Macrae sat down next to him. The wino had opened his mouth and begun to snore. Macrae could smell the mingling of his inner and outer effluvia all the way from the other end of the car.

"Let's divvy," he said.

"Here?"

"Where else?" Macrae said.

Charlie pulled a roll of twenties from his pants pocket and ran his thumb along it, counting by the edges, and passed a portion to Macrae, who began to count it out. The conductor walked through the car, swinging a brass key chain, and Macrae covered the money on his knee and looked aimlessly about him. Directly across from him was an ad for hemorrhoid cream in Spanish. He found he could make out most of the words. The conductor went out and Macrae counted the bills over again. Ten.

"You got some out of their pockets, too," he said.

"Don't miss a trick, do you?" Charlie said. "What about that cab fare?"

"It wasn't no thirty dollars' worth," Macrae said.

"How much you think that coat you give him back would go for?" Charlie said. "Seems to me I'm being mighty generous—" He looked at Macrae. "Don't get excited," he said. "I'll buy you a drink."

The train stopped and Macrae followed Charlie out and up the stairs to Forty-second Street, the corner across from Port Authority. A beat policeman took a look at them as they came out, but Macrae was no longer much impressed. Charlie was walking like he had a destination and humming in time to his steps as he went. Macrae went after him across Eighth Avenue.

"Living it up, living it up, oh yeah . . . ," said Charlie. "Friday night . . ."

"It's Saturday," Macrae said.

Charlie raised his eyebrows. "So it is," he said, and turned and walked up Ninth. A tall black woman in red vinyl hotpants reached for him as he went by and then she turned to Macrae.

"Going out?" She had a big puff of straightened hair and white eye shadow and white polish on her nails. Macrae's left leg veered toward her but he corrected it and went on after Charlie.

At the next corner Charlie turned into a railroad bar; Macrae didn't take in the sign. A row of steam tables was next to the door and when he smelled the food he thought for an instant he was going to faint. But at the counter, a young Irishman in a white apron had already set up drinks for Charlie without being asked. A shot of bourbon and a draft beer. The bartender said something in an accent so thick Macrae couldn't understand it.

"What'll you have?" Charlie said.

"Same," said Macrae.

The bartender reached back to the shelf behind him.

"They know you," Macrae said.

"More or less," Charlie said. "They don't know my name."

"What is your name?" Macrae said.

"Charlie," Charlie said. He pushed a bill across the counter as the bartender set down Macrae's drinks. "You?"

"Macrae."

"First or last?"

"It'll do either way."

"However you want it," Charlie said. "You sound like you're from down home somewhere."

"Tennessee," Macrae said. "You?"

"South Carolina." Charlie turned toward the bartender. "Throw me a pack of Lucky, will you?"

"You hadn't got much accent," Macrae said. He threw down his shot. It rolled in his shrunken stomach like an orange ball of fire.

Charlie shrugged. "I travel around a good deal," he said. He lit a cigarette and suddenly reached around to thump Macrae on the back.

"Homeboy!" he said.

"Is that something white people say?"

"Do I look white enough to you?" Charlie said. He tapped the pack and a cigarette poked itself out. Macrae took it and picked up the pack of matches from the bar and lit it. The second deep drag dizzied him. He hadn't had a smoke all day.

"Whoa, there," Charlie said. "Steady, sailor. Just a minute, I'll be back."

Macrae's elbows had slipped forward on the counter and the side of his head was on the damp varnished wood. From here he could see how the bar ran away a long distance into the building, and two-thirds of the way back, stairs climbed up to an upper level with some rickety tables scattered behind a railing. The long perspective began to spin, but he couldn't seem to move his head. Instead he shortened his focus, with an effort, and looked at the twin ripples of smoke rising off the cigarette in his numbed hand.

When Charlie came back and put a plate down beside him he pushed himself upright. Cabbage and potatoes and a sandwich on a kaiser roll. Macrae attacked the sandwich so hard he bit through the corned beef into his lip. He swallowed the blood along with the food. Both tasted good to him.

"Don't strangle," Charlie said. He had brought a plate of his own but had stopped eating to watch Macrae.

"Full of advice, aren't you?" Macrae said. He put the remains of the sandwich on the edge of his plate and took a desultory forkful of potatoes. "I believe you're the crazy one. You never had any gun or knife in that pocket, did you?"

Charlie turned toward the mirror and laughed at his reflection.

"You'd be laughing out the other side of your mouth if we were sitting in jail right now," Macrae said, and took a bite of cabbage. He felt better, his head was clear.

"Two white boys in an unarmed robbery?" Charlie said. "We'd

of been out in fifteen minutes. Didn't they just about offer to give us the money?"

"All them things you told that girl about me? And you never even knew my name."

"I doubt she would have married you anyway," Charlie said. He took a drink and Macrae looked at his hand on the beer glass. There were small shiny scars on the backs of his fingers, between the knuckles and second joints, symmetrically placed as if by design. Macrae emptied his own glass and pushed it and the shot glass onto the lip of the counter for the bartender to refill. He remembered the small points of the girl's teeth whitening her lower lip as they dragged across it, and he felt that he had not come to the end of all she reminded him of; the notion made him a little uneasy.

"They had cameras in those banks," he said. "Cops could have been all over us in a minute."

"Do I hear you complaining?" said Charlie. "You got money in your pocket, a drink in your hand . . . Food on the plate—when was the last time you had some of that?"

Macrae looked away from him. He saw his own bluish face in the mirror. There were shadows under his cheekbones and in the dim lighting he could see only hollows for his eyes.

"Still," he muttered. "We ought not to try it that way again."

"All right," Charlie said, and touched him on the shoulder. "But don't worry about it. Ain't nobody watches those cameras." He lit another cigarette and blew smoke toward the mirror where both their faces were together. "Ain't nobody cares that much what you do."

two

The dirty white cue balls were gathering in a metal trough, fed one at a time from a chute above. Four, five, six, seven—each fell with a deep ringing sound. When the eighth had dropped, the trough overbalanced on its hinge and dumped them all. They raced around an S-curved track and passed through a trapdoor that sounded a different bell each time it gated one of them, and then into an elevator that towed them to the top again. All through the rest of the big machine other balls were spinning and traveling, falling and rising, and every movement rang a different chime. Macrae liked to think of it as a perpetual-motion machine, though he knew better. He had spent hours on end staring at it in the days before he met Charlie.

Balls re-collected in the metal trough. Macrae rocked to one side, automatically checking the faint reflection in the glass case to be sure that no one was too near behind him. Through the two glass layers of the case he could see across the dim brick floor of the bus station to a bank of phones where the hustlers hovered over legitimate dialers, trying to make out the pattern of tones that composed a credit card calling number. It was a lame hustle, if you asked Macrae. Reaching his hand into his right pants pocket, he touched three keys on a ring and smiled to himself. The shadow of his reflection on the glass remained unchanged.

Macrae shrugged and went out onto Eighth Avenue and stopped at the corner of Forty-second Street. It was late afternoon and the light had turned blue. Cold cloud had shelved in close on the tops of the buildings, sealing the streets into tight, narrow tubes, through which the cars and people interminably shuttled. In his days of staring and musing, before Charlie, Macrae had understood that the big machine was made to describe for him no other thing than this. But now it didn't worry him. He looked up. The sagging belly of the sky was the vague no-color that meant snow, though Macrae knew it might not fall. It was rush hour and the westbound traffic shimmied haltingly toward the tunnel. Macrae started walking across Forty-second Street in the opposite direction.

He was cheerful and so everything interested him, it didn't much matter what. He loitered along the storefronts, keeping out of the flow of hard-pressed pedestrians, most going the opposite way from him. At a narrow shop he stopped to admire the weapons hanging behind the gate, mace sprays, tear-gas guns, a thicket of long knives, and then the Oriental section, with nunchuks and *kubotan* and multipointed stars for throwing. He moved on idly, under the theater awnings. Kung Fu or porn was what they all showed. Macrae studied the posters indiscriminately, ripped muscles and overinflated breasts. He passed to an electronic discounter and stopped to look over the rising ranks of music boxes and cameras, with interest but no particular desire, turning coins over in one of his pockets and the ring of keys in the other. His hands were warm in the cloth against his legs.

A barker from the strip bar next door started braying at him, and Macrae walked around him, then hesitated before a display case. The barker kept after him, talking to his back, trying to bully him inside. Macrae stared at a clumsily painted picture of a topless woman on a piece of posterboard sagging damply in the case.

"Best five dollars you ever spent . . . ," the barker said. Macrae shifted position to block the reflection on the glass. Beneath it, the invitation of the woman's smile was twisted by the warp of the cardboard. Dry paint was cracking from her lip. Macrae turned around toward the barker.

"What would you give for that?"

"For that?" the barker said. "Nothing."

"Well somebody must have paid somebody something for it," Macrae said.

"What if they did?" the barker said. He was confused. Macrae had made him think that he was crazy, which was okay with Macrae. The barker faced out into the street again, calling louder, trying to catch somebody's eye. Macrae looked back at the cardboard woman slumping in the case. He had seen tattoos that were more convincing than she was. He thought he could do better himself without half trying. This woman had been executed without understanding—it was an outline without a body inside. At the same time her chrome yellow blondness reminded him of someone she was not.

"Wouldn't you rather have a little live action?"

It was a woman's voice, and Macrae turned quickly and looked down, because she was small, so small it was almost weird, she barely reached up to his rib cage. She wore red tights under a leopard-spotted shorts suit. The cuffs of the shorts were rolled tight into her crotch and the top was unzipped to the ends of her breasts. Macrae saw her lemon skin was paling in the cold.

"Why, are you?" he said. The girl pushed an olive beret back on her hair and cocked her head at him. Almost a glare. Over the top of her beret Macrae saw two more cops carried along in the crowd's current toward them, swinging their nightsticks and talking to each other. The girl twisted around and saw them too.

"Walk with me?" she said, and without waiting she uncrossed her ankles and started off toward Seventh Avenue. Macrae noticed that the beret had a little beaded tail that flopped in her hair, which was dark, with dyed yellow streaks, and ran in permed wavelets over her shoulder blades to the small of her back.

He caught up with her in one long stride. She was an energetic walker but she needed to take three steps to his one. Her face was a little long, but pretty and unlined, with high Indian cheekbones and a small pert nose.

"Like it?" she said.

"Sure," Macrae said. "How old did you say you were?"

"Nobody asks me that," she said. "Do you want to go to the hotel?"

"I don't think . . . ," Macrae said.

"What don't you think?"

"I don't think I want to go to the hotel," Macrae said.

"Doesn't cost much," the girl said, taking one-two-three steps to keep pace with him. "I'll leave you happy."

"I might buy you a beer," Macrae said. "If you're old enough to drink, that is."

The girl's heels clicked to an irritable stop. "You're a waste of my time, big fella," she said, and reversed herself, stalking off the other way. Macrae paused to watch her go until she slowed into a stroll, rolling her hips up and showing her red legs. She had long legs for such a little girl, he thought. He pictured that poster again for a second, but the memory behind it had fallen away, and he was relieved, but without knowing why.

He went into a drugstore and bought a pack of cigarettes and a pad and a pencil, the fat roly-poly kind of pencil little children use in school. In the shelter of the doorway he lit a cigarette and then went out into Times Square. The wind came up as he turned the corner and though the cold was blunted by the moisture hanging in the air above, Macrae turned his coat collar up. The feel of the navy serge against his cheek made him smile again. He had bought a heavy pea coat secondhand on Canal Street, and he was happy with the deal. Charlie had taken the ratty old raincoat from him and dropped it over a bum they'd passed sleeping on the street. So much for that.

Head tucked against the wind, he walked up the concrete triangle, past the ticket booth, and stopped on the curb by the recruiting station. It didn't bother him anymore to be so near it, though a few weeks back he wouldn't even have set foot on the block. But that was a superstitious attitude. Macrae dropped his cigarette and then kicked it into a subway grating and leaned over slightly to watch the sparks go showering away into the dark. There was still an invisible filament that connected him to the recruiter and the station and to everything behind it all, but so long as no one knew of it but Macrae it had no power over him. He tapped the pad and pencil in the pea-coat pocket and thought of the teenage hooker he'd been talking to. Then he saw her coming toward him on the crosswalk from the west side of the avenue.

"Hey, pretty," Macrae said.

"Yeah, and I'm for sale," the girl said. "What you gonna do about it?"

Macrae shrugged.

"You're following me," the girl said.

"Nah," Macrae said. "You're just walking in circles."

"Why don't you want to go to the hotel?" The girl stamped her right foot on the pavement. There was something childish in that.

"You wouldn't enjoy it," Macrae said.

"You're nasty," the girl said.

"I don't mean to be." Macrae shook a cigarette out of the pack and held it toward her. She used her lips to take it from his hand. Macrae flicked a light and she drew in.

"What's your name?" Macrae said.

"Bea." The girl rolled the cigarette between her thumb and forefinger and looked down on it as if the name were written there.

"What's that?"

"Bay-*yah!*" the girl said, drawing out the vowels.

"I like it," Macrae said. Across the street, the light flashed WALK. "Okay, Bea, see you around."

At the far corner he looked back, but she must have already gone behind a building. He walked across Forty-fifth Street, passing Eighth Avenue again. It was starting to get dark. The sky had settled onto the building tops and was bulging down toward the street. Across Ninth Avenue, halfway down the block, Macrae walked up the steps of a tenement, slapping the rail with his palm just to see it rock on the loose bolts. He opened the steel-plated door with a key from his pocket and pushed it in. Rafael was holding out a fresh-lit joint toward him from where he sat on the radiator.

"Hey, cat-daddy," Macrae said. "You been sitting there all day?"

Rafael looked at him with a peculiar fixed expression, cheeks drawn in and lips pressed tight. Macrae pulled the joint from his fingers and took a cautious hit. Rafael opened his mouth for a long exhalation. Only a shadow of smoke emerged.

"Waste not, want not," Macrae said, and breathed out himself. He unrolled the end of the joint and looked at it and then retightened it. "Green as the grass," he said.

"It's Hawaiian." Rafael ran his hand over the oily wing of his hair to the point where a red rubber band cinched it tight into the base of his head. With his other hand he accepted the joint from Macrae and sucked. When he tried to pass it back Macrae shook his head at it.

"Ahhhhh," Rafael said, exhaling, rolling his red-rimmed eyes at Macrae. "What's the matter?"

"Two is two too many," Macrae said. "This is some more of your creeper weed, I expect. Let's wait and see."

Rafael shrugged and wet two fingers and pinched the head of the joint out. He slipped it under the cellophane of a pack of Camels and drew out a cigarette and lit it. Macrae turned to the little square window and looked out through the pattern of wire checks. His breath fogged on the pane and he wiped it away.

"Hey," he said suddenly, and snatched the door open and ran out. Rafael followed him sluggishly onto the stoop.

Macrae was standing down on the sidewalk, head craned back and one finger pointing up.

"What's the matter," Rafael muttered.

"Nothing," Macrae said. "Snow." Snow was coming down in long spiraling trains from the colorless sky. The flakes dampened and vanished when they touched his upturned face. The patterns were concrete but changed too fast for him to completely grasp them.

"Yeah, it's snow," Rafael said.

Macrae brought his head upright and rubbed at the back of his neck with one hand. "First snow," he said.

"It doan do this in Santo Domingo," Rafael said.

"You never saw snow till you came here?" The snow was wetting Macrae's hair. He pulled the plastic bag loose from the pad and pencil and stretched and knotted it over his head.

"Just rain," Rafael said. "Big rain, though. Hot where you come from too, right?"

"Oh, we get snow," Macrae said. "We get all the winter you want." He closed his eyes for just a second. On the palm of his hand he could feel the snow coming thicker and faster. When he opened his eyes he saw it had begun to stick on the sidewalk. On the other side of the street, a small figure was coming along in the shadows where the streetlights didn't work. When she passed into the light of the entryway opposite, Macrae saw that it was Bea.

"*¡Hola!*" Rafael called from above him. Bea glanced over and saw Macrae and tossed her head and walked on. There was enough snow on the ground now for her to leave footprints behind.

"You know her?" Macrae said.

Rafael snapped his cigarette over the loose railing toward the middle of the street. "Yeah, she go to my school. Did go."

"She don't look old enough to be out."

"She took herself out," Rafael said. "This city no good for women, man." He walked back in through the open door and sat down on the radiator.

Macrae climbed back up the steps and looked back over his shoulder. The snow was already filling in the faint trail Bea's feet had left. A little stoned now, he thought of the cue balls in the big machine, how they would scatter and reconnect.

"Come in or go out," Rafael said. "Kick that door shut, okay?"

Macrae stepped over the sill and slammed the door with the back of his heel. He scuffed his foot at a puddle on the cracked tile.

"I watched her walk around about an hour," he said. "Don't look like she's doing no good."

"Too early," Rafael shivered all over, then wiped his nose with his fingers. "But she got a mean old man, what it is."

"Oh," Macrae said. "Well. You plan on staying down here awhile?"

"I guess so," Rafael said.

"Dig you later," Macrae said, and began to climb the narrow stairs. The wall was painted dung brown to waist height and then a soiled cream to the ceiling. At the first landing a lacy graffito declared *Chinga Su Madre*. On the second landing lay a crack vial and Macrae turned and punted it down; it rebounded off the lower wall and tinkled down the steps into the entryway. Macrae heard Rafael snicker as it fell. He went up four more flights of stairs to the apartment.

The front room was empty except for Charlie, barefoot and bare chested, down on the floor in a push-up position.

"I said *down,* you maggot," Macrae said pleasantly.

Charlie peered up at him, his chin a quarter inch from the bare floor. "If it ain't Aunt Jemima," he said.

Macrae tore the bag from his head, balled it, and pitched it in a corner of the room. Charlie pushed up and went down and held.

"You expect me to pick up after you?" he said.

"No," Macrae said. "Would it help any if I stood on the back of your neck?"

"Don't you want to do a set?" Charlie said.

"No, I don't," Macrae said. "That's one thing I told myself when I went over the hill—ain't nobody going to make me do another push-up."

Charlie pushed up and went down again. "You'll make yourself, before you're through," he said, through gritted teeth. "Just wait till you get old."

"What's old?" Macrae said. "Keep your back straight, you spineless maggot."

Charlie did ten more push-ups fast and sat back on his heels, gasping. Sweat ran down his neck into the hollows of his collarbones and down his scrawny stomach through the yellowed hair around his navel.

"How old are you, anyway?" Macrae said.

"Forty-some," Charlie said. "I expect I could be your daddy."

"No, you couldn't," Macrae said. "That part's already taken." He walked into the kitchen, which was also unfurnished except for a couple of folding chairs and a card table pushed up under the window, took a beer out of the refrigerator, and popped off the cap under the knob of a drawer. The cap clicked on the linoleum and rolled to a stop under the radiator.

"Were you raised in a barn?" Charlie said.

"Pretty near." Macrae sat down and put the pad and pencil on the table. He shrugged his pea coat off onto the chair back. "We hadn't got no pencil sharpener, do we?" he said.

Charlie heaved himself up from the floor and leaned in the kitchen doorway. "Not that would do a twelve-gauge pencil," he said.

"Why, have we got some other kind?"

"No." Charlie moved around the table and ran some water from a tap into a glass. He drank, and wiped his forehead with the back of his hand. Macrae stretched toward the sink, tilting his chair, and pulled a kitchen knife off the drainboard. He began whittling the fat pencil down to a point.

"So, you feel like making any money tonight?" Charlie tipped a little water from the glass into his palm and ran it back over the kinks of his hair.

"Nah," Macrae said. "We got cash in the pocket and the rent's done paid."

"It's Friday night," Charlie said. "We'll miss that weekend theater crowd."

"They'll still be there tomorrow," Macrae said. "They'll be back next week." He took a swallow of beer and looked out the window through the diamonds of the gate. The dark pane threw back his own reflection and Charlie's under the dull light of the kitchen fixture, but through it he could just make out the snow continuing to descend in ropes and coils, whispering down all over the outdoors. He leaned forward and then stopped moving altogether.

"You turned to stone?" Charlie said.

Macrae came up from his daze with a shake of his head. "Christ, I'm higher than a kite," he said.

"So that's your problem," Charlie said. "That loco weed will just destroy your motivation."

Macrae wasn't listening. The dope had stolen up on him as he thought it would, and Charlie's voice might have been coming from the bottom of a well. His mouth was sour and puffy, and he sucked at the beer bottle again. Cottonmouth. He closed his eyes and made a picture behind them and then, only half looking at the paper, made a few quick strong strokes with the pencil.

"Huh," Charlie said, and leaned over the table. "Where'd you learn how to do that?"

"Just picked it up," Macrae said. "Fooling around." Bea's face stood out from the blue ruling on the paper, turned up in three-quarter profile. He wet his finger and ran it over the dark pencil blot and with his fingertip began to shade the line of her cheekbone.

"That's a fair likeness of somebody," Charlie said. "I feel like I've seen her."

"You could have." Macrae felt in his coat pocket, extracted a cigarette, and held it unlit in his left hand. "She's out there walking around on the street."

"That's something," Charlie said. "You can knock out anything you want just like that?"

"Depends," Macrae said. The face looked up at him from the page. The ruled lines were beginning to distract him a little. "Color," he muttered, half under his breath. He had forgotten to pay attention to the color of her eyes. He hitched his chair halfway around and looked at Charlie's feet.

"I used to draw tattoos," he said. "When I was in the service."

"You're a tattoo artist?" Charlie said.

"I didn't do the needles," Macrae said. "I used to draw for a guy, though. I'd draw them and he'd trace them out and all. If anybody wanted something special besides what was in the book."

"Any money in that?"

"Not no whole lot," Macrae said. When he looked back at the drawing it no longer pleased him. He tore off the sheet and pushed it aside and lifted the pencil to begin again, or something else, but his mind went numb; he was too high. Charlie picked up the drawing for a closer look.

"How come you never got a tattoo?" he said.

"They don't come off," Macrae said.

Charlie glanced at the back of his hand. "Not easy," he said.

"Right," Macrae said. "I never saw anything I liked well enough to have it stuck onto me all the rest of my life."

The pad was before him, framed in his hands, so whitely glimmering that the blue lines crossing it fractured and seemed to fade away. He was drawing again before he knew it. Charlie leaned in close behind, a faint tang of sweat drying on his skin.

"Now there's somebody special," Charlie said. "You saw her walking around today, I'd like you to tell me where."

"No," Macrae said. His tongue curled heavily in his mouth. It was the truth but not the whole of it. He leaned over and reached through the gate to heave the sash window all the way up. A gust caught the pad's cover and flipped it shut.

"Have you lost your mind?" Charlie said. "It's freezing out there."

"It's snowing," Macrae said.

"Yeah, that too. Are you trying to give me pneumonia?"

Macrae wasn't listening to him. It was like snow coming down inside his head, inside or outside, no difference between them.

He sat and watched the snow keep falling, shading itself in every-where. At the back of his eyes he saw a cue ball poised on the lip of a hinged gutter with the snow silting over its curve, thickening, gaining weight like a purpose, until it would have to fall.

three

Most of the snow had been hammered down into hard-frozen piebald patches. A drift that lay between two stoops, against a building wall, was crossed diagonally with an acrid yellow slash. The streetlight picked out the color plainly. Macrae wrinkled his nose as they walked by. He walked mincingly because it was slippery underfoot. But Charlie was stomping ahead in an angry gamecock strut.

"Wait up," Macrae said. "What's the matter, anyhow?"

Charlie gave him a hot look over his shoulder. His arms had tensed and risen a little clear of his sides. "Well, what are you poking along back there for?" he said. "Don't you know what time it is?"

"Just getting along toward the right time," Macrae said. "You don't want to have to cut'm out of the crowd, no way. Want to get the last ones coming out of Lindy's."

"Lutèce," Charlie said in a singsong. "Tonight, Lutèce."

"Lettuce?" Macrae said.

"You're an ignorant redneck, aren't you?"

Macrae's heel caught in a pool of slush. He recovered himself and stopped on the corner, by a wire trash bin. A bearded bag man with a knit cap pulled down to the rims of his eyes was rooting through the garbage, taking out strands of stained spaghetti and arranging them in a tinfoil go-plate. Macrae waited for Charlie to turn and stalk back.

"You have to do it, don't you?" Macrae said.

Charlie stood before him, a bantamweight tremble of redhead rage. "Do what?" he said.

Macrae pulled the piece of copper tubing out of his pea coat pocket and slapped it in his hand like a swagger stick. Behind him the bag man made a loud eating noise. "Get all worked up that-away," Macrae said. "You know, just beforehand."

"What's it to you?" Charlie said.

Macrae spun the pipe up into the air between his two hands. The torn copper edges caught the light and twisted it. He put the pipe back in his coat pocket. "The hell," he said. "Come on, let's do it."

"You ready now?" Charlie said. "I wouldn't want to rush you." He turned and started across Ninth Avenue. Macrae could see the cords in his neck were still tight. In his pocket, the copper warmed to his hand; he touched the torn end, then the smooth one. His stomach was on a slow perk from all the coffee he'd drunk in the bar. He had been drinking coffee for hours, it seemed, mostly to keep himself off the whiskey. Then there was the hollow, cool spiral below his belly button he could remember from when he took the paratrooper course, for instance. Not the jump itself, just climbing the tower, hearing the snap and groan of the harnesses as the other guys threw themselves down ahead. He sped up and came abreast of Charlie.

"You know, I once had a dog like you."

Charlie glanced at him, without speaking. He had started a cigarette. Macrae took one from his own pack and held it in his mouth unlit.

"Little fice dog," he said. "Not any bigger than a coffeepot. He was slick, though." He plucked the cigarette from his mouth and whistled. Ahead, the street was almost all dark, except for the lights of a basement nightclub halfway up the block.

"What was so slick about him?" Charlie said.

"How he used to bring in the cows . . ."

"The *cows?*"

"Figured it all out on his own, too," Macrae said. "Didn't nobody ever teach him. He'd stalk and creep up on a cow till he thought he had his distance right, and then he'd flatten down on his belly on the ground and start to bubble along—same way you do, exactly . . ."

"Same way I do what?"

"He'd sizzle and simmer till he thought he had him a good head of steam and then he'd take and run and jump way up high in the air and nip that cow right on the base of the tail. You never saw such a startled cow."

"I don't doubt you there."

"He'd have'm all in the barn inside of ten minutes," Macrae said. "See, it wasn't just the height he could get, it was the accuracy."

"What kind of a dog was this?" Charlie said.

"I don't know," Macrae said. "He had some spots on him. He just came down the road one day. Kind of a volunteer dog, you might call it."

"Shame we don't have him here right now," Charlie said. "We could all have us a big time, I'm sure. Except we hadn't got any cows."

"Hey, shut up, Charlie," Macrae said. He pointed up the block with his cigarette. "Hey—looka there."

"You see a cow?"

"I see what it is we're looking for, what do you see?"

Macrae thought he could feel Charlie's hackles rising, over there where Charlie was. He himself was now walking up on the balls of his feet. Up the block, a heavyset man in a big brown overcoat came out of the stairwell of the basement club, slipped on the trampled snow, and caught himself on the stair rail. He was laughing. A middle-aged woman with a stiff balloon of hair climbed out and stood beside him, balancing carefully on her chunky high heels. She was wearing a short silver-fox jacket. The man straightened up and said something to her that made her start laughing too.

"What do you know," Charlie said.

"Not much," Macrae said.

A second woman had come out the stairs to stand with the

first pair, smiling thinly, nodding, a little outside the circle of their laughter. She had flat shoes and a cloth coat and a much less elaborate hairdo.

"What's the matter?" Charlie said.

"Don't you see there's three of them?"

"What about it?"

"If they got another guy down there?"

But the man had taken the first woman on his left arm and was moving down the street toward Charlie and Macrae. The first woman leaned into him, laughing at something he was saying. The second walked a little apart until the man reached out with his other arm to draw her in.

"Coming at you," Charlie hissed. He looked to his right; there was a doorway, barely lit, with the outer door ajar.

"Hey, *Charlie*—"

The three were almost there. Macrae saw the man—he wore a suit with a fancy vest, a patterned cloth in his breast pocket, and the kind of patent-leather shoes that would match a dress uniform. He had a full head of whitening hair that stuck up like a shock of hay, and he was still laughing loudly at his own jokes. Charlie took Macrae by the elbow and pulled him toward the wall.

"Just let'm go by now . . . ," Charlie muttered, and bowed his head.

Macrae also looked down at his feet. "I don't like it," he said. Too late. He was there, feeling the total unattachment, looking down through the hatch of the plane to see the guy ahead of him falling like a matchstick cross down into the checkerboard green, those nasty first seconds before the chute popped. And what if you were chained to that guy? Macrae whiffed a cloud of liquor breath as the three of them came alongside.

"Let's *do it!*" Charlie was screaming, as he snatched the guy by the scruff of his coat and rushed him into the unlocked entry. Macrae stepped out half a beat behind him and caught the sleeve of the silver-fox jacket. He turned up the waistband and pressed the smooth end of the copper tube into the woman's back so she could feel it through the cloth of his coat pocket.

"He's got a gun, Foley." The woman's voice was slightly nasal, detached and uninflected, as if she might have been reading the news. She hadn't moved, except to turn her head toward the entryway, where Charlie had smashed the guy into the wall. The slack of his jowl was mashed into the grimy buzzer plate, and his face looked green in the bilious light.

Charlie had a hand in the back of his hair, pushing his head more forward. "Come on, fella," Charlie said. "Put some weight into it." He hooked one of the guy's feet out from under him, unbalancing him further into the wall. The intercom crackled and someone spoke so unintelligibly you could hardly tell it was a human voice. The guy grunted and the inner door buzzed open.

"You damn fool, you're ringing the doorbell with him," Macrae cried.

"Oh." Charlie jerked the guy off the buzzer and popped his cheek back against the tile. He flipped up the tail of his coat. "Cashmere," he said as he took out the wallet.

Macrae turned his head toward a yelp. The second woman spun around and started to run, but one leg shot from under her on the ice and she fell hard to her other knee and stayed there, stooped and gasping.

"Now what did I tell you?" Macrae said to Charlie, who was thumbing into the wallet.

"You can handle it," Charlie said. "Hey, Foley, you barely got cab fare here, you know?"

Macrae pivoted around the first woman and reached his free hand down toward the second. "You okay?" he said; and when she didn't answer, "Come on, I guess you better get up."

"Enough plastic, you could make your own Tupperware set," Charlie mused. "That's modern life for you, now ain't it?"

The woman looked up at Macrae, her lips set in a tense white line, from pain or fear he didn't know. "Come on, now," he coaxed her. "You'll be all right." She took his hand and hauled herself up.

"Jesus, Eve," the first woman said, and shook her head just slightly.

"You got to watch your step," Macrae said. "This kind of weather. Oh, by the way, I think he'll want that purse." He passed both purses to Charlie, who sniffed as he opened them and flipped through. The second woman, Eve, shifted her feet and winced. Macrae kept his tube pressed into the first woman's back. Fox fur pricked against the skin of his wrist, a ticklish feeling.

"Disco purses," Charlie said. "Barely hold a subway token." He passed the purses back to Macrae and looked at Foley's card carrier again. "Holy Moley," he said. He plucked loose a card and passed it to Macrae.

"Don't bother me," Macrae said. Two people to watch was making him jumpy, though he thought Eve was too sore to try another bolt. He felt the paper edge of the card and stuck it in his pocket without looking at it.

"We got a veep on our hands here, boy," Charlie said. "Foley is a regular Vee-Pee." He pulled Foley off the wall and hustled him back down to the sidewalk. "Ain't that right, Foley?" Charlie held him facing the other woman—his wife? He reached across his shoulder to stroke the silver-fox fur, then lifted her earlobe to see the stone there better.

"That real jewelry?" Charlie said. "Or just green glass?"

"Forget about it," Macrae said.

"You see what a hard case this fella is?" Charlie said to Foley. "You don't do me right, he's apt to eat these ladies all up. Come on, let's go look at the business." He pulled Foley around and started walking him away. Foley twisted to look back at his women, but Charlie thumped him on the neck to make him face straight.

"Let's walk a little," Macrae said. "Too cold to be just standing here." He let go of the pipe in his pocket and took Foley's wife's right hand in his left. With his other hand he reached for Eve, who came along haltingly as they began to move.

"How's that knee?" Macrae said. He was in much the same position between them that Foley had been, he thought.

"You *bastard,*" said Foley's wife.

Macrae looked at her with mild surprise. He couldn't tell how old she was—an over-made-up forty- or a struggling fifty-so. She had a hawk face, handsome in its hard-edged way, but leathery from too much time in the tanning machine.

"What did *I* do?" Macrae said. He glanced back at the hitching steps of the other woman. Eve wore a midcalf skirt, so he couldn't see the knee, but she flinched whenever she set down the game leg. Macrae couldn't figure what put her with the Foley couple. She didn't seem at all their type and wasn't enough like either one of them to be a poor relation. She had her hair cut in a stick-up thatch like Rod Stewart's hair, and was awkwardly tall and gangly, like Big Bird on TV. If she had been walking by herself Macrae would have made Charlie let her alone.

Foley's wife pulled a little away when they turned the corner of Eighth Avenue. Macrae reeled her back in, put her hand in his coat pocket and held it there. The hand was lumpy and jagged with all her rings; the palm of it was dry. The wind came sharply up the avenue from the south, chilling Macrae's open throat; he would have liked to close his collar but didn't have a hand to spare.

"You son of a *bitch.*" Foley's wife hissed like she meant to bite him.

"What's the matter?" Macrae said. "Don't want your hand to get cold, do you?"

There were more people on this block, though mostly johns and hookers, or the homeless jumbled in the doorways. Another uptown couple, furs and a fancy dress coat, came hurrying by the other way; Mrs. Foley screwed her head around to track them as they passed. Farther down the block a hooker was leaning into the driver's side of an old Lincoln, her red-striped hotpants sticking up in the air. Macrae watched her spring back from the car; she yelled something after it as it screeched away. Then someone spoke to Macrae, and reflexively he stopped.

There was a gaggle of Asian tourists near the wall to one side; he hadn't noticed where they came from. Three were conferring over a map and a book, while a fourth said something that sounded to Macrae like "*Ooh ah eh ahoo-ah?*"

"What say?" Macrae said.

"*Ooh ah eh ahoo-ah?*" The foreigner ducked down slightly, squinted, and waved his hands expressively, looking up at Macrae with a face full of hopeful tension. Macrae turned to Eve.

"Can you make out what he wants?"

Eve stood rigid, tilted onto her good leg. The foreigner turned back to the group and they spoke excitedly in their own language, then looked all around. The spokesman addressed Macrae once more.

"Ahmboogah," he said, definitively. Macrae stood agape. Beside him, Eve shifted and snapped her fingers.

"Hamburger!" she said. "Do you know where McDonald's is?"

Macrae stared at her. "*Ooh ah eh ahoo-ah?* Yeah," he said, smiling at Eve. "You don't know where they can find one?"

"No," Eve said. "But there's a Burger King a couple of blocks east, I think. On Forty-first, or Fortieth?"

"Jesus, Eve," Foley's wife said. She made a sudden yank but Macrae managed to keep her hand securely in his pocket. With her other hand she began to bat Macrae on the face and neck. "You bastard, you son of a bitch," she cried. It was not quite a fist and not quite a claw. Occasionally one of her long lacquered nails snagged at Macrae's skin almost by accident.

"That's telling him, Sissy." From an electronics shop doorway, the hooker in hotpants nodded approvingly. "Let's see you draw blood."

"Goddamn, will you stop it?" Macrae said. "You're gonna make the cops come in a minute." He caught her hand with an effort and turned to the Asians, who had drawn a little away and were watching in postures of respectful attention. "You'll have to excuse her," Macrae said. "I think she's had a little too much to drink."

The lead Asian made a half bow and held out the purse Foley's wife had flung away in her struggle, but she and Macrae were too engaged to take it, so he turned, bowed again, and handed it to Eve. Foley's wife snapped one of her hands free and raked at Macrae's face again; then she spat at him. Macrae pulled back.

"That'll *do*," he said. "All right, come on." He caught Eve by the elbow and awkwardly jockeyed both the women through the double doorway just behind them.

TOUCH HERE TO SPEAK ENGLISH, said the bank machine. Charlie crowded in close beside Foley, head tucked away from the automatic camera, leaning into the cavity that shaded the screen.

"I'm proud to know you, Foley," he said. "You know, this is my favorite bank. Do you know why that is?"

Foley hesitated, a thick finger hovering over the buttons.

"Take the maximum," Charlie said, "of course. What I like is how it lets you in here off the street so nobody can come along and bother you or whack you over top of the head while you're trying to do your business."

Above the screen, the chrome cylinder began to turn; inside, there began a shucking sound.

"That's what I call a slick idea, you know it?" Charlie said. "Maybe it was you that thought that one up, hey?" The cylinder unrolled to its opening, and Charlie reached over Foley's arm to take the stack of bills.

"Another thing," he said. "How does it count out all this money? How would it know a ten from a twenty? You get involved with that side of things, Foley?"

Foley turned his head to the side and breathed through his parted lips, without speaking.

"Go on," Charlie said. "Do it again."

Foley's jowls were dully lit from below by the blue glow of the screen: HELLO, HOW MAY I HELP YOU? "That's the limit," he said.

"For me it would be, maybe," said Charlie. "But for you?"

"I'm the same as anybody else," Foley said.

Behind them, the door clicked open. A young woman in a quilted floor-length overcoat came in and went to the other machine, tapped for a second, sighed, then drew back to wait for Charlie and Foley to finish. She set down the portfolio she was carrying and let it lean against her booted calf.

"No, you're not," Charlie whispered.

"Okay," Foley hissed. "Watch, you'll see . . ." He pressed the buttons and dipped his card. The machine said it was sorry that he had already made the maximum withdrawal for a twenty-four-hour period.

"I don't believe this," Charlie said. "Did you jigger it up some way?"

"Hey, you were watching," Foley said.

"You mean to tell me you are *vice president* of the goddamn bank and it won't let you have any more money than that?"

Behind them, the woman shifted her weight and tapped her foot. A puddle was forming by her boot toe; she stooped and shifted the portfolio out of the wet, then straightened, tossing back her hair. "Doesn't that machine work either?" she called.

"In a manner of speaking," Charlie said. "Hang on, we won't be a minute." He turned to Foley. "I told you, if you don't do right by me—"

"Look." Foley's voice got thinner as it rose. "The machine can only hold so much cash. That's what the limit's for. So it doesn't run out before the bank reopens. Same for me, same for anybody."

"Then we'll just have to go to another branch."

"No different," Foley said. "It goes on the main computer."

Charlie pushed away from the ATM. "Go ahead," he said to the woman, "go on and try it for what it's worth." She gave him a quizzical look as she scooped up her portfolio and stepped in.

"Well, I say the hell with it," Charlie said. "What's the use of being vice president, anyhow?" He stuck the money into his front pocket, turned, and headed out the door, but Foley stepped after him and caught him by the shoulder.

"What about—?" Foley said. "I did everything you wanted."

Charlie came around and smacked Foley's hand smartly away. The woman at the terminal had turned to stare at him; he wanted to tell her to mind her own business.

"Maybe you did," he said to Foley, "but can't you see I'm not satisfied?"

The interior of the peep show was painted a blobby robin's-egg blue, at least in the front area, where it was brightly lit. Behind the high counter the attendant was studying a slick magazine about breast bondage. His bald spot looked oily under the fluorescent tubes. He seemed like a young man, though, with acne on his pudgy face and a head shaped like a peanut.

"Lemme have a roll of quarters," Macrae said. He stuck up a ten-dollar bill. The attendant laid down his magazine and gave Macrae's money a slow wet blink. Then he took the bill and passed back a paper tube of coins. Macrae rolled it in his hand.

"I guess we can go on back," he said, a little uncertainly. He was still holding Foley's wife by her wrist, but Eve came along without any prompting. Together they passed through a curtain into the back.

On the other side of the curtain was a honeycomb of black-painted plywood partitions. The swing door of each cubicle was marked with a number sketched in silver fluorescent tape; a black-light tube on the floor helped them glow. The partition walls didn't come all the way to the ceiling or floor. If Macrae had stretched himself he could have seen over the tops of them. There was a click of the viewers' sprockets in a couple of cubicles and in one a deep, rheumy cough was repeating itself.

Macrae led the way to a cubicle near the end of the row. Number nine. He opened the swing door; the paint was blobby, tacky to his touch. "Go on in," he suggested. Foley's wife entered and Eve went after her. Macrae followed them in and pulled the door shut. There was a gasping sound coming out of the next cubicle. Macrae wasn't sure if it was live or from one of the film strips, possibly.

"You can sit down," he said. "We can . . ." Foley's wife sat on the bench, uneasily adjusting her skirt around her thighs, then Eve sat too. Their knees were almost brushing the opposite partition. Macrae squeezed himself in on the far side of Eve, the spot nearest the swing door—he was pleased to have something separating him from Foley's wife. But the bench was narrow, never meant for three, and all their legs were mashed uncomfortably between the partition walls.

"You got the time?" Macrae said. "Either one of you?" But it was too dark to read a watch or even see if they had one between them. Macrae peeled some paper from the roll and pried a quarter loose. He had to lean across Eve and Foley's wife to reach the coin box. The timer began to whir, and the light came on. On the screen a woman with a short curly cap of reddish brown hair sat facing them on a bench much the same as theirs. She was wearing a pair of fraying denim shorts and a tank top that for no apparent reason she suddenly hauled off. There were freckles all over her breasts and her belly. A man with a mustache, fully clothed, entered the screen and sat down on the bench beside her. There was no sound.

"You bastard," Foley's wife muttered.

Macrae sighed. He looked at both women in the flicker of the light from the screen. Neither one of them had a watch. The timer buzzed and the screen went dark. He reached across and lobbed in another quarter.

"You sick perverted son of a bitch," Foley's wife said. There was a distant, reflective quality to her words, as if she was no longer really hearing what she said. She watched the screen with apparent avidity. The redheaded woman's shorts had disappeared and the man's hand moved between her legs. She hooked her bare heels on the edge of the bench and fanned out her knees like a butterfly's wings.

"I know you think that," Macrae said. "But when the man

walks by, he don't see the projector running, he's supposed to flush us out of here."

The screen went dark. Macrae reached over and fed the coin box. Foley's wife made a sound of repulsion deep in her throat, like the sound she'd made before she spat at him earlier.

"You don't have to look at it," Macrae pointed out. "You could close your eyes or whatever. Besides, it never was *my* idea to kick up a big commotion out there on the street." But he was getting uncomfortable about where he should be looking himself. The redheaded woman grabbed the man by his ears and pulled his head down to her breasts. Macrae turned to look at Eve. Her face was rigid under the shadows shifting over it. She would have looked a little better, he thought, if she just fixed her hair some other way.

"I guess we could just have a look at that knee." He pulled back the hem of her skirt a couple of inches. Certainly the joint was puffy, but in the uneven light from the screen he couldn't tell the color.

"You ought to get some ice on this, the minute you can," Macrae said. "And after that, hot soaks . . ." He touched the knee-cap lightly with his forefinger. Not broken, though it was slightly displaced by the swelling. Eve flinched. Packed in as they were, the movement made the whole cubicle rock.

"That sore?" Macrae glanced up: her face was frozen, turned a quarter toward him; the back of her head and every bump of her spine was indented into the plywood behind her as she struggled to shrink as far away from him as possible.

"Oh, for God's sake," Macrae said. "I'm not planning to bother you." The projector stopped. He could still hear that cough a few doors down.

"You sick bastard," Foley's wife said.

"Why don't you just be quiet?" Macrae said. In the dark he found Eve's nearer hand, turned it over, and began to shell quarters into her palm. "You pump this in till it's all gone. Don't leave before the money's all spent, or something bad's apt to happen to you. You understand?"

Eve nodded, Macrae thought, the way the bench creaked. "All right," she whispered.

"Here," he said, and flipped out two more quarters. "You can save these last ones for the phone." He folded her fingers up over the coins, got up, and backed his way out of the cubicle, dropping what was left of the quarter roll on top of the copper tube in his pocket.

"Pervert," Foley's wife said in the dark.

"Same to you, lady," Macrae said. "Y'all have a nice night." He swung the door to, walked loudly down the corridor between the cubicles, then tiptoed partway back. It was still dark in booth number nine. When the light came on he stopped. Under the lower edge of the partition he could see both women's shoes facing forward toward the screen.

There was a clock behind the attendant's peanut head, which showed it was getting on for one o'clock. Macrae was sure that Charlie had to have made it back to the bar by this time. It seemed colder on the street, and he buttoned the top button of his pea coat and stuck his hands deep in his pockets. He was hurrying by taking lots of short steps, careful not to slip on the ice and fall.

four

Rafael took a pawn with his knight, forking Macrae's two rooks. It took Macrae almost a minute to register the trap. He tilted back onto his chair's hind legs, bracing one elbow on the balcony rail. In the bar's main room below, there was a clatter of glasses and plates amidst the general hum. It was after five and the shifts were changing. Something was playing on the jukebox but Macrae could just hear the bass flubbing along, over the noise of talk. He rocked the chair's front legs to the floor, pinched the bridge of his nose, and stared at the position. Rafael's chessboard was so old he could barely tell the light squares from the dark ones. Paper peeled back from the cardboard around the middle crease. Macrae yawned. His head felt thick, from being indoors almost all day.

"No way out," Rafael said. "I got you, man." He grinned at Macrae through the thicket of a new-grown beard. A week or so back he had stopped shaving.

Macrae touched his beer stein, but it was empty except for a patch of yellowed foam on the bottom. He rotated it a quarter turn on the dirty oilcloth and began counting up the pieces on the side of the board. Already he was a knight and a bishop down, not to mention a couple of pawns, which he never thought were very important.

"Make you mine up," Rafael said. "Goan lose one or lose the other."

"You want to rub it in or something?" Macrae closed one eye and flicked his king with thumb and forefinger. The plastic piece shot across the board and tumbled down several men on Rafael's queen side.

"Eh, what you do that for?" Rafael was still smiling, though. "You doan like to lose, ah?" He bent sideways to gather the spilled pieces from the floor. "You loss, you buy some drinks, ah?" he said when he straightened up. "I take a Seven and Seven."

Macrae collected the handles of the steins and went down the rickety steps from the balcony. Out beyond the bar's plate-glass windows a cold rain was pelting down Ninth Avenue, gnawing at the frozen piles of graying snow. It had been raining for most of the day. Macrae went to the counter and wedged his way in between two stools. The bar was packed from end to end, with three Irishmen in white shirts and black vests frantically working the length of it. Macrae pulled out a ten and held it high.

"Draft and a Seven and Seven," he shouted, pushing the empty glasses onto the inner lip of the bar. Evan the barman, who was older than the other two, whirled toward the bottle behind him and began to mix the first drink. He whacked down the Seven and Seven, squirted some beer into one of the glasses, and plucked the bill from Macrae's hand.

"And a shot of bourbon," Macrae said. "Straight up."

Evan grunted as he stooped for the bottle. In the mirror behind him, Macrae saw Bea, perched high three stools over from him. A baggy-pants guy in a crush hat, one of the sort the bar was full of, appeared to be buying her drinks. She was wearing what Macrae had come to think of as her guerrilla hooker outfit. It was what she almost always wore. Macrae caught her eye in the mirror and winked.

"It's the Live Lady!" he said.

Bea stuck her tongue out at him and turned rapidly away. Of a sudden something small and heavy dropped about four inches from behind Macrae's navel, like one of those balls falling down a chute in the Port Authority perpetual-motion machine. Evan sloshed whiskey into a short glass and pushed the change across the counter. Macrae was much surprised at himself. The thing that had shifted inside him was hot and cold at once where it had landed, burning like cold metal will burn to wet skin. But he had always thought of her as a kid, because she was. He swallowed his shot with a snap of his wrist and climbed the stairs with the other two drinks, feeling a little shaky.

Rafael had set up the chessboard again. Macrae sat down and slid him his drink. "What's the point?" he said. "I don't see where you get any fun even beating me, really."

He sipped on his beer and wiped his mouth on the back of his wrist. Rafael shook a Camel out of his pack and broke the filter off of it.

"Where'd you learn to play so good, anyway?" Macrae said.

Rafael glanced up, stroking his hair back to the rubber-band cinch, and shrugged. "I read a few books," he said.

"It's a game," Macrae said. "You read books about it?"

"How you get good," Rafael said. He turned the torn end of the cigarette over the ashtray and began rolling it in his fingers, working loose some shreds of the tobacco.

"How far you go in school, Rafael?" Macrae said.

"Eight grade I go to in Santo Domingo," Rafael said. "Over here, I go high school three, four year." There was contempt in his tone. He craned his neck and looked up at the smoke-stained squares of the pressed tin ceiling. "I doan know, I doan like to go here so much. I doan know nobody, once a week I go to school I probably get in a fight . . . But I use to go sometime anyway." He laughed and rolled his head forward to look at Macrae. "You?"

"Oh, I finished high school," Macrae said. "Didn't do good but I finished it. I even took a couple college courses in the—" He clicked his lips and looked out over the balcony.

Rafael shaped the empty half inch of the cigarette's tube into a perfect circle. "Bobby Fischer, you know I think he doan go to school either."

"Is that a fact?" Macrae said.

Rafael took out a worn piece of foil paper from his cigarette box and refolded an old crease down the center. "I doan know why, but anyway, he stay home. With his sister. The mother is working somewhere, I guess. So one day, the sister she buy a chess set. Just little plastic men and a board like this one." Rafael nodded at the board between them. "They have the rules inside the box top, so Bobby and his sister they start to play . . . Eight years old, he beats the grand masters. The sister is not so bad either, I hear."

"Hot diggity," Macrae said. With one hand on the rail, he hitched himself up a little and peered out. Charlie had come into the area below and was standing in front of the steam tables, flipping a plastic tray back and forth in both hands as he examined the pans of food. Macrae put his finger in his mouth and let out such an excruciating whistle that most of the people in the bar looked up at him. Charlie nodded and Macrae settled back in his chair.

"Yeah, I remember when he play what's-is-name," Rafael said. He took a tiny Ziploc bag from his pocket and shook some leaf from it into the white side of the creased foil paper. "The Russian?"

"Spaz-something," Macrae said. "That's a long time gone." He watched Rafael's forefinger working the leaf in the paper crease. The dope was a pale, cidery color, almost as fine as a powder.

"Spastic," Macrae said.

"Spass-kee!" said Rafael. He tilted the foil-paper fold and tapped the high end of it so that the powdery leaf ran down into the emptied cigarette tube. "I was a little kid back then, man."

"You all paid attention to that back in Santo Domingo?"

"It was America against the Russians, you know?" Rafael said. He tamped the cigarette on the oilcloth a time or two to settle the dope and then sealed the end with a twist, like the twirl at the top of a Hershey's Kiss. "He beat the Russian so bad, they took the Russian's car away. His apartment too, I think. I think the Russian, he even defected. Bobby Fischer," Rafael said with reverence. "You know, he is good at bowling, too."

Rafael reached for the board and moved his queen's pawn forward. Macrae shook his head at it. Rafael shrugged, lit the doctored cigarette, drew in deeply, and stopped breathing. He passed the smoke to Macrae, who followed suit. Macrae sat still, feeling a single vein beat in his temple. Below, someone cut the volume of the jukebox with the dial behind the bar. As in slow motion, Macrae saw Evan turn and crane his neck and begin to shout at them. Whenever he raised his voice, his accent thickened unintelligibly.

Rafael exhaled some faintly stained air and stood up to yell back down at Evan. "Whaddaya, crazy? You smelling things? This an American cigarette I got here." He waved the pack, then looked at it. "Turkish tobacco, thas what you smell."

He sat down. Below, Evan snarled a few more times on a declining note, then bent to the panel of switches and turned up the TV. Local news; someone was giving the weather report. The rain would freeze and turn to snow.

"This guy . . ." Rafael proffered the cigarette to Macrae, who pushed his palm out to decline.

"Yeah, it's down to the tobacco," Rafael said, and blew a small smoke ring through a large one as he leaned back. "This freaking Irishman."

"Nose like a bloodhound," Macrae said. He took out one of his own cigarettes and lit it, though his mouth was cottony dry. Charlie was coming up the stairs with his tray loaded.

"You hear the one, the Irishman rapes the nun?"

"A hundred times," Macrae said.

Charlie sat down, bumping the chessboard to make room for his tray, whose edge was notched with old cigarette burns. He had Salisbury steak and mashed with gravy and baked beans, white bread and butter and a glass of beer. His wool hat was still wet from the rain outside; he pulled it off and squeezed it and hung it on a knob of his chair back before he lifted his knife and fork.

"Hungry?" Macrae said.

Charlie made use of the salt and pepper shakers with which his tray was also furnished. "Stoned?" he said. He cut a piece of meat and chewed it. "You two gonna get us barred from this place one of these days."

"Never happen." Macrae turned his head away from the thick gravy steam. It was getting good dark outside, and the TV set, on a shelf high in the corner above the outer door, was the brightest point in the ground-floor space. The door opened and Big Tee pushed in. He folded an umbrella and pushed the maroon velour hood of his sweatshirt down on the collar of his leather jacket.

"Huh," Rafael said. "Look like a new one."

Macrae blinked slowly. He thought he could feel his brain move in its casing anytime he shifted his head. Indeed the girl on Big Tee's arm seemed distinctly unfamiliar.

"Got to be," Rafael said. "You see him open the door for her?"

"Right," Macrae said. "Umbrella too."

The crowd at the counter parted and a couple of stools vacated for Big Tee and the new girl. Big Tee spoke to Evan, who picked up a pair of extension grabbers and snagged a dusty bottle of Remy Martin from the high shelf over the mirror.

Rafael pursed his lips to breathe a whistle. "Man, I think she new to*day*."

The new girl raised her haunch over one of the stools and set her purse on the other, which Big Tee was not using. She wore electric blue stretch jeans and a short white jacket of synthetic fur; her hair or wig hung straight and dark among the fake-fur tendrils. Big Tee toasted her with a balloon of brandy, then leaned to kiss her on the cheek. The new girl bridled as if she would blush. Her eyes were black and almond shaped.

"Chinese?" Macrae said. "Don't see much of that around here."

"I doan think," Rafael said. "She have some Indian blood, I think, with eyes like that, maybe she from South America somewhere."

"Window-shopping?" Charlie said.

"Don't make so much noise while you eat," said Macrae. His eyes tracked down the bar; it was the dope that made him preternaturally aware of these tiny physical operations. Bea was looking hard at something in the mirror. With an apparent effort she broke the stare and returned to the baggy-pants guy who was buying.

"Yeah," Rafael said. "I wonder . . ."

Macrae's dry tongue was so thick in his mouth he thought it would almost block his throat. The tumbling feeling in his groin was matched to a current that flowed from the glands underneath his arms—though all that was the dope, he knew, and if he thought of something else he could stop it. He raised his eyes to the TV set, whose light was needle sharp. An image moved and then seemed to repeat. It was black and white, or gray looking.

"Goddamn," Macrae said. Without taking his eyes from the television he reached behind him and caught Charlie by the upper arm.

"What's the matter," Charlie said. There was a click as he set down his knife and fork.

Macrae stared at the TV screen. Over and over two figures kept entering the glassine cubicle of an ATM, one broad, the other thin and wiry, both shot at a sharp angle from above. The video was thick and grainy. A digital readout in the lower corner gave the date and time. Macrae couldn't seem to make out what the announcer's voice was saying.

"You can't tell who it is," Charlie said.

"It's Foley," Macrae said. The image changed to a young woman working at a drafting table, and Macrae told himself the story was over, told the pins and needles stitching all over his skin to stop. It was doing something to his eyes to stare at the television so hard—around the sides the screen was beginning to shimmer and run. At the dim flickering edge of his peripheral vision he saw Big Tee lean to kiss the new girl one final time, flip up his hood, and stroll out onto the glistening dark street. On the screen, the woman looked up sharply and pointed her pencil toward the camera.

"Wait a minute here—" Charlie jerked forward suddenly enough to jostle over a couple of pieces on the chessboard. "I know where I last saw her . . ."

The image changed—a pencil sketch of a man in a wool hat. Beneath it a set of letters wrote themselves in brilliant yellow:

$400 BANDIT?

The drawing shrank, slid to the left above the caption, and was joined by another. Artist's conception of Charlie with his hat off, but she had done his hair straight and dark. Macrae's head had a cannonball weight as he pivoted it to look at Charlie and then back at the screen.

"Could be anybody," Charlie said, with shrinking conviction. He clicked his tongue between his teeth.

"I could have done better," Macrae said, "but still . . ."

"I don't see what they're making a TV show out of it for," Charlie said. "Little thing like that must happen a few hundred times a day around here."

The picture changed. Foley sat behind a desk of dark wood, bulking out his pinstripes. Below, the yellow letters wrote his title out.

"You and your vice presidents," Macrae said. "You ought to walked away from that guy the minute you saw his card."

"Shut up, Macrae." Charlie jerked his head at Rafael, who was shifting his sights curiously between the television and the two of them.

"Hey, this is *Rafael*," Macrae said.

"What have you told him?"

"No more than he asked me. Not a damn thing."

"Well, he knows now."

"What about it?"

"I don't like it."

"Eh," Rafael said, turning to Charlie, flipping a hand over his shoulder toward the TV. "I doan know this guy, okay? I never see him before my whole life. You hear me?"

Charlie said nothing. On the screen, a column of dates and places scrolled back across the pair of drawings.

"Hey, look at that," Macrae said bitterly. "Now they're doing the résumé."

"Shut up, Macrae."

"Why don't you?" Macrae's cigarette had burned out on the filter. The long dead ash tumbled as he turned back toward Charlie. He dropped the butt in the ashtray and swept the ash off the sticky oilcloth with the back of his hand.

"I don't like people to know, that's all," Charlie said.

"Do we have to keep going over it? What gets people to know is being on the freaking *Tee-Vee*, understand?"

"All right," Charlie said. He found his fork and scooped up a final blob of mashed and beans. "Forget about it."

"Eh," Rafael said. "I think maybe you should buy a new hat."

Charlie looked at him, slitting his eyes, the fork suspended halfway to his plate. Rafael was smiling on one side of his mouth.

"A big Stetson, maybe," he said. "Like a Marlboro man."

Charlie gave out a short barking laugh. He let the fork clatter down, picked up a bread end, and chased the last streak of gravy to the edge of his plate. Macrae drained his glass and sighed. Charlie, still chewing, leaned back in his chair to dig a bill from the front pocket of his jeans.

"Buy us a round," he said.

"You got legs, ain't you?" said Macrae.

"I'm buying."

"Didn't they teach you not to talk with your mouth full?"

"All right," Charlie said. "I'll flip you."

"Nah, I'll go," Macrae said, thinking that after all it might break his dopey torpor if he moved around a little. He stood and picked up the money, and as he passed behind Charlie's chair he paused to drop a hand on his shoulder.

"It'll be all right."

"I know it will," Charlie said, looking straight ahead of him, out over the bar.

Macrae was so high, though, he had almost forgotten what they were talking about. Ten-minute creeper, Colombian probably.

From the color. But Rafael was the expert on vintage dope. Macrae stopped at the foot of the stairs and put a hand on the plate-glass window that faced the side street. The pane fogged around it, leaving a print of his palm and five fingers. Outside, the wind was sweeping waves of rain against the glass, and the water was stained with colored lights as it ran down. Macrae watched the palm print fade, then shuffled back into the rear of the bar, to the area underneath the balcony. There was a small pool table back there, with four men playing, and he watched for a minute before he stooped over the jukebox. A ring of red and white lights, bulbous like the lights of a makeup mirror, were racing around and around the arch above the panel of selections, and they kept distracting his eye. Finally he picked out a Whitney Houston and with an effort of memory punched in the number. Nothing happened. Evan had cut the jukebox back in favor of the TV news. Or had he forgot to put in the money? The news. The video and the indifferent sketch of Charlie resurfaced, a cold bubble floating on the top of his mind.

It felt as though his throat were closing. He turned toward the TV. The first thing he saw was some baggy-pants guys springing back from the counter; one of them knocked over a tiny table in the middle of the bar. Bea lunged across the freshly opened space and sank her nails into the new girl's scalp. Wig. It came away so easily it threw Bea off balance. Before she could recover, the new girl caught her with an open hand across the face, hard enough to spin her half around. Under the wig her real hair was netted to her head in a nappy bundle, and without it she looked older, uglier.

Bea caught her balance, threw the wig in the new girl's face, and under cover of this diversion stepped forward and slugged a fist into her belly. *Good shot!* Macrae said to himself, seeing it was a nice straight punch instead of the usual whore's haymaker. Without knowing it he had moved in a good deal closer behind Bea. On the balcony above, Charlie and Rafael had risen to cheer.

"Cheap tinsel hairless bitch," Bea said breathlessly. The new girl was bent over, gasping. Red circles bloomed on her yellow cheeks when she straightened. She took a breath, snatched a straight tumbler off the bar and broke the rim with an efficient crack on the edge of the counter. A couple of melted ice cubes showered out with the broken glass. The new girl lunged with the jagged edge and Bea jumped back, raising a forearm over her face. She jostled into Macrae and without thinking he snatched her by a shoulder and leg and pressed her into the air over his head like a barbell.

The new girl didn't know what to do; at first she didn't even seem to know where Bea had gone. Then she cocked back her arm as if she might throw the glass, but Evan made a long reach over the bar top, caught her wrist, and twisted it. The glass came loose and broke some more on the floor inside the counter. Spraying saliva, the new girl whirled to scream and claw at Evan, but the other two barmen came over the counter almost instantly, caught her elbows, and were ferrying her out the door. Evan stood up straight. The weighted billy club he used on such occasions rotated on its leather loop and smacked into his palm. He slid it back into its place below the cash register. Bea shivered like a fish in Macrae's hands, came free, and slid down to the floor.

"Come on," Macrae said. Evan was looking consideringly at the pair of them as the other two barmen turned back from the door. Macrae switched Bea around and aimed her toward the stairs with a palm at the base of her spine.

"Go," he said. He stooped to pick up the beret, which had fallen on the floor during the fight. The heel of his hand was warm where it had touched her. He followed her up the stairs, turning the hat in his hands and brushing at it.

"Where's my drink?" Charlie said.

Macrae waited a beat, then burst out laughing. "I got distracted," he said, and gave the bill back. "Maybe you better go yourself."

Charlie stood up with a smirk and went down the stairs,

shaking his head. Macrae pointed at the chair he'd been in and Bea sat down in it. Rafael passed a hand over his hair and turned his one-sided smile on her.

"*¿Cómo sientas?*"

"*¿Qué quieres?*" Bea snapped. She was still breathing hard from the fight, as Macrae could see in close detail. He broke his glance from the top zip of her jumpsuit and sat down.

"Bald-headed old skank," Bea said. She touched her own streaked hair affectionately; it had come loose and was on the fly.

"Forget about it," Rafael said.

"Here's your hat," said Macrae. Bea looked at him, blankly. It took her a second to recognize the beret and reach for it.

"Hey, let's have a look," Macrae said, catching her wrist. Bea tugged a little, without answering. There was a cut on the inside of her forearm.

"Don't get excited," Macrae said. He let go her arm and leaned over the railing. "Charlie!" he called. "Bring a rag when you come."

Charlie looked up from the counter, where he was dealing with Evan. Beside him, Macrae saw that Big Tee had appeared. He had taken off the jacket and sweatshirt and was holding them clamped under his arm.

"A clean one," Macrae called, and settled back. Bea unsnapped a compact mirror from her purse, gasped at her tangled hair, and began to rearrange it. Behind her, Charlie was coming up the stairs with a lot of glasses bunched in his hands.

"Don't put your thumb in it," Macrae said. In back of Charlie, Big Tee's face was an inky patch shifting ahead of the old brown paneling. With the gold satin stripe, the maroon sweatpants stood out best. Also the gold chain on his chest, with the oversized initials cut out in a flat square of the metal. The gold lay on a black dress T-shirt of some slinky synthetic material.

Charlie set the drinks down, slopping on the chessboard. Rafael cleared his throat irritably and began to scoop the pieces into a cloth bag. He moved the glasses off the board and folded it. As Big

Tee floated up behind her, silent on his fat-laced sneakers, Bea clapped her compact back into her purse and clutched it with both hands, not looking back. He wasn't quite big enough for the tag, Macrae thought. Thick in the chest and shoulders, like he might do weights, narrow hipped and light on his feet, but if Macrae stood up he'd be a good head taller. Big Tee took the lobe of Bea's ear and rolled it between a thumb and forefinger, then tugged. Bea jumped up and stepped clear of the chair as he sat down.

"Say my bitches been misbehaving," Big Tee said. His hair was cut close; a razor line of beard ran from one small ear down the edge of his jawbone and up to the other. The face was handsome as a jet-carved idol. Macrae caught a whiff of leathery perfume as Big Tee leaned in close.

"Say you help out, thass what they say." Big Tee's voice was silky and low. His hands were rather small, so that the big square rings overpowered them. Macrae felt for a cigarette, then changed his mind. Charlie was dangling a white dishcloth in one hand and Macrae reached across and took it.

"Nobody ass you," Big Tee said contemplatively. "You just step in."

Bea opened her mouth with an audible plop of her lips, but before she could speak Big Tee had whirled up and half out of his chair. He crouched, twisted toward her. *Fast,* Macrae thought. Big Tee let himself unwind into the chair again. His voice was even softer and smoother than before, but Macrae knew he was speaking for her to hear. He set his teeth on the dishrag and tore off a long strip loudly.

"Would never happened," Big Tee said, "she been out there rolling her moneymaker like she spose. Steada sitting in here trine keep her moneymaker warm and dry."

Macrae crooked a finger at Bea, and after a moment's hesitation she came to him. The arm was limp as cold spaghetti when he turned it over.

"A scratch," Big Tee said. "She's lucky."

Macrae dipped an end of the cloth into a glass of neat whiskey on the table before him and dabbed at the dry blood near the cut. Bea hissed just slightly at the sting.

"You're right," Macrae said, without looking at Big Tee. "But you don't know, sometimes these things'll take a stitch."

"Oh yes," Big Tee said. "I like how you do that."

Macrae let go of the arm and it swung away from him like a pendulum.

"Way I think," Big Tee said, "my bitches wants to fight, they should put on gloves. None of this cutting and marking up and all like that. I like how you done—I'm giving her to you. All night long. You do what you want."

Macrae pulled out a cigarette and held it unlit. "I didn't know she was yours to give," he said.

"Yes, you did." Big Tee stood up. His manicured fingertips grazed the oilcloth. The chunky rings were in brass-knuckle arrangement, the initials again, and others with carved or colored stones. "She's my bitch, white boy, you know that all along."

five

Outside, the rain had finally stopped and the cold had dropped and constricted so sharply that the puddles were already glazing on the uneven sidewalk. Macrae's shoes crunched with every step he took. He had swiped Charlie's wool hat off the chair back when he left the bar, thinking Charlie would be better off not wearing it for a while anyway, and now he put it on and tugged it down over his ears. Bea stamped along grimly, an arm's length from him. She had zipped herself into a blocky red jacket that looked as if it were made of rubber. It cinched in at her waist, leaving her legs bare under the shorts of the jumpsuit, except for the long tights.

"Hadn't you got any more coat than that?" Macrae said.

Bea shot him a laser look and tramped on. Tonight she wore little high-heeled boots whose tops turned over loosely around her ankles. They lashed down like clubs beating the sidewalk angrily again and again. She tucked her face into the red wings of the jacket's collar and watched the whipping movement of her feet. Macrae led her into the Times Square subway. They rode downtown, holding onto a pole and looking away from each other.

In the dark reflection of the car window Macrae saw that Charlie's hat made him look like a fuzzy ballistic missile. He yanked it off and stuck it in the pocket of his pea coat. His hand and Bea's were locked above each other on the chrome pole, like hands seizing up the handle of a baseball bat. Her nails were black, to match her lipstick, and chipped white along the pointy edges. He touched the backs of her knuckles gingerly and her hand contracted and slid a couple of inches down the pole.

The train screeched into Fourteenth Street and they got off. Out on the street the sleet had started, settling with a steady ticking sound. An east wind brought it corkscrewing into their faces as they walked the long blocks crosstown. The conversation with Big Tee had squelched the effects of the dope for a while, but as Macrae watched the long glittering ropes of sleet whirl toward him he felt the high beginning to return.

"Where we going," Bea called to him. "The moon?"

Macrae turned his head to see her silhouette gliding along before the backlit diamond gates that guarded the show windows of the knockdown clothes stores along Fourteenth Street. He threw an arm around her red rubber shoulder and drew her, in spite of her irritable stiffening.

"I was married once," he said. The words seemed to break apart and scatter away from each other as they tumbled out of his mouth.

"What about it?"

Macrae turned, guiding her onto an avenue—a couple of doors down was a narrow entry to a bar. Bea shook loose of him as they came in the door. She looked about herself without unzipping her jacket.

"Come so far for this?" she said. The bar was little different from the one they'd started in, only smaller and sleepier. The counter running along one wall, and against the other a portable railing that fenced off a drum kit and a couple of amps. The bartender was dozing on a stool, and in a cubbyhole at the rear a couple of men in dirty work pants droned slowly around a small pool table.

"What'll you have?" Macrae said. He pointed her to a seat at a table edged into the railing near the drum set. The whole bar was swimming in a sour yellow light. A waitress appeared near Macrae and wiped back her hair with a damp hand. She stood there a minute before he figured out what she was there for.

"Gimme a B and B," Bea said finally. Macrae ordered beer and she went to the counter.

"Yeah," he said. "It was a whole lot like riding the subway with you." With concentration he felt that he could mold the words and force them to accrete into usable packets of meaning.

"What was?"

"Being married." Turning the words was like rolling a stone. When he looked at the agglomeration at a few seconds' distance he wasn't so sure it meant anything after all.

Bea snorted. "Some marriage."

"It didn't last long." Macrae shook a cigarette from his pack and offered it to her; she looked at it for a second and then took it. The waitress set down the drinks with a *clonk* and walked away. Macrae took out a pack of matches and flipped it one-handed, folding a match and snapping it alight on the back striker. Bea leaned toward the flame and drew.

"You'll know what to do when they cut your arm off, won't you?" she said.

"Something to do sitting around the post," Macrae said, "teach yourself little tricks like that, it's where I learned how to blow smoke rings." He shifted his feet uneasily under the table—he never had intended to bring up the post or anything to do with it. A slim black boy of about sixteen negotiated the railing and turned on a couple of amps.

"I hate sailors," Bea said.

"Good, I wasn't one."

Bea ran her tongue around the sticky rim of her small bell-shaped glass. "You one of those Vietnam guys?"

Macrae burst out laughing. "How old do you think I am?"

Bea shrugged. "I hadn't thought about it."

"Nah," Macrae said. Beyond the railing, the amps hummed deeply. The door of the bar opened and shut and several more people came in together, shrugging out of damp hats and coats.

"Only jungle I ever was in was Panama," Macrae said.

Bea looked at him sidelong, turning her lemon face in profile against the wall. "They send you to go get Noriega?"

"It was before that," Macrae said. "Just training." The bar door swung again and he felt a damp draft for a second on the back of his neck.

"No war or anything, and you just go off and leave your wife and go walk around in the jungle?"

"What?" Macrae said, confused.

"You said you were married, you said it was like—"

"Right," Macrae said. He hooked a fingernail under the label of his beer and began to peel strips of it away from the wet brown glass. "It started out, me and some fellas drove into town, we went to Tootsie's to have a drink or so and listen to some music . . . And next morning I wake up somewhere; I thought, *Where am I at? And who's this funny-looking woman here with the dyed hair?* It was some trailer park to hell and gone out the Murfreesboro Road somewhere. Little Airstream trailer about the size of one of them subway cars."

Macrae listened to himself with wonder at his fluency and at all he was revealing so effortlessly. Bea had pursed up her lips in an odd expression and was resting her blackened fingernails across her mouth.

"Well, she ups and tells me we had gone and got married somewhere the night before. You know, *Dontcha remember, honey? Dontcha remember whatcha said?* And I couldn't even call her name. You might say it was getting off on the wrong foot if we intended on being married for a very long stretch." Macrae snorted. "I don't know what she thought she wanted either. I wasn't but seventeen or eighteen and here she was forty-five years old, at least."

Bea was tittering through the bars of her fingers. "What *was* her name?" she said, glancing to the side again as two more men edged around their table and climbed into the railed space with the amps. One picked up an electric bass and the other got on a stool behind the drum kit, shoving the bass drum out a little from the wall. The man with the bass bumped a long, low note that Macrae could feel buzzing through the table into his palm.

"Julie," Macrae said. "Pretty name, really. Oh, she wasn't a bad woman, either, but—that trailer, it was like trying to live inside a tunafish can."

Bea dropped her fingers from her face and began to laugh openly. "You stayed?"

Macrae shrugged. "A month or two, yeah, I hung around. What do you do? I kept thinking at least I might finally remember what happened. I mean, she might have been fooling me all along, but you got somebody telling you you went and married'm, well . . .. You want to go and say, *Now you* sure *you remember this right, the way it really happened?*"

Bea jiggled in her chair, rocking slightly from the waist as she laughed. "You make me choke on my drink—" She gasped.

"Yeah," Macrae said. He was rather pleased with the way the story had turned out. "I never knew for sure till it came divorce time. Then, sure enough, there was the paper. Now I still don't know how she found people to do all that swearing and signing in the middle of the night like that . . ."

Bea sighed with fatigue from the laughing fit. The cigarette Macrae had lit for her had burned down to the filter, and she reached to stub it out completely. "You're a funny guy," she said.

"I thought you said I was nasty," Macrae said, and kicked his ankle jumpily under the table. This was a wrong fork in the criss-cross trails of conversation, which he momentarily pictured as fluorescent lines webbing over a map. Bea's eyes had smoked over and she looked rather sad. Macrae glanced uneasily around the bar, which had filled up considerably. At the rear, the bartender and the waitress were maneuvering a big sheet of plywood over the pool table; one of the players hung alongside them, complaining.

The light dimmed as a fourth man walked out from the back, holding a red guitar, and swung over the railing. There was an instant of loud ground-out hum as he plugged in his cord. The younger boy, meanwhile, was stroking something on another guitar, turned to the wall, his hip twitching slightly to whatever he was fingering. The red-guitarist said something to him off-mike, and both of them took a step forward, toward what had become the audience. The red-guitar man hit a trembling A chord, and the boy, whose guitar was white, bent all the strings of it and spun up the neck into a slow blues intro.

It wasn't the regular house band, but better than that, Macrae saw. They sang their choruses in three-part harmony, the drummer craning his neck toward a boom mike to pick up the third. Macrae didn't recognize the tune. He leaned in, over Bea's shoulder, watching the lead guitarist work through his solo.

"Look at him," he said softly, barely knowing he had spoken out loud. The boy stood stock-still now as he played, only his fingers moving. His face was dark and shadowed so you couldn't see his eyes.

"You play?" Bea turned toward him curiously.

"Not like that," Macrae said with a whistling exhalation.

The song wound down to a final cymbal crash, and out of the shimmer of it the white guitar took up a fresh new line, old and utterly familiar, but the new turns he was taking it through sent an electric ripple up Macrae's spine into his back brain, where there was a plush explosion.

" 'Black Magic Woman,' " he said, and pulled at Bea's hand. "Come on, let's dance."

"Here?" Bea said. She rolled her eyes around the bar, now mostly packed.

"Let's go," said Macrae. There was a half-inch residue of liquor in her glass and as he stood he took it and tossed it off. The burn was distant under the syrupy sweetness. He tugged at both Bea's hands and she leaned back, away from him—but it was mock resistance. There was a place, between the clutter of tables and the people lining the bar where there was just room to move, sway together like trees in a wind, and as the music turned them they started others turning, and the area around them broke up into slow Brownian motion. When the band switched into something faster, Bea led Macrae in a jitterbug, though the space was small for it. She was grinning, her teeth were white. Macrae could feel his elbows snapping into people behind him as he whirled around, but no one was getting angry. Everybody jostled as they danced. Near him a yuppie woman was flinging her long blond hair into her boyfriend's face, flushed and sweating as she pogoed back and forth with him. A couple of old black men in two-toned shoes and snap-brim hats were two-stepping languidly with their hands raised toward the ceiling, and they were smiling, everyone was.

They danced two sets, with a couple of drinks in between, but Macrae felt sober by the time they left the bar, and had come down completely off the dope. He'd danced it all out, only his head hurt a little. The snow that had been called for didn't amount to much. It filtered down in a fine grainy dust, just filming over the old ice on the street. As they went back toward the West Side subway their hands came disconnected and they were walking with a space between them again, as if they didn't know each other or didn't want to. Macrae pulled on Charlie's hat and jammed his hands into his coat pockets. He squinted up his eyes against the blowing powder of snow.

It was late and the subway platform was empty except for one bundled man, faceless and shoeless, his feet bloody clubs sticking out of the rags. Macrae walked past him, with Bea trailing after, and they stood at the end of the platform, hanging out every so often to look for the light of the train. A couple of rats were scuffling through the litter inside the nearest rail and Macrae pointed these out to Bea, but she only shrugged and ducked her head deeper into her red-wing lapels.

Away down the tunnel was an invisible dripping sound. It was fifteen minutes till the train pulled in, a slow night train nearly half-full, but there was room for the two of them to sit without touching. Macrae's head was humming, his ears ringing a little. Every so often there came a brief brilliant flash of pain, like two nodes of a battery connecting for an instant on either side of his brain. The blues tunes ran over on top of each other behind the hum. In the bar he had danced artfully close to Bea, drawing her in with a hand at the small of her back, above the curve, feeling her open and attach herself warmly to the front of him. There was the same flutter behind his navel when he thought of that. Her smallness was such that he could lift her with one hand. Now, in the windows of the car, he saw their dim and featureless reflections. Over the window was a poster of a woman in a white one-piece bathing suit, stretched tautly on her back and arching toward a blinding sun. Ad for some sort of island tour.

"Where you from?" Macrae turned to Bea, who was chewing black lipstick off the inside of her lower lip. She muttered something indistinct and kept looking at the toe of her left boot, crossed over her knee and gently rocking there. A trembling hunchback in a long grimy coat came staggering down the aisle, rattling change in a cup and muttering, but she seemed too disoriented to beg. The jerk when the subway stopped at Times Square almost threw her into Macrae's lap, and he slid down the bench to avoid her.

Then he got up and went out through the turnstile. On the step he turned back and saw Bea still coming along a step or two behind him.

"Well," he said, as they emerged, "it's been real."

Bea stared at him. "I got to stay with you," she said. "All night, you heard Big Tee."

Macrae rubbed his open hand down the grooved iron of the railing post. A gaggle of other prostitutes hung near the subway stairs on the south side of the street, watching them quietly.

"There's nothing Big Tee could make me do," Macrae said. "And I don't take no presents from him."

Bea stepped in on him jerkily, like a windup toy; she clamped her hand between his legs, arched her neck, and stuck her tongue up and out to the root. As grisly a transformation as if she'd been changed to some completely other order of thing.

"Cut it out," Macrae said, and scissored himself free.

"What's the matter," Bea said. "Too good to pay? Well, you

don't have to, it's free this time. You heard the man." She turned around in a tight circle, wobbling a little on the boot heels. "I don't like how you do!" she yelled. "What you treat me this way for?" The shout echoed off the high walls all around and faded into some raspy laughter that came from the whores across the street.

"I been treating you nice," Macrae said quietly. Bea ducked her head and held her eyebrows in her palm.

"Listen," Macrae said. "I'm not—I one time did go with a woman for money. She was nice looking, had a nice voice. Older than me. I liked her. So we went to the hotel and I paid her and all—I climb on top of her and pretty soon I figure out she ain't there. I mean she might as well have been on the moon. Would rather been. Here was her arms and legs right there doing this job of work, but the rest of her, I couldn't tell where she was at. So I quit, and she goes, you know, *What's the matter* . . . I laid there and I said to her, *Don't you have anybody you like to do it with?*"

Macrae stopped talking. The pain flashed brightly across his head and vanished. Bea was looking up at him with an angry shine in her eye. "You were some kind of son of a bitch to ask her that."

"Yeah," Macrae said. "Yeah, you're right about that. I thought about that. Later on. But she did answer, she says to me, *Everybody's got somebody.*"

"Oh yeah?"

"Right," Macrae said. "Then she says to me, *What are you doing here?* And I didn't have no answer to that one."

"Who was she?" Bea said.

"The bitch, I'll kill her," Macrae said, falsetto, and then resumed a normal tone. "It was in Texas. A while ago."

Bea hung her fingers on the fold of coat cloth at his elbow. "I'm supposed to make you happy," she said.

"I know that," Macrae said, "but can't nobody make you want to."

"I got nowhere to go," Bea said. "I can't go in till morning. If I stay out here he's gonna catch me."

"I never met a pimp I liked," Macrae said. "All right, you stick with me."

There was no light under the door of Charlie's room; he was out, or sleeping, maybe. Macrae guessed out, without knowing why. He hung the hat on Charlie's doorknob, took Bea's jacket, and draped it over a chair back.

"Swell place," Bea said. She kicked at a large ball of slut's wool, which turned over lazily a couple of times on the bare wood floor.

"Want a drink?" Macrae said.

Bea shook her head, hitched up her purse, and wandered around the walls of the room. She stopped in front of a lot of large black-and-white photos of pretty young white people that had been pinned up in a checkerboard pattern between two windows. "Who's all this?" she said.

"Actors," Macrae said. "You know all those theaters east of here. I found them in the trash."

Bea shrugged and moved away. Macrae went into the kitchen and opened a beer. There was a bottle of aspirin on the edge of the sink and he shook out three and swallowed them. When he came back out he saw Bea framed in the doorway to the bathroom at the end of the hall. She had pulled her hair back and taken a tiny jar of cold cream from her purse and was dabbing at the makeup on her face. When she felt Macrae looking at her she turned toward him.

"Can I take a shower?"

"You think you have to ask?" Macrae said. "Use the red towel."

The door shut. Macrae went into his own small room and sat down on the edge of the mattress on the floor, which was wrapped in a faded blue coverlet. There were two army-surplus blankets piled at the end of the mattress and a small space heater plugged into the wall beside it. He turned on the heater and pulled off his shoes. There was a little high-intensity lamp on the same outlet as the heater and he switched it on and rotated it so the light softened, bouncing off the wall. Inside the walls the pipes lurched and began to roar as Bea turned on the shower. Macrae picked up his sketch pad from a litter of papers near the heater and looked at it and put it back down. The heater creaked as the metal warmed, its coils glowing red in the shadows. Macrae flipped up a corner of the coverlet, found his bag and papers, and rolled a skinny joint.

In the bathroom the water shut off with a bang. There was a dribbling sound. In a moment Macrae heard a loud stage whisper: "*Hey!*"

He rose and went to the door. Bea's face was framed in the crack, the light bright behind her. She looked at him inquiringly. Her hair was pulled back sleek and tight away from her forehead.

"Right," Macrae said. He got an old flannel shirt from his closet and passed it to her through the crack. The door closed, and he went back to his pallet and sat there turning the joint over in his hands, fiddling with the little paper twists at either end. He heard the click of the bathroom light switch and Bea walked into the room. The red towel was wrapped in a turban around her head and the old checked shirt hit her well below the knee.

Macrae lit the joint and drew. "Want some?" he said.

Bea knelt on the edge of the mattress and reached out her hand. She put the joint to her lips and held the smoke while she looked all around.

"It's a big place," she whispered, exhaling. "Lotta room . . . two bedroom?"

"Yeah," Macrae said softly, as he puffed.

"Nothing left for furniture, huh," Bea said. She picked at the edge of a blanket. "You don't got sheets?"

"Don't need'm," Macrae said.

"It's like a monk or something," Bea said.

"Some monk," Macrae said.

They laughed together. Bea stopped first. She tucked the coal of the joint expertly inside her mouth, hollowing her cheeks around it. When she beckoned to him, he leaned in. Her hand was light on his collarbone, her tight lips dry, just brushing his. A column of smoke broke on the back of his throat like water blasting from a hose. He swallowed and pulled away, straining successfully to choke back a cough. Bea reversed the joint and took a delicate drag for herself.

"I'm done," Macrae said. He picked up the beer and swallowed across the ragged place in his gullet. "You can finish it."

Bea crawled forward to stub out the joint in a jar lid on the floor near the stack of papers. "Warm in here," she whispered, with an approving nod.

"What are we whispering for?" Macrae whispered.

Bea giggled. "Hey, what's this stuff?" Her normal voice was oddly loud.

"Pictures," Macrae said.

Bea sat back with a sheaf of them. "You draw all this?" The big shirt tented around her, covering her completely, sticking to a damp spot here and there. No part of her showed but her face and her hands. A tinge of natural color surfaced on her lemon cheek. It was almost frightening to Macrae how young she appeared without makeup.

"Hey, what you do, anyway?" she said. "You know, for money."

"Steal," Macrae said. A silver shiver crossed inside his belly. "We're muggers, actually."

"Come on," Bea said.

"Where to?" said Macrae. "Weren't you there for the evening news?"

Bea frowned. A piece of towel came loose from her turban and she tucked it back. Macrae picked up his pad and pencil. He closed his eyes to concentrate; behind them something dark was heaving. He looked again and quickly drew the face of Charlie in the hat—a little wrong, the way the other artist had.

"You knock it out just like that!" Bea said eagerly, taking the new picture. "You could sit on the street and draw people go by. And get paid, like they do down the Village."

"Not in this weather," Macrae said.

Bea looked at the picture a moment more and shuffled it to

the bottom of the stack. If she was making the connections between it and Charlie and the news she didn't seem to think it was worth talking about. Macrae's unease turned in on itself and rolled a short distance away from him.

"*Mira*," Bea said, and looked up at him smiling. In her hand was the first drawing he had done of her on the blue ruled paper. She scooted around and set her shoulders on the wall next to his.

"It's not *that* good," Macrae said.

"You just do that out of your head, huh?" Bea said. "What for?"

"I guess I thought you were good looking."

She turned her head toward him. "What you think now?"

"I'm wondering how old you are," Macrae said. True, but it was the dope had decided to say so aloud.

"We don't give out that information," Bea said primly.

"I'm thinking if you give me more time," Macrae said, "I could probably draw a better picture."

"Oh yeah?" Bea's voice lowered in her throat. "What you plan to put in this time?" She reached across his knees and dropped the sheaf of papers on the floor; Macrae stretched over to shift them out of range of the heater's glow. When he rolled back against the wall she arched over him and her head came down quickly and surely to his. Her lips were long, prehensile, muscular, pulling at his mouth like a warm wet hand. A clear hot sparkling fluid flowed between her mouth and his. An end of the towel came undone and she groped for it falteringly. Macrae pulled the towel free and tossed it to a corner of the room. He pulled back to watch the weight of her hair come splashing down over her shoulders.

When she pushed into him again, the shirt opened and her small breast came naturally into his hand. The nipple was long and stiff as the first joint of his little finger which grazed on it. He stroked her damp hair in a fan shape over her shoulder blades down to her hips and with the other hand opened the rest of the buttons with a sure speed that surprised him. The skin below her navel was taut between the bones and trembled like a harp string when he touched it. She turned and sighed a windy rush into the hollow of his collarbone. Words were hidden in the breath.

"What," Macrae whispered.

Her fingers curved inside his waistband and pulled the cloth out. "Get your stuff off," she said. "Hurry."

Sulphurous bright bursts of light seared through the shrouds of Macrae's dream. He was blinking at Lacy, who manipulated a camera with one hand and an old-fashioned flashgun with a hemispherical silver reflector with the other. Each time she fired it Macrae went half-blind and stumbled among the stones that had scattered away from the wall. He wanted to say to her that since they were outdoors and it was daylight there was no need to use the flash. But either he was unable to speak or else she couldn't hear him.

Why don't you smile? Lacy flashed and flashed like a strobe light. *Why won't you smile for me?* Then she said something more in Spanish and he didn't understand.

With a jackknife snap he sat up from the pallet, sweating and breathless. A police spotlight raked across the windows, brightening the room violently, leaving a scorched darkness when it passed. Bea was tossing, moaning Spanish phrases. He stilled her with his hands and rocked her awake and she came up gasping, her eyes blurred.

"Oh," she said. "Oh ma—I didn't know where I was."

"That's all right," Macrae said. "You're right here, now." He stroked her and drew her down under the blanket and made a hollow in his shoulder where she nestled.

"I didn't know where I was," she mumbled.

"All right, all right," Macrae said. "Neither did I."

A stiff east wind blew off and on across Forty-second Street, picking up bits of newspaper and cardboard and scattering them back against Macrae's ankles. He walked with his head tucked in, and when the wind rose it slicked his hair back against his skull like the fur of a wet beaver. When it stopped, his hair tumbled forward and fell into his eyes. There was almost enough fog from his breath to blow rings.

Charlie walked an arm's length away from him, hands jammed in his pants pockets, shoulders bowed tight. He cut sideways suddenly, veering into a doughnut shop. Macrae followed. Meeting the damp cushion of warmth inside, he straightened up and blinked and wiped his nose on the back of his wrist.

"Better get you a hat," Charlie said.

"You ought to get rid of that one you got."

Charlie peered up at him from under the rolled wool rim. "What for?" he said.

"You know—," Macrae began.

"Pipe down," Charlie said, but without urgency. A weary Egyptian counterman in a brown polyester service jacket was wiping a rag over the snake bends of the counter, lazily moving toward them. Macrae reached around Charlie and took a napkin from a dispenser to blow his nose. There were three whores with big hair sitting at the counter's tail end, in the corner with the pay phone, and one of them looked up and began to giggle, Macrae didn't know if it was at him or not. He folded the napkin over and stuck it in his coat pocket.

"Don't need any hat," he said. "What my daddy use to say, long as you keep your bosom warm you don't need to worry about the rest of you."

"Your bosom?"

Macrae reached to give Charlie a thump on the breastbone. Charlie tensed up for a bare instant, then relaxed into a chuckle. The pay phone rang in the back and one of the hookers got up to answer it. She wore a short fuzzy jacket and Lycra tights striped like a candy cane. Charlie pulled his hat off and wadded it in his hand.

"You're a case," he said to Macrae. He spun on his stool and spoke to the Egyptian, who was waiting. "Coffee, black, and a cinnamon roll."

In the rear the hooker let a laugh fly jingling into the phone. She turned and swayed from side to side, leashed by the receiver's cable. As the Egyptian turned to Macrae a dagger of light cut through the show window and slapped against his cheekbone.

"Coffee light to go, no sugar," Macrae said.

"What's the matter?" Charlie slapped the streaked vinyl of the stool next to his. "Don't you want to sit down and eat a doughnut?"

Macrae shook his head, watching the hooker hang up the phone and prance back to her seat. He was wondering where Bea was this minute, and if these women knew her, or how well. "No bag," he said to the Egyptian as he paid. He tore a small half circle from the lid and replaced it on the steaming cup.

"Where you off to in such a hurry?" Charlie said.

Macrae shrugged. "No hurry. I'm a man of leisure."

"Until tonight you are," Charlie said. "We'll get together around dark?"

Macrae shrugged again and swung through the door. Only a little short of the lunch hour, the street was relatively bare, because of the cold, probably. It was bright, though, as if a pane of light had shattered and come ringing down in jagged bursts. Macrae had to squint as he continued. A couple of doors down he stopped in a smoke shop barely larger than a phone booth and bought a pair of sunglasses for five dollars, dark green and styled in aviator teardrops. Then he jaywalked to the south side of the street, near the library, and climbed the stone steps toward Bryant Park. As he cornered the building his toe caught on a crack and he stumbled. The coffee sloshed back to scald his wrist and he swore at it.

"Smoke, smoke," a voice said, sarcastically. It was Rafael, passing the other way.

Macrae switched the coffee to his other hand and shook his dampened arm. "Doing any good?" he said.

Rafael snorted and rolled his eyes. "I'm going in, man," he said.

"You'll miss the lunch crowd," Macrae said.

"Too cold," Rafael said. "For them or me. You don't need anything?"

"I'm set." Macrae paused and set his coffee on the concrete balustrade, watching Rafael walk down to street level. Ten feet below, he broke into a jog, then leapt up and took a hook shot at the cup, which Macrae snatched back with both hands. Rafael landed in a crouch and jogged off, laughing.

The clumps of ivy around the tree trunks in the park looked a deeper green through Macrae's new shades. He walked to the south side of the rectangle and sat down on a wooden bench, sipping his coffee through the tear in the lid. Across the cobbled path from him a dead man lay spread-eagled on a backless concrete bench like a sacrifice on an altar; at least he looked like he was dead and when the wind lashed his long hair over his face he did not stir. Macrae took a box of Marlboros out of his pocket and found a big roach tucked between the silver paper and the cardboard. Narrowing his lips to hold it, he struck a match.

A policeman came through on foot, snapping his club against his dark glove leather, turning for a brief glance at the corpse laid out on the bench. Macrae cupped the roach out of sight, dropping his hand toward a drain near the bench's foot, until the cop passed by. Then he tore off the cover of his matchbook and rolled it as a holder for the roach, and so he got the last of it. When he was done he dropped the scorched twist of paper into the drain. The cop had turned and was coming back; he stopped before the corpse, stooped, and wrinkled his nose. Taking the body by its swollen foot, he gave it a vigorous shake. The dead man sat partway up and cursed him ferociously, then made to lower himself again. The cop prodded him inquisitively in the ribs with the butt of his club. Like a kid teasing a caged dog with a stick, Macrae thought, only no cage. The cop had a pleasantly round black face and he smiled amiably as he poked. Finally the dead man swung his legs down to the cobbles and stood with an effort and began to stagger off across the bars of shadow cast by the tree trunks, looking back resentfully at the cop, who followed him at a short distance, smiling yet more broadly now.

The wind rose and fell. Macrae lit a cigarette, wasting one match. His fingers were red and stiffening from the cold, but he felt happy here, regardless. He smoked and drained the dregs of his cup. A scurf of spilled coffee was hardening on the sleeve of his coat. Macrae raised his cigarette near his eye and studied the ash lengthening on it and the smoke coiling upward in the cold clear light. The wind picked up and teased the ash loose and carried it away. Macrae's shanks were beginning to freeze to the slats of the bench. He stood up creakily and moved to the grating in the center of the cobbled path and lowered himself onto it. Steam from a tunnel down below held him in a column of invisible warmth. He was eye-to-eye with a fat squirrel who picked through the ivy not a yard from him, looking at him with a glittering dark eye. If I was home, Macrae thought to it, I'd shoot you. Skin you out and fry you up . . . The squirrel turned its back and cocked up its tail in a question mark.

A pair of secretaries, or so they looked, came from the library side and settled themselves on the concrete bench where the dead man had lain. One set a folded newspaper to the left of her while the other lifted cartons of hot soup from a paper sack. Macrae let his eyes drift shut. The talk of the two women was an empty chittering blowing past his ear. He shifted on his haunches and winced slightly. His pelvis was sore, from a pounding by Bea last night or the night before. She came to him two hours before light, not every night, but often, and often they'd still be at it when the dawn leaked in at his windows. He could see her then, punching her hips forward, astraddle him, her breasts molding soft shadows under one of his ribbed undershirts she liked to wear in bed. Her eyes were half-shut and her mouth soft and slack but her free hand had gathered a clutch of the mattress cover and with her every breath her nails cut into it sharp and taut as the talons of a hawk.

The wind blew, the cone of heat swung away from Macrae, and his eyes opened as he leaned from the hips, tilting after the ghostly warmth. The secretaries were getting up from the bench, telling each other it was too cold to sit out. Macrae watched them tap past him. Their coats were bright solid colors, one red, one electric blue. The wind died down and the shell of warmth fastened itself around him again. He was drowsy, his eyelids thickening. Just on the near side of the border of iron hoops that hemmed in the ivy, a red cardinal hopped on the rough-cut cobbles. It twisted its head for a sidelong look at Macrae and then the wind picked up and blew it away.

There was a rattle behind him and he turned. The secretaries had abandoned their newspaper on the bench, and now the wind turned it open to the centerfold, then scooted the whole thing onto the ground. It spread out fanwise with the wind shuffling the pages and Macrae craned over, into the cold, to see the news flick by. Karate murder, a Mafia trial, cartoon, something about the subway, the mayor, a starlet, a mugging . . . The sketch of the man in the wool hat turned over and Macrae reached to snatch the page. The picture was as usual captioned $400 BANDIT. A middle-aged couple from Greenwich accosted on Broadway and Fiftieth Street, the woman held hostage while the man, some sort of Wall Street analyst, was escorted to his ATM . . . Except that the muggers had taken watches and jewelry, it could have been Macrae and Charlie, but it wasn't, that was the hell of it. Macrae stared at the grubby newsprint, tight to the tearing point between his hands. At his insistence they had shifted operations across town, and besides, they had done nothing for more than ten days.

The wind stopped for a single beat and then hammered down on him so hard it made his eyes run. He double-folded the sheet of newspaper and crammed it in his pocket, then took out the wadded napkin to blow his nose again. So cold his ears were getting numb. He got up and walked quickly back to the doughnut shop but Charlie was no longer there. The place was more crowded now, with lunch business. Macrae sat down indecisively on one of the few free stools, just under the cash register, by the door. He wasn't altogether sure if the clipping was good news or bad, but when he tried to not think about it at all his mind was overgrown with tendrils of a nonspecific cannabis paranoia. His tongue was thick and gluey in his mouth, and when the Egyptian stopped in front of him he couldn't think what to say immediately. Then he ordered eggs and hash browns. When the food came he was surprised at his hunger, and he ate eagerly, stooping over his plate.

The door swung open and shut with gusts that chilled the back of Macrae's neck. He looked up and saw Bea standing at the cash register, calling snappily for a pack of Salems and a coffee to go.

"Hey," Macrae said, pushing back his plate as he straightened. Even sitting down, he was not much below her eye level when she turned to him. Her eyes were pinched in a headache expression.

"Want to sit?" Macrae said.

"Where at?" said Bea.

Macrae looked around. There were no stools. He shrugged. "Here," he said, digging in his pocket. "I'll buy you coffee."

Bea crossed her eyes at the crumple of small bills. "Look at all that money," she said. The Egyptian handed her the coffee in a white paper sack and she rolled the top of it in one hand.

"You're in a good humor," Macrae said uneasily. He stood up and backed away from his stool. "Sit a minute?"

"No time," Bea said.

84

"Where you going in such a rush?"

"Sell my snatch," Bea snapped. "What you think?"

Macrae flinched. Bea held the glance. "Got egg on your face," she said.

Reflexively Macrae dabbed at the corner of his mouth with a napkin, watching her stalk out. "Mood swings," he said, to no one in particular. Knives and forks clacked uninterrupted all through the little room. Macrae paid his check and went out. The sidewalks were busier than they had been earlier but he didn't see anyone he knew.

Near midnight Macrae and Charlie caught up with a pair of women walking together down Vanderbilt Avenue toward Grand Central Station and ran them into a doorway. College girls, as it turned out, probably on their way home for the vacation. Both had Columbia IDs when Charlie turned out their purses, and one had a Vermont driver's license.

"Convenient," Charlie said, snapping the blue-and-white Citicard between his fingers. "This won't take a minute, will it?" He ran his hand up under the wide waistband of the girl's leather jacket and locked it around her belt. Fastened to the small of her back, he turned her and propelled her down the street toward the bank awning beside the station. Macrae watched them walk away; from a dozen yards it might have passed for a lover's touch.

"What's going to happen?" the other girl said to him in a small voice. She was a little shorter than her friend, and more plainly dressed—a dark cloth coat, but funny multicolored knitted gloves, like what a little kid might wear. The glove felt plump and scratchy in Macrae's hand.

"Take a walk," he said, and led her across the street. A taxi came roaring out of nowhere and pinned them in its lights. Macrae yanked the girl to the opposite curb, away from the blaring horn. "New York drivers . . . ," he muttered.

"You're not from here?"

"This hellhole?" Macrae looked down on the girl. She wore little round glasses with dark wire rims.

"Look," she said. "Just tell me. Are you going to hurt me?"

"No," Macrae said. He looked at their linked hands, embarrassed. The girl nodded thoughtfully. Macrae pulled her a step backward, to clear a passage for an older couple in bulky overcoats who were walking arm-in-arm toward the station.

"What if I run?" the girl said. "What if I start screaming?" She tugged her arm from his, experimentally. Macrae tightened his grip a little.

"Don't do that," he said. "There'll just be a scuffle. Like a boyfriend and a girlfriend, having a fight? And anybody'll just go the other way if they see it, you know how it is around here."

"But what would *you* do?" the girl said.

"Hey," said Macrae. "It's not about anybody supposed to get hurt. We're a little short of cash is all."

The girl shuddered from her hips to her shoulders. "I'm cold," she said. "Do we have to just stand out here?"

"Let's see," Macrae said. He led the girl across Forty-third Street by her hand and peered in the window of McAnn's. On the far side of the dingy Christmas scene in the display case, a lone bartender sat on a high stool, looking generally in the direction of MTV jerking silently on a highset screen. Deep inside the place a couple of old-country drunks slumped on the counter and that was all.

"All right," Macrae said. He swung the door open and steered her to a table by itself in the front corner, by the pay phones and the Lotto machine. When she was seated he let go her hand and she took off the gloves, finger by finger, and stuck them in her coat pocket. Under the coat she wore a cream silk shirt with a monogram. She was pretty in a severe way, with narrow crisp features, her hair cut short and plain like a boy's. Macrae stepped toward the bar, keeping himself half turned to her, in case she might try to come out of the alcove. He pulled out his money and frowned at it. Charlie had taken all that was in the purses and he could barely make up five dollars now, change included. He shrugged and rapped on the bar with a quarter, then ordered a couple of drafts.

"Best I can do," he told her, sliding her one of the glasses. "Like I said, we're a little short at the moment."

"Oh," the girl said, "oh, I don't want anything." Her teeth were chattering.

"Hey, you really are cold, aren't you?" Macrae said. He reached to touch her, then changed his mind. The girl tensed and controlled her trembling.

"You're okay," Macrae said. "It's just business. Fifteen minutes and you're back on your way."

The girl nodded. "But that other guy. He's rough."

Macrae shrugged. "It's just his way. He wants you scared. You know."

"This never happened to me," the girl said. "Everybody said, but it—"

"Now listen," Macrae said, but he couldn't think what she ought to listen to. He scooted his stool so he could rest his back on the edge of the counter. On a triangular shelf above the girl a second television with the sound turned off swirled in an MTV delirium.

"Brigid was raped," the girl said suddenly.

"Brigid?"

The girl twisted her head toward the window. Macrae looked past her into the display shelf, at the seedy back of Santa's red coat, the moulting reindeer dispersed on a crumple of sheet dotted with stick-on stars.

"Your friend?" Macrae said.

"She knew the guy," the girl said. "She didn't go out with him or anything, but he walked her home from a party one night, late. And he followed her into her room and he did it to her, just like that."

"Jeez Louise," Macrae said, feeling vaguely outraged. Groping in his pocket for his cigarettes, his fingers grazed the clipping and he frowned. He pulled the pack out and lit up. "Then what happened?"

"Nothing." The girl took off her glasses and folded them on the table. Her eyes were liquid and brilliant. "She went to the dean but there wasn't evidence, they said. Because she didn't go to the cops first and she didn't go right away, she waited . . ." The girl was staring at him like she expected his help. Above her, Madonna was slithering around the TV screen, working her lips in the humming silence and describing large looping figures with her bare navel.

"There ought to be a law," Macrae said.

"He's still in school," the girl said. "He smiles when he sees her. He's probably done it to other people. He could do it to her again."

"How old are you?" Macrae said.

"Eighteen, why?"

They ought not to let you run around loose, he thought. Then he remembered that when he was eighteen he had spent his first days in the county jail, waiting a week, two weeks, for somebody to make bond . . . But the girl was still expecting something.

"Relax," he said. "I'm not a rapist. I'm a thief."

The girl pursed her lips together. Her eyes appeared to swirl for a second and then she burst into tears. Macrae twisted his head to look all around the bar. The bartender took note that a woman was crying and quickly averted his eye.

"What's wrong?" Macrae said, fidgeting with his cigarette. "Come on, what's the matter?"

"The train," the girl blubbered. "We won't have the money for the train."

"Oh, Christ," Macrae said. "Look, just give me the purse already. Just give it to me, I'll give it back—" He set his cigarette in the dented ashtray and dug into the purse for the billfold and its clutch of cards. On the Visa card a name was embossed: Mary S. Cleveland.

"Mary?" Macrae said. "That your name?"

The girl looked up at him through her swimming eyes.

"See this?" Macrae said. "You buy your ticket with this here. Like you would have anyway. We don't take credit cards. Just cash."

"Okay," the girl said. "Okay, I didn't think."

"I don't carry no credit card myself." Macrae leaned over to the shelves behind the counter and snagged a couple of napkins off a stack. "Come on," he said. "Blow your nose, it'll be all right."

The girl dabbed at her eyes with a napkin and settled her glasses back on her nose.

"I'm sorry," she said.

"Don't worry about it." Macrae drained off his beer and tapped the second glass. "You really don't want this?"

The girl pushed the glass toward him. "What's your name?"

"I—come on, you know I can't tell you that."

"Sorry," the girl said. "I forgot."

"You don't have to keep apologizing," Macrae said. He read her wristwatch upside down; it was half past midnight. "Okay," he said. "It's time."

"Are you going to leave me here?"

"You'll be fine," Macrae said. He gulped at the second beer and then stood up. "Give it five more minutes, then you just walk across the street and buy your ticket. Your friend's going to be there, she'll be all right . . . Or if you rather, you can sit right here and call nine-eleven. But if I see you come out that door before five minutes, I'm going to cut your arms and legs off with a chain saw."

The girl jumped in her seat.

"Kidding," Macrae said. "You see a chain saw on me anywhere? Well. You have a good Christmas, now."

Charlie had beat him back to the table on the balcony, and he pulled out the sheaf of bills as Macrae climbed up.

"Nothing to drink?" Charlie said, cutting the pack and passing Macrae his half under the corner of the table.

"I'm down to about a dollar," Macrae said, counting the bills out onto his knee. "Was. Hey, what happened? Ain't but a hundred and thirty here."

Charlie sighed out a breath of smoke. "All she had. I'd of come back for the other one but I didn't know where you took her."

"You cleaned her out?"

"I had to, didn't I, she didn't have but two-twenty in the account."

"God, Charlie," Macrae said, "they were just kids."

"Rich kids," Charlie said. "What's eating you?"

Eighteen years old, Macrae thought, my Lord. In only a couple of years Mary Cleveland and the like of her seemed to have moved a whole generation away. But I never knew anybody like them, he reminded himself, not hardly. He'd sat in the jail cell, snapping the chain that held up the bunk and watching the light creep around the walls, breathing delicately because one of his ribs had been cracked in the fight. His left dog tooth was loose in the socket and his tongue could shift it with a distant dull pain that was almost pleasant. In a day or so they set the bail and Lacy came right away to tell him. It was a little jail, old-fashioned. They stacked their hands one above the other, fingers wrapped round a paint-crusted bar.

What's the good word, Macrae said, and touched the loose tooth with his tongue.

He's going to live, Lacy said. *He's going to be all right, I guess.*

Reckon you'd say that's good for me.

It'll sure make it easier to get up the bond. She shook her head. *What in the world did you do it for?*

Ah, Macrae said. *I couldn't tell you.*

Lacy looked at him, shaking her head again, her eyes sad, liquid, seeming to recede. Macrae shifted his tooth again, to feel that twinge. He knew she thought he meant he didn't know.

"*Yo.*" Charlie snapped his fingers in front of Macrae's nose. "Macrae, Macrae. How many fingers?"

"Enough." Macrae swung away from Charlie's hand and pulled the scrap of newspaper out of his coat. "You seen the paper?" He shrugged the coat off and let it fall over the chair back, watching as Charlie scanned the clipping.

"Copycat," Charlie said. "No big deal. How long you been carrying that clip?"

"I don't like it," Macrae said.

"What's not to like? They catch them, they'll hang our stuff on them probably."

"Yeah," Macrae said. "And if they catch us, they'll probably hang their stuff on us."

"You can look at it that way if you want to," Charlie said. "What do you want to do, get a job?"

"It's been done."

"By you?" Charlie said. "Employment record: AWOL from the army. Two months New York City mugger, hands-on experience."

Macrae looked out over the railing. The place had emptied out, except for the night stalkers. Big Tee and a few others were playing cards at a table by the window. Also there were some probable homeless with money enough to buy a place to sit by the glassful. Evan sat idle behind the bar.

"You're not laughing," Charlie said.

"Knock it off."

"There's always pimping," Charlie said.

Macrae turned back toward him. "Watch out, Charlie."

Charlie spread his hands on the table. "Hey, I didn't mean anything."

Macrae kept staring at him.

"I didn't," Charlie said. "Go get yourself a drink, Mac, you need an attitude adjustment. You can buy one for your . . . girlfriend."

"You didn't say, *your* whore *girlfriend*."

"I didn't think it." Charlie reached in his shirt pocket and peeled a ten from his own roll. "Go ahead, I'll buy."

"She's here?" Macrae said, relaxing. "I didn't see her."

Charlie pointed a finger straight down at the floor. Macrae stood up and craned over the railing. Bea was sitting by herself at the back corner of the bar, chin propped on her hand. As he watched, her elbow slipped off the counter and she momentarily lost her balance on the stool. Macrae straightened and glanced back at Charlie.

"You tell me." Charlie turned up a hand. "I got nothing to do with it."

Macrae heaved himself up again. "Is this my day, I wonder?" he said.

"You tell me," Charlie said. "So far, you didn't get arrested."

Approaching the corner of the bar, Macrae gave Evan a whistle just loud enough to get his attention. Bea had stretched both her arms across the counter and was clutching its inner edge like a desperately seasick person clinging to some fixture of a rolling ship.

"One and one?" Evan said, uncorking a bottle.

"You're the doctor," Macrae said. He snapped his fingers, but Bea didn't stir, and he took her by the chin and turned her head around to him. Her yellow-green irises had eaten up her eyes; there were no pupils left but a pair of dark pinpricks. Like this her face was as alien as the face of a feral cat. Evan set down the glasses with a clink. Bea's head lolled away from Macrae as he reached for his drink. He drained the shot glass, sighed, and reached for Charlie's ten.

"On the house," Evan said.

"Thanks." Macrae pocketed the bill. "I don't suppose *she* wants a drink."

"Pa—" Evan blew out a burst of air through loosened lips and turned his back.

"Come here," Macrae said, pulling Bea's face around to him

92

again. Her hands rose and waved in front of him like seaweed underwater. "What did you do?"

In the bar mirror he saw her head rolling slackly by his, and behind both of them the card players at the table, Big Tee with his back to the room. The reflected view was broken up by some small cardboard Santas with movable joints, taped here and there to the mirror glass. He lifted Bea off the stool and set her on her feet; her knees wobbled, then locked to hold her. He put his arm across her back and got a grip in her far armpit so as to move her across the floor.

"Lemalone," Bea mumbled, as if she had just now become aware that someone was trying to engage her somehow. Her toes turned under and her feet began to drag.

"Pick it up," Macrae said, aiming her for the stairs. Seemed like he would always be ferrying some woman around whether she was willing or interested or not. "One. Two. Pick'm up." He supported her up the stairs with both hands on her back. At the table she flopped into a chair and let her arms swing down below the edges of the seat.

"Take a picture," Charlie said. "Here she is, now what do we do with her? Hey, don't get salty, now."

But Macrae was staring glumly at Bea slumped all over the chair. He had come up the stairs without his beer because he lacked a hand to carry it. Bea's head lay all the way over on her shoulder, like her neck was broken. A rim of white showed under her eyelashes. He took her by the shoulders and gave her a rattle; her head swung back and forth disconnectedly.

"Mmmmm," she said. "Mallri . . . Malone . . ." She lost momentum. Macrae let her sag back.

"You been smoking rock?" he said, and looked over his shoulder at Charlie. "Dust, you think?"

Charlie scratched the side of his nose. "Could be scag."

"Well, goddammit." Macrae switched back to Bea. "Did you stick a needle in your arm?" He took her wrists and pulled them out, but the pale skin of her inner arms was clean except for a few freckles.

"Try the leg." Big Tee was walking in an arc around the table, swaying his torso lightly from the hips, enough to jingle the rows of gold chain on his chest. Macrae flicked his eyes away from him and looked at the hem of Bea's shorts.

"Mo high up," Big Tee said. "Right round where she start charging. To some people."

Macrae raised his head reluctantly. Big Tee had halted about a yard away, between his chair and the balcony rail.

"You know where it is," Macrae said, "it must have been you that jabbed her, huh?"

Big Tee lifted his acetate shirttail to scratch his belly, then snapped his elastic waistband. "You know she not a virgin," he said silkily, inspecting the cling of the fabric to the ridges of his stomach muscles. He took a step backward and set one buttock on the rail.

"It'll kill her," Macrae said. In the chair next to him he could hear Bea breathing lightly through her mouth, the way she did when she was sleeping.

"Don't let it bother you." Lazily Big Tee turned his head to look out over the bar below. "Plenty mo where she come from."

Macrae closed his eyes and massaged the bridge of his nose. Twin flashes of white light pulsed briefly under his lids. He looked again. Big Tee was lowering his head toward one hand; a knot of weight-lifter muscle came up on the back of his neck like a buffalo hump. Macrae thought of the girl Brigid meeting her rapist in class or at meals. He didn't really remember what she had looked like and doubted Charlie would either. Had she been blonde? He thought he heard Charlie start to shout as he dug the balls of his feet into the floor and lunged, striking Big Tee lower than he'd aimed, around the waist. The railing cracked open and Big Tee went sailing out over the floor as light and gentle as a falling leaf, or so it appeared to Macrae during the long period of frozen time when he himself was hovering in midair.

He dragged himself back, clutching at a length of railing that had held. Charlie had seized his other arm. Below, Big Tee lay among the splinters of the table his fall had shattered, moving his arms and legs weakly, like a bug turned on its back. Evan vaulted over the counter and ran to check him, then straightened and looked up. He indicated Macrae with a slightly shaky forefinger.

"Out," he said. "Both of you, out now. You're barred."

Charlie twisted his hand on Macrae's upper arm, like he meant to give him an Indian burn through his shirt. "What did you think was going to happen?" he said. "Now look what you done."

seven

Now I got you, Macrae said, *what am I going to do with you?* He kept the question to himself. Bea came out of the nods next day, more than a little hung over, but quiet at first. A glassy slick of silence had closed over the night for her and she didn't know what had happened until she talked to Rafael in the stairwell and came back up to Macrae with her eyes glittering.

"What you do that for, huh?" she said. "Huh, huh?" She was half-laughing and half-afraid.

"Tired of him all the time in my face," Macrae said. "I don't know, I didn't plan it."

"Rafi says you broke his back."

"Couldn't tell you," Macrae said. "I hadn't been to visit . . ." He got the gossip, though, the same as her, but never just one story. Big Tee was paralyzed or merely sore, laying out for a while on the Upper West Side or sealed in a body cast down at Saint Vincent's. The only sure thing was that nobody seemed to be seeing him out on the street anymore. His ladies were mostly going independent; a couple took up with other pimps. Bea, so far as Macrae was concerned, was supposed to be retired.

"What I'm supposed to do all day?" she said, glaring at the dust bunnies in the corners of the room from where she slumped on a stained and swaybacked sofa. "When you don't even got a TV or nothing . . ."

"Hey, you're right," Macrae said. "Charlie, let's go steal us a TV somewhere."

"People don't carry'm in their pocket," Charlie muttered.

"A Watchman," Macrae said. "What the hell."

Charlie stood up without replying, zipped up his jacket, and with a sour yellow-eyed glance at the pair of them, he slid out the door.

"At least you oughta have a boom box," Bea said, kicking her heels against the bare board floor. "I mean, *nothing* to do around here."

"You should be in school," Macrae said.

"It's Christmas, dumbass," Bea said. "School's out."

They spent so much time in bed it got wearing. "What you looking at?" Bea began to say whenever Macrae gave in to his nagging impulse to scope out every inch of her skin for needle marks. Her arms were clean but he found the one jab more or less where Big Tee had suggested he should look for it, along with some other spots on her inner thighs that were more ambiguous.

"What you looking at," Bea said.

Macrae turned over and lay back, a little farther than he'd planned, thumping his head on the wallboard behind him. "Can't just be doing this all day," he said.

"Wanna bet?" Bea rose to her knees and set her hands on her hips, stretching her spine up so the skin of her stomach pulled into a tight triangle.

"Shut up about it," Macrae said. "I'll take you to the movies."

Sex stuff bored her and no wonder. Macrae too. She liked kung fu, or Schwarzenegger or Stallone. In the huge half-gutted theaters down Forty-Second Street, she liked to wander from clump to clump of the loose-joint dealers and street rappers with their blasters beating low who came to the movies like they were cocktail parties. Macrae stayed slumped down in his seat, his back to a post if he could manage it, chain-smoking till his mouth was sandpaper and looking at the screen through the snarls of smoke. It bugged him to wonder how she knew all the guys she seemed to know, and that she usually spoke to them in a street Spanish too fast and urgent for him to have any hope of following. None of them ever glanced up at the picture until some slugging or shooting started.

"Might as well be back on the firing range," he said, clutching Bea's elbow and pointing to *Cobra* on the screen. "Except they don't even bother to make any sense which way they point the guns. We got to go see something else for a change."

"Like what?" said Bea

"I don't know," Macrae said. "Something with a story to it?"

The johns still turned to look at her out on the street, and if she stood still long enough, then somebody would be sure to come over.

"You got to get better clothes," Macrae said.

"You think so?"

"It's winter, ain't it?" Macrae said. "You need some jeans and like a long coat. Can't always be walking around in your underwear."

"I hear you talking," Bea said. "You buying too?"

"Business been slow," Macrae said. "I maybe could take you down to Canal Street."

"Yeah, right," Bea said. "I think I want to go to Fiorucci."

So maybe that was where she went, sometimes, when she was gone for hours or a day, though she never seemed to bring back much in the way of clothes. There were signs of her having money she never got from Macrae, though, and that nagged at him. He never saw her comatose again but he didn't know for sure it didn't happen. When she came back, he'd look obsessively for fresh tracks but never found them. And when she started out again they'd argue.

"What you talking?" Bea flashed at him. "This isn't no convent, man, I don't see no nuns around."

"All I asked is where are you going," Macrae repeated dully.

"Whaddaya think, you're my *father?*" Bea flung out. Macrae watched the door shivering in the frame. Someone down the hall was calling out dimly in Spanish to protest the slam. Like her father was exactly how he was beginning to feel, though he was only a few years older than she was and had surely not been expecting it. Sometimes he wondered if she had any father, mother, family of any kind. Rafael might have helped him here, but at this stage of the game he was embarrassed to ask.

"You could always take her key back," Charlie said.

"What's that?" Macrae called. He walked down the hall and opened the bathroom door. Charlie came dripping out of the shower, ducking under streamers of panties and hose that dangled from the rod. He wrapped a towel around his waist and turned back to brush an undergarment with his thumb.

"What I want to know is, where did all this stuff come from?" he said. "Did she unload it all out of her pockets, or what? Looked like all she had was on her back when she came here."

"What was that you said before?" Macrae said.

"Take the key back," Charlie said. "That was it."

"You mean you want her out?"

"I never said that," Charlie told him, picking up his razor and turning to the mirror to wipe off steam. "It would give you a little more control, is all . . ."

Barred from Evan's place, they'd switched to a Blarney Stone a few blocks farther up. It didn't much matter, there were dozens of bars. The new place was smaller, darker because it was set in the middle of the block, and had no balcony. Charlie bought Macrae drinks to cheer him up.

"What's the deal?" he said to Macrae. "You got to think it through."

"There is no deal," Macrae said. The mirror behind the bar was warped like one in a funhouse, compressing his and Charlie's faces and molding their heads to points.

"You got it," Charlie said. "At least with Big Tee, she knew what was happening."

"You think I should go into being a pimp?"

"I don't know, do you want to marry her?"

"Not especially," Macrae said, choking as he drained his drink.

"There you go," Charlie said. "I mean, you're *not* her father, the girl has got a good point there."

Macrae turned to look at him, tired eyes like holes to the back of his head. "What about you, Charlie, what do you do about it? I don't see you bringing nobody home."

"Home," Charlie said, as if he'd never heard the word before. He squeaked around on the vinyl stool. "Who, me? I just do what I have to."

They knocked over an odd couple on Eleventh Avenue—the girl a dark teenage voluptuary, the boy spindly, prematurely thin haired, his face a brilliant mass of pustules. East Orange, New Jersey, the IDs read. Macrae held the girl lightly by her hip and the nape of her neck; he could turn her head more easily than a mannequin's. She kept chewing her gum with a light smacking sound and blinked her eyes slowly and automatically, as if she had no idea where she really was or what was really happening. Charlie made the boy pull off the motorcycle boots he was wearing, and out plopped a fat white envelope.

"How'd you know where he had it?" Macrae said, crowding next to Charlie in the single toilet stall of the Blarney Stone.

"Feel this thing," Charlie said. "It was giving him a limp." He opened the envelope and took a quick count. "Three *thousand* dollars?" he said. "They must of been planning to coke up a whole high school."

"We better get out of here," Macrae said. "People gonna think we're fairies."

"Just let me look at this a second," Charlie said. "Well, well, well. Santy Claus is coming to town . . ."

The big score didn't make the papers. Dope dealers wouldn't report, was Charlie's read. In fact the copycat had been making more press for them than they had themselves lately. Macrae didn't worry, for once. He bought a boom box and a small color TV—"A Sony of your own-y," he said when he plugged it in for Bea. He also got a pawnshop guitar, a cheap undersized Yamaha with next to no tone. The idea was that Bea would learn to play it. Give her something to do, Macrae argued, be learning some kind of something at least. Bea refused to cut her nails, though sometimes she'd strum a little, awkwardly, with Macrae's arm around her shoulder, his left hand framing the chords. It amused her more to hear him play a few simple tunes and sing a bit in his cracking voice.

G—C, G—D . . . "General Washington and Rochambeau—," Macrae sang, and stopped and went back to the G chord. "General Washington and Rochambeau—"

Bea turned from the TV to look at him with a smile. "That all there is?" She giggled.

"All I remember." Macrae slid the guitar down on the floor.

Charlie bought a bag of blow—where, Macrae didn't know, but not from Rafael, who didn't usually handle it. But once he had it he didn't seem very interested. He took a snort or two in the evening, not more, and not even every day.

"Be all gone before you know it," Macrae said, corkscrewing up from the refrigerator with a beer in his hand. In the next room, Bea had built a crystalline hillock on a blue plastic plate and was eroding a slope of it with the ballpoint-pen barrel attached to her nose.

"Nothing to me," Charlie shrugged. "Just get rid of it."

Macrae hesitated, twisting the top of his bottle, then handed it to Charlie and stooped to the refrigerator to get himself another. "What did you get it for, then, if you don't want it?"

"Fair question." Charlie shifted, setting his tailbone against the edge of the sink. He reached behind himself to tip ashes into the drain, then turned his head toward the window; beyond it the night street was oily with slow rain. "It was those kids put it in my head, I think," he said. "I knew where that money was planning to go."

Macrae lowered his voice, under the radio bopping out funk in the next room, where Bea was flying. "What, did you used to have a habit?"

"Hmmm." Charlie dropped his cigarette butt in the sink and began picking at the blotchy pink scars on the backs of his fingers. "That was a long time ago, buddy boy."

Macrae watched Charlie's hands with a stoned fascination. The tips of his first two fingers were streaked yellow and brown from the Lucky Strikes; the stains were stronger on the left hand. When he raised his head his eyes were flat, a depthless unreflecting green. "You could always call it your Christmas present," he said.

"Handsome of you," Macrae said. "Anything you want from Santy Claus?"

Charlie rearranged his legs and stroked the line of his jaw, looking through the doorway into the other room; Bea had got up from the couch and was standing loosely before the window, swaying and twitching slightly to the music.

"I think not," Macrae muttered. "There's trouble down that road."

"Not if you're not looking for it," Charlie said. "And why would you be?"

"What do you mean," Macrae said.

"I mean, what's the problem," Charlie said, still looking past Macrae to Bea in the other room, as she raised her hands, shuttered her eyelids, and made reptilian twists around an invisible axis. "You know," Charlie said, "just like she says, you ain't her daddy. And you're not married, like *you* say—"

Macrae moved a little forward and made as if to speak, but Charlie stopped him with one finger raised. "Hey, she's a pro, that's all I'm saying. What else has she got to do?—I could maybe take a little time off her hands."

"Starting to remind me of Big Tee," Macrae said, "the way this conversation is going."

"Well, let's can it, then." Charlie shifted his weight off the sink, though he wasn't backing up. "I wouldn't of brought her in here, myself. She's here already, that's another matter. But it was just a thought, don't let it get to you. Especially while you're doing coke."

"Okay," Macrae said. He tried to take a deep breath, but his jaws were tight. "All right then, forget about it."

"That's the way," Charlie said. "Got to be careful with that stuff, or it'll get you in a temper."

It was true he hadn't had much experience with coke. Never

so much, so strong, for so long. He liked the way it lit the inside of his head, though the insomnia that came with it was a bother. Rafael copped him Valium to take care of that, prescription grade, a bottle of punctured pellets like tiny blue life rings. One of those dissolved on his tongue and Macrae could drop off if he needed to, after the strenuous and ingenious combinations he and Bea had reinvented on the mattress, when they each seemed to ride the same endless wave of sinuous sparkling energy. In the lulls, he drew her, sleeping or waking, naked or half-clothed. It was better than Rafael's dope for that; with the coke what he saw moved effortlessly from his eye into his hand.

All in all, he had known worse Christmases. A lot worse—he could count them. When the coke ran out, he felt a little antsy, needing the little blue pellets, even during the day sometimes, to settle him. Bea was more than a trifle bitchy, he noticed. Then one day she was just gone.

A night, two nights—on the third Macrae knew it was different this time. He didn't really want to go out but sat on his mattress, his head propped on the baseboard molding. The gooseneck of his lamp was twisted so the light bounced off the wall. Pictures he had drawn of Bea fluttered on their pushpins, in the draft that leaked under the window sash. Outside it had turned cold again; again it had begun to snow.

Charlie stuck his head in the door. "Hey, Macrae, don't you want to make some money?"

"We got money," Macrae said. His arm declined mechanically from his mouth to stub out a cigarette beside a pile of butts accumulating among ashes on the bare floor.

"Take your mind off it," Charlie said neutrally.

"Off what?" Macrae snapped, sitting up with a jerk. "Do you know something I don't?"

"Not me, bud," Charlie said, and showed his empty hands. "None of my business, you made that clear."

Macrae leaned back again and retracted his head into the shadows. Charlie withdrew, leaving the door an inch acrack, and after a couple of minutes Macrae heard the lock tumble as he left the apartment. He didn't know how long it was before he jacked himself up and put on his coat and went out also. Snow blew lazily into his face as he trudged east with his head tucked in, licking at the flakes that clung to the corners of his mouth.

At the old corner bar he went in without hesitating and walked immediately to the counter. It was slow, and Evan caught his eye at once.

"I thought I told you—" He interrupted himself, popped the dishtowel, and folded it into his apron string. "All right," he said, and put two glasses on the bar. "All right."

"Don't I do good time?" Macrae said. He paid, drank, pushed his change around on the sodden wood. Idly he looked around the place, distracted by the vague movements of his own head in the mirror beyond the rows of bottles. The broken balcony rail was nailed up in wooden splints. There was no one up there now, and no one anywhere he knew well enough to speak to. He chimed his empty glasses together and Evan came to pour again.

"You seen—" Macrae paused to clear his throat. "You seen Big Tee anywhere around?"

"What, are you looking for him?" Evan snorted. "Yeah, he's been in a time or two, last couple days. Say he popped a couple ribs, is all. Lucky."

Macrae squinted at his short glass of bourbon and dipped his tongue in it, like a cat, before he knocked it down. It tasted a little off, somehow. A smoky dislocation was setting up in the top of his head—signs he might be catching a cold. He locked on his own hooded eyes in the mirror. What happens already happened, he thought, and I'm just waiting to find out what it is.

The explosion of a gunshot in his dream was still throbbing when he lunged up from the mattress. From the street came a long hysterical ululation, in Spanish so far as it contained any words at all. Rubbing wouldn't clear the fog from the window, so he heaved up the sash and leaned out, gooseflesh pricking up on his bare chest and arms.

Big Tee stood three stories down, against a backdrop of clean snow, moving Bea here and there in his hands like a posable figure. "Come on down, Mac," he called cheerfully. "She wants you to see this, we both do."

He came down the stairwell, pacing his steps; not until his feet crossed the outer threshold did he notice tangentially that he had forgotten even to put on shirt or shoes. All he had on was the pair of pants he'd slept in. Bea twisted and turned in Big Tee's hands, thrashing her hair across her face, but it was unclear if she were struggling or dancing. On the second floor of the tenement across the street a light snapped on and Macrae saw a shadow cross the blind.

"Come on," said Big Tee, conversationally, "let's get a little bit out of the way." He shifted his left hand to the top of Bea's head, yanked, and twisted it down to waist level. Macrae didn't know he had started forward; he saw the muzzle flash and heard the boom a nanosecond later, as Big Tee raised his free arm toward the sky. Macrae stopped, rooting himself in the inch-deep snow. A big chrome revolver, magnum by the size and sound. He looked where the pistol pointed: in the high crack between the buildings a random arrangement of stars could just be seen.

"Take it slow, now," Big Tee said. "Don't spoil it. One step at a time." He dragged Bea away, holding her head so low she stumbled and had to catch herself several times on her hands. Macrae followed them to the mouth of the alley, not trying to close the short distance. He could no longer feel his feet. As he turned in he kicked into something and lifted his foot to pull the triangle of glass from the ball of it and continued.

Big Tee had stopped a third of the way down the alley, near a double-duty Dumpster with a heap of wet cardboard teetering beside it. He was out of the angle of the streetlights but Macrae could still see him well enough. Bea's babbling streamed on in a continuous regurgitation. Macrae could catch a word or two he understood—*mother . . . please . . . Mary . . . I . . . look . . .* Her hands flew around her face in movements of prayer or convulsion. Macrae did not think he was being addressed, it was more like he was watching the scene unfold from behind a sheet of one-way glass.

"Watch close," Big Tee said. "The hand is quicker than the eye." He jerked Bea suddenly upright. Macrae saw the side of her head come open and its contents blossom out to splash a scarlet snowflake on the alley wall. The roar of the shot began an instant later and went on and on. Big Tee released the corpse's hair and it dropped forward with a limber movement to its knees. Its mouth hung open still, and the lopsided features were still composed in an expression of some kind, so that Macrae felt relieved in a minor way when it toppled over face down in the snow.

"My final offer," Big Tee said. "All yours. She's still warm . . ."

"There's something wrong with you," Macrae said. "Something out of the ordinary. You'll come to a bad end."

Big Tee turned the huge pistol in his hand and looked at it as if it were completely unfamiliar. "You're not gonna drop a dime on me," he said, "'cause you're the four-hundred-dollar bandit."

"You're right," Macrae said. "I won't do that." His voice sounded funny and remote.

Big Tee shrugged, slipped the gun into his jacket pocket, and flipped the hood of his sweatshirt up. "So, Merry Christmas, Mac," he said. He scuffed his toe at the foot of the corpse; its shoe came loose, disclosing a small frayed hole in the heel of the blue sock.

Macrae nodded. "Happy New Year," he said, hearing his estranged voice coming back to him from a howling long distance away. There were splotches of blood marking his way into the alley, but now the cut had frozen and he left no stain on going out.

eight

At four in the morning Charlie hailed a prostitute standing lonely in a side street north of Times Square. Price negotiated, they went through the whole routine at the hotel. *Mister and Mrs. John Q. Smith*, Charlie signed a grubby index card. Married for an hour, or till the meter should part them . . . A flabby person of indeterminate age and sex, head bound up in a rip of sheet, mopped a slime trail down the hall, as if intending to paint the floor with dirt.

Inside the room, Charlie paid, then watched sidelong as the whore divested herself of her nether Spandex. She crossed the floor, storklike on her skinny legs, to fit him with a condom. At his gesture she sighed and rolled up her striped top into a bundle under her armpits so that his skin could meet hers there. They lay awkwardly on the bed, tilting toward the hammock in the middle. Her black Andean eyes sank half out of sight behind her heavy brown wedges of cheekbone; her wig rubbed slightly askew against the grimy mattress. Charlie put his hands on her upper arms and gripped. Foolish disconnected thoughts rattled together inside his head. In prison he had been raped himself a number of times and his mind had wandered similarly during those experiences. He pushed himself partly up from the woman and looked around the room. Two dim bulbs were stuck in wall brackets either side of the door, above them plume-shaped stains of soot on the dun-colored wall as if torches had once burned there. In the far corner a yellowed sink with a broken faucet dripped a spiral rust mark toward the drain. Charlie let himself down a notch. Under him the woman's skin was dry, rubbery, and rather cool. She breathed long and evenly in the studied manner of a marathon runner. Charlie turned his head toward the door. Beyond it he could hear another door open and close and a titter or shriek cut off by a slap. He finished, got up, cleaned himself perfunctorily, and put on his pants. As he checked the pockets the whore sat up, straightened her wig, and looked toward him.

"See you, Cholly . . ."

She was Big Tee's new girl, the one who had fought with Bea—had been new a couple of months before, at least. Charlie had been with her in this way a time or two previously but he never thought she knew his name.

Outside the matte black sky had just begun to liquefy toward dawn. Charlie felt freshened, as if from exercise, and he was more sharply aware of the cold. He had been good drunk when he picked up the girl but now he felt sober and airy. Dome lights were flashing red and blue and red in an uneasy tickling rhythm from an ambulance and police car parked at the mouth of the alley alongside his building. There was a knot of tense activity in an oblong of stark searchlight near the Dumpster in the alley. Because of the hour there were no rubbernecks bystanding but lights had come on in a few windows of the tenements across the street and Charlie saw some shadows standing there, and heard a voice calling from one window to another. He crossed the street to give the police more clearance, then buttonhooked back to his own doorway without looking again.

A muttering came from Macrae's room as Charlie passed toward the bathroom. He took a long shower, then dried off and inspected himself methodically and dispassionately for any symptoms of disease. The whispering continued when he came out of the bathroom door, just one voice, and he couldn't make out the words. Charlie smiled sourly at the thought that the little slut had come back to the boy. Although the complications of having her there had become wearing, it might be worth it to have Macrae easy in his mind. Although, come right down to it, if your peace of mind rested on the fidelity of a whore that was apt to make it a hard thing to protect.

Fully dressed again, he catnapped on his mattress for an hour or two, and rose when it was full day. The muttered monologue was still leaking through the crack under Macrae's door. A lot to catch up on, Charlie supposed, shrugging as he locked the apartment door behind. He ate a meal in the vicinity, found a paper to read his horoscope and the funnies, played a few games in a video arcade, and returned to the apartment about noon. He could hear the one-sided conversation issuing from the kitchen this time, over the sound of running water. But when he turned the corner there was nobody there but Macrae, leaning crazily against the sink. He had twisted the swivel of the spigot so that the stream of water broke on the lip of the basin and came splashing into his bare midsection, then ran down to pool on the floor.

Charlie's first thought was that Macrae must have stumbled upon some new drug of unsuspected potency. He reached around him to shut off the water, and Macrae instantly stopped his mumbling, as if to this cue, and made a strange paddling movement in the air with his hands. Charlie caught at one of them and found it blazing hot.

"Cha . . . Chawl . . . ," Macrae said vaguely. "M'sick, Chawl . . ."

"No lie," Charlie said. Macrae slumped forward and Charlie bent his knees to receive his weight, then hauled him to the couch in the next room. His head would not keep upright but went lolling over the seat back.

"Wadda . . . ," Macrae muttered toward the ceiling.

Charlie stared a moment, then went to the kitchen and filled a glass. The tiles below the sink were squelching and shifting underfoot from the spillage. Charlie had to raise Macrae's head with one hand, tilt the glass to his lips. Macrae's bony Adam's apple bobbed a time or two, and then his throat appeared to lock so that water ran out and down his neck into the hollows of his collarbone. The doorbell rang.

It was Rafael, gesturing with a cigarette, drinking from a

half-pint of rum in a paper sack. Charlie was surprised at that. Rafael was usually a light drinker, preferring his weed, and it was early too.

"You hear?" Rafael said to Charlie, and then looked past him. "Yo, Macrae, you heard?"

Macrae had twisted over on the couch and slumped with his cheek against the fabric, showing the whites of his eyes.

"What's with him?" Rafael said.

"What's to hear?" Charlie said.

"They shot Bea," Rafael said, staring at Charlie out of bloodshot eyes. "Blow the side her head off, man."

Charlie nodded. "They who?"

"Doan know . . ." Rafael took a belt from the bottle, wiped the neck, and cleared his throat with a strangling sound. He stepped around Charlie and went over toward Macrae. "What is this?"

"He's got fever," Charlie said. "You got any ideas?"

"Should take him to the clinic." Rafael stubbed out his cigarette in an old tuna can converted to an ashtray. "Man, he doan look good . . ."

Charlie masked his mouth with a hand. There was almost nothing he liked about the idea of a delirious free-associating Macrae in the hands of welfare doctors.

"Would he make it?" he said. "I doubt he can even stand up."

Rafael knelt down and lifted one of Macrae's bare feet. A track of dried blood ran from between his big toe and the next one, blackening under the ball of his foot. Both his pants legs were still stained with wet.

"Look, he been walking around outside this way," Rafael said.

"What, barefoot?"

"Look like it." Rafael dropped Macrae's leg, letting the heel thump on the floor. He stood up, bracing himself on the couch arm, and turned toward Charlie. "He do her, man?"

"Love is a funny thing," Charlie said. "Where'd it happen?"

"The alley there," Rafael said, flapping one hand at the wall.

"Ah yes," Charlie said. "There's one thing, though. He don't have a gun."

"No?" Rafael arched his eyebrows and pulled at the cinch on his ponytail. "Then how you . . ."

"Finger," Charlie said. "Finger in the pocket or a stick or something."

"You *lie* . . ."

"Hey, people are stupid," Charlie said, and then added piously, "Besides, gun's a year mandatory in New York."

Rafael burst out laughing. "Okay," he said. "All right, man." He stooped to brush the back of his hand against Macrae's cheek, then yanked it back. "Huh," he said. "You not taking him in."

"I'm against it," Charlie said. "There could be some problems."

Rafael nodded. "I gonna try to get you some medicine, then, bring down this fever. You make him drink a lot, okay? Water, juice . . . You got soup?"

"Soup powder," Charlie said.

"That's all right," Rafael said. "You put in garlic too." He nodded again and then went out.

Charlie spent the next few hours helping Macrae to and from the bathroom and the bed, offering him drinks or mugs of soup base. Macrae talked continuously and Charlie did his best to ignore what he said, which was easy enough since most of his words were unintelligibly slurred and what was clearly enunciated seemed senseless altogether. At dusk Rafael returned, shaking a bootleg bottle of Keflex in his hand like a rattle.

"This got the mojo?" Charlie said.

"It's strong," said Rafael. "You give him four times a day, it gonna stop this fever." He looked at Macrae, who lay drawn up on the couch, whistling dry air through his parted lips.

"Where'd you get it?" Charlie said.

"Pet doctor."

Overnight and the whole next day, Charlie fed Macrae the pills. The pills or something seemed to silence him, which was a relief.

But often he had to work his throat with a hand to make sure he swallowed them. The same with anything Macrae took to drink; he was messy as a baby. Charlie did what he had to, hating the job. As a child he had been witness to his mother's death from cancer, had seen her contorted with nausea, crazed with painkillers that failed to work. Now as then he wanted out, to abandon the apartment and whatever was in it. Find a new place, new city even. But on the second afternoon, Macrae's fever finally broke.

He slept for twenty hours, a relaxed and silent sleep, his breathing easy and regular. Around the middle of the next day Charlie was roused from a stupor in front of the TV by a noise in the hall, and he lifted his head to see Macrae come tottering into the room, weak but apparently rational.

"What time is it?"

"What day is it, is what you probably want to know," said Charlie, swinging his feet to the floor.

"That bad?" Macrae said.

"You been sick as a dog. Sicker."

Macrae made his way around the room, leaning on the walls for balance. "Goddamn, I'm hungry," he said.

"You got the right," Charlie said. He watched Macrae go groping into the kitchen, listened to the refrigerator door swing open. When he heard the tab of a beer can rip, he smiled inside his hand. Macrae came creaking back into the room, carrying the beer and two slices of Roman Meal bread folded over each other, and lowered himself cautiously onto the couch.

"Damn, I'm hungry," he said again.

Charlie reached over and snapped off the television. "You been on a liquid diet," he said. He lifted the bottle of Keflex from the windowsill and handed it to Macrae, who tilted it curiously to the light, squinting at the label.

"Supposed to take them till they're gone," Charlie said. "Every six hours or whatever. You missed a couple times, I didn't want to wake you up."

"What is it?" Macrae said.

112

"Some antibiotic," Charlie said. "Ask Rafael. Hey, what happened to you, Macrae."

Macrae shrugged evasively and chewed on his bread. "Just a bug, I guess."

Charlie snorted. "Like a four-hundred-pound bug, yeah, right."

"We got anything to eat around here other than bread sandwiches?"

"I been scared to go out," Charlie said. "Afraid you'd die on me. You might always try a mayonnaise sandwich."

Macrae swallowed the ends of his bread and chased it with a long gulp of beer. With thumb and forefinger he slightly indented the walls of the can and then squeezed it elsewhere to watch it pop back. He brushed a palm across his bare chest and frowned.

"You got a cigarette at least?"

Charlie threw him the pack. "Smoke'm in good health," he said, and stood up. "I can go out, tell me what you want."

Macrae lit up and rocked his head back, looking up at the blobs of hastily rolled paint depending from the ceiling. He blew a twin spout of smoke from his nostrils and brought his head back to the horizontal. "A baseball bat."

"Say what?"

"Baseball bat," said Macrae. "A wooden one." He opened the medicine bottle, shook out a capsule, and rotated it in his fingers before he swallowed it. "A little hacksaw, bow saw or something. Epoxy glue, some solder, three or four rolls of heavy solder, and a drill."

Charlie gave him a wondering look. "Electric drill?"

"Don't have to be," Macrae said. "A brace and bit would do the trick. Get a big bit like an auger."

"Check," Charlie said, closing his mouth with a definitive click. "Anything else, boss?"

"Bring me pizza," Macrae said. "We're low on beer, too."

———

Outside it was raining a gray cold rain that took the old stained snow in gritty streaks down the gutters. Charlie's paper sacks were soggy and beginning to tear by the time he got back with Macrae's shopping list. Rafael was sitting inside the door, halfway up the stairs to the second-floor landing, and he got up to help when Charlie lurched in.

"You goan play some baseball?" Rafael said. He took the hardware sack and peered in. "What you do, you goan operate?"

"Better ask him," Charlie said, beginning to climb. A slick pad of paper skated out from under his foot and he staggered and caught himself against the wall.

"He better, then," Rafael said.

"He's up at least," Charlie said, trudging around the turn of the stairway. "If he's in his right mind or not, I'll let you judge."

In the kitchen Charlie laid out pizza and beer, pulling the kitchen table out of the corner to make room for three to sit. Macrae ate a slice, laid the crust down beside the box, and drew the baseball bat out of the bag.

"Thought you were starving," Charlie said.

Macrae slapped the thickness of the bat into his palm, then laid the end across his knee. He rooted the bow saw out of the bag and made a cut an inch or so from the bat's tip.

"Did I buy that for you to just tear up?" Charlie said.

Macrae didn't answer. The saw bit through the bat and the end clacked on the floor. Macrae picked up the round of wood from the floor and set it on the table next to the pizza box, then bit into another slice of pizza.

"Macrae," Charlie said, "what're you doing, bud?" He turned to Rafael. "What's he doing?"

Rafael pushed aside his napkin and began to nod at Macrae, arms folded across his chest. His eyes were dark and shining, concentrated. Macrae gripped the bat between his knees, the handle propped down on the floor, took up the auger, and started to bore. The long spiral bit went corkscrewing into the wood, kicking back sawdust and little chips. When Macrae was satisfied with his hole he blew out the last film of sawdust and tested the interior with his forefinger. Digging into the bag again, he found the solder and began to unroll it into the cavity. The snaking twists of metal had a dull mercurial gloss. When the first roll ran out Macrae picked up a table knife and tamped it with the handle. The solder flattened easily and seemed to compress a good deal. Macrae got the second roll and repeated the procedure.

"Hit a home run with that, wouldn't you," Charlie said. "I think they got some rule against it, though."

Rafael was continuing to nod, as rhythmically as a junkie riding the slow decline of his rush. "You didn't shoot her," he murmured. "You didn't shoot her, did you?"

Macrae kept his eye on the job. The hole in the bat took half a third roll of solder, and he twisted the metal to break it from the spool and tamped it down with the knife handle. "Throw me a beer, somebody," he said.

Charlie tilted back in his chair to open the refrigerator. Macrae popped the can top and sighted through the ring of the tab at Rafael. "If you knew who killed her, then what?"

Rafael considered. "I'd be angry."

"Yeah?" Macrae flicked the tab toward an empty sack in the corner under the windowsill, then leaned forward to tear a long strip of cardboard from the pizza box. The epoxy was packaged in a double syringe. Macrae cut the tip off and pressed the plunger and began stirring the glue and resin together on the cardboard.

"You'd be angry," he said. It was so quiet in the room that the people calling on the street outside sounded like ghost voices from another world and when the refrigerator shut off it was loud as a shot.

"Sad, too," Rafael said. He flattened his palms on the tabletop, a finger tapped at a grease-spotted paper napkin. "Sad."

"Right," Macrae said. He smeared epoxy onto the circle of wood he'd cut from the bat and pressed it down to cover the leaded cavity. "So you must know how I feel."

Charlie reached into the refrigerator for another beer. It cut back on when he had closed the door, the hum of the motor swelling to fill the room. Macrae picked up a napkin and wiped beads of excess glue from the seam. He pushed back his chair and stood up, letting the bat slide through his hands so it swung low by its handle.

"Better let that glue set awhile," Charlie said.

"It'll hold," Macrae said. "Ain't nothing like epoxy." He made a tight turn and lashed out with the bat, whose end whipped grazingly a quarter inch from the rain-streaked windowpane and swept away a large spiderweb from the corner of the frame. Startled, the spider came scrambling over the sill and scuttled across the wallboard toward the kitchen cabinets.

"I suppose that means you're feeling better," Charlie said.

Macrae watched the spider. He brought the bat up to the horizontal and made a peculiar motion with his wrist. The bat shot straight out toward the wall with a rifled spin in the loose ring of Macrae's thumb and forefinger, and its weighted end printed the spider onto the wall as neatly as if it had been stenciled there.

"Don't you think that's overkill?" Charlie said.

Heels together, Macrae turned back to face the other two. He held the bat in both hands across his chest in the "present arms" position. "Well, I didn't shoot her, boys," he said. "Might as well have, though."

Macrae walked to build back up his strength. The long rain had rinsed the weather almost clean, and there followed several brilliantly clear and cold days, the sky in its narrow tracks above the building tops an oddly jolly blue. Macrae squinted in the sudden wealth of light, which set off electrical flashes of headache in him. At first he could only stay out for an hour or so before he was exhausted, but after a few days his headaches stopped and he figured he was back to normal.

He switched to a nocturnal schedule then, back to his usual habit. The only thing he didn't do was drink, at least not much.

Soon he was outlasting the hookers at night, holding on till the streets cleared perfectly, in that vacant predawn hour of silence.

Quietly he studied the comings and goings of the several of Big Tee's girls he knew by sight. They made confusing crisscrossed trails, among a couple of hotels, a few bars, and coffee shops they seemed to favor. He tried to keep his profile low, not wanting to be noticed following, suspected as a crazy john, a stalker. So it took a while for him to fix on the one apartment all of them seemed to visit. A six-story tenement on Eleventh Avenue, not much different from where he lived. The girls would head there late—or early, depending on your point of view—clocking-out time. Only a favored one or two stayed long.

The downstairs lock was a piece of junk. Macrae was through it in under five minutes. There appeared to be less hanging out in the hallways than in his own building, which was convenient. He climbed a couple of flights of stairs and found a good place off the second landing to wait out of the way, the alcove for an elevator that a scribbled sign downstairs said to be broken. He squatted on his heels, not smoking, hardly looking at anything, holding the doctored bat half-concealed under the skirt of his pea coat. The building was stone quiet, oddly so, even for the time of night. Full of warehoused apartments, must be.

At the click of the door opening downstairs, he could scoot forward a couple of yards and peer down through the stair rails to see who had come in. For the first couple of hours, no one came. Then the girls began to show, alone mostly, one or two pairs. Macrae flattened himself into the alcove as they entered, listening to the click of heels ascending, the slow purr of weary voices, if there were two. Always they turned the opposite way, heading for the apartment at the end of the hall. Most came back out soon after; only the newest girl stayed on. Big Tee never appeared, though once Macrae thought he heard his voice when the apartment door was ajar. He waited until the traffic stopped and he saw the first light bleeding through the small mesh window above the turn of the stair.

Next night he tried a little earlier, sometime between two and three. An hour wait, no murmur, only the muted thump of a stereo somewhere high in the building. At last the door lock clicked and Macrae shuttled forward toward the stairwell. It was the newest girl, bewigged and bedizened, coming in early, and alone. She opened the apartment at the end of the hall with her own key and went in and slammed some bolts behind her.

Out of boredom, Macrae risked a cigarette. A sound like a baby crying came and went, floating up the elevator shaft behind him; he assumed it was only a cat. He wore a cut-off leg of Bea's red pantyhose rolled on the crown of his head like a beanie or a yarmulke. The prickly fabric scratched his scalp and cut a taut band into his skin. The door lock clicked and Macrae slipped forward to the stairwell. In the queasy green light of the tiny foyer he saw Big Tee turning back in the direction of the closing door as if he were speaking to someone there out of sight. But he had only paused to light a short black cigar. He threw his match down, exhaled, and raised his eyes. Macrae rolled back from the gap between the rails, hooked a finger under the fold of red stocking, and dragged it down over his face and his chin. Big Tee coughed once and Macrae heard the squeak of his fancy tennis shoes on the tile as he turned on the landing below.

He could see quite clearly through the thin weave of the stocking, although it turned everything a gory red. He had taken up a batter's stance and was already starting his swing when Big Tee came out of the stairwell. Once again the speed and grace of Big Tee were something to admire as he spun toward Macrae and reached his left arm toward the small of his back, his cigar still tight between his lips, but the bat caught the upper arm against his side and Macrae heard the bone pop like a rotten stick. He braked on the follow-through and wiped the bat backward, brushing Big Tee on the edge of his jaw and jarring him away, into the stair post. The cigar was loosed from his lips and rolled smoking down several stairs to the landing. Big Tee was reaching behind him with his other arm when his foot slipped down a step and as he twisted around Macrae saw the good hand trying for the gun grip that stuck up from a clip holster at the back of his belt. Macrae clubbed the bat down vertically, striking not at the arm, this time the spine. Big Tee shouted aloud at the point of impact and the big shiny magnum went clattering through the stair rails and discharged itself once when it landed butt down in the hallway below.

The door of Big Tee's apartment flew open and the newest girl rushed out screaming, her natural hair frizzing an inch or so from her head, heavy makeup cracking along new fault lines of her face. Macrae raised his masked head toward her for just an instant, and she fled back behind her door yelling and locked it. He went after Big Tee, who had slid to the lower landing and lay with his good arm reaching back up across the corners of several steps. Macrae stamped the arm just behind the elbow to smash the joint and then kicked Big Tee lightly in the shoulder, just enough to flip him over. The back of his head hit the tile with a nasty hollow sound. Macrae thought fleetingly that if he puked, the vomit would back up on the stocking and strangle him. It was not working. As he shattered Big Tee's kneecaps and shinbones he could feel the sadness to which Rafael had referred breaking open inside him to gnaw like an acid at his core. Every blow was struck for nothing and his anger had been lost, unconsummated. He only had to keep on with it because it had all been determined from the moment when Bea first spoke to him on Forty-second Street. Therefore he planted a foot either side of Big Tee's head and let the end of the bat fall onto his clenched jaws many times like a piledriver. Splinters of bloody tooth fanned out over the tile all around. Macrae took a step back from the ruin of Big Tee and beat the bat frantically against the walls and floor and the ceiling not caring where he struck. The weak bulb in the wall fixture exploded and in the dark Macrae went on beating everything until the weighted end of the bat sheared off and he was left with only the peculiar lightness of the handle in his hands. He dropped that too and staggered down into the entryway, rolled his face against the metal mailbox plates and sobbed.

The stocking was soaked with tears and snot and Macrae got himself enough under control that he could tear it off and breath more easily. He turned and rested the back of his head on the row of thin metal mailbox doors. The lost cigar was still smoldering where it had fallen on a step. Big Tee breathed somewhere above it in the dark, with a difficult gurgling inhalation.

"Macrae?" Big Tee made a spitting sound, after which he spoke a little more clearly. "You there, Macrae?"

"I'm here," Macrae whispered. He became still.

"Gommee back dinya, Macrae?" Big Tee foamed toothlessly. "Gommee back, allri . . . How it feels?"

"It don't," Macrae said. He shifted his foot and the big revolver spun away from him, rotating on its cylinder and glinting in the light of the street outside. Above, Big Tee hawked with a roaring sound from inside himself and spat another time.

"Macrae?" He coughed and breathed out with a whistle. "Hey, babe, don't leave me here this way."

Macrae closed his eyes and saw the mazy paths of the Port Authority machine with all its balls helplessly ringing and falling in their chutes. Big Tee breathed in the dark above him with a rasping catch.

"You got to kill me," Big Tee said. "You got to kill me, Macrae . . . I've had it, man . . ."

Macrae hesitated, then opened his eyes. "Do it yourself, you son of a bitch," he said. He brushed the pistol with the side of his foot and the butt clicked against the baseboard as he went out onto the street.

nine

Charlie was hungry, he didn't know why. He'd had a doughnut for breakfast, a hero for lunch, and it was only four in the afternoon, but he felt hollow all the way to his backbone. There was something he wanted, he didn't know what. He walked with his head down, hands jammed tight in his pockets, palms cupping his hipbones through the cloth, on the cross streets south of Port Authority. It was sleazy wet and cold March weather, the sky sagging low between the building tops and rumbling now and then like a greasy belly. Charlie turned suddenly into a small Spanish diner, smaller than a boxcar, close as an oven. A paper sign hung above the griddle, stained with oily smoke, each letter done in a different color crayon:

NO REFUND OR EXCHANGE
ON EDIBLE MERCHANDIZE

Charlie smiled when he saw that, but his lips were tight against his jaws.

He ordered a full meal, soup, rice and beans, liver and onions and green peppers. When the food was given him he ate at the counter facing the show window, still standing, facing out toward the street. The beans were red and the rice was yellow; together they filled a plate. The liver was served separately, in the sort of tin pedestal dish they used at cheap Chinese restaurants. Charlie ate quickly, angrily, hardly chewing the meat, not looking at his plate either but staring out through the glass. A little commuter traffic was beginning to appear along the side street, some women in businesswear and running shoes, striding out grimly, a suit or a pair of suits walking and talking together. It had got windy suddenly, Charlie could see from people's windblown hair. Old newspaper and bits of litter from the sidewalk were picking themselves up and whirling as though there would be a sudden change of weather.

A couple of umbrellas were beginning to go up, and an occasional isolated drop of rain was smashed on the glass before Charlie's face. He saw the wind rip one umbrella inside out, and watched the man struggle, cursing, with the twisted spokes. When he had eaten everything on the two plates he mopped up the gravy and juice with a piece of white bread that had come with it and then turned his attention to the soup. *Sopa de mondongo,* just a clear liquid with a thick webbing of tripe stirring lightly in it a quarter inch below the surface. Charlie picked up the bowl with both hands and drained off the broth, then began to cut pieces of the tripe with knife and fork. It was tough, rubbery, and altogether tasteless. He ate it all, then turned to the register to pay.

The mound of food was pressing out against his waistband, but at the back of his throat he still felt a need for friction, still wanted to tear at something with his teeth. As he came out the door, a man walking hunched under an umbrella slammed blindly into him, heavily enough to jostle him back against the wall, and mumbled something, threat or apology Charlie wasn't sure. A magnesium flare of rage lit up inside his head. He began to follow the man, automatically, around the corner and up Eighth Avenue, threading his way rapidly over the increasingly crowded sidewalk. It was not yet raining enough to pay attention to, just sputtering a little here and there, a sudden chilly drop on his face. The man ahead of him wore a tan camel's-hair coat, stretched at the seams across his back. He walked with a swiveling motion of his hips, as though he were accommodating a big stomach. As they came opposite Port Authority Charlie sped up and cut around in front of him.

"Hey, yo! Fat bastard!" He spat toward the man's face, snapping his neck to project the gob, which went a little wide and short and stuck to the camel's-hair lapel. The man looked down, and up, incredulous. From the front he was not so old as Charlie would have guessed, and not so much fat as massive, refrigerator size. He lunged and Charlie stepped backward off the curb into the surge of northbound traffic, and like a bullfighter caped the fender of a speeding cab that separated the two of them. As he moved the storm broke instantly and completely, rain slashing down in solid layers continuous as fabric. Charlie flipped the finger at the man still gaping at him from the sidewalk, then ran across the other lanes and into the ground level of the bus station.

Inside, he took off his wool hat and wiped the back of his neck and shoulders with it. But he wasn't really very wet, he'd only been caught for a few seconds. His sudden movement had unsettled the heavy meal; he exhaled a large bubble of gas from both ends of himself simultaneously. The rain was driving others in from the street, a few ordinary citizens, but mostly the homeless. There were many of these already encamped on the wide dim expanse of the empty brick floor. Charlie thought the wet ones smelled the worst, as though the rainwater had sharpened their stench. There was a long slurry of them lumped against the walls around the area, while others roamed the floor gibbering at each other or at nothing.

The wave that had come in with Charlie was breaking up, the separate members looking for somewhere to be. Charlie glanced back toward the street, where the rain went on, so sudden and immense the drains couldn't handle it. Dirty floodwater was running level with the curb. Charlie started diagonally across the floor toward the escalators, cutting a straight way through the people who milled around him, bleary eyed and disordered. There was one who looked particularly dissolute and unstrung, standing before the kinetic sculpture sealed in a glass cube in the center of the area, slack jawed and glazed as though drugged or entranced. He was a long, rickety scarecrow, sunken eyed and shaggy. In fact he looked a little like Macrae.

Charlie stopped dead, twenty yards short of the sculpture in the cube. Someone jostled him from behind and went around, muttering. It was like one of those trick drawings where you might see either a white vase or two dark faces staring each other down, depending on how your eye happened to catch it. Macrae and not and then Macrae again. It unnerved Charlie to see him standing so loosely and staring in that dull way. He shook his head and walked across to slap him on the shoulder.

Macrae wanted to keep his eye on just one ball. To see where it went and know if it ever completed a cycle and understand everything that happened to it along the way. The balls were of several different colors but still there were many alike. He had tried to pick out one with a smudge or blister, settling finally on a white cue ball with a distinguishing crack, a blue marbled star spreading over one hemisphere. But as often as not the mark spun away from him and he would confuse the ball with the other white ones and then lose it down in the works of the machine. If it reappeared it was never where he would have expected and then he would have the whole task to try over again.

A hand came down on his shoulder and clamped. Macrae spun away, twisting at the waist to break the grip; when he saw it was Charlie he softened the punch he had started and let it rest as a light open-handed touch on the ribs.

"Slipped up on me," Macrae said.

"What are you doing?" Charlie said. "What do you think you're *doing* here?" He stepped closer. Macrae's back stiffened, automatically. For an instant he was almost at attention. Charlie's face had partly flushed and his neck was swollen and tense as a drill sergeant's. Macrae relaxed and took an easy step back, stroking a hand along his jawline.

"Nothing," he said. "Just standing here, why?"

Charlie made a mock-spastic motion, rolled his eyes to show their whites, slackened his lips to a drooling O, and let his head dangle to one side. Inside the glass, the balls continued to fall and ascend while the clockwork whirred and the chimes kept ringing.

Charlie snapped himself alert. "Standing here," he said. "Man, you looked like you were swinging from a hook."

"What's it to you," Macrae said. "Off my case, Charlie."

Charlie swept his hand in a semicircle away from the glass cube. "Don't you see these people, Macrae? I mean, look at the sorry sons of bitches."

"What about them?"

"You know the difference between them and us?"

Macrae looked into the cube. The blue-starred cue ball turned up its mark as if in a wink, then whirled and disappeared again.

"Do you?" said Charlie.

"We got an apartment." Macrae scratched his ear and frowned.

Charlie stared up at him, bulge eyed and vibrating. "Can't just stand here," he said. "We got to do something."

"Come on, Charlie," Macrae said. "We got money to make it into next month."

"No, I mean we got to *do* somthing." It was almost the tone of a plea this time.

"What, now?" Macrae said. "This time of day?"

"Yes," Charlie said, with total definition. "Now now now now now."

The rain had stopped as quickly as it had begun, though the gutters were still swirling by the time they reached Times Square. Macrae stopped at an intersection and stared across at the recruiting station, there on the cement island dividing the traffic's stream. "I hate this town in the springtime," he said. "Can't even tell the difference."

"Why don't we make some money," Charlie said. "Then you can go on a cruise or something."

"Cruise?" Macrae rubbed his thumb over a streak on his jaw where his razor had missed. "You know, sometimes I think the army wasn't so bad."

"No worse than prison," Charlie said.

Macrae looked at him curiously. "You ever in the service?"

"No thank you," Charlie said. "I've done the other, though."

"Yeah..." Macrae was still looking at the recruiting post, almost wistfully.

"Forget about it," Charlie said. "You never told me—"

"Damn right," Macrae said.

"—but what I think, if they once get their hooks in you again they're going to send you to Leavenworth."

"I could re-up under a phony name." Macrae muttered. "I've heard of that."

"Yeah?" Charlie said. "You want some excitement, we can get it right here. And don't have to sign any papers."

Macrae sighed. "You know it's too early. Look at these people all swarming around, it'd be crazy to do a deal in a crowd like this."

"We don't want to lose our momentum."

"What momentum?" Macrae said. "All right. All right, but we're headed the wrong way. We got to go west, where it's a little quieter."

They backtracked the long crosstown block, passing the bus station one more time. Macrae was peering up; the rain clouds were breaking apart and the bare sky showed dull smoky white beyond them. At the corner of Ninth, Charlie stopped and pulled out his pack of Lucky, but the last cigarette was broken in the middle. He wadded it and snapped it to the sidewalk.

"I got one," Macrae said. But Charlie had already started for a small storefront halfway down the far side of the avenue. Macrae shrugged and went after him. A long line of Jersey buses was lumbering down the ramp with saurian lethargy. Macrae went around the nose of one, crossed the street, and followed Charlie into the store.

The place was a box, barely big enough to hold three customers. At the counter, an old lady on a walker was counting out coins from a cracked leather change purse, to pay for several cans of tomatoes. A balding Korean waited at the register, his face heavy, smooth, inexpressive. At the back, which seemed only inches away, a younger Korean woman in a gray work smock was using an extension grabber to stock the highest shelves with toilet paper. Charlie stood behind her, shifting restlessly from foot to foot.

The old woman completed her payment to the penny and limped out, cans strung to a knob of the walker in a plastic carry bag. The late sun had broken through, outdoors. Macrae saw it shining through the thin furze of her hair as she went out. The door was thick scratched Plexiglas and as it closed it dulled the light. A little brass bell tied to the push bar gave out a faint jingle as the door settled in the frame. The first thing Macrae noticed was the extension grabber falling sideways; he saw with a weird clarity how a crack in the pole had been secured with rings of silver and black. The rubber-tipped tongs swept some jars of pickles from a shelf as the pole came down. One cracked and began to drain over the floor.

"Get that register, boy!" Charlie yelled. He had lifted the stocker off her feet in a full nelson. She shouted something in an Oriental language and kicked backward at his shins. It was like the first time in Battery Park, doing the thing before you knew what it was. Macrae turned toward the cash register. He could see the light of the fluorescent fixture reflected in the smooth, sweaty skin of the cashier's head. The cashier's eyes were round and black and in his right hand he held a small black water pistol. Macrae heard a snap like a mousetrap and felt a beesting on his arm. He slapped his other hand over the spot.

"Holy Christ!" he said. A vermilion stain gloved the inner seams of his fingers. "What did you do that for?"

There was the same popping sound again and some more jars broke on the shelves behind. Charlie pushed in between Macrae and the counter, bulling the woman ahead of him as a shield. Clutching his arm, Macrae ducked low and charged like a football tackle. He smashed the door open with the top of his head. Charlie came out alongside him, shoulder-to-shoulder. Above the door frame and the store sign an alarm siren was howling all over the street. A few passersby glanced over incuriously and went on without slackening their pace. Macrae shook some blood from his fingers and closed his hand over his coat sleeve again.

"Come on," Charlie said, eyes darting either way on the street. "*Don't* run." He took Macrae by the elbow and and in a sort of strangulated walk they crossed the street and entered the back of the bus station.

"Goddamn you for a fool," Macrae said, as Charlie steered him toward an escalator. "You freaking lunatic . . ."

"Who, me?" Charlie said. Macrae turned his face away from him, making a spitting motion. This back escalator wasn't busy; they stopped on a stair and let themselves be carried. The pale greenish walls shut them close around. A Spanish boy with a backward-turned cap was riding down with a shouldered boom box pushed into his ear. Salsa echoed back up the shaft as he passed in his descent.

"Can you move it?" Charlie said.

Macrae bent his left elbow experimentally. There was a pulling sensation in his upper arm but no real pain to speak of.

"Move your fingers," Charlie said.

Macrae turned his palm up and let his fingers wiggle like underwater seaweed.

"Good," Charlie said, leading him around a turn onto a second rising escalator.

"What's good about it?"

"Looks like it missed the bone. You're lucky."

"*Me?*" Macrae hissed. "Why, you—where are we going, anyway?"

"This way." Charlie pulled him off the escalator and hurried him up the gentle slope of the third level. Old mold-colored plastic chairs were bolted in rows alongside the gates to the bus ramps, some few with small coin-op TV sets attached. Charlie supported Macrae by his wounded elbow, frowning at the spot where the pea coat's fabric was matting under the bloody hand. At the end of the corridor they went around the last corner and through the swing door of the men's room.

"Let's have a look," Charlie said. He plucked at Macrae's coat sleeve. Macrae rested a hip on one of a line of sinks. His pale face doubled back at him in the mirror. Charlie undid the coat and peeled it back from the shoulders. Macrae sighed as it came free of his arm. Beneath, he wore a long-sleeved baseball jersey. Charlie cut through the sleeve with his pocketknife, near the shoulder seam.

"Hey . . . ," Macrae mumbled. The cloth rolled away with a slight sucking sound. There was a small black-rimmed puncture in the meaty outer part of his upper arm. Charlie pinched the flesh and twisted it to examine the exit wound.

"Clean through," he said. "Not bad at all . . . Bleeding a bit much, though."

"What?" Macrae looked down, slightly dizzy. The blood that lipped over the bullet hole's edge was shockingly bright on his sallow skin.

Charlie folded the cut-off sleeve into a packet and placed it between the exit hole and Macrae's ribs, then took Macrae's right hand and positioned it over the outer wound.

"Mash down good," he said. "Stop that bleeding."

Macrae nodded and improved his grip. Under his stiffened palm his arm felt numb.

"Stick with it," Charlie said. "I'll be back."

"What, are you leaving me here?"

"Yeah, you better get in a stall or something," Charlie said. "Be cool, I think there's a drugstore right in the building. I doubt I'll be long."

A bit dizzy, Macrae rolled his head back against the dented metal of a stall partition. He could feel only a sensation of pressure between his palm and his rib cage, and a little diffuse pain that was very dim and distant. He half closed his eyes. The gun had seemed so small, not even real, not able to harm him. Some twenty-two target pistol probably. Roundabout there were steps, a flush, the sound of running water. It seemed a long time since Charlie had gone, and Macrae knew he might not come back, that he might have decided not to come back himself if he were Charlie, but this possibility seemed no more real to him than the gun had earlier, and he had no idea at all what he would do if it came to pass.

Steps crossed the floor and the stall door pushed in on him. In the tin frame stood a stranger, eyes moist and bright with a peculiar urgency. His pants were unbuckled around his knees and a long erection wavered up toward Macrae like a deranged mushroom.

"Good God," Macrae said. "Wrong number, buddy, get out of here." He caught the stall door with the point of his shoulder and swung it shut. Keeping his right hand sealed over the wound, he managed to flip the latch closed with his left. His head swimming, he sat down on the closed toilet seat and let it sink. From another stall there came some panting and slurping sounds and a low tense moan. Macrae raised his head again, then let it slowly droop.

"Macrae?" A soft whistle, then Charlie's voice again. "Hey, Mac?"

Macrae came uneasily out of the stall. "Did you know it was queer central up here?"

"No cops, though," Charlie said. "What do you want?" He took a bottle of Pepto Bismol from the drugstore bag he was carrying, broke the seal, and swigged from the bottle neck. "Upset stomach," he explained.

"You poor thing," Macrae said. "What, does the sight of blood upset you?"

"All right, already," Charlie said. "Here, have a few." He held out a bottle of Advil and a cardboard carton.

"You're bringing me orange juice?"

"You're in shock, boy," said Charlie. "You need the sugar."

Macrae shook out a handful of pills and swallowed them with

a slug of juice. After a moment it did seem that his head began to clear somewhat. He drank again.

"Let's have it," Charlie said, opening a bottle of peroxide. He took Macrae's wrist and straightened the arm, then poured a generous amount of peroxide into the wound. The liquid foamed up like a bloody volcano from both the holes and splattered sizzling on the floor.

"Ai yai yai," Macrae said. "What are you doing?"

"Hurt?" Charlie said, meeting his eyes.

"Not that much," Macrae admitted.

"Well then," Charlie said. "Ready steady." He opened a bottle of Betadine and slopped it into the bullet holes. Macrae yanked his arm back powerfully. "Stings a little," Charlie said. "Hold still, now." He began binding up the wound with a roll of gauze.

"Hey, Charlie," Macrae said. "I need a doctor, you know. This is great, but I got a hole through my arm here."

"Well," Charlie said, "we get you home, find Rafael, maybe see what he can do."

Macrae's voice shrilled close to a scream. "I said a *doctor,* not a witch doctor. I don't want voodoo, man, I need a white doctor, with a degree."

"They got some of those in jail, I hear," Charlie said.

Macrae glared at him as he finished off the bandage with tape.

"Okay," Charlie said. "Okay, we'll get it figured."

Two blue-and-whites were spinning their dome lights outside the store when Charlie and Macrae came down the back escalator. The shopkeeper and his assistant stood on the sidewalk waving their arms while the cops stood around waiting them out like a storm.

"Jesus, Charlie . . . ," Macrae said.

"We'll try the other door, I think," Charlie said. "He never should have had that gun anyhow. You think he had a permit for it?"

"All I want to know is where is the freaking hospital," Macrae said.

"Keep your hair on."

They crossed back to the Eighth Avenue exit. Charlie had begun to sweat. He stopped Macrae in front of the door. "Wait here," he said. "Just watch for me." He went out without looking back, and began walking east on Forty-first Street, wondering if he would ever see Macrae again. It was time to leave town but he didn't know exactly how this would be accomplished. He stopped and bought a tube of street Valium from a hawker who wore fancy sunglasses with the name BUSTER cut in the wide gold temple. Putting the pills in his pocket, he walked on.

A car was coming along behind him at a creep, enough the wrong speed to make Charlie turn his head. BUSTER swung up to the driver's side, leaned down for a second, and then rebounded. No sale. The car eased toward Charlie: a green vintage Mustang, Jersey plates. The driver was a kid with multicolored punk hair, alone, looking inquisitively at Charlie from his bare pinkish eyes.

"Sens, sens," Charlie said. "Windowpane." He made the whip motion of one hand he had seen crack dealers make. The driver's window glided down and the kid's head came turtling out. *Dumb*, Charlie thought. He grabbed an ear and twisted, groped open the inside door latch with his free hand, kneed the kid hard in the face and belly, and landed a rabbit punch on the back of his head as he started to fall. He was behind the wheel and off, it seemed, before the kid had hit the pavement altogether.

The crosstown street was clear, Seventh Avenue slow and syrupy. Charlie doubled around and started up Eighth, crawling in the traffic, tires hissing on the wet street. As he drew near the bus station he leaned on the horn. Macrae came loping out and jumped in the passenger side. Charlie tossed him the tube of Valium.

"What is it," Macrae said.

"Poison," Charlie said. "Try it, it'll settle your nerves."

Macrae shrugged and worked one of the tablets down his dry throat. "What's the idea?" he said.

"You want a doctor," Charlie said. "I recommend an out-of-town doctor. That's my medical advice."

"You're the doctor . . ." Macrae laughed giddily. Charlie turned the car toward the Lincoln Tunnel. Buses hemmed him in on either side. The traffic was barely oozing.

"Tearing up the track here, aren't we." Macrae peered around, then leaned forward to fiddle with the knobs of the tape deck. "Blaupunkt," he said. "Class. Where'd you get it?"

"Borrowed it," Charlie said shortly.

"Big day for bad risks, huh, Charlie?" Macrae fumbled out a cigarette and put it shakily in his mouth.

"Are you getting a ride or not?" Charlie said. "Get off of me, why don't you."

"Well, you did get me shot," Macrae said. "I think I got the right to complain."

"Blame it on Bernard Goetz," Charlie said.

"What the hell are you talking about?"

"He shot those muggers on the subway, remember? Gave all the patsies an attitude."

"Give up, Charlie." Macrae groaned. "Just shut up and drive the car."

charm city

Porter walked haltingly up the last block of York Road and turned left by the liquor store on the corner. He went a third of the way down the length of the long, low building and, forcing the hesitation out of his step, swung open the heavy door of the bar. At his left hand a double counter ran a short distance toward the back wall, turned a right angle, and went all the way across to the restaurant wall. Right at the angle of this L a stool was free, just under the mount of the smaller television. Porter went there immediately and sat down. He shook some rainwater off his canvas hat and fixed his eye on one of the two bartenders working, the shorter of the Italian ones, with the long nose and the gunmetal blue sheen of beard growth spreading on his ax jaw. Porter couldn't remember his name, if he had ever known it, and if the bartender recognized him he gave no sign. No real reason why he should, Porter thought, it's been this long. And what am I doing back here, anyway? He sniffed and sneezed the thought away.

"Lemme have a Seven and Seven," he said, unrolling a twenty from his pocket and smoothing it flat on the bar. It was a new synthetic stone countertop, he noticed now, and he looked up. The bartender had turned to reach down a Seagram's bottle; behind the liquor shelves the paneling and the mirrors were all new. The place had been remodeled, in a manner of speaking, though the total effect seemed much the same as before. Porter looked down the long leg of the L toward the restaurant partition. Most of the seats at the bar had been taken by the ageless career boozers, damp tangled clothing twisted into their wrinkled skin, leaning in tight to their ashtrays and glasses. Still, he had seen the whole place busier. This was a lull between the get-off-work-ers and the late-night crowd, which would include a fair number of young punks from colleges round about. Porter was the only black on the bar side at the moment, same as the last time he'd been in the place, about twelve months before. Not that the bar was officially segre-gated or anything like it, it just seemed to naturally evolve that the ofays used the barroom and the homeboys bought their sauce on the liquor-store side to carry it off somewhere else and drink. Porter had only started coming in here because of Carole, who'd been introduced to the place by the pack of white girls she ran with at work.

The bartender spritzed Seven-Up into his glass from a multi-tracked hose and picked up the twenty to pay himself. Porter eyeballed the change when it came back, the fan of bills limp and humid with beer. He'd cashed a week's paycheck before he came over. Since he got out of jail he'd been signed on with ManPower, only until he could get something better, and the jobs had come steady so far. Day shift, too, which was lucky. He'd said he'd work swing or night too if need be, anything they could get him. The ice was sizzling in his drink. Porter picked up the glass and took a swallow and put it down. A sweet warmth spread over the back of his throat. He felt in the pocket of his damp field jacket and found a pack of Salems. No matches, though he thought he'd had some.

Across the double counter of the L's short leg, fluorescent lights bore brightly down on the liquor-store side. Porter had always liked this seat, where he could watch the traffic there, which right now was steady. Everybody strolling in for the Friday-night buy, six-packs and half-pints as a rule. The buy line formed across the counter from where he sat. There was a turnstile at the York Road entrance so you couldn't get back out that way; the only exit door was right by the cash register on the short leg of the L. Porter didn't recognize the kid in the cashier's slot tonight. He was young, certainly, with a round olive-skinned head with a haircut so close it was almost a shave. He wore some strange New Wave costumery, big black-and-white checks on his shirt, an X of suspenders on his back. In his ear swung something that looked like a spinning lure. He faced away from Porter, into the liquor-store line, punching the register and serving up the cigarettes and half-pints, which were shelved on racks above and below the counter.

All sorts of people coming in, shaking the rain from their clothes, old folks, young bloods, high-stepping ladies getting their primer for the evening. Porter stared at them all openly, as though he were looking through one-way glass or just staring into a bar-room mirror. He knew that from the liquor-store side it was hard to see much in the dim of the bar. When he recalled the unlit cigarette in his fingers he stood up and leaned across the counter to dip a book of matches from the bartender's plastic tackle box, which also held cherries and lime wedges and the like. He lit the cigarette, exhaled, and swiveled his stool the other way.

Basketball played on the projection TV mounted down there on the wall between the bar and restaurant sections. Porter didn't know if that was new or not; there had always been some kind of an oversized TV down there, he thought. Below and to the left a thick-legged, heavy-breasted waitress was waiting for the bartender to relay her a hamburger plate that had just been shunted out from the kitchen through a small rabbit hole beside the main cash register in the middle of the bar. The girl was attractive in her slatternly way, black oily hair draining toward the corners of her half smile. There was a sexual weight in the shift of her hips as she turned away from the service hatch with her tray. Get your mind running that direction, Porter thought with a grimace, if you get yourself locked up a few months and come out with a dog all you got left for company. God keep me away from some Italian white girl anyhow.

He turned in the other direction and when he saw Carole standing in the liquor store he almost fell off his stool. No. Well, maybe. Porter took a long drink that left him sucking ice. The girl was standing in front of the cold box that held the Asti Spumante and the cheap sparkling wine. She wore a bright red vinyl raincoat, calf length, and shiny from the wet. Carole had just such a coat, though Porter didn't recall the little matching hat that hung down her back on an elastic thong. Cute touch just the same. The hair looked the same, straightened, teased up high with a foot-long fall over the shoulders. She opened the case, took out a bottle, and came tripping along toward the cash register. Slim ankles and high heels ... She was smiling a little, not at him, of course. Long fingernails curving around the gold foil of the bottle neck. Porter saw she was nothing like Carole, really. They both had a very slight resemblance to Janet Jackson and that was it. She smiled at the New Wave cashier as she paid. Plenty good looking and if he'd been in a different mood he'd have wanted to try and follow her home, though it looked like her plans for the evening were already set. What a stupid idea to come in here, Porter thought. He ordered another drink.

Stupid now, and stupid then, the last time he'd been here. One false move and you're dead—well, that's just the way it goes sometimes. Things with Carole had been going so well up until that night, in spite of her being pregnant. As a matter of fact it had become clear to Porter, as he thought it over while doing his eleven-month bit in the workhouse, that the pregnancy was the very reason why everything seemed to be happening so nice, even though it was unscheduled; they didn't even have a plan to marry. A year before, Porter would have thought it a nuisance at best to have some girl pregnant, and with one of the wrong girls it would have been a disaster, but now when he looked at Carole he felt a light floating pleasurable sensation he'd only got before from butyl or speed or sex itself.

She wasn't showing yet, only her breasts had grown much larger. Although she complained about this, Porter could see that it pleased her as much as it did him. Carole, who had always known what she wanted and gone after it in the most disciplined and purposeful way, who had completed two years of community college and was on the management track at the telephone company, was pleased and proud to be carrying his baby. Porter, therefore, was surely going to straighten out and fly right for good this time. He'd been on a long way back from dropping out of school, some time on the street, a little drug traffic, a few inconclusive skirmishes with the law. Then he met Carole again, after ten years, and saw how she'd hauled herself up hand over hand from the old neighborhood. He passed the GED and got himself apprenticed to a master plumber. Was pulling down good money and soon would have a wife and baby to spend it on.

He felt that to be true, at least, though nothing had been said. When they talked about the pregnancy it was still along the lines of *What are we gonna do about this?* Porter knew that they would just let it ride until abortion was out of the question. Then he would ask her and she would say yes.

Carole was officially still living in her own apartment, but about 75 percent moved into the duplex Porter rented in Govans. Porter had even gone to the pound and got himself a dog, an outsized six-month-old puppy he named Sooner. The dog was a collie-shepherd bastard, with short hair and a great plumed tail and an expression you could call either soulful or egg sucking, depending on your mood at the time. A dog made things homier, Porter thought. Carole laughed at him for this, saying that what the dog really made things was smellier and messier, but Porter had always wanted a dog, had wanted to be able even to consider having a dog, from when he was a kid on East Eager Street, where the tenements crumbled straight down to the pavement and there was no place even a blade of grass could grow. Back of the duplex was a patch of yard with a wire fence around it where Sooner could stay when he was at work. He had that and he had Carole too, most nights.

She was sleeping over the night she began to spot, just a little at first. "Probably nothing," Carole said, but Porter knew if she really thought that she wouldn't ever have brought it up. She sat on the edge of the bed, slumping slightly inside the white lace baby-doll nightie Porter had got her for Valentine's and staring across at the phone. There was no one really she knew to call; she hadn't been to a doctor yet, and she hadn't told her mother or anyone else but Porter. Finally she phoned up her aunt Luanne, who was only six or seven years older but already had a string of babies, all living on welfare down Eager Street.

Luanne said it was probably nothing, *Why honey, you know that do sometime happen and it usually don't mean a thing. You just take it easy a day or two and try not to be on your feet so much. And girl? I didn't have no idea you all was pregnant. That's something now, it surely is . . .*

Carole put the phone down and stared at it like she thought a look would destroy it. Porter didn't know what had teed her off so, till finally she lay back and said to the ceiling in a small tight voice, "That was a big waste of time. Should have went straight ahead and called up the newspaper and the Tee-Vee." Then Porter closed his own eyes and got a life-sized picture of Luanne putting it all over the street, *Well, you won't never guess what happened to Miss Priss, got herself knocked up after all her big talk, Miss Biggety-Britches, and with that trashy Porter too . . .*

So, let the bitches talk. He went to sleep himself, uneasily, with Carole lying rigid beside him. In the morning he decided to blow off work, which turned out to be a good idea because by eleven or noon she was bleeding heavily, the glow draining out from under the copper tone of her cheeks. She sent Porter out for jumbo Kotex and she still didn't want to go to the hospital till he dragged her there at two or three in the afternoon. A long time got wasted horsing around with the insurance, till Porter finally told the lady, under his breath so Carole wouldn't hear, "If you don't get her in to see somebody quick, she's going to bleed to death all over this waiting-room furniture." After that it appeared to be as bad as a birth itself except they didn't expect him to stand there and watch it. He went to the cafeteria and bought himself a pack of cigarettes, although he had quit six weeks before. It was good dark by the time they called him. Carole was so wasted by shock and painkillers she didn't even start to cry till he got her back to the duplex.

All this while, Porter had been tightening his hand on his glass without being aware of what he was doing. Wet and slippery with beaded moisture from his last drink, it shot out of his fingers and shattered on the floor behind the counter. Porter twitched on his stool as heads turned from everywhere to stare at him; the bar had been filling up, the last half hour, while he wasn't paying attention. Two strange white men had shoved up to the bar beside his stool, one scroungy, rail-like dark-haired guy, and another, shorter one with fading red hair. They were watching him too. The tall one tapped a finger into his palm as sarcastic applause. *Whatchoo looking at?* Porter thought. *Yo, I'm talking to you!* He didn't say it. The bartender was also giving him the fisheye.

"Clumsy," Porter said. "Sorry . . . I'll pay for it." He looked at his table money, which had dwindled to a couple of singles and a scatter of coins, so he took out another twenty and displayed it. The bartender was sizing him up, for relative sobriety, or else maybe the sound of breaking glass had jogged his memory back to the other time.

"Forget about it," the bartender said finally. " 'S only a glass . . . What was it, a Seven and Seven, right?" He turned and reached for a broom in the corner. Porter relaxed. Sort of. The moment had passed. The bartender was brushing glass and ice tinkling together into a dustpan. Porter got another drink and the bartender tried to wave away his money, but Porter insisted. The two white guys had turned toward each other again, the redhead with his back to Porter, somewhat uncomfortably near. Automatically Porter scooted his stool deeper into the corner. Don't want to get into anything silly. The moment could always cycle back around again.

He had sat next to Carole on the broke-back couch in the duplex, unable to think of anything to say or do, for something like a thousand years. Sooner kept trying to push his long nose into her crotch, and finally Porter tried to relieve his feelings by giving the dog a slap and a kick and getting up to sling him outside. Didn't help much. He paced around the kitchen, opening cabinets, the refrigerator. Nothing to drink but a couple of light beers, which didn't seem to suit his mood. What to say, what to do . . . *Come on, honey, we'll get married anyway. We'll try again.* Hell, they hadn't

143

been trying the first time. Upstairs in the bathroom, Porter yanked open the medicine cabinet, mainly just to get away from his reflection on the mirrored door. He hadn't been doping at all for months, so he couldn't have been expecting to find anything. Nothing there but antacids and toothpaste anymore. It was dumb luck, really stupid luck, for him to happen on the two black beauties wrapped in a wad of foil.

He undid the wrapper and looked at the two capsules, fat and sleek with their obsidian gloss there on the pale tan palm of his hand. Then he crumpled the foil around them again and shoved them down his front pants pocket. Carole hadn't shifted from her huddle on the couch.

"You hungry?" Porter said. "You want to lie down or something?" He bent to rub around the back of her neck and lifted her hair to press into her shoulders, but the tendons were stiff and didn't soften. He straightened up. Carole mumbled that she would need more pads for the bleeding, probably. Before the drugstore closed. Porter was relieved to go.

Outside, he drifted to his backyard fence. Sooner looked at him mistrustfully, then dropped his head and loped over, with a little whine, to get his ears scratched. There was a thin rain settling down like spiderweb, but it wasn't all that cold for the time of year. Porter worked one of the pills loose in his pocket and licked it down his throat. The dog looked up at him, rain streaking his yellow eyes. Porter wandered over to York Road and turned north.

The drugstore would be open for another hour, at least. He passed it by; he hadn't formed any intentions but he was in no hurry to complete the errand and return. The speed began to kick in, almost as if he felt the capsule break wetly open upon his insides, releasing its chemical roar. He got increasingly jittery as he walked on. The rain was like mist, sticking to him as he passed through it. He had no umbrella or hat, and as the crinkles of his hair got soaked, sour-tasting water ran into the corners of his mouth. It was too much speed to take, especially after so long off it altogether. He should have chopped up that capsule and had a smaller taste.

And the more his nerves were overdriving themselves the more he felt his mind sinking away from his body, leaden, drowning. When he came to the liquor store he went in and bought a bottle of CC. Drinking might blunt the edge of his high and help him pull himself a little tighter together. He waited to pay, blinking irritably in the bright light by the cash register, staring into the dark over there on the bar side. With the bottle in a paper sack under his arm, he went out the one door and back in the other beside it.

Canadian Club straight up and a beer back. He drank and reordered but it didn't seem to help much. On the surface he still felt sprung tight as a rat trap, while his inner self was sealed deeply away, welded into a lead casket, nailed up in a coffin, which in turn was wrapped in a heavy length of chain. It was physically difficult for him to breathe, and the smoke of others' cigarettes bothered him even though he was chain-smoking himself. He had the same seat in the corner of the bar, under the small TV. The grumble of the sound was giving him a headache. On the larger screen at the opposite end of the bar he could see they were playing some dumb teen movie, *Porky's,* maybe, and that annoyed him too. Did the guy jostle him first or the other way around? Porter didn't even notice him until they were already shoving, a sizable dude with hair in some kind of white-boy process and muscles built up under his polo shirt like a bouncer from some college bar.

One punch was thrown. Porter ducked under it and came up with his glass still in his hand, unspilled, even. With a snap of his wrist he broke it on the counter, half hearing the jingle of ice and shards, and scrubbed the jagged butt in a vigorous counterclockwise spiral across the other guy's face. Blood came whirling up in a kaleidoscope design, and the next thing Porter knew he was waking up in a puke-smelling jail cell downtown, rubbing the spot behind his ear where somebody, the bartender probably, had cold-cocked him. He called Jerome, a running buddy from the days before Carole, whom he was ashamed to call, since he was already pretty damn late and hadn't even run her errand yet . . . Jerome dug up a lawyer who wasn't too bad, bargained it down to an assault and battery plea, so never mind the leftover black beaut in his pocket, never mind the guy showed up in court with his face looking like a jigsaw puzzle with some significant pieces lost, Porter came out under a year. Fairly freaking lucky, all things considered, even if Carole never answered a letter, never took a phone call, never spoke to him again.

Well, who could blame her? Who could blame her at all? There wasn't a lot Porter could do about it. He could sit in the bar and hate himself, or he could go home and try to feed his dog. It would be the best idea to get out. The place was filling up fast, getting noisy, getting on his nerves. Porter was looking at his last drink, thinking he'd just leave it there half-finished, when the little red-haired guy swung his arm out blindly behind him, reaching for something, an ashtray perhaps, and swept the glass into Porter's lap.

There came the same old snap and sizzle, the white flash expanding rapidly behind his eyes. Through this he could dimly see that Charlie was squared off and bristling, that *Make something of it* look branded on his face. Then Macrae slapped him on the back of the head with the heel of his hand and spoke in the cracker accent that had been vaguely bugging Porter for the last half hour or so.

"Shut up, Charlie," Macrae said, though Charlie hadn't said a word at all. "Why don't you buy the man a drink since you spilt one on him, hah?" He picked up a napkin dispenser and reached over Charlie's shoulder to set it down in front of Porter. "Here you go, bro, clean yourself up. My friend ain't got any manners much but he don't really mean any harm."

"*Bro?*" Porter's mouth felt slack. His drink was drizzling from his knees. He turned over a sticky hand and pulled loose a wad of napkins.

"That's the spirit," Macrae said. "It'll be all right. What're you drinking, anyway?"

eleven

"**Which way,** captain?" Charlie had said, once they had finally poked through the Lincoln Tunnel.

"I'd pull for south," Macrae said. "Maybe the weather's gonna improve."

Charlie swung onto the New Jersey Turnpike and edged his way into the cars-only lane. The traffic was heavy but moving fairly fast. It had cleared enough he needed to bring the visor down and adjust it carefully to block the sun, which was low and coming in strong, though rain still slicked over the pavement. Macrae groped the bottom of his seat for the lever that adjusted it and lay back, mouth-breathing and showing a line of white under his eyelashes. They had gone about thirty or forty miles before he sat up with a jerk.

"Hot in here to you?" he said.

"No, why?"

"How long you borrow the car for, Charlie?"

"It's open ended." Charlie smirked.

"Get off it," Macrae said. "What's the story?"

"Some New Jersey kid on a dope buy," Charlie said. "Fifty-fifty he's gonna be scared to even call a cop."

"Hell, it's probably his mommy's car." Macrae fingered the upholstery. "Man, the car is smoking hot, and they ain't hardly any way off of this highway. Plus which, it's the most obvious way to go."

"If you were going to leave town," Charlie noted. "Don't forget, we're already out of state."

"True," Macrae said. "But still—"

"Nag, nag, nag," Charlie said. "Look, it's only about an hour to Delaware. We cross that line, we'll look to make a change, all right?"

"Whatever," Macrae said. Though it was nervous talk his manner had been peculiarly serene throughout the conversation. His eyes slid easily from point to point, as though their mechanism was freshly oiled. Charlie watched him settle back and pillow himself on the headrest.

"Arm bothering you?"

" 'S all right," Macrae mumbled. "Whatever that street tranq is, it's pretty good."

"Have some more when you get in the mood," Charlie said. "And you can load up on those pain pills every four hours. Take three or four and it brings it up to prescription strength."

Macrae cracked an eyelid. "How you know that?"

"Always suspicious," Charlie said. "A dentist told me, now do you think a dentist would lie?" But by the time he finished speaking Macrae appeared to be asleep.

At a huge rest stop between two tollbooths on the Delaware Turnpike, Charlie pulled off and stopped the car. A couple of football fields of parked cars; it was better than a showroom, he supposed. Macrae woke when he heard the trunk pop.

"What's going on?"

"Looking to see if our boy's got a toolbox," Charlie said. "Oh yes. Here we go." He came back around the end of the car with a long flat-blade screwdriver hanging in his hand. Macrae blinked at him, red eyed.

"Tell me you're not looking for a customer."

"Relax, will you?" Charlie said. "I'm shopping for a car."

Macrae nodded, then yawned so wide it pushed his eyes momentarily shut.

"Well, don't just sit there," Charlie said. "You want to bleed your lizard, now's the time."

"I suppose I could do with that," Macrae said, unfolding himself through the car door onto the pavement. He stretched himself. "Dark, ain't it?"

"No lie," Charlie said. "Just wait out front there when you're done. I'll be by and pick you up."

It didn't take him more than ten minutes to happen upon a blue Honda Civic with the keys left in it. He drove around to the opposite side of the lot and exchanged plates with a tiny Brat pickup truck. Virginia, that seemed good enough. He slung the screwdriver into a cement-ringed island of grass. Macrae was waiting in front of the food service pavilion, shifting from foot to foot, backlit by the yellow glow of the glass wall behind him.

"They'll know we're southbound," he said as Charlie raced out the ramp. "'Cause they ain't no other way out of here."

"I changed the plates," Charlie said. "We'll be in Maryland in under an hour. Less than half an hour, probably."

Macrae squinted at him across the green glow of the dash lights. "Know these roads pretty good, don't you?"

"I've driven them," Charlie said.

Macrae thumbed open the cap of the Valium bottle. "I still say we ought to get off this highway."

"We can bail out in Baltimore," Charlie said. "That suit you all right?"

"Don't know much about the place." Macrae sucked up some saliva and swallowed a tablet.

"Me neither," Charlie admitted. "I think they're big on seafood."

"Wasn't there something happened there with Paul Revere and the Indians?" Macrae said. "Back there in the War We Won?"

"What're you talking about?"

"The Baltimore Tea Party," Macrae said. "Something like that."

"You idiot," Charlie shouted. "That was the *Boston* Tea Party."

"You watch who you call a idiot," Macrae said. "How come you to know so much anyhow?"

"I been to college," Charlie said. "I graduated the University of Chicago, as a matter of fact." He shook his head and sniffed.

Before his eyes the bright road wedged ahead to its vanishing point in the dark. "Jesus Christ, the Baltimore Tea Party."

Macrae said nothing; there was no sound but the wheels hissing up under the car. A match flared in his corner, lighting the end of his nose and the lips thinned to pinch a cigarette.

"Never figured you for a college puke." Macrae exhaled.

"Live and learn," Charlie said. "Say, what're you calling the War We Won?"

"Instead of the War Between the States, don't you know," Macrae said. "Which, if you remember, we lost."

"Ah hah," Charlie said. "Okay. I get it."

"Oh, I know some history," Macrae said. "Even if I never went to no Yankee university to find out about it."

A spur of the highway dropped them onto Charles Street. Charlie hadn't picked the exit, it just sort of seemed to come up. A still area, nothing alongside the road but trees. They were still headed south, he thought.

Macrae stirred and raised his head. "This it?"

"Best I can figure," Charlie said.

"Dead, ain't it? I don't see no motels or whatever."

"No nothing," Charlie said.

Macrae wound down his window and trailed a finger in the dark damp breeze. "Rich people," he said. Charlie pulled up at a red light, the intersection of another four-lane street.

"This road looks like it ought to go somewhere," Macrae said.

"Yeah," Charlie said. "Which way you rather?"

Macrae shrugged. "Why not hang a left?"

Charlie turned, drove through another light, then up a rise. In the dip on the far side the lights of a shopping area appeared.

"This looks more like it," Macrae said. "Are we looking for fun or a place to stay?"

"I see fun," Charlie said. Two bars flanked the intersection: one a storefront and the other taking the whole corner.

"What's your pleasure?" Charlie said.

"Take your pick," Macrae said. "I see a parking place right over there."

Charlie pulled the car to the curb and cut the motor. He looked at Macrae with some curiosity. "Weren't you yelping for a doctor there awhile back?"

Macrae shook his head. "I don't know. It don't really hurt anymore, just stiff is all."

Charlie reached across to feel the bandage on Macrae's upper arm. "Don't really appear to be bleeding," he said. "It's not too tight, not numb anywhere?"

Macrae flexed the fingers of his left hand. "Feels good enough," he said.

"I guess you'll do," Charlie said. "Only you better not go in there showing that for an armband."

"You're right about that," Macrae said. "What's the plan?"

"Guess I'll change shirts with you," Charlie said, already hauling his V-neck over his head. Macrae unbuttoned and made the switch.

"Christ, it's a little short," he said. When he stood out of the car, the hem of the shirt was riding somewhere around his navel.

Charlie snickered, thrusting a hand through the ripped armhole of Macrae's shirt, then rolling up the extra length of the other sleeve. "Like one of those shortie shirts the muscle boys wear," he said. "Only you ain't really built for it."

"Shut the freak up," Macrae said amiably. They passed the liquor-store entrance and turned the corner toward the doors to the larger bar. A light mist hung over the street, particles glistening in the street lamps, but it was barely cool.

"Weather agree with you?" Charlie said.

"I love it," said Macrae. "Don't even need a coat."

The bar was crowded, but they wedged in at the counter, standing room only and other bodies pressing them. Macrae had ordered his beer and a shot before the thought struck him and he turned to Charlie.

"Am I okay to drink on whatever I'm taking?"

"It's just Valium," Charlie said.

"Who says?"

"Guy name of Buster. I bought it on the street."

"Buster? You sure it ain't some heavy down, like I have a few beers I'm gone to wake up dead?"

"Well, you're tough enough to take a bullet...," Charlie began, but Macrae had stopped listening. He was looking over Charlie's shoulder at a young black guy who was mumbling to himself and clutching his glass so tight that it fired out of his hand and smashed against the shelves behind the bar. Macrae laughed as Charlie turned to see and tapped his finger in his open palm, but the black guy shot him such an ugly look he stopped at once and turned toward his drink.

"If it ain't Valium, it's probably ludes," Charlie said. "You can drink on that, in moderation."

"Moderation is our watchword." Macrae dropped his shot and took a sip of beer. "Hey, my cigarettes still in that shirt pocket?"

Charlie produced the pack.

"You see an ashtray?" Macrae said.

Charlie shot out an arm behind him, not looking, and dumped the black guy's fresh drink in his lap. In one second the whole thing had tilted toward fight, but Macrae wasn't in the mood. He put a hand on Charlie's shoulder and began to mediate, his voice running out him like syrup. The black guy was staring at him, rings of pale around his eyeballs. Macrae saw he wasn't as drunk as he'd first thought. Something else was eating him. A wrong guy for Charlie to jangle, or just the wrong night. He was very dark and handsome in a chiseled way. His hair was short and sidewalled, a double part cut in it with a razor. Macrae guessed him about his own age. Still smiling, Macrae put out his hand and said his name.

"Porter," Porter said. His grip was strong, a little sticky from the spilled drink.

"Proud to know you," Macrae said. "Let's move over yonder, what say?" He jerked his thumb at a few small tables in a mirrored niche opposite the counter. "Where it's a little more safer, don't you know."

Porter nodded and they made the switch, threading their way through what looked like a crowd of college jocks, a few musclebound and horsy girls among them.

"Tippy table," Porter said, rocking it with a finger as he sat down.

"Keep your drink in your hand," Macrae said.

Porter hesitated, then cracked a thin smile. "Where you two come from, anyway?"

"Oh, we just—"

"—drove up from Virginia," Charlie said. He put his toe across Macrae's instep and worked it lightly, like tapping a brake.

"That right?" Porter said. "West Virginia?"

"Sure," Macrae said. Charlie's foot pumped across his again. Irritably he kicked free.

"Whereabout exactly?" Porter said.

"Charleston," Charlie said. "Around there."

"Charleston's in South Carolina, ain't it?" Macrae said. "Guess you must not have majored in geography, college boy."

Charlie pushed back, the table's edge digging into the heels of his palms, glaring at Macrae. The table shifted on its uneven base and Macrae's two glasses chattered against each other.

"There's a Charleston in West Virginia," Porter said smoothly. "Believe it's the capital, as a matter of fact."

"I wouldn't know," Macrae said. "Better ask Joe College here."

"Jesus, Macrae . . ."

"What have we got to hide?" Macrae snapped.

"Hey," Porter said. "What I always like best is mind my own business." He stood up. "Thanks for the drink."

"Buy him another one, Charlie," Macrae said. "Look yonder." He pointed at a gang of lacrosse players, whatever they were, all going out together. "There's room back at the bar."

Birds on a rail, they settled again in the corner where Porter had been first, overlooking the liquor store. Business had slowed but the door was still open, the oddly dressed cashier still in his station. Macrae rattled his knuckles on the counter, trying to make him turn around.

"He don't tend bar," Porter said. "You got to get the other guy."

"Whatever." Macrae spread a twenty on the mottled counter-top. Charlie gave him a dig in the ribs.

"Big spender."

Macrae shrugged. "We'll get more."

"How's that?" Charlie said. "You got a plan?"

Macrae cast a drifting look over the liquor store. "Why not here?"

"Are you crazy?" Charlie said.

Mockingly, Macrae laid a finger on his lip. The bartender had come to serve them. All three were quiet while the drinks were poured, staring straight ahead while the smaller TV crackled and hummed above them. Macrae sipped from his shot glass, poked in the pile of his change. He was blinking frequently, heavily, Charlie noticed, and every few beats his eyelids seemed to stick in the closed position.

"Maybe you better slack off on the whiskey," Charlie said. "Might get a bad mix after all."

"Look," Macrae said. "See how they got the register just right by the door?"

"Get out of here," Charlie said. He swiveled a slow three-sixty degrees on his stool, surveying the kitchen hatch, the swing doors that led to the restaurant section. "You'd need three guys at least to hold this place down."

"Ain't talking about holding the territory," Macrae said. "Just easy in, easy out."

"You'd go out in cuffs and a waist chain," Charlie said. He rotated toward Porter. "What do you think?"

"I don't think about things like that," Porter said.

"What's the difference," Charlie said. "We're just talking."

Porter turned out the palm of his hand; it dipped with the tilt of his forearm, like a ragged tan flag. "Guess I'd have to go with you then." He turned his hand over and pointed it to the rabbit hole to the kitchen. "Even three guys probably wouldn't do it. They got a door back there and phones too, I bet."

"Sheee . . ." Macrae lowered a foot to the floor. "Hundred bucks says one guy could take it off."

"You hadn't got it," Charlie said.

"Not yet," Macrae said. He pushed up from the stool, wobbling slightly. His step steadied as he went out the door. Porter was left staring at Charlie, his eyebrows arched in a question mark.

"Time to run?" Porter said.

"Nah," said Charlie. "He's on medication. Probably just went to the car to sleep it off."

The cool braced Macrae, cut through that glassy remote sensation that had settled over him after his first couple of drinks. In the bar, he'd begun to feel almost like a fly trapped in a paperweight, trying to move through Lucite gel. His ears felt funny, ringing like they'd just come away from some overpowering noise. He was walking around the back side of the bar, where there was a parking lot with eight or ten cars, and then an alley. Where had Charlie parked the car? In a Dumpster niche off the alley, a white truck with mud on the fenders was parked cattycornered. A fly rod and a shotgun hung on a rack against the rear glass, behind a decal reading I AM A COON HUNTER AND A SPORTSMAN. Picture of a raccoon sitting in a tree . . . Macrae smiled at that; you wouldn't see such a truck in Manhattan, no. Behind it, two black kids sat in a Bondo-speckled Chevette, smoking and playing the radio.

At the end of the alley, Macrae emerged into the street where the stolen car was parked. Charlie hadn't bothered to lock it. He'd left his wool hat lying on the passenger seat. Macrae got in, closed his eyes briefly, rubbed at his temples. The seat space was a little too short for him to straighten his legs completely. He picked up the hat and began to fidget with it, pulling loose loops from the weave and breaking the yarn. In a couple of minutes he saw that what he had made was an eye hole.

The Chevette was gone from the alley when he went back. He was walking lightly, high on his arches. It felt like he was walking on rolled puffs of air. High. Too high for what he was going to do and he was going to do it just the same. If. Two boxes of shells lay on the seat of the truck. Macrae walked around between the driver's door and the bar's rear wall. Around the corner he could hear the sound of clashing dishes coming out the kitchen door Porter had been worried about. At his feet lay half a brick, as if placed there to confirm his intentions.

When he smashed in the window a cat shot out from under the truck like a rocket, but that was all. Macrae crouched behind the Dumpster with a box of shells, number-ten shot, and the gun broken open across his other hand. A smell from the Dumpster of tainted fish and old fry oil. He hadn't messed with an over-and-under before but it looked reasonably simple. In fact he hadn't messed with any kind of gun since the day before he went over the hill. Loping around the parade ground to the drill sergeant's order, brandishing his M-16 over his head and batting at his crotch with his other hand. *This is my weapon—this is my gun. This is for killing—this is for fun.* He snapped the breech closed. The figure-eight barrel was cold to his hand, gunmetal blue, and a blue shooting sensation ran from his armpits into his fingertips. He took a deep breath and adjusted the roll of the wool hat on his brow.

"Got a light?" Porter said, and pointed his Salem at Charlie. He'd lost track of the matches again when they changed up seats. Charlie passed him a Bic. Porter was cupping the flame when he saw out of the corner of his eye the liquor-store door pop open and in come a rangy shambling dude. He was moving a little more quickly than most but what really got your attention was the woolen face mask, which looked like cheap homemade Halloween. Porter burned his thumb and dropped the lighter. His instinct was to try to beat it to the floor, but Charlie stopped him, a hand on his back.

"Just don't move," he said in a tense whisper. Porter froze as Macrae slid the shotgun barrels tactfully across the counter to push against the cashier's ribs. The voice was muffled through the wool but Porter realized he'd already learned to recognize it.

"Drop that cash drawer in a sack for me, would you?" Macrae said. "Just the folding money, you can keep the change."

The cashier was a little fumble fingered, moving like a marionette. He had enough sense not to say anything. Porter watched him put a hand under the counter for a bag. A club handle protruded next to the brown-paper stack, but he didn't go near it. Macrae was stooping slightly over the gun barrel, almost like he was lining up a pool shot. Then he folded the filled bag once over and darted out the door.

Porter had lit his cigarette somewhere around the middle of the tube. He stubbed it out, untasted, and leaned down to retrieve the lighter. When he straightened up again, the cashier was still standing where he had been, shoulders shaking, leaning forward on his palms. Porter could see his lungs working through his checked shirt. He hadn't yet raised the alarm. The bartender was working the other end of the place and no one seemed to have noticed anything unusual. Porter looked at Charlie.

"So, you got that hundred bucks?"

"Not on me," Charlie said. "What about you?"

twelve

Porter and Charlie slipped out before the bar went crazy, leaving their drinks standing. But around the corner, the blue-and-red lights were already flashing on the walls. Two cars had hemmed in the Delaware Honda.

"That was quick," Charlie said.

"No lie," Porter said. "Don't see how they could get here that fast."

"They didn't," Charlie said. Now he could see that the car was empty. A cop was stooping to check the stolen plate, then calling something to another one, who was on the radio. A third cop, this one a woman, looked up surprised as two bartenders came shouting out of the liquor-store door.

"Well, so much for that," Charlie said. "The hell with it."

"What?" Porter said.

"Nothing," said Charlie. "It's nothing to do with it." He spat on the pavement. The mist appeared to be lifting now and a little wind blew chill, teasing the loose threads around the hacked-off armhole of the shirt he'd traded from Macrae. The bartenders were still shouting at the cops—one hit the radio again and then all three began marching toward the corner, the woman with her pistol drawn. She was heavyset and short, as short as Charlie, a fringe of black curls hanging from her hatband. The pupils of her eyes were small. Charlie saw this in the glow of the liquor-store show windows as the police and the bartenders turned in. Off to the south a siren wound to a crest and descended and rose again as it came near.

"So where's your friend at?" Porter said.

"Friend? You mean that crazy fella you were talking to?" Charlie said. "Beats me." He jerked his head toward the bar on the opposite corner. "You want a drink?"

This was a smaller place, maybe slightly upscale, maybe not. A cubicle about phone-booth size was indented behind the front door; left was the restaurant; right, the bar, considerably shorter than the one in the other place. Macrae sat on the first stool, his usual pair of glasses set up before him.

"Hey, fellas," he said. "Where you been?"

"Taking the air," Charlie said. "You buying?"

"I guess I ought to," Macrae said. "You know, I had to ditch your hat."

"Don't worry about it," Charlie said.

"I'll try not to," Macrae said. "Luck's about run out on that hat anyhow."

Porter's duplex was a shingled house, with many shingles fallen away and lying in the yard. Once upon a time it had been green. The front walk ran to a concrete porch framed by a spade shape cut out under the roof, like a hole in a jigsaw puzzle or something from a movie set, not quite real when you got close. The foundation had settled and the concrete was cracked and buckling underfoot. A barricade of old planters, bent lawn furniture, and derelict toys divided Porter's side of the porch from the other.

Hitching the beer bag under his arm, Porter worked the key and pushed the door in. He flipped the wall switch. A spherical paper shade yellowed the light of the bulb overhead. Sooner got up, yawning, from the corner and came over to sniff. Charlie kneed him aside and the dog approached Macrae, who stooped to scratch his ears. Macrae sat down in a flaccid armchair that wheezed up a cloud of dust and mold as it took his weight. Feeling in the corner of the cushion he found a quarter and held it up.

"Ho, look what I got," he said to Porter. "Finders keepers?"

Porter shrugged and passed him a bottle of beer from the bag. Macrae yawned and twisted off the cap. The dog laid his head on the arm of the chair and looked at him, yellow eyes deep and rich with the sadness of infinite resignation. A black stripe ran back the length of his nose and split into arches over his eyes.

"Thought you were rich," Charlie said.

"Don't know." Macrae dug deep in his waistband and pulled out the folded sack. He shook it out from the bottom, scattering a dull green crumple of bills on the floor.

"Count it?" Charlie said.

"Hell yes, I counted it," Macrae said. "Right down on the bar at that other place. Got the bartender to hold my shotgun so I could use both hands to count with."

Charlie picked up the bills and ordered them by the edges. He sat down beside Porter on a vinyl couch patched here and there with silver tape. At the far end of the room hulked a single bucket seat from a car, and that was all the furniture. Through the wall a radio was playing. Voices raised and were cut off by the slap of a door.

"Eight hundred and change," Charlie said. "Can't complain. You loan me a hundred?"

"For what?" Macrae said.

"For love," said Charlie. "And pay off my bet."

"Sure, Charlie," Macrae said with a thin smile. "I guess you owe me a hundred, okay?" He slid down deeper in the chair, his heels rucking up a furrow in the old hooked rug. The dog opened his mouth and breathed across Macrae's face. Macrae choked and shoved his head off the chair arm.

"What you been feeding this dog, corpses?" he said.

"He hadn't been eating much at all, actually," Porter said.

Macrae looked at the dog, down the bony length of his flanks. Sooner looked back at him with profound affection. His plumed tail waved grandly and he exhaled again.

"My God," Macrae said. "Smells like he been eating out of an open grave."

"We got a disagreement going . . ." Porter stopped and held up a finger. A hissing sound came from the back of the house. "*God*damn," Porter said. He rose and went into the kitchen in a silent velvet run. Charlie hauled himself up from the couch and followed him. A hose with a nozzle attached was coiled in the kitchen sink. Hastily Porter connected it to the spigot. The hose stiffened and shifted slightly when he turned the water on. He crept to the back door, nozzle cocked in his hand like a pistol, and slid it open quietly. From the back steps adjacent, a greasy white kid with a cap turned backward on his head was urinating in a high arc that collapsed on Porter's section of the yard.

Porter fired the nozzle, hitting the kid where his hands were joined, then raising the stream to blast into his face. There was enough pressure concentrated to knock off the hat. The kid lurched back against the railing, moving in a slow, narcoticized torpor, like a turtle on its back.

"Aw, man," he said. "What you do that for?"

"Told you people not to do that into my yard," Porter said, and slammed the door.

"Aw, man . . ." The voice trailed unhappily off. Porter turned off the tap and shook his fingers dry. A little water had pooled on the linoleum and he kicked at it with his toe.

"What's all that?" Charlie said.

"This place took a nosedive while I was in the pokey," Porter said. "Used to be a family next door, now it's some kind of a shooting gallery. What they do with the bathroom I don't know."

"Probably sold it," Charlie said.

Porter snorted. "Yeah, right."

In the front room Macrae was snoring, the dog's head draped on one of his legs. The dog was snoring lightly too.

"Lucky man," Porter said to Charlie. "Looks like you get the couch."

———

Early next morning when Charlie woke up, the light had barely yet turned gray. He was in a sweat from sleeping on the vinyl. Macrae had slipped down from the chair and in his sleep disputed the dog for a share of the worn-out rug. Out on the back stoop it was no more than pleasantly cool, a little foggy. Charlie drew a glass of water from the sink and went into the yard to sit on one of several milk crates that were arranged around a big old cable spool turned on its side. Presently the back door of the other half of the duplex flew open and out came a lean angry woman driving an older man before her with a broom. The man was balding, his scalp and his face mottled piebald from drinking, and there was something impeding his speech as he tried to complain. He slipped backward down the stairs, knocking his head against the wall, then slowly pulled himself upright. Charlie watched him shuffle off into the alley behind the houses. His pants were unbelted and so loose he had to hold them with both hands to keep them up.

The dog's cold nose pressed Charlie's elbow and he slapped it away. Sooner trotted in a half circle that led him to his dish underneath the back steps; he sniffed and turned aside with an air of disappointment. Macrae and Porter had come into the yard, carrying mugs of coffee.

"How you feel?" Charlie said to Macrae. "Better have a look at the arm."

Macrae winced, pulling up his sleeve.

"Bad?" Charlie said.

"Just stiff, is all."

"What happened here?" Porter said, leaning to look at the blackened hole.

"Cut myself," Macrae said.

"On a bullet, I see."

"Hunting accident," Macrae said.

"You know, we left that disinfectant in the car," Charlie said.

"Buy some more," Macrae said. "We're flush, ain't we?" The dog's head was in his lap. He stroked absently the length of his head and then down the back. Protruding ribs counted themselves into his palm.

"Believe this dog is fixing to starve," Macrae said.

"He's starving his own self," Porter said. "He don't want to eat what I give him."

Macrae walked over to the stairs and picked up the pocked aluminum dish, an old cookpot with the handle gone. The pellets of dog meal were gray-brown and partially disintegrated.

"Maybe he don't like it," Macrae said.

"He gets hungry enough, he'll eat it," Porter said.

"How long he been off his feed?"

"Four, five days." Porter shrugged.

"Hell," Macrae said.

"My dog and my dog food." Porter took out a pack of cigarettes and laid it on the spool. Macrae stooped to set the dish down with a clatter, swung upright, and was still. His left eye shriveled partway shut as he stared across the patchy yard at Porter.

"Y'all be sweet now," Charlie said in a saccharine falsetto.

Porter's fingers rattled a tattoo on the cellophane of his cigarette pack. Charlie flicked at his elbow, and Porter turned his way.

"What about you, you hungry?" Charlie said in his normal tone. "Come on and let's hunt us something to eat."

Macrae watched them down the alley; it was brushy and overgrown and a couple of steps took them out of sight. The dog worked along the fence, moving with high, anxious steps, pushing his nose into the squares of woven wire. Macrae crossed the yard and sat on the edge of the spool and let his head hang heavily. He was tired, in a woozy way, not from drinking but from too long sleeping too little, or that was how it felt. The edges of his bullet wound were itchy. He rubbed at the crust with a fingernail and winced at the deeper ache inside. The spool tilted with the involuntary shift of his weight. He yawned and let his head loll back. There was the sky, slate gray and breaking into blue. It seemed awhile since he had noticed it, and there was a lot of it visible here; it wasn't like New York.

He pushed himself up and followed the dog's track along the fence, which was threaded through with weeds and tumbled over with a mass of honeysuckle vine. The bugle-shaped flowers were shut at the bell, just on the point of opening. When he brushed his finger over them they were powdery and damp from dew, or else it had possibly rained in the night. He could see Lacy just that plain, sitting on a rotted log with her back against a redbud sapling just in bloom. He'd broken a clump of honeysuckle for her and watched her pinch the flowers at the base and suck the ghostly trace of sweetness out of each. She looked back at him, her eyes merry, and rolled a yellow blossom in her lips, the long twin stamens waving at him teasingly. Down the side of her neck over her collarbone and into the white V of her T-shirt ran a chain of fresh strawberry marks, and he wondered if they had come there from something she liked or something she didn't. The pulse was beating in her throat. He might have liked to ask her but he didn't want the answer and now, however much later it was, he only wished he could rub the whole picture out of his mind.

The dog yipped from the middle of the yard and Macrae turned. Sooner was scrubbing the top of his head across the weedy dirt and batting at his ears with his paws.

"I know how it is," Macrae said, walking toward the dog. "Hard to scratch the inside of your head."

Sooner scrambled up and came to him. Macrae brushed dirt from the fur covering his skull. The dog leaned a flank against his thigh.

"Dog's life, ain't it, pup?" Macrae said. "Well, now, let's see what we can do for you." He moved to the fence, which was only waist high, and swung one leg over and then the other. Sooner approached, arching his mandarin brows.

"Stay," Macrae said, raising the flat of his palm. "You stay, now, I'll be back shortly."

Porter wrinkled his nose as he climbed the back steps, a damp spice-stained sack clamped against his hip. "What could be that awful smell?"

"Your guess is as good as mine." Charlie came along behind him, carrying beer and a drugstore bag. Porter shouldered the kitchen door open with a creak. Macrae was standing at the stove, stirring a pot with a long-handled spoon. Porter sniffed the steam above it.

"Liver," he said. "I do believe. Son, we brought you something better than that."

Macrae took a fork and probed in the boiling water. The mass of liver moved like it was swimming; it unfolded a purple lip.

"Glad to hear it," Macrae said. "This here's dog food."

Porter set his bag on the edge of the sink. His voice was low and smooth as butter. "You wouldn't feed my dog when I asked you not to."

"Don't and you'll kill him," Macrae said.

"He'll eat what I give him," Porter said. "Listen, I come out of jail, bunch of junkies moved in next door, my running buddy sold off my goddamn *furniture*—I got nothing left but my dog and my dog food."

"Sounds to me like your dog food is stale," Macrae said. "What I'm gonna do, I'm going to mix up some this liver with some of your dog meal and that way maybe he'll eat both together, so everybody be happy, all right?"

Porter tilted his head to look at Macrae, who was halfway turned toward him, one hand lightly circling the handle of the steaming pot. Porter's eyes had widened enough that Macrae could see white clear around their light brown irises. In the corner of one eye a little bloodshot starburst waited like a spider.

"Always hated liver," Porter said. "Just the smell of it'll just about make me sick." He opened the door of a pantry closet and took out a sack of dog meal. "You're a diplomat, Macrae," he said. "Fair enough."

Macrae forked the slab of liver drizzling onto the counter by the sink, and while Porter refilled the dog's dish with meal, he hacked the meat into small chunks with a knife. Sooner, meanwhile, stood with his head pressed into the screen of the kitchen door, his tail curved up above him and ticking back and forth.

"Can he come in to eat?" Macrae said.

Porter shrugged. "You're the doctor."

"What's his name, anyhow?"

"Sooner," Porter said. In the corner of the kitchen, Charlie sneezed a sort of laugh, and Macrae's mouth twisted into half a smile.

"How'd you pick that one?" Charlie said. Porter didn't answer.

"You know what it means?" Macrae said.

"Hey, it's a name, is all," Porter said. "I like the sound of it. Maybe I heard it on some other dog one time."

Macrae wiped the smile off his face and opened the kitchen door. "Okay, Sooner," he said. "Grub's up." He mixed some liver into the dog meal, poured in some juice from the pan, and stooped to set the dog dish on the floor.

"So what's it mean?" Porter said.

"You really don't know?" Macrae said. "It's short for *Sooner suck eggs than hunt meat.*"

In his corner, Charlie turned his face away and strangled another laugh. Sooner was hovering over the bowl. He nosed at it, looked up at Porter and Macrae. His head dropped again and he began to eat.

"Look at that," Macrae said.

"Don't count if he just picks out the meat," Porter said.

"He's eating it all," Macrae said. "Look at him there." The dog's head gouged into the bowl like a steam shovel. His flanks were pumping, his shoulders thrust up from his back like knives.

"Dog's hungry," Charlie said, retracting his head from the refrigerator. There was a pop as he cracked a beer.

"And asking for more," Macrae said. Sooner raised up his head and looked at Macrae feelingly, then tried to wipe his dripping muzzle on Porter's pants leg. Macrae picked up the dog-food sack and scooped out a handful. He made to drop it in the dish, then stopped and began to finger through the pellets in his palm.

"Look there," he said, holding out his hand to Porter, showing him the small black droppings mixed all through the meal. "Mice been using in that bag."

Porter squinted into Macrae's hand. "You're right," he said. "No wonder he didn't want it. Okay, I'll buy him a fresh batch."

"Good deal," Macrae said. He dumped the remains of the liver and stock into the dish and patted the dog's skinny shoulders as he pitched in. Charlie clinked his nails on his beer bottle.

"Glad we got that problem solved," he said. "You think it's time for us to eat?"

Porter upended the sack over the spool and scattered out a couple of dozen crabs, coated with spice and boiled deep red.

"God help us," Macrae said. "You mean to eat them things?"

"That's my intention," Porter said, adjusting a milk crate to sit down.

"Hadn't you ever seen a crab before?" Charlie said. He pulled the claws off one and cracked them with the butt end of an empty beer bottle.

"Not up close," Macrae said. "Not to get acquainted with."

"What you get for living in a landlocked state," Charlie said. He sucked up some claw meat and licked his fingers.

"How you get at it?" Macrae said. He raised a crab to look at it more closely, staring at the multiple gates of its mouth. The black eyes on their stalks looked like the heads of small straight pins.

"Do like we do," Porter said.

"Ugly little sucker, ain't he?" Macrae said.

"He's a she," said Charlie.

"Nah," said Macrae. "You can't tell that."

"Sure," Charlie said. He flipped his crab over and tapped the undershell. "If this latch here is wide this way it's female. Male's got a little narrow thing." He flipped up the latch with the blade of his pocket knife and tore back to remove the top shell, then scooped up a clot of bright orange roe and ate it.

"Now what is that there?" Macrae said.

"Eggs," said Porter, chasing some claw meat with a long swig of beer.

"And you eat that?"

"It's good," Charlie said. "Go on, you'll get some." With the knife he split the body of the crab down the middle as you might split a muffin, exposing the white backfin meat in sections.

"You're a quicker picker," Porter said.

"Yeah," said Charlie. "I copied off the old ladies do the picking down on the docks."

"Hell of a way to make a living," Porter said.

"You know it." Charlie speared a good chunk of backfin meat on his knife point and offered it to Macrae. "Free taste," he said. "After that you're on your own."

Macrae rolled the bite between his fingers, then popped in his mouth. "Sweet," he said. "You're right, I like it."

"Funny what good eating they are," Charlie said, reaching for another. "Considering what they eat themselves."

"Hey, I just want to eat my breakfast here," Porter said. "Do you mind?"

"Talk about eating corpses," Charlie said blithely. "Nothing a crab likes better than old rotten meat. The nastier it is the more they want it. You get some old piece the maggots been in it for a couple days and it'll draw crabs from a hundred miles."

"That sure is interesting," Macrae said, cracking some claws open for himself. "How come you to know so much?"

"I grew up with crabs," Charlie said.

"And you go right ahead and eat'm just the same?"

"Oh yes," Charlie said. "I'd a lot sooner pick them than have them picking me."

thirteen

"Put out that cigarette," Porter said from halfway up the staircase. "You can't smoke up here." He paused, one foot on a higher step, and twisted back to see himself obeyed. Macrae, who had just lit up, took a good-bye drag and snapped the cigarette through the half-open door, over the curb of the Eager Street sidewalk, where it hissed out in a runnel of spring rain.

"Can't cuss either, I see," Macrae said, reading a banner draped down one wall of the steep stairwell. Drinking and spitting were also proscribed. "I reckon I could take dope if I want to, hey? Don't say nothing against that."

Porter turned again at the top landing. The wall behind him was completely covered with an enormous poster: a half-length portrait of a rather handsome, solemn-looking black man with a little mustache, dressed in a white suit and tie. "Come off it," Porter said. "Don't be making those cracks up here."

"Where are we, church?" Macrae said peevishly, but Porter had already turned out of the landing and disappeared into the adjacent room. Macrae coughed and cleared his throat. The narrow stairwell seemed to suck everything up toward the poster. The black man's left forearm was propped on the lowest edge of the paper, floor level here, and his giant's face stared down the steps with a tense, alert expression. It made Macrae a shade uneasy. He swallowed back phlegm—smoking too much, as a matter of fact—and climbed the rest of the way with his eyes lowered.

Beyond the landing a row of heavy bags hung like a screen,

one dancing and swaying under a storm of punches from a young man in gray sweats. He was hitting the hell out of it, Macrae saw. Porter stood by, watching him work. Macrae sidled toward the windows, a line of them overlooking Eager Street, where the sun appeared to be just cutting through the cloud cover. It was a long loftlike room, with two rings roped off and the wood floor covered with canvas inside them. The crumbling plaster walls had been patched and papered over with dozens of fight posters. Macrae recognized Ali, Joe Frazier, but most he'd never seen. One of the rings was empty and in the other two young boys were shadowbox- ing, each alone, practicing some drill. A trainer turned sharply from the pair and crossed the floor to Macrae.

"Help you?" He was slightly cross-eyed, with a face that seemed amiable, though it looked smashed too.

"I'm just with him," Macrae said, flipping a hand in the direc- tion of Porter, by the bags.

The trainer turned. "Yo Porter!" he called, raising his voice over the *crack-crack-crack* the other man's gloves made hitting the bag. "Long time, boy."

"Long time, Toadfish," Porter called back. The trainer smiled at him with a long slash mouth and went back to the two boys in the second ring.

Macrae squinted through the gritty window. The sun came clean out, sudden and sharp; he felt it make his eyeballs shrink. There were a few rickety metal chairs scattered along the wall of windows and turning away from the light he placed himself on the edge of one of these, still ill at ease, half wishing he'd stayed back at Porter's house with Charlie. Boring though, getting to be. He'd taught the dog all the tricks he was willing to learn. And Charlie was getting the jitters, the way he would do whenever money was low. That was nervous company there. The eight hundred had held out around a month, with no rent to pay, but carrying Porter. This town was cheaper than New York, except you really did need a car, what with no subway worth the name. Macrae despised to ride a bus. Charlie was still stealing cars for short-term use but you'd run through your luck too fast that way.

Macrae closed his eyes and pressed on the lids. The whip crack of the gloves on the bag pressed on him louder and he opened his eyes back up to watch. The guy was slipping imaginary punches and ducking to slam his own in low. Macrae's temples pulsed to the beat, not quite painfully. He figured this guy to be shy of middleweight, though he'd never been much of a boxing fan. The guy stopped his round suddenly and began to towel off his face, talking to Porter in a low voice. Macrae decided it must be Jerome. He pushed out of the chair and eased in their direction.

"What do you know, big bro?" Jerome gasped. He rubbed the towel over his shaven head; a fresh gleam of sweat pulsed through as soon as it had passed.

"Not a whole lot," Porter said. "You look pretty crisp on the bag there, son."

Jerome smiled. His front two teeth were capped with gold cut through to the white: the shapes of a card-deck club and spade. The dogtooth next to them on the left was missing altogether. His eyes were cool, passing over Macrae, who stood just back of Porter's shoulder.

"Trying to tighten it up," Jerome said. His sweatshirt, soaked through, clung like a layer of skin, with the action of his heart and lungs showing through it. "I been sparring with Jaybone, you know."

Macrae pushed the bag, gently, and felt it come back against the flat of his hand. He shoved it a little harder, stepped back, and looked up to where its chain connected to a swivel up there in the shadow of a beam in the high ceiling. *Swinging from a hook*, he thought, *swinging from a hook*. It was Charlie's voice ringing in between his ears. The bag came back, its rind of tape chafing against the butt of his palm. They might have been coasting a little too long, he realized. Something was due to happen any day now and it wouldn't necessarily be for the better.

"Jaybone got a fight?" Porter said.

"He want to fight Breland, man." Jerome's breathing was coming under control. He hung the towel over his shoulder and narrowed his eyes as Porter started laughing.

"Hey, Jaybone come a long way these last few months," Jerome said. "In the national rankings, now."

"No lie?"

"I'm telling you," Jerome twisted his head toward the vacant ring. "You want to climb in there with him, you're welcome to it."

"I don't guess," Porter said. "I been smoking and all."

"Bad for you," said Jerome.

"It's dull in jail," said Porter. "You got to do something."

"How it is."

"You're not training him for Breland now," Porter said.

"Nah," said Jerome. "Kid named Figuero, think he's number eight."

"No lie?"

"What I tell you. Jaybone looking real good lately." Jerome's eyes cut toward Macrae, who was fingering the bands of tape that wrapped round the heavy bag nearest him. Something made him take his hand away and stand up straighter.

"You coming back, Porter?" Jerome said. "Get yo'self together?"

"Not yet awhile," Porter said. "You want to know the truth of it, I was looking out a way to make some money."

Jerome shrugged. "Ain't no money in this here. You know Mist' Leggett can't pay sparring partners. Jaybone neither, where he's at now."

"You know what I mean."

Again Jerome's eyes swept over Macrae. The gold teeth sank out of sight below his heavy lip.

"He's all right," Porter said.

"You can't be talking that talk up here," Jerome said. "Not in Mist' Leggett's place."

"Sorry," Porter said. "I been having a problem finding you anywhere else. You fighting shy of me, or what?"

Jerome picked at the tape on his left hand. "Yo, I kept the rent paid, didn't I?"

"Sure," Porter said. "What's a little furniture here and there?"

"I was messed up then," Jerome said.

"You owe me," Porter said. "I didn't even ask you for the money. Just let's go make it. Couple of runs."

"I'm trying to get right, Porter. Can't be making no couple runs right now."

"You let mice get in my dog food."

"Dog's still there, ain't he?"

Porter's face was too studiously blank; bad things were turning underneath it, Macrae was sure. He took a long step away as Porter moved in. Jerome's white-bound hands were rising, but Porter put his arms around his neck and kissed him on the corner of the mouth.

"You faggot." Jerome's teeth flashed gold again. He wiped his mouth on the back of his taped wrist.

"Yeah boy, okay," Porter said. "All right for you. You keep out of trouble. Tell Jaybone I wish him luck. And say hello to Mister Leg."

"You ain't gone wait till he comes in?"

"He'd smell it on my breath, son," Porter said. "You tell him I love him, Jerome." He turned away sharply, ducking his head, and started for the stairs. Macrae followed. They were halfway down when they heard Jerome's voice again from above.

"Yo, Porter, don't mess up, man."

A slight echo in the stairwell magnified the words. Macrae twisted around and looked back up. Jerome stood on the landing, blocking part of the giant portrait. He had tied the towel around his head in a sort of yashmak.

"I won't," Porter said.

"Don't mess up *too* bad, you hear me?" Jerome stepped off the landing, out of sight. The outsized face on the poster gazed down the steep steps, nothing interrupting it now.

"Who's that?" Macrae said.

"Jerome?" Porter was standing below with one foot through the street door.

"No, him." Macrae pointed.

"Don't you know who Joe Louis is?"

"Sure I do," Macrae said. "I just didn't know what he looked like."

The sun had come out altogether, and after the indoor dim it made a terrible glare. A temple came loose from Macrae's sunglasses as he fished them out of his shirt pocket. Muttering, he stooped to pick it up and straightened with a piece in either hand. Porter paused and looked over his shoulder.

"You got a paper clip?" Macrae said. "Piece of wire or something?"

Porter shrugged and shook his head. Macrae cast about on the sidewalk. Beer tabs, plenty of broken glass, something that was maybe dog dung, but nothing of use. Weeds were growing tall through the cracks in the concrete. He put the loose temple in his pocket, balanced the sunglasses on his nose, and followed Porter around the corner of Broadway to the bus stop.

The lozenges of grass down the middle of the boulevard were tattered at the edges, as if some giant rats had been chewing on them. The bare patches were muddy from the recent rain. There were cherry trees planted in a line, and some pink dogwoods just beginning to break into bloom. On the far side of the street a group of men stood, staring in various directions, not speaking to one another, near the steps of a boarded building that looked as if it had once served some public function. Macrae took off the sunglasses, bent the wire frame for a better purchase, and put them back on. The bus continued not to come.

"We need to get hold of a car some way," Macrae said.

"I can't push Jerome," Porter said. "Not when he's trying to clean himself up. Not at Mister Leg's."

"Did I ask you to?" He wiped his face. The air was gravid, rimed with grit, though hardly hot as yet. "There must be some bar around here somewhere," Macrae said.

"What you do down here," Porter said, "is get you a shortie and sit down and drink it on the street."

"Let's do it," Macrae said. "My standing-up muscle is tired."

Porter led the way east on Eager Street again. Dozens of young men were waiting vacantly at different posts all along the way, many already supplied with brown bags from the liquor stores. Few women around, and no children at all. That was a bad sign, in Macrae's experience. Several expensive late-model cars, with phone antennae curling up from them, were parked among the rusting junkers against the curb. A current of drug money running through the neighborhood. There were liquor stores on every corner and some in the middle of the block. Macrae waited on the doorstep while Porter went into one of these. The eyes around seemed to harden then and he felt his skin crawling with its paleness.

Porter came out with a bag in one hand and beckoned with the other. A few doors over he climbed the stoop of a boarded form-stone row house and kicked a mass of molded newspaper back down the steps to clear sitting space. Macrae rubbed his palm over the concrete top step. An overhanging eave had sheltered it from the rain, so it was hardly wet at all. He sat down, straightened his glasses, and sniffed; they fell back cockeyed. He watched as Porter cracked the seal on a half-pint of 151 rum and drank and proffered the bottle.

"Arrghhh," Macrae said, yanking the bottle neck out of his jaw. A billow of boiling gas wrinkled through his nostrils and burned in cavities behind his eyes. "Tell me you got a chaser, Porter."

Porter handed him a malt liquor tallboy. Gratefully Macrae closed his hand around the damp can.

"Look out for the bull," he said. "God amighty. That should do it." He wiped his eyes and looked around. On the surface of the splintered board that covered the window holes beside the door, someone had penciled a drawing of a man with a long bumpy nose, life size or a little larger. Macrae appraised it. The sketch was done with short underconfident strokes, but it appeared a fair likeness of somebody or other. Below was a note scrawled from one child to another about homework and what the parents wanted.

"You spend a good deal of time round here?" Macrae said.

"My momma brought us down here," Porter said. "Had to move when my daddy died. I lived here from twelve to seventeen."

"I see you lived through it," Macrae said. He took a more cautious pull on the bottle and passed it back.

"Yeah," Porter said. "Mister Leg took care of me. I'd be up in that gym every day after school."

"You a pretty good boxer, then?"

"Not really," Porter said. "I did okay. What it is, you got to be angry, you got to go in and really want to hurt that guy. I don't have that. Jaybone, now, Jaybone can get that up."

"What was it you did your last little stretch for, you said?" Macrae sipped on his beer and reached for the shortie.

"Cut the face off of some peckerhead there in that bar where we first met."

"That's what I thought," Macrae said, passing the bottle back. "I'm having a little trouble putting this all together."

"Hey," Porter said, flicking his eyes toward him and away. "I was just in a bad mood that one night. You want to get ranked in the ring, son, you got to feel that way all the time."

"If you say so." Macrae pushed his sleeve back and scratched at the closed wound, a red knotted welt still scabby at the edges.

"While we're letting our hair down," Porter said, "what were you hunting when you had that accident?"

"Snipe."

"Yo, I told you the truth, son."

"Ah, we was just trying to bluff some money out of a cash register is all," Macrae said. "Firepower was all on the other side, it turned out."

"That armed robbery is a dangerous trade," Porter said.

"You ought to try it unarmed some time."

Porter laughed and passed the bottle. "Count me out," he said. He waited for Macrae to drink and then took it again for himself.

"Poison," he said, clearing his throat. "Who knows, maybe I'll go back up to the gym sometime, get myself in shape." He took out a cigarette. "Yeah," he said. "Mister Leg, he saw me through high school all right. Up every morning before it was light, he'd be knocking on my house . . . Be running a pack of us, Jerome, Jaybone, all those guys. We'd run all through this neighborhood and over through Patterson Park and back in time for school every morning."

"Sorry I missed this Mister Leg," Macrae said.

"He's something," Porter said. "He was an old man already, going on those runs. He must have been sixty at least. Him and my old man was friends and all, they was about the same age I guess."

"I know what you mean," Macrae said.

Porter glanced at him, setting the bottle down with a clink on the step between them.

"I was born late too, I mean," Macrae said. "So far as my father was concerned."

"Huh," Porter said. He flicked his lighter and breathed out smoke. "Your daddy fight the big war?"

"He got in just before it was over," Macrae said. "He was in the Pacific Fleet."

"Yeah," Porter said. "My daddy was in that Quartermaster Corps. Lugged him a pick and shovel all over France and Italy. He was too old for the draft but he went and enlisted after Joe Louis did."

"Is that a fact?"

"They were both Alabama boys, him and Joe Louis," Porter said. "Joe Louis fought for all of us, what my daddy used to say."

"I heard that." Macrae nodded. He picked up the half-pint, drank, and passed it. "When he whipped that Nazi boxer."

"All of *us*," Porter said. "Not all of you."

"I thought it was all of us," Macrae said. "I never heard Joe Louis meant to limit it to just niggers."

The bottle rotated in Porter's palm. He clutched it butt down like a hammer cocked to strike.

"Just wondered if you were listening, is all," Macrae said pleasantly. "Way I see it, you share whiskey with somebody you get to say what you think. Don't make me no difference what skin you got on."

"Sheeee . . ." Porter relaxed his fingers and handed over the bottle gently. Macrae drank and held it to the light.

"Went through this quicker than I'd of thought," he said.

"You're crazy, Macrae," Porter said. He pointed across the street. "What you do now, take and throw it against the wall so you can see it break."

Macrae looked. The building across the way was sealed up also, with tin this time; graffiti signatures crawled across the metal and the darkened brick. A youngish woman in a tight skirt was passing before, towing groceries in a two-wheeled cart, moving fast, with her eyes slightly lowered. Macrae waited until she was well out of the way, feeling a warmth building up from his wrist to his shoulder, inevitably as the heavy bag must swing back, every time he might push it away from him. He drew back his arm and fired. The bottle burst like a snowflake on the sill opposite and rattled piecemeal to the pavement. A few other loiterers looked briefly toward the sound.

"How's it feel?" Porter said.

"So-so," said Macrae. "Ain't the first time I done it."

fourteen

Charlie was out when Porter and Macrae finally made it back to the house. No telling where. It was getting dark. They sat in the backyard, smoking and watching the light decline. No beer in the house, and they were too tired of walking to hump it to the store for more. Macrae could feel a hangover building as he came off the rum they'd drunk in the afternoon.

"Days getting longer," Macrae said.

"You know it," said Porter.

"C'mere, Sooner," Macrae said. The dog, who lay with his head stretched over his crossed paws, pushed himself up, hindquarters first, and approached.

"Sit," Macrae said. He took a dog biscuit from the half-empty box on the spool and balanced it on Sooner's nose. The dog crossed his eyes to look at the biscuit and hung his red tongue out.

"Stay . . . ," Macrae said. "All right, *get* it!"

Sooner flipped the biscuit off his nose and caught it in the air with a clop. Macrae shook another one out of the box.

"Sit . . . ," he said. The dog gave him a disgusted look and walked back to the corner of the fence, where he flopped down with a sigh and relaxed himself over the weeds and dirt.

"Not gonna make him mind?" Porter said.

"He's just bored, like the rest of us," Macrae said. "I had a steak to stick on his nose, I bet he'd go for that . . ." He flapped his hand in the stagnant air. "Gummy out, ain't it?"

"Yeah," Porter said. "This town gets miserable come summer."

"I believe you," Macrae said. "We don't got any beer, do we?"

"Want me to check the fridge and see if some grew?"

Macrae rubbed around the bone of his eye socket, the area where the headache seemed to be concentrating. "Why don't you order a pizza?" he said.

He lit another cigarette and smoked in the twilight while Porter made the call. It was breathless and so damp and still that his smoke hung all around his head without dissipating. He had to fan his hand at it to shift it away. A greasy white kid with a cap turned backward came out of the junkie half of the duplex and wandered over the litter in the yard. From one hand trailed the plug end of a heavy orange extension cord that issued from the house. When Porter came back outside the kid hailed him.

"Hey, man . . ."

"Hey, man," Porter mimicked.

"Man, uh . . ." The kid lost momentum. His mouth hung slack and lusterless; inside, his tongue was gray. The plug of the cord swung pendulously a foot or so below his hand.

"Bugs gonna fly down your throat, *man,*" Porter said. In his corner, Sooner lurched up and scratched his ear desperately with his hind foot and then with a groan resettled himself.

"Uh, they cut off our electricity, man, you know?" The kid squinted across at Porter.

"Is that right," Porter said. "I bet you didn't pay your bill."

"Gonna be dark," the kid said. He hung the plug out across the woven wire fence. "You think you could plug this in on your side, man?"

Porter exhaled heavily. "You just want to borrow a little electricity."

"That's all, man," the kid said, relieved by the ease of communicating the concept.

"What's the matter," Porter said. "Can't hit a vein in the dark?"

"Hey, man," the kid said, offended. "I might smoke a little rock but I never put a needle in my arm."

"Proud of you, *man,*" Porter snapped. "You don't get your arm back on your own side of the fence, I'm gonna chop it off and feed it to my dog."

The kid looked down at the hand with the plug in it, stupefied.

"Get me the hatchet, would you Macrae?" Porter called over his shoulder. The kid yanked his arm away, letting the plug drop in the dirt in the junkies' yard. Uncertainly, he shuffled back toward the house, using the orange cord as a guideline.

"Don't care much for the neighbors do you?" Macrae said.

Porter sat down on a milk crate and propped his elbows on the spool. "Don't care if I say it out loud," he said, and raised his voice to a sudden shout. "*Those people are trash!*"

"Oh well," Macrae said. "You get pepperoni?"

It was dark by the time the pizza came. They ate in the glow of a yellow bulb over the back door. Moths circling the light sent queer shadows floating over the yard. They debated saving a piece for Charlie and decided against it. Macrae dropped his last crust into the box and rocked back on the corner of his crate.

"Might gimme the strength to go for a six-pack," he said.

"We could always just walk over to the bar," Porter said.

"Carryout's cheaper," Macrae said. He levered himself up and climbed the back steps. Looking back, he saw a firefly drifting down the alley in the dark. He reached over the door and unscrewed the bulb.

"What you do that for?" Porter said.

"Lightning bugs," Macrae said. He came back down the steps and sat down again. There were more of them winking and hovering in the damp shrubs along the alley. A few carried their faint green phosphors low over the tangled weeds of the yard.

"Used to be, they'd fill my daddy's whole field," Macrae said. "Lightning bugs all in the high grass."

"Yeah." Porter crossed his legs. "Me and my sister used to pull the tails off of them, when we were little. Stick it on a finger and call it jewelry. You ever do that?"

"Time or two," Macrae said. "It's sorta mean, though."

They were quiet for a minute or more. Macrae drifted. Ten

summers or so back, when he was twelve or thirteen he'd slip
across the field at twilight, through tall grass that wet him to the
waist if it was damp, scaring up the fireflies from the long stalks,
watching meadowlarks settle into the hay as the light faded. Tucked
in the swag of his shirt belly a pack of cigarettes stolen from his
father's pack, maybe a joint in amongst them, maybe a couple cans
of beer. Lacy would be waiting in the lane, by the rusted fence that
used the tall old cedar trees for posts. With luck she might have
a bottle of wine . . . He'd help her lift her bike across the fence
and hide it, and then they'd climb the slope together, sit on a bare
patch of the limestone bedrock and drink and smoke and hardly
talk, while the fireflies formed and reformed constellations in the
field below.

He'd looked at her then but never touched. Now to reach back
over the years just tore a hole in the one memory through to
another, when they were little children, really, some family picnic.
After supper they were catching fireflies in the grass. There was
another boy, some fat-faced cousin, tearing the green lights off the
fireflies and putting them to the backs of Lacy's fingers, showing
her how they'd stick with their own glue. It made his stomach flip
to see her holding her hand out like a little queen accepting tribute,
to see the two of them together so. Old Beaverface, whoever he
was. Macrae walked over.

Quit it, he said.

Quit what, said Beaverface.

Let'm alone. You're hurtin'm.

They're just bugs. What's it to you?

So then they were on the ground and tumbling, Macrae out-
weighed and getting the worst of it until he got an arm crooked
around the fat boy's neck and choked him till he lost his breath
and socked him in the nose and made it bleed. His father dragged
him out to the barn and took down a harness strap and said, *What
have you got to tell me?* and Macrae said, *He's biggern me, is what,* and
his father let out a hack of a laugh and said, *Yeah, and you got the
drop on him, didn't you,* and he hung the strap back on the wire.

That once at least he'd hung it up, that once. Macrae shifted on the crate, crossed his legs and uncrossed them again. Spring fever taking a funny turn, that was what got you thinking this way, wishing you'd done the things you hadn't and could undo the things you had. A memory could rise and lift you with it like you were riding in an elevator and finally drop you down and rolling in some groove you never carved. Not the least bit of use in it, he told himself, and yet he could feel it tingling to his fingertips.

"What's that?" Porter said.

"I didn't say nothing."

"Your lips're moving."

"Might be eating in my sleep."

Porter's chuckle died away. Somewhere just in earshot somebody spun a few bands of a radio and shut it off. Next door a woman's voice shrilled instantaneously to hysteria and then broke off just as abruptly. A car was crawling down the alley, mist swirling in the headlight beams. The untrimmed bushes dragged over the doors of the sleek black sedan. It stopped at the back gate and Charlie got out, leaving the lights and motor running. He rested his hand on the top strand of the fence.

"Hi there, boys," Charlie said.

In the fence corner the dog raised his head and pricked his ears for a moment, then sagged back. Macrae got off of his crate and strolled toward the gate, his belly swagging with pizza. Porter followed a step behind.

"You stole a BMW," Macrae said.

Charlie shrugged and glanced over his shoulder at the richly humming car. "I changed the plates and all," he said.

"Hell, they'll be pulling those over on description," Macrae said.

"You ever drive a car like this?" Charlie said.

"No."

"Well"—Charlie waved a hand at the driver's door, which he'd left open. "Be my guest."

The gate was wire on a wood frame, fastened with a loop of

184

rope. Macrae opened it and slipped through and into the driver's seat of the car, a deep, sweet-smelling bucket of leather. Dials and instruments glowed intimately toward him from the dashboard. With one hand he stroked the polished pommel of the gearshift. Porter had come through and shut the gate behind him and was headed toward the door to the backseat. Sooner stood on the inside of the gate, alert now, whining half-audibly and watching them all.

Charlie got into the passenger seat and swung the door shut with a dampered clap. Macrae turned to look at him.

"Where to, boss?"

Charlie shrugged. "Your choice."

Macrae caressed the pedals with the balls of his feet. He pumped the clutch and put the car in gear. The glide from stillness to motion was completely seamless. Overgrown forsythia and honeysuckle feathered along the sides of the car as its low speed carried it out the mouth of the alley. Macrae turned west and headed for the Jones Falls.

"Smells new," Porter said from the back.

"It's not," Charlie said. "It's vintage. Been restored."

Macrae snorted. "Christ, Charlie, you stole a collector's item?"

"Quit complaining, boy, ain't it a smooth ride?"

Macrae crossed Falls Road and threaded the car through the corkscrew ramp that dropped onto the southbound expressway. At once he swelled into the center lane, the speedometer needle lifting to seventy, seventy-five, eighty.

"Don't even feel the speed," Macrae murmured.

Charlie's eye flicked over the dial. "Better cool it down a shade. You wouldn't want to get a ticket."

On the right, the vinegar tank whizzed by. The lit sign of the Stieff Silver factory . . . They were already on the edge of downtown. Macrae coasted off onto Maryland Avenue and continued farther south. The radio was tuned to a classical station and playing soft. When Charlie reached for the knob, Macrae stopped him.

"Leave it," he said. "It's right."

They drove on in the bright cloud of a string quartet, surging and slowing easily with the flow of the weekend traffic. At the corner of Mount Royal Avenue there appeared a large liquor store.

"Calls for a celebration, I'd say," Charlie said. "Why don't you pull it over?"

Macrae slowed alongside the liquor store, passing up a couple of empty spots just under its windows. He swung into the curb a bit farther on, by a long warehouse wall that was out of the light.

"Ah, I don't know about just sitting here," he said at large. "Can't turn the sucker off, can we?"

"Where's your faith?" Charlie said. "Just shut the lights. It'll be here."

The liquor store was bright and large, narrow in the front but very deep. The stock looked huge. The three of them walked by the two cash registers and looped their way toward the rear of the place. The store was medium busy for so late at night. Evidently a discounter, the sort of place people shopped with a cart.

"What'll it be," Charlie said. "Something special?"

"Champagne," Porter said.

"Not if you don't want a hangover into the middle of next week," Macrae said.

Porter stopped in front of the shelves of brandy and hooked down a bottle of Remy Martin. "This is good."

Charlie squinted at the label. "For that amount of money it better be."

They tossed a coin. At the register Charlie paid, wincing a little and staring straight through the cashier, a pretty, dark girl, about twenty. The second cashier looked even younger, a blond kid with a pimply chin, chewing a matchstick and trying on a grim expression. Charlie twisted the sack around the bottle and swung it by the neck going out.

"God, I hate to pay that price," he said.

"Don't be a bear about it," Macrae said. "You might scare off the car." But the BMW was still purring evenly against the curb, where they had left it.

Charlie tapped Porter on the arm. "Want to give it a whirl?"

"Nah," Porter said, climbing into the back. "I like to have you white boys drive me."

"Whatever you say." Charlie slid behind the wheel, rolling the bagged bottle onto the passenger seat, where Macrae collected it as he got in. He twisted off the cap and took a sip and passed it over the seat back to Porter.

"Smooth," Macrae said. "Goes a good deal easier on you than that rum."

"Get what you pay for," Porter said. He leaned forward to dangle the bottle over Charlie's shoulder.

"No lie," Charlie said. "They just must coin money in that place. Which reminds me, boys, we're getting mighty low on cash these days."

"For somebody that far as I know never worked for money, you sure do worry about it a lot," Macrae said.

Charlie snapped his head around, annoyed, but Macrae signaled him for silence, finger over his lips.

"I want to hear this," Macrae said. The sound of the violins was wearing at him gently, softening and rounding a ragged edge. Turning his head, he watched the storefronts gliding by, some still lit and others locked down for the night, light and dark and light again. He could remember from when he was little the exact feel of the tiny legs of a firefly crawling out of his loosened fist onto the joint of his thumb, winking its green taillight up at him. The storefronts kept strobing by and framed against them he could picture the profile of the first girl, the one from Battery Park, her hand loose and dry in his, just that same way.

The music stopped and the announcer's featureless voice began pronouncing credits. Macrae cleared his throat. "Guess we ought to start thinking about ditching this car."

"Not quite yet," Charlie said.

"Pushing our luck," said Macrae.

"Hey Porter." Charlie twisted his head toward the back. "Need a tiebreaker."

"Let's keep it awhile," Porter said. He switched his feet up to the seat and lay back longways with an arm between his head and the padded leather.

"Living it up, living it up, oh yeah . . ." Charlie drummed his fingers on the wheel. Macrae looked at him with uneasy curiosity.

"You got money," Charlie said, "you can have a car like this forever."

"Shame I wasn't born a stockbroker," Macrae said.

"Don't believe you can get born that," Porter said. "You got to have education."

"What to do," Charlie said. He rattled his fingers on the wheel and hummed the tune. "What to do . . ."

"How'd you swing it in New York?" Porter said.

"People on the street would give us money," Charlie said.

"Panhandling?" Porter rolled sideways on the leather seat. "You don't seem like the type."

"Bigger amounts," Macrae said.

"You're muggers," Porter said.

"Such an ugly word," Charlie said. "We used aggressive solicitation."

"I don't see that's gonna go over here," Macrae said.

Charlie braked to a gentle stop for a red light and looked toward Macrae, a corner of his mouth twisting down. "Yeah, you don't seem to catch people off their turf around here, you know? All these little neighborhoods. Everybody's always close to home."

"What this town needs is more tourism," Macrae said.

The light changed. Charlie shifted and the car passed on down the street. Macrae's head swiveled, tracking a pair of ornately got-up mannequins in the window of a lingerie shop. A man and a woman clung to each other in the door of a restaurant, the woman's head thrown back in laughter.

"Let me have a drink," Charlie said. "Yeah, Porter, where's the tourists go around here?"

"Harborplace," Porter said. "You've seen'm."

"That's no good." Charlie licked brandy off his lips and wedged the bottle upright between the gear housing and the edge of his seat. "They're too bunched up down there."

"And nowhere to hide," Macrae said.

"Where's the vice crime at around here?"

"Like what?" Porter said.

"You know," said Charlie. "Forty-second Street. Times Square."

Porter swung his feet to the floor and sat up, scratching the back of his neck.

"Take a left here," he said. "And another left and go back north." He reached for the bottle and took a drink and shoved it back in where he had found it. "Take a right here on Baltimore Street."

"Doing okay?" Charlie looked back over his shoulder.

"Next block," Porter said.

Then it was there, both sides of the street aglow with gaud and sleaze. GIRLS, GIRLS, GIRLS, blinked the marquees. The usual big-breasted, big-hipped silhouettes, and doorways ringed with colored lights. From some of the doorways music thumped. Despite the strenuous invitation there seemed to be little trade. Charlie stopped at the first intersection; the street before the car was dark. Macrae rolled his head to the side. The big corner building was painted to resemble a circus tent and a large sign declared it to be THE BIG TOP. Sexual aids and other commodities were on offer inside, each indicated on the painted wall by an oversized pointing-finger emblem lacquered there. Down the side street a white illumina-ted cross overhung the walk and there was a sign for the Union Mission.

"Pretty small," Charlie said. He slid the car on under the green light. Macrae looked to the rear, seeing Porter's face outlined against the receding blaze of lights, his features indistinct.

"Guess that's why they call it the Block," Porter said. "Used to be a good deal bigger, I been told."

"What is this?" Charlie said tightly. Macrae swiveled to the front. On the left of the street were twenty-some police cars parked parallel and angled back like the ribs of a fish.

"Police station," Porter said.

"I see it is," said Macrae. "Could we get the hell out of here, please?"

The car roared and bucked in place. Charlie had broken a sudden sweat.

"You're shifting the freaking *bottle,*" Macrae hissed. He knocked Charlie's hand to the right position. "Get yourself together, would you?" A slight skid, and the car jumped to the end of the block.

"Take it easy," Porter said. "Left here. That ramp puts you back on the Jones Falls."

Macrae peered back through the rear windshield as Charlie took the car onto the northbound expressway. Something was coming up the ramp behind them, headlights but no blue ones yet. Charlie slowed and let it overtake: a yellow T-roof Z with two girls chattering and giggling in the seats, the wind flouncing their big blond poodle hair.

"Convenient arrangement they got back down there," Charlie said. "Very cozy."

"Bet you can get DUI the minute you unlock your car," Macrae said. "Bet they do all right on public drunk too. Yeah, we can cross that pleasure spot right off the list."

The radio had been spouting egghead news for what seemed the last half hour. Macrae snapped it off and lit a cigarette. He cracked the window and the smoke straightened to a thin line sucking out.

"You're right," Charlie said. "We got to notch up."

Macrae blew a twin column of smoke from his nostrils. "Notch up to what?" he said.

No answer. Charlie drove, the traffic thinning as they went north. The chain of lights of the oncoming cars dropped away behind a wooded strip of median. Charlie merged into the beltway, amongst a convoy of double-trailer trucks, one fishtailing considerably across two lanes.

"Stay away from that thing," Macrae said irritably.

Charlie took a random exit. He pulled into the parking lot of a shopping center and began to circle slowly.

"That liquor store," Charlie said.

"It's closed," said Porter.

"Not this one here," Charlie said. "I mean the one we were at downtown." He kept cruising the lot, one hand on the wheel, just holding the car in a gentle curve. There were a handful of cars parked around the twenty-four-hour Giant Foods but the rest of the lot was empty. The car looped the three walls of shuttered stores. Record World, liquor store, T-shirt Barn. Pizza parlor. A bank branch, a shoe store . . . Sporting Goods: Hunting and Fishing. A fish restaurant, still open for late-night bar business. Charlie swung the car toward the street side, then circled back, deeper into the lot.

"What about it," Macrae said.

"Neighborhood like that," Charlie said. "They get the winos. Plus they get all that bulk-buy business. Liquor store like that is as good as a bank. If you were to go in on a Saturday night . . . They got that lottery counter in there too."

"And they got that show window about half a block long," Macrae said. "Whatever was to happen in there people would see it from a mile away."

"Wrong," Charlie said. "They got boxes stacked so high along that window, you can't hardly see in the place at all."

"Checked it out, did you?" Porter said. The car cruised the pickup lane of the grocery; lights from the store's awning played over their faces. A perky black girl was collecting carts along the curb, a bounce in her step, her hair whirled up high on her head and frozen there like a double-dip chocolate ice-cream cone.

"Couple of punk kids running the place." Charlie was staring at Macrae over the wheel. "Sitting on that stack of money . . . It'd be easy in, easy out, just the way you like."

"Out where?" Macrae said. "How you plan on getting away through that downtown traffic?"

Charlie shrugged. "Not all that much traffic late Saturday night."

"We just come from there," Macrae said. "There was plenty."

"The expressway's right there, though," Porter said. "There's another way too."

"My man," Charlie said, looking over the back of his seat. "You can be the driver."

"Watch where you're going," Macrae said. The stores were flashing by again. Hairdresser, Sporting Goods, the fish restaurant again. "What are you riding us around this way for? You're gonna make me seasick."

"Think about it," Charlie said.

Porter lay back on his seat and let out a throttled laugh toward the roof.

"What's the matter?" Charlie sheered away from the wall of shops and let the car drift toward the empty center of the lot, crossing haphazardly over the white lines of the vacant parking places.

"Just talk is all it is," Porter said. "No way you're really gonna do this."

"You think not?" Charlie said softly. The car glided on a curve, turning its nose slowly back toward the storefronts.

"Well, son . . ." Porter stuck a finger up toward the ceiling. "You not going to do no liquor store with a stick in your pocket." He raised another finger. "You hadn't got no guns." The third finger went up. "You hadn't got money to *get* no guns."

"Is that all your problem?" Charlie whispered. The car had floated almost to a stop.

"Charlie," Macrae said. "Charl*eeee!*" He was shouting as the car rocked and shot forward. Porter jerked himself upright and the punch of the takeoff threw him against the door. The car hit thirty, maybe forty, launching over the curb to shatter the glass and smash in the gate of the sporting-goods store. Charlie spun the wheel—a bootleg turn that splashed racks of clothes in five directions. The indoor walls doubled the shriek of the skid. The alarm sirens were already howling by the time Charlie jumped out, and he was washed in a crisscross of emergency spotlights. For some reason the sprinkler system had come on also. The pistols and long guns were locked in display cases along the side wall and Charlie was smashing these open with an ax he had found. He threw his weight on a row of shotguns chained to the wall through their trigger guards and ripped loose the whole fixture in a shower of plaster. Macrae saw him fall over backward with the sudden release. The arcs of sprinkler water softened and yellowed the swiveling spotlight beams. Charlie got up and rammed the guns into the backseat, bundled like firewood.

"Ammo!" Charlie yelled. Macrae, slipping on the wet floor under the sprinklers, was gathering boxed pistols and flinging them into the car.

"Shotgun shells," Charlie shouted. "Hurry it up." With the ax he sprung open several wooden drawers behind the counters. Macrae collected awkward cubes of shells and ran toward the car, scattering them on his way. Charlie, trying to carry too much, slipped in a puddle and fell full length again, cutting himself on the broken glass and losing a lot of his load. The car's wheels spun on the wet concrete floor. Porter was leaning out the driver's window.

"*I am going to leave you suckers.*" Every word crisp and clearly pronounced. Macrae noticed that he had turned on the windshield wipers. Charlie got up on one knee, dripping wet and bleeding from a forearm and one side of his face. He turned back in the direction of the gun racks.

"*Right now,*" Porter said. Macrae grabbed Charlie by the roots of his hair and snatched him into the backseat. Wet gun barrels gouged into his kidneys. The car door cracked shut on them as Porter scraped the window frame going out. He caromed the car off a parking meter, straightened out with a squeal, and floored it for the street. The first few people were just coming out of the grocery and stopping short at the curb to stare. Then the shopping center shrank away behind them. Porter was back on the beltway, threading pinhole gaps between the trucks. He took the fork for the southbound expressway, then a sudden dogleg onto Falls Road. No cars ahead or behind. He slowed down a little. Macrae sat up and pushed some guns to the floor to make room for himself on the seat. Charlie was crumpled against the dented door, breathing like a marathoner. Through the rear window a lone streetlight fell back and dwindled off into the dark. The road was silent and so were they.

fifteen

In the backyard, Porter put Sooner through all the tricks
Macrae had been teaching him—sit, lie down, roll over, jump the
milk crate, flip the biscuit . . . When the biscuits ran out, the dog
got disgusted and went to press his nose against the screen of the
back door. Porter stood up, hands on his hips, facing away from
the house, straining to inhale the heavy air. The hulk of the battered
BMW was heeled up under some bushes in the alley; he could just
see the nose of it in the dark. There was no streetlight in that area
and he was happy about that much at least.

Sooner peered at the screen, shivered and whined, looking in
at Macrae, who knelt on the floor over a fan of newspaper where
he had spread out the parts of eight disassembled shotguns. Since
there was no table he had plenty of room on the floor to work.
Sooner yipped and scratched on the screen, and Charlie stretched
out an arm from the folding chair he sat on to let the dog in.

"God—" Macrae started and twisted around as Sooner snuffled
at the back of his neck. "Get out of here, dog." He pushed him
back. "You want him to scatter all this stuff?" Macrae said to
Charlie.

Sooner slunk into the front room, the black-edged tip of his
plumed tail dragging the floor. Macrae rubbed the breech of one
of the shotguns dry and shiny and put some oil on it with another
rag. The sweet piercing smell of WD-40 was strong in the room.

"You really think they got all that wet?" Charlie said.

"You really want to take a chance on it?" Macrae snapped.

The spring of the screen door stretched and whined as Porter came in and stopped just over the sill. "Huh," he said. "Think you're going to be able to get all that back together?"

"Weapons maintenance is my specialty," Macrae droned. His lips twisted into spitting position as he spoke. He picked up the brandy bottle from the floor and rinsed his mouth with a swallow.

"Have a chair," Charlie said graciously, standing up and motioning to Porter.

" 'S all right."

"Go ahead, I got to go out."

"Where to?" Macrae said.

"Think I'd better trade the car in, don't you?" Briefly Charlie showed his teeth. "Need anything?"

Macrae lifted the oil can and gave it a shake. A dry rattle answered back from inside. "We could use some more of this D-forty," Macrae said.

"Stores'll be closed this late," Charlie said.

"I don't see why that should hold you back," Macrae said. "Can't you just cave the door in with your knotty old head?"

Charlie made a face and went out without answering. Porter stood by the chair he'd vacated, a hand on the metal back of it. In the front room, Sooner stretched his legs out, shuddered, and snored. Porter stepped to the sink and snapped on the boom box on the sill above it. A rapper. He turned the volume down.

Macrae had reconnected the pump to a twenty-gauge shotgun. He fed three shells into the breech and then pumped them back out one at time, staring at the action.

"Those all right?" Porter said.

"The shells?" Macrae said. "They're plastic. Didn't really soak through the boxes anyway." He rubbed a little more oil on the breech, then stood up and gave the gun to Porter, who held it a little awkwardly, upside-down.

"How many shots this give you?" Porter said.

"It's plugged for three," Macrae said. "Otherwise you get a few more."

"You know how to unplug it?"

Macrae shrugged. "Good deal of trouble. Besides, I don't hope to fire it even once."

"Ay Lord," Porter said, and leaned the shotgun against the side of the refrigerator. The motor cut off inside, as if from the touch.

"You know guns?" Macrae said.

"I've shot a pistol," Porter said. "Never had any call to do much with a shotgun. Are we planning to just waltz in there with'm over our shoulders or what?"

"Beats me," Macrae said. "Maybe Charlie's planning to crash the car through a music store and pick up a trombone case or something."

Porter tittered, his voice breaking high. The angry voices of the rappers kept muttering on the radio, bass ticking low behind. Porter stooped for the brandy bottle and took a drink.

"Help yourself to a pistol, then." Macrae pointed at a stack by the corner of the newspaper. "Boxes kept them pretty dry."

Porter bent down and hefted a magnum revolver with a six-inch barrel. "Feels like a hundred pounds," he grunted.

"Should do you," Macrae said. "Clint Eastwood hisself would be proud to own that."

Porter broke the pistol and spun the cylinder, which coasted a considerable time before it stopped. It was unloaded. He snapped it shut and raised the gun two handed, aiming through the doorway at the car seat in the front room.

"Yeah, you'll need two hands for him," Macrae said. "Else he'll jump up and crown you—wait."

Porter twisted, waist and knees, lowering the gun two handed to his crotch. Macrae was staring at the stove top.

"Wait a second," he said. "There, see there?"

A small gray mouse put his nose up from the vent of the oven to survey the stove top. He twitched a whisker, looked to both sides and scampered forward, then took a flying dive into one of the burners. Porter could hear his feet scratching down under the metal. He raised the pistol and sighted on the vent. One thumb drew back the hammer with a precisely machined click.

"Heavy artillery for a mouse," Macrae said. "You wouldn't find the least piece of him afterward."

"Bet he's hungry," Porter said, lowering the pistol.

"Probably," Macrae said. "He can't be finding much to eat around here lately." He stood up, balancing a twelve-gauge double-barreled shotgun with the breech broken over the palm of one hand.

"You taking that one?" Porter said.

"Nah," Macrae said. "Fire one of these a few times, your shoulder'll hurt you for a week."

"I thought you weren't planning on firing anything at all."

"Yeah," Macrae said. "That's right."

Porter stood with the magnum hanging down the outside of his right leg, the long barrel reaching below his knee. The weight of it dragged his shoulder down.

"We hadn't really thought this through, have we," he said.

"We sho ain't," Macrae said. With a one-handed whip he popped the twelve-gauge shut. "But it looks like we're fixing to do it, just the same."

"Red car," Macrae muttered from the backseat. "Don't you know red cars have more accidents?"

"Ain't the cars," Charlie said. "It's the people driving them. Long as Porter's satisfied, I don't see what it is to you."

"Ahhggh." Macrae slouched down as best he could. Charlie had knocked off a Scirocco this time, for the high performance, but it was cramped in the back for somebody Macrae's height. His knees were jammed against his chin. With a struggle he extricated one foot from behind the driver's seat, and then the other, and unfolded his legs partially into the well on the other side. That was better, but not a whole lot better. His feet slotted delicately amongst the butts of two shotguns and an egg-shaped plastic panty-hose container.

"Handles good," Porter said, pulling a left turn onto Northern Parkway. "Nice pickup from scratch." He lifted his hands off the wheel and let the car right itself, the wheel spinning back under his palms. A single set of headlights bored in on them from the opposite lane and then fell away. It was late, around eleven, getting time. Macrae twisted his hips and pulled a roll of LifeSavers from his front pocket. He had been smoking too much to choke down another cigarette just now. The mint adhered to the roof of his mouth; he could hardly get up enough spit to loosen it. By mutual agreement there had been no drinking all day.

"How about high speed to higher?" Porter looked at Charlie. "We got overdrive possibilities?"

Charlie shrugged. "I ain't read the manual."

"We'll see about it." Porter turned and raced north on Falls Road. Nothing so smooth as last night's car; Macrae was pinned to his seat by the thrust. He watched the speedometer needle roll through its arc to the right.

"Not bad at all," Porter said. "Now, what about—" As the needle hit seventy he jammed the brakes and ripped the wheel to the left at the same time. The car luffed up onto its right tires, every joint squealing. Macrae's head bounced off the window. Rear end dragging, the car burned through a tight buttonhook and slid into the southbound lanes. Porter straightened out the fishtail and shot for the interstate ramps.

"God help us," Macrae said breathily. Great spurts of adrenaline were frothing on the roof of his brain. "You better save that one for when we really need it."

Porter found his eyes in the rearview mirror. "Deal I heard, we not gonna need no fancy maneuvers. Deal I heard, this is just a convenience stop."

"You got it right," Charlie said. He twisted toward Macrae, his fingers laced around the headrest of his seat. "You ready?"

"Ready as I'll ever be," Macrae said.

Charlie kept looking at him.

"What do you want?" Macrae said.

Charlie uncoiled himself and looked forward down the road. "Okay, boys," he said. "Time to go downtown."

Macrae groped on the floor for the plastic egg and broke it open on his lap. With his pocket knife he hacked off the legs of the hose and passed the ragged panty portion forward to Charlie.

"What's this?"

"Bozo hat for Porter," Macrae said. "Got holes for his ears and the works."

With one hand Porter shook out the wad of polyester and let it dangle. He hissed at it and tossed it out the window of the car.

"Is that wise?" Macrae said. He gave one of the cut-off legs to Charlie.

"Too late now," Porter said. Air dragged at the edges of open window. He raised his half-burned cigarette and tipped the ash out, over the brushy canyon where Falls Road dropped below the expressway. Charlie was stretching the stocking between his hands like a cat's cradle.

"What is this whorehouse rag?" he said, touching the pattern with a forefinger. "Are these supposed to be grapevines or what?"

"Kudzu, probably," Macrae said. "Sorry. I don't generally shop for pantyhose."

"Complains about a red car and comes home with electric blue stockings." Charlie shook his head. "I just don't know." He pulled the stocking down over his face. It flattened his nose and lips and mashed his cheeks down on the bone, leveling his every feature into formlessness.

"Wooo-eeee," Porter mocked. "Great Googly-moogly. If you ain't scary I don't know what is."

"Quit your fooling," Macrae said as Porter pulled off onto Maryland Avenue. He passed one of the twenty-gauges through the space between the seats. "Let's lock and load."

Charlie was twisting the gun around, trying to get it right way to. Porter flinched and the car jerked as the barrel scraped across his lap.

"Can't you keep that thing on your own side?"

"There's no room in here."

"Yeah? Whyn't you steal a bigger car?"

Macrae pushed shells into the pump tube, one, two, and three. A cold spot gathered and turned in his stomach, shimmering like mercury. He jacked the first shell into the chamber and laid the gun flat across his knee with his forefinger on the outside of the trigger guard and his thumb in the half-open breech. The metal seemed to bind to his hand like an ice cube will freeze to your wet tongue.

"This is it." Porter slowed to a crawl just over Mount Royal Avenue.

"Let me hear it," Charlie said. "One more time."

"I'm gonna make one block, one time," Porter said.

"You know it," said Charlie. "We'll be coming out that door with bags of money."

"And if you don't?"

Macrae swallowed. The LifeSaver dislodged and almost choked him. He'd forgotten it was there.

"We'll be there," Charlie said. He got out of the car and Macrae pulled the mask down over his face and followed, cracking his head on the door frame, not feeling it at all. He was aware of the ridged plastic of the shotgun shell just under his thumb and his left hand tight on the tooled wood of the pump. A drop of sweat unrolled from his armpit. He spat his mint onto the asphalt as Charlie's shadow passed into the liquor store. The glass door began shutting itself gradually against the pressure of the air hinge. Macrae slid the pump glossily forward and the chamber closed with a definitive snap. He walked in after Charlie, raising the gun to his shoulder as he moved.

The dark-haired girl appeared above the bead of his front sight. She was taking out a piece of gum, but seeing Macrae she froze, neatly and immediately as a deer in the woods, and held tranquilly still, with one stick of Wrigley's protruding from the pack she held in her left hand. Macrae's focus narrowed so sharply it was like he was looking down the inside of the gun barrel. "It's all right," he said. "I wouldn't hurt you."

Behind the other register, the pimply boy was backed against the half-pint shelves, his mouth opening and closing, his fingers working on the air.

"Let's see," Charlie said musingly. "I think I'll have . . . half-pint of Smirnoff."

The boy gaped. His skinny shoulders rubbed the shelves in back of him.

"Get it down for me," Charlie prompted. "The black label. Or I'm gonna kill you, boy."

The boy gulped and turned toward the shelves. His head seemed to stay in place, staring rigidly at the shotgun, as his body rotated underneath it. He took the front bottle, fumbling, and brought the second one down behind it. It slapped onto the rubber mat on the floor by the register but didn't break.

"Open it for me," Charlie said. "Go on."

Shakily, the boy's hands broke the paper seal. Charlie held the twenty-gauge one handed, the barrel weaving, his hand around the pistol grip and finger on the trigger. With his left hand he pulled the stocking up above his upper lip. He picked up the opened bottle and at the same time gouged the gun barrel into the boy's belly, just to the right of his belt buckle.

"Safety's off," he said. "Don't jostle anything. There could be an accident." He fit the bottle neck between his teeth, threw back his head, and let it bubble.

"Ah yes," he said, wiping his lips on his shirt sleeve. "Hadn't had a drink all day."

Macrae's eyes were nailed to the girl. He was unaware of anything else. Her face was translucently pale and a blue vein partly encircled her right eye; on her, a beauty mark. Only the slight pulsing in the hollow between the tendons of her neck reminded him that time was passing.

"Quit messing around," he said, without turning his head.

"Be cool, be cool," Charlie said, taking another gulp. "We got time."

"Are you crazy?" Macrae said.

"You better believe it." Charlie was talking to the boy again. "Show me how you open that cash register, now."

From behind him, Macrae heard the drawer ring open and Charlie's voice continue. His arms were stiff, holding the gun, his trigger hand so numb it felt like it belonged to some other person.

"Okay, come out of there," Charlie said. "Let's have Little Sugar out here too."

Released by this, Macrae lowered the gun to his hip. He took his left hand off the pump and motioned. "Come on this way," he said. "You can go on and get your gum."

"I don't want it," the girl said, her voice calm and sweet. It was the first thing either of them had said. She put the pack of gum on the counter and smoothed back her hair with both hands as she came out from behind it. Macrae saw her hips were trim in white painter's pants. She wore soft-soled cotton sandals that were silent on the floor.

"That's right," Charlie said. "Now, why don't you two hold hands?" Taking them by their shoulders, he arranged them in the aisle between the registers. "Both hands. That's right. Cute." He slapped the boy lightly on the cheek with his fingertips and looked at Macrae. "Anything happens, shoot Pizza Face the first."

Macrae didn't answer him. He stood still pressing the gun against his right hip, about two yards back. No range at all for a shotgun. Boy and girl were positioned with both their hands clasped, as if they were waltzing. They looked back at him as if he were perhaps the photographer at a high school prom. Each wore the same cut of V-necked shirt, his red, hers blue. High on the swell of her left breast lay the silk-screened emblem of the liquor store.

Charlie went from the first register to the second, cramming bills in a paper bag. "Problem," he said, coming back from behind the girl's counter.

"You got it, didn't you?" Macrae said. "Come on, let's go."

Charlie shook his head. "Not enough," he said. "There's not but three, four hundred dollars here."

Porter made a right turn, the car gliding slowly, close to the curb, like a big lazy fish. His left foot, removed from the pedals, was twitching uncontrollably. It took a major effort not to speed up. An announcer was reading news on the radio . . . the president, the economy . . . the volume was low. Something was funny about her voice, as if maybe she had learned English on Mars. Porter turned again, one hand checking the butt of the big magnum pistol jammed down below the edge of his seat.

The third turn. He withdrew his hand from the pistol and plastered it claylike to the wheel. He was alongside the big display window of the liquor store, but Charlie was right, the boxes were stacked so high you couldn't see anything, at least not at this angle. He made the last corner, dry lips parting. Two black kids, hardly in their teens, were snapping their skateboards on and off the curb, two or three doors down from the liquor store. They wore over-sized surf-shop T-shirts, and one had a beanie with a propellor on top. No kidding. Too late for them to be out, Porter thought automatically. Except for them, the sidewalk was empty. His throat closed as if he had been garroted. Charlie and Macrae were nowhere in sight.

Charlie walked idly toward the boy and the girl, still standing half-embraced under Macrae's gun. "Must be a safe around here somewhere," he said.

"Bh—," the boy started. "B-Behind the lottery."

Charlie circled the pair and walked on slowly to the lottery machine. He dipped forward, his left leg rising as a counterweight, like he was taking a long leaning shot over a pool table. Set in the concrete floor was a circular safe door with a slot for bills above its keyhole.

"Mmm-hmm," Charlie, swinging back on both feet and coming back, his shotgun held crossways over his chest. "Where's that key?"

"We don't have it," the boy said. "We du—we put money in the slot every hour. The day shift takes it to the bank."

"Where's the key," Charlie said, as if he had heard nothing. "Let go of your girlfriend, now, Pizza Face. Just step away from her."

The boy dropped the girl's hand and backed against the chrome rail between him and the counter. He looked at the palms of his hands and rubbed them on his pants.

"Pizza Face," Charlie said. "I want that safe to come open for me." Under the blue mesh of the stocking mask his features swirled and tightened. Still rolled partway up, the fabric cut a white line across his upper lip.

"I told you, we—"

Charlie cracked him on the corner of the jaw with the side of the gun stock, then drew back deeply and drove the butt into his stomach. As the boy folded up he swung the stock into his face again and then kicked him over onto his side, where he lay with his nose bleeding over the green-and-white checks of linoleum and a tendril of vomit running out of his mouth. Charlie put the ball of his foot on his temple and turned toward the girl.

"Now, sugar," he said, "all I want is the money out of that safe."

"We really can't open it." The girl's voice was so dreamily calm that Macrae wasn't sure if she was naming a fact of the situation or just a personal decision she had made. Charlie shifted his weight forward and the boy screamed underneath his foot. Charlie cupped one hand behind the girl's neck and drew her near. Macrae saw her head drop back, her hair running down toward the floor like a dark waterfall. She was bonelessly relaxed. Charlie's thumb stroked over her cheek and traced the underside of her full red lower lip.

"This is serious," he said. "Don't be stubborn, sugar pie. After all, it's not your money, is it?"

Porter edged the car into the curb, leaning sideways to try to see into the store, but he couldn't make out much. Macrae's back was to the door but Porter couldn't tell what he was doing. Whoever else was in there he couldn't see them. Another car zipped up behind him and the driver began leaning on the horn.

"All right, all right," Porter muttered aloud. The sound of his voice was queerly detached. He pulled away and began to make the block a second time. Faster now, definitely faster. His palms were slick with sweat and shaky on the wheel.

"They're telling the truth, Charlie," Macrae said. "Come on, we been in here twice too long."

Charlie's head made a lazy revolution Macrae's way. "You jackass," he said. "Did I hear you call my name in this place?"

The nose of Macrae's gun covered Charlie as much as the girl. "You got a nerve," he said. "I spoke to you once about calling me a jackass." He paused, listening to a hum building, not in the back of his head but really behind him, outside. It peaked and broke and it was a siren.

"Oh, God," Macrae said. "A silent alarm."

"Nobody cares what *I* want," Charlie said. "What *I'm* after. Me." He stepped off the boy's head and pushed the girl a few feet away. "Little miss," he said, as she recovered herself and shook back her hair from her face. "Did you trip it? Don't you know I can splash every bit of you across that wall?"

Macrae snatched Charlie's gun barrel and twisted it away from her. He half expected it to go off but it didn't. One hand over the other, he reeled Charlie past him and then shoved him in the direction of the door and went after. A police car was barreling up along the westbound lane and the Scirocco wasn't there at all. Nowhere. Macrae's head lashed back and forth. Charlie shouldered his gun and fired, and one of the dome lights on the police car shattered. He pumped and the hot shell spiraled out, grazing Macrae's cheek. Charlie took a lower aim and fired again. Pellets raked noisily over the metal. The police car jumped the curb and halted, the driver's door burst open and from behind it, low, came a pair of pistol shots. Charlie fired again and there was the sound of pellets scraping metal.

"You're shooting at the cops," Macrae said, stupefied. Charlie pumped the gun and fired. The glass of the open police car door starred without completely shattering. No return fire came this time. Macrae could see a cop's blue knees on the asphalt below the edge of the car door. Not far from that a skateboard lay upside down across the curb, fat red plastic wheels spinning on their bearings. The third shell came singing out of Charlie's breech and he pulled the trigger again but there was not even a click. A siren was winding down from the opposite direction, but the rise and fall of the sound made it hard to tell if it was nearing or receding. Charlie flung his shotgun at the police car like a spear and turned sidelong to grab at Macrae's. His eyes showed burning through the blue stocking mask. Macrae twisted away from him, breaking his grip, cracking the gun barrel across his ribs hard and only half by accident. That smash and ring was a heavy-caliber slug striking a utility pole a yard to the side. The cops were firing their weapons again.

Macrae flinched, spun on his heels, half lost his footing, recovered, and ran. Nowhere in particular, just away, still holding the shotgun. The Scirocco materialized at the opposite corner and he ran for that. Porter didn't quite stop, but he leaned into his skid to flip open the passenger door and immediately regathered speed as Macrae dove in. Macrae's gun barrel swept around like the boom of a boat. As it crossed Charlie, running to catch up, the thought flashed in and out of Macrae's head that he might just pull the trigger. He got the back door open as Porter powered through the red light and into the intersection. Charlie was running all out, stocking-swaddled head thrown back, his fingers dragging at the edge of the back door. Porter jabbed his brakes as a car creased the nose of the Scirocco with a burst of broken glass and swept away. Charlie came half into the backseat on his belly like a snake or a salamander but the lurch as Porter took off threw him mostly back out. His elbows plowed backward along the vinyl of the seat and Macrae screwed around and caught him by the forearms. Charlie's feet turned under, the tops of his shoes burning through on the pavement. The door clapped open and shut against his ribs. Macrae was so contorted he could only hang on, not really pull, but Charlie choked up, teeth gritted below the blue tourniquet of stocking, and flung himself all the way in.

The door banged shut and caught on the latch. There was an instant of pure silence, then a siren exploding just in their path as a police car sliced sideways into their lane, blocking them off from the interstate ramp. "Jesus!" Porter screamed. "Jesus is Lord, I testify!"

The car turned almost on its side and Porter was roaring into the mouth of a street Macrae hadn't seen; he could hardly see anything because a grape cluster from the weave of the ridiculous stocking had curled across his eyes. He ripped the mask off and threw it out the window and saw it unfurl on the windshield of the police car that was latched to their rear bumper. Macrae faced front to look out where they might go and saw a line of brake lights, cars stopped at a signal. Porter swung the car into the opposite lane, full in the face of the oncoming traffic. The police car was sticking tight, and dead ahead were twin caves of head-light—something big, a van or a truck. Porter flattened his foot on the gas. "Chicken!" he yelled, "you better give," but the truck, whatever it was, had nowhere to go and it was exploding into the windscreen altogether when Porter whipped up onto the sidewalk.

Two newspaper boxes flew up as if equipped with personal rockets and collided with each other in midair. Porter sheered the

208

sideview mirror off on the corner of a building and the car jounced down hard onto the street again and shot north, the bottom briefly scraping. Ahead, the train station; and on the other side another ramp to the JFX. Macrae clutched at Porter as he passed this up. Porter grinned back at him like a skull, skin stretched tight over the bones of his face. He looked like a cat on fire. "We'll whip it," he cried, a lilt in his voice like he was singing to himself. "There'd be no game, brothers, if no one would play . . ."

Macrae could hear sirens all over the place, but nothing was behind them, nothing in sight. They ripped past the movie theater, a line waiting outside the *Rocky Horror* midnight show, faces revolving toward them in a blur. The bottom of the car smacked ground again as Porter took a left. They launched over a hump and were airborne and seemed to turn again in flight. "Yes!" Everything changed. Porter shouted "Yes!" again, hammering the wheel with one hand as he gunned up a narrow, winding ribbon of pavement, lacing among the warehouses that suddenly appeared, the claws of uncut brush raking by, stanchions of the interstate overpass. They were down below the level of the city, sheltered somehow, alone on the road. Porter fired across a sudden open space, over some railroad tracks that rattled Macrae to the roots of his bones, and hauled the car up short behind an abandoned switching station.

Macrae was out of the car before it was stopped good, running across the decaying concrete like a cockroach in fear of the light, the shotgun still fixed to his hands. A dark wall of woods seemed to rise sheer ahead of him, but first there was a ditch—actually a shallow creek that he was splashing through before he ever saw it. On the other side the slope was steep but Macrae didn't falter. Branches lashed across his face. When he heard a siren from the hollow behind, he wheeled and braced the shotgun across the fork of a sapling handy by.

"Easy," Porter said, coming up the grade with the magnum swinging from one hand. Charlie had stopped a way below, head down, gasping, one hand locked over the branch of a scrub cedar. Out over them both, Macrae saw a fan of light spreading on the road and then the police car came in view, just one. It howled past the station without stopping, and its siren faded along the walls of the ravine. It was quiet then, except for the drone of cars over the elevated highway and some sirens there too. When those had faded, Macrae could begin to hear insects singing in the brush near him. His feet were cold and squelching in his shoes. Below, the Scirocco stood crabwise across a section of uprooted track, washed in the ambient glow of the city light reflected from the cloudy sky.

"Nice piece of driving," Macrae said to Porter. He craned his neck and squinted up. A sound of blades thrashing the air swelled, not directly overhead, but hovering near the expressway. A beam of light cut a wedge out of the misty sky and swiveled.

"Goddamn cop chopper," Porter hissed.

"Don't tell me that," Macrae said.

"It's all right," Porter said. His profile was plain against the sky glow, framed by the lace of new-leafed branches. The beam tilted away and the helicopter dropped off to the south. "They don't know where to look."

Still breathing raggedly, Charlie pulled himself straight. He hawked and spat on the ground and came limping up toward the others.

"What happened in there?" Porter said.

"Charlie lost it," Macrae said. "Charlie lost it big time." He turned to look up the slope behind them, to the edge, where the trees thinned out and they could see a few lights glittering. "What's up there?"

"Hampden, should be," Porter said. "You want to maybe give me a couple more details?"

"Not especially," Macrae said. He touched one finger to a seep of blood from a shallow cut a branch had flicked into his cheek as he ran up the hill.

Charlie pulled the stocking off the back of his head, wiped his face with it, and tossed it away. It snagged on a twig and unrolled down, the stretched-out foot dangling like a deformity. "They had a safe—," he began.

"Shut up," said Macrae. "I don't want to hear it out of your mouth."

"Ay, Lord," Porter said. "Did we get anything at all?"

"Not much," Charlie said.

"Enough to leave town on," Macrae said. "If you still even got it."

"Oh, I got it." Charlie patted his hip pocket.

"That bad, is it?" Porter tried to stick the magnum in his waistband but it was too heavy and he stooped to lay it on the ground. Straightening up, he got himself out a cigarette.

"You tell me," Macrae said. "Old Charlie here just emptied his shotgun into a police car. That's bad enough for me."

Porter's match flared and he sighed on the exhalation. Macrae couldn't see his face in the dark.

"He get one?" Porter said.

"I don't know," Macrae said. "You could probably find out from the morning paper, except I hope to be somewhere by then where they don't sell it."

"I hear you," Porter said. The coal on his cigarette glowed and as it darkened he sighed again. "All right," he said. "But what about my dog?"

down home

Struggling with the worn-out clutch, Lacy drove to the new shopping center, to the new grocery there. They'd widened the road that went by the thing, put in an extra lane each way, to keep the cars running smooth toward Nashville. The fields around were subdivisions now—a bedroom community in formation . . . Well, it couldn't all have happened since she'd last been back, only that it seemed that way. She parked and entered the brand-spanking-new grocery and glumly pushed a cart up and down the wide empty aisles, under the greenish aquarium-style lighting. The place was oddly empty, though it was midday. Muzak played for nobody but her and a few old ladies who looked dazed and lost, the idle cashiers, and a couple of stockers strolling around in their red aprons.

She shopped like a person with practice being poor, loading the cart with rice and dried beans, carrots and onions, the cheapest cuts of meat, for soup. There was a little nut of money she'd saved in Philadelphia and she meant to stretch it as thin as she could. In the right place, she knew she could make good money as a waitress or a barmaid, probably working only half a week, but she didn't have the stomach for it now. The right kind of place, where she'd have the eyes on her, less frequently the hands on her maybe, dumb jokes and false friendliness and *Honey, when do you get off work?* In the right place you'd get that certain breed of businessman, overfed and overpaid, "getting over" his divorce or just on his way to one, tie undone, breath hot and sweet, sweating alcohol through the Arrow shirt. Yeah, they were big tippers. The money would be good, but right now she didn't want it. Blinking in the unfamiliar outdoor brightness, though it was overcast, she crossed the parking lot with her arms hugged around her bags, admitting sourly to herself that right now she didn't quite know what she wanted.

The car bucked out of the parking slot and she wrenched it onto the road again. Not even prayer would hold the clutch much longer, that was sure. She didn't feel like going home—to the house, she should say. Well, she might still be in Philadelphia, with the spring rains washing the garbage over the sidewalks, getting braced for another summer in the ghetto. It wasn't a thought that especially appealed. She turned off between ranks of orange-striped barrels where another road was being widened, to cut from one highway to the other, farther west. But still between the highways there remained a wedge of land that was all farm or forest. Ahead of her the sun broke through the marbled sky and she reached to the dashboard for her sunglasses. Her mood improved a little. In another mile she was on a dirt road.

On the downside of a hill she stopped and backed the car into a set-back gateway. The gate itself had long fallen down and the gap was freshly fenced across; there'd be no one needing to come through. With her elbows braced on the top strand of new wire, she focused her Leica on the boards of the fallen gate, scattered through the new spring grass and whitening like bones. Finally, she didn't take the picture. She zipped the camera back in the bag and pushed the whole business up under the driver's seat, out of sight, before she locked the car. Better sometimes to go without a camera, use your eyes instead of it, and try to really see.

She climbed the fence, swinging her jeaned leg high over the barbs of the top strand, landing with a soggy thump on the spongy turf on the other side, heels of her cowboy boots digging in. With a toe she flipped up one of the loose boards from the gate. Beneath it the grass was pale and wrinkly, like noodles. Someone had mowed this patch of hillside pasture, though, within the year. At its edge it went back to buckbushes and blackberry bramble, threaded through with animal trails she saw when she got nearer—ground-hogs, foxes maybe. Beyond the thicket were old apple trees in rows of an untended orchard, and among them the wild black-berries had grown in hedges higher than her head.

She picked her way around the briar patch. At the far side of it, the hill got sharply steeper. There was a shaley slope she couldn't climb; she circled her way around to an area where the footing was firmer and climbed up, holding on to saplings for support. It half winded her to reach the crown of the hill—because she was smoking again, no doubt. The cigarettes were on the dash of the car, where she had left them. She stood with a hand on the earth-caked roots of a fallen elm and looked to the west. The trees had not yet leafed, so the view was clear between the trunks and spectral lacing of bare branches, all the way across the valley to the other hilltops that rolled around to enclose it. Their wooded flanks were copper and blue, a patina like old bronze. Into them crept a network of new roads, new driveways, spreading like varicose veins or a rash. It was all being eaten away, she thought. On the far side of the valley the windows of new houses winked at her in the spring sunshine, but where she was she felt gray and ancient, winter still cold in her bones. It occurred to her that if Macrae were there he wouldn't be thinking such thoughts. He might feel it but he wouldn't be thinking it so plain. Sometimes there were virtues in obscurity, she thought, sometimes, and felt the corners of her mouth binding in a dry and slightly bitter smile.

She descended from the hill's round head and struck a trail and followed it. When it petered out she climbed again to the backbone of the ridge. The circle of linked hills kept leading her north, northwest. Sometimes she saw below her through the naked trees a barn or a house, and once a doll-sized man on a tractor whose engine noise came to her as a distant, staticky crackle. All the while she kept well back in the trees, though at one time or another she'd known all the people who owned this land and she'd have been welcomed to wander if only she'd asked. But she hadn't gone calling, hadn't presented herself . . . There was something she didn't want to see them wondering—*Did you give it all up and come home this time? Or are you just passing through?*

Maybe it was loneliness, she thought, that made her want to keep away from waitressing right now. She'd only feel it deeper if she had to drift among those packs of drunken people, pretending that there was really something between them, some connection that would last. If her parents had been here it might have made a difference, but they'd sold up and gone to Arizona for her father's emphysema, they were done. She thought of Marvin's cheap cocktail psychology—regression, sure, just show me how.

She didn't know where she was going, maybe, but she did know where she was. Stepping over a jumble of old wire brought her onto Macrae's place, his daddy's, theirs. She kept following the ridge until she overlooked the barn lot and the yard. A small International pickup was pulled alongside a tree halfway between the house and the milk barn. It looked deserted down there, deadly still. She felt her breast pocket for the cigarettes that weren't there, and wondered vaguely where Macrae might be this minute, *just passing through* somewhere, she'd bet.

A sound behind her turned her head, a breath. A few yards up the slope a brindled dog sat on its haunches, panting, watching her from yellow eyes. It sucked in its tongue briefly and assumed a serious expression, then let it hang again and seemed to smile. Lacy snapped her fingers and beckoned. The dog once again became grave, then picked itself up and went off quietly through the trees.

There was a stump and she sat down on it. Flat diamond-shaped stick-tights coated her jeans legs. She began to pick them off and peel them, eating the tiny, hard seeds inside. On the cover of old leaves there was a ticking sound, a small brown rabbit foraging. It raised its folded ears and looked at her with a black bead eye. She was still. The rabbit's attention shifted; it hopped along. Of perversity she reached for a worm-eaten stick and threw it. The rabbit fled in springing bounds that carried it in effortless high arcs, crashing over the dead leaves. Farther downhill the brindled dog reappeared and chased it out of sight.

Lacy stood up, her mind gone agreeably blank at last, and wandered along the inner slope of the hill, into a dense cedar grove. Here it was dim, and cool enough to make her shiver. Underfoot were moss and fragrant dry fronds from the cedars. Crossing a hummock, she came upon a dairy cow who rounded on her with a bellow and a snort. Startled, Lacy took a step back, placed her palm on a shaggy cedar trunk, and froze. The cow watched her a moment more, then dropped her head and went back to licking the spotted calf curled there in a hollow of the moss.

It must have been born just minutes before, Lacy realized. It was still wet, hair matted in twirls, still a little bloody. The cow's heavy tongue passed over its neck and shoulders. Not far away was a glistening swirl of afterbirth. She watched the calf struggling to get up, hind end first. The skinny legs braced and the forequarters came up shakily. The calf lifted its heavy head, opened its mouth, and tottered toward the bursting bag. Its muzzle brushed the teats but the cow swung away and the calf fell to its front knees. It rested, rose again, and staggered to the cow. A knot of tension came undone in Lacy when she saw it latch on successfully. The cow sighed and lowered her head while the calf's kinky tail lifted just enough to wag.

Lacy batted at her hip for the camera bag, which also wasn't there, and reminded herself that this time she'd only come to see. The calf lunged, thrusting at the bag, lost the teat, and recaptured it. Its one eye rolled white with pleasure. Lacy sat down on the moss and wrapped her hands around her knees.

It needs a human eye, she told herself, that's what it takes to see these things. Or show them. So this is what you'll do. You'll go around and see these people and you'll admit you know them. Take their pictures if they'll let you . . . And let them think whatever they want. She picked a patch of lichen from a stone and crumbled it between her fingers. That was what her pictures had been lacking, she thought now; they needed people in them.

seventeen

Macrae missed the turn, once on the southbound pass, again coming back, driving slow, turtling his neck to peer out over the wheel of the Dodge minivan Charlie had stolen for this leg of the trip. Though it was only midafternoon the sky had darkened under a festering shelf of cloud, and the tempered light dyed everything bruise purple. A stiff crosswind rocked the van on its wheels and turned back the pale undersides of the leaves, but most of the trees he remembered were gone.

A car blew past him, blowing its horn, as he made a limping turn into the drive of Willowmere Estates. The lurch threw Sooner off his legs and he yelped, scrambling for balance among the shotguns scattered on the shifting floor. Porter, who'd made a sort of seat of a folded blanket in the back, irritably told the dog to sit down.

"How long you say you lived in this place?" Charlie said. Macrae groaned and dragged the van through a U-turn and stopped it facing the highway again. He was jittery and lightheaded from driving straight through. Another car zoomed by, southbound. Macrae wiped his face with the back of his wrist. The van had no air-conditioning and the humidity was pressing sweat out of them all like a juicer.

"There wasn't none of this here before," Macrae said, flipping his hand out the window toward the rows of jerry-built houses. "Not none of it . . . There's nothing left to go by." A bend of the highway curved smoothly to the south, and just at the curve on the far side of the road was a flat square high school building he'd never seen before, the asphalt of its parking lot black, oily, brand-new.

"I know it's north of those gas stations," Macrae said. "It ought to be right here." He shut his eyes and pictured the road the way he'd known it. The wind dropped off shortly and the sky pressed down harder than before. He looked again, then put the van in gear.

Alongside the new school parking lot a white board fence abutted on a heap of stones beside the old turnoff. Macrae swung the van into the lane. It was newly paved but he recognized the ancient rock-wall fence that ran back beside, unmortared stone piled craftily and overgrown with a century of vine.

"Got it?" Charlie said.

"Sure enough." Macrae twisted his head to look back at the school. "But this stuff just comes up like toadstools after the rain. Nothing but cows in that pasture last time I was here."

The pavement ran out suddenly at the crest of a low rise and beyond it the road was potholed and ribbed with the underlying limestone. The car slewed and shivered over the washboard surface.

"Take it easy," Porter said, grabbing hold to a strut with one hand as the base of his backbone slammed the floor.

"Can't help the road," Macrae said cheerfully, mashing the gas. Ahead, the lane dipped low and turned off sharply to the right, and just at the corner two deteriorated cairns of stone marked off the gateway. Uphill from there, above the ridge, a wide glittering shaft of lightning reached out of the eerie silence of the sky and clove into a grove of cedar trees. The sulphurous flash of light washed over them well before the shock of the thunderclap.

Charlie flinched and righted himself. "Think it'll rain?" he said.

"Might do," Macrae said. The van jounced over the cattle gap between the crumbling posts and followed a rutted track to the left, curving around the base of a gently rising hill where shelves of pitted stone thrust out among the trunks of the scrub cedars. Round the bend appeared a long one-story house of bare board weathered silver-gray; without the phone wires and the raised porch it could have been taken for a barn. Off to the right a rusting International pickup with the tailgate missing was parked underneath a black oak tree. The wind rose, turning back the club-shaped leaves.

The creak of the van door seemed to carry a mile through the charged atmosphere when Macrae got out. The wind lifted his hair in a spiral. Three dogs came barking from under the porch, a black shaggy one, a little fice, and a brindled dog with yellow eyes like a coyote's. Sooner had jumped down out of the van's side door, his plumed tail alternately pricking and descending. Macrae rested an elbow on the hood of the van. His knees were stiff, and his stomach had soured from the caffeine poisoning of the night and day. Porter and Charlie climbed out and shook themselves. The dogs, sniffing urgently nose to tail, turned in tight anxious loops around and around. The little fice kept yapping nervously. Sooner's tail sagged; he let out a howl and bolted up the grade into the woods.

Porter went a little way after him at a tottery run, calling and stumbling over the rocks, then stopped and turned back helplessly.

"Just leave the van door open," Macrae said. The wind ripped his hair to one side, then the other. "He'll come back to that, probably he will. Come on, let's get indoors ahead of this storm."

Rain was gunning down on the tin roof of the porch as they dashed up the steps. The home dogs were sheltering under the floor, scuffling and nipping at each other. Macrae struggled with the door; it was unlocked but warped tight to the jamb. Inside, it was musty and very dim.

"Pappy?" he called. "Pappy, you home?" He went partway into the room, muttering back to the others, "Truck's here, any-how . . ." He walked deeper into the gloom, his silhouette just visible against a cloudy wall, the others picking their way after him. The windows were streaked with dirt and cobwebs, and the interior was almost fully dark with such a dense rain. Macrae felt his way through the kitchen door and found the pull chain for the light.

"Pappy," he said. "What're you doing sitting in the dark?"

The bare bulb at the end of the paint-stiffened cord swung slightly from the touch that had ignited it. Below, the old man rotated around gradually in a straight chair set before a square Formica table.

"Huh," he said, tilting his head sidelong like a bird. The whiskery edge of his ear thrust up at the doorway. "Come back, did you?" He wrapped one arm around his rib cage. It was apparent that he had once been a heavyset man but had fallen off lately, the frame of him hollowed halfway out.

"Brought some fellows," Macrae said. "Charlie and Porter."

"Hello there," Porter said.

The old man let his head drop away, then raised it back toward the door. One hand raked through the thick shock of his white hair. The joints of his hand were large as marbles, but his fingers had lost flesh. His eyes were blue and swirled with white; they passed over the three of them without stopping.

"Bringing trouble, I don't doubt," he said.

"Sure," Macrae said. "I'm happy to see you too."

The old man bunched his shoulders and shifted away, flexing his hands uncertainly on the mottled surface of the table. The rumpled place in his hair was slowly settling.

"One of you's a nigger," he observed. A raindrop slapped down on the table between his thumb and forefinger, while another struck into a crusted coffee cup a few inches away. Macrae craned his neck. Rainwater was beading rapidly all along the joins of the ceiling boards; he couldn't pin down one particular leak.

"Ain't been doing much for this roof, have you?" Macrae said, and turned around in the doorway. In the room they'd come in through, the rain was starting to come down everywhere as if the roof was no more than a temporary interruption.

"Hell with this," Macrae said. "Let's try the barn." He went out through the front door, shaking his head, paused a half beat, and swung down off the porch. Rain sluiced down over his head and shoulders like a waterfall but he kept standing there, letting it drain over him. The yard was filling up with water because the ground was rock hard from drought and couldn't take it in. Twin brown rivers ran down the ruts of the track. Macrae slicked back a mass of his wet hair as Porter appeared at his elbow. Porter had taken off his shirt and braced it over his head like a sail, but it was already soaked through.

"Where we going," Porter shouted, barely audible above the racket of the rain. Macrae pointed past the truck and the black oak tree, and they both began to run, Porter a step behind. Charlie was bringing up the rear. They ran through a stand of walnut trees and, stepping over a tangle of wire, came into a lot before a large barn, two stories high with a peaked roof, and more impressive than the house. Two odd creatures looking like a cross between jacks and mules brayed at them and cantered away, tossing their heads. The hard-packed surface of the lot was just forming a thin skein of mud, so Macrae's feet went slipsliding. A flash threw cold light over the three of them as another lightning bolt drove into the hillside. Thunder rolled away behind it. Somewhere out of sight a cow was lowing painfully, over and over, a long bass note going ragged at the end. The barn door was open, and in a wide half circle before it the mud had been whipped up by animal hooves and hardened into crests and peaks that the rain had only begun to soften. They broke off clods from this patch, stumbling over it and into the dusty hay-smelling hall.

Macrae coughed and leaned on the wall. His wet clothes clung to his skin seamlessly as a coating of oil. The stutter of the rain on the roof was muffled by the loft ceiling, and the desperate lowing of the one cow now sounded a little farther off. Macrae pulled off his shirt and wiped it over his head, but the cloth and his hair were both too wet for any exchange of moisture to take place between them.

"Let's have a look," he said, slinging the sodden shirt over a wire where some rusted horseshoes hung. He opened a door and mounted a set of wooden stairs that passed through a board-floored room, completely dark and windowless, and emerged into the gray-ish light of the loft above. The sound of the rain was louder here and through the square loading hatches at either end they could see the rain streaking down. The floor was covered with loose hay, and some bales were stacked around irregularly, not very many. Some holes had been cut through the floor along the walls, for feeding hay directly into the stalls.

"Watch your step," Macrae said, indicating these. He moved toward the western loading hatch, pulled down a bale of straw, and cut one band of twine with his knife. Holding the other band, he drove his knee into the bale and broke it outward. The straw spread on the floor in a crescent of pale gold slices. Yawning, Macrae picked up a flake and shook it loose, then another and the next.

"A snooze," he said. "I'm overdue."

Porter sneezed.

"Just lie down there like a dog?" Charlie said. He took out a cigarette but before he got it in his mouth Macrae struck his wrist with the edge of his hand and the cigarette went pinwheeling out the hatch, into the stream of rain.

"Can't strike a light in here, that's for damn sure," Macrae said. "Not if you don't want it burning down all round your head."

Charlie squeezed the jarred wrist with his other hand, made a fist, and then wriggled his fingers.

"Hey," Macrae said, conciliatory. "Dogs I've known didn't have it so good. Drier than the house is, anyhow."

"No drier than the van," Charlie said.

"Do what you want to." Macrae turned sideways and let himself drop like a tree falling. He landed on hip and shoulder in the straw bedding and rolled over on his back. "Just don't get struck by lightning, boy."

Porter stood over him a moment, listening to the shuffle of Charlie's feet going away down the stairs. He let himself down more gently, his joints snapping, and rolled on his side in the straw. Macrae lay with his eyes half-shut, breathing with a hiss through parted lips. The lightning had stopped but the rain seemed even heavier. Above them a gray cat crouched on the ridgepole, studying them warily, and higher yet the rain dashed against the roof in a steady drone. That one cow's lowing lifted again from its lowest note and broke into a sort of scream. Macrae sat up and hugged his knees.

"Now I remember why I left," he said. "It ain't never over with." He stood up, putting his hands on his hips, and stared at the rain through the hatch. Bits of straw clung to the damp white skin along his knobs of backbone. "Things're going to hell in a hand basket around here, aren't they?" he said.

Clicking his tongue, Macrae went down the stairs. Porter propped himself partway up to look out the hatch. In a minute he saw Macrae come out into the rain, carrying a feed can and some loops of orangish baling twine. He went down the slope from the barn, skidding over the mud, and toward the brush where the cow kept crying. Porter lost sight of him around the corner of the barn, but after a little while he came trudging back, towing a yellow cow at the end of the baling twine he'd noosed her with. A calf of a darker shade came shambling behind, knocking its nose at the cow's hind legs. The cow balked, rolled her eyes white, and jerked her head hard enough to pull Macrae off balance on the slippery grade. He turned and shook the feed can at her and with a gentle pressure on the twine kept bringing her along.

In a stall Macrae tied the cow to the feed box and dumped in the can of grain. The cow nuzzled eagerly at the feed, but when he stooped to touch her bag she backed up sharply and the whole stall shivered, nails groaning in the wood. Macrae moved to her head and shortened the rope, stroking her ears and murmuring. The four-month calf came in to suck and the cow kicked at it, rolling her eyes and moaning.

"I know," Macrae said, and stepped back for another look. "I know." The bag was awfully distended, blue veins throbbing on the white-haired curve of it, the swollen teats sticking out almost at right angles. He found a bucket, and a tub to sit on. The cow kicked inefficiently as he closed his hands on the near teats.

"Easy," Macrae said. "Easy now . . ." He stroked her flank,

then took the teats again, gripping at the top and closing his fingers down. The first stream of milk rasped against the bucket's metal floor. Macrae leaned forward, drowsy again. His forehead rested in the sweet-smelling hollow just above the swelling of the bag. The warmth of the cow and the milk combined put him nearly into a trance. When he raised his head, Porter was standing in the doorway.

"What's the matter with her," he said softly.

"Look like Pappy ain't milked her in two three days," Macrae said. "Calf can't take all what she makes, you know. You'd holler too if you were in that fix." The calf butted the far side of the bag, as if to deny this. The stall was full of the milky smell, and the regularly alternating streams cut shafts into the thick froth on the bucket.

"Think I caught it," Macrae said. "Few more days and she'd be getting mastitis and I don't know what."

"What for your old man hadn't been doing it?"

Macrae sat back, frowning, and shook out his fingers. "Bet he couldn't catch her," he said. "Appears to me he's gone stone blind."

"He can see good enough to tell a nigger," Porter said.

"Nah." Macrae leaned in and recommenced the milking. "He guessed by your voice is all. He can't see daylight, I don't think. Always having trouble with his eyes but it never was as bad as this."

"What kind of trouble?"

"Beats me," Macrae said. "He's too mean to go to a doctor, that I know."

"Well," Porter said. "You need any help in there?"

"Look by the steps and see if you don't find another bucket," Macrae said. "This here's about full up."

When Porter returned, Macrae passed out the full bucket and took the empty one. He reached in and began to strip the hind tits, which were wet and doubly warm from the calf's busy mouth. The cow sighed in relief and shifted her feet as she chewed her cud. Macrae milked in silence till he was done, Porter watching him, leaning on the door frame. When Macrae finished he untied the cow and brought the other bucket out half-full. Porter was trying the foam on the first bucket with his forefinger.

"Like beer," he said.

Macrae laughed. "Not hardly." He went to the feed room and found a tin cup, came back, and dipped it full of milk. He drank, tipping his head and swallowing steadily till the cup was dry. His tongue swept a line of froth from his upper lip and he refilled the cup for Porter.

"Just straight up that way?" Porter said.

"All comes from the same place," Macrae said. "Milk don't grow in cartons."

Porter shrugged and took a sip, then drank again more eagerly. "That's different," he said.

"It'll settle your stomach." Macrae lifted the buckets and set them on a high shelf. "Help you sleep too . . ." He yawned. "You never drank fresh milk before?"

"Never saw a cow before," Porter said, putting down the empty cup, "outside of TV."

eighteen

Macrae woke up throwing a roundhouse punch at someone who'd attacked him in his dream. The follow-through almost
rolled him out the hatch, but he caught himself short and came up
uneasily onto his knees, unsure just where he was at first and still
wary of some new sally from the dream opponent. His eyes cleared
slowly. He'd slept clear around into the night and it was moonset
now, the irregular orb hanging low in a cleft between two hills.
The air was freshened, washed to softness by the rain. Behind him
Porter was breathing gently, a wisp of straw stuck to the corner
of his half-open mouth.

Macrae lifted himself to his feet, one hand on the wall, and felt
his way delicately down the stairs into the hall of the barn. The
moon shone over the metal gate at the back and sculpted out the
two milk buckets in clean silvery light. Cream had risen to a thick
layer on the top, heavy and sweet tasting when Macrae tried a dab
on one finger. He took a bucket in either hand and started for the
house, the new mud in the barn lot sucking at his shoes. The milk
ought to have been put to cool but he didn't want to go crashing
around in the lightless interior. He set the buckets inside the house
door where the cats couldn't get them and stepped down from the
porch.

The side loading door of the van was open and Charlie slept
inside on the folded blanket, one arm hooked over his head and
the other grazing the stock of one of the several shotguns rowed
out neatly alongside him. Loaded too, Macrae would bet. Sooner
had come back to the van as he'd predicted and was sleeping in a

229

compact curl near Charlie's feet. Macrae walked around the nose of the van, stroking his fingers over the moisture beaded on the metal. The track was sloppy and he walked on the grass beside it until he had come back to the stone gateposts. It occurred to him then that his father would not be expecting the buckets and if he were blind, as Macrae supposed, he would probably kick them over when he got up. But he didn't go back to shift them. Placing the balls of his feet carefully on the pipes of the cattle gap, he crossed over onto the road.

The rain had settled the limestone dust into a damp sheath of grit on the spine of bedrock. Macrae walked till the moon had gone down altogether. It was flat dark then, until his eyes adjusted to the starlight, only the opalescent sheen of the ribbon of road before him, unwinding down the corridor of indistinguishable trees. Across a field to his right two screech owls were calling. He walked on till the stars retracted up and away and the first stains of blue leaked under the black lid of the sky. Where the road peaked near a hilltop he climbed a fence and went up a steeply sloping pasture to the grove of trees that sat on the crown like a derby hat askew. Just inside the treeline he sat down with his back against a trunk and rested, drowsing, eyes slipping shut.

Sunrise woke him fully again, the first rays splintering through the trees on the next ridge and reaching to touch him where he sat. He crossed hastily back to the road so as not to be seen trespassing. The uncut hay was standing tall, full of dew and rain-water; it wet him to the thigh. He went back down the road the way he'd come. The sun had not yet reached so far, and in the tunnel of overarching trees was still the first shell-colored light of dawn. When the road leveled off at the bottom he heard the creek running strong with rainwater through the ribbed cul-vert. From the far side, through a screen of trees, came the sound of a hoe chopping into the dirt and every so often ringing on a stone.

Macrae stopped at the post where the garden fence turned a

corner along the road. Over the wire, Laidlaw was chopping a row of corn, his back turned to him.

After a moment he spoke without looking around. "Morning, Macrae."

Macrae jumped. "How'd you know me?"

"Seen you coming out of the woods." Laidlaw said. He hoed to the end of the row and straightened up and leaned the hoe against the fence on the far side. Slowly he came walking back toward the road. His graying hair was gathered in a leather thong on the back of his neck, and the necklace of odd little bones clicked on his clavicle. His chest was caved in on one side, under a cluster of ridged starburst scars, like a school of small octopi clinging there.

"What happened to you?" Macrae said. In all the time he'd known Laidlaw he'd never seen him shirtless.

Laidlaw glanced down. "Walked into a door."

Macrae snorted. "Who was behind it?"

"Nobody you know." Laidlaw took a box of Marlboro out of his hip pocket and flipped up the lid.

"You're out early," Macrae said.

Laidlaw nodded, striking a kitchen match on the zipper of his jeans. "Beat the heat."

Macrae sniffed hungrily at the first cloud of smoke and Laidlaw passed him the box and a match over the top strand of the fence. "Obliged," Macrae said, lighting up. He laid the box on the corner fence post.

"See you're out of uniform," Laidlaw said.

"Yeah," Macrae said. "I had to muster myself out awhile back."

Laidlaw nodded. "Matter of fact, some fellas came by asking after you."

"Did they," Macrae said. "When was that?"

"Oh, it's been about a year. I didn't tell'm anything."

"Good of you."

"Wouldn't known what to tell'm no way."

"Yeah, well." Macrae posed his lips to blow a smoke ring. "I been seeing the world at my own expense."

"Can be costly." Laidlaw flicked off a cylinder of ash and stirred its peppery flakes into the dirt with the toe of his cracked brogan. "You mean to stay long?"

"Ah . . ." Macrae looked up and down the road. "I don't know. I doubt it."

"How's your daddy?" Laidlaw put his head to one side, a slight squint in his left eye. The sun was higher risen, light straining through the trees that lined the creek.

"Don't hardly know," Macrae said. "We just pulled in yesterday . . ." He dragged on his cigarette and inspected the tip. "So far he seems a little surly, you might say."

Laidlaw nodded. "I wondered if he might've been under the weather. Had stock coming down to the road fence and bellering and carrying on sometimes over the winter. I drove down there and thrown some hay over . . . Tried to get back in there to see him once but he didn't appear to care for no company."

"Appreciate the effort," Macrae said.

"Time was, he'd done it for me." Laidlaw threw down his cigarette end and trod it under.

"You got your band going still?" Macrae said.

"Oh yes," Laidlaw said. "Gonna play you-all's family reunion, matter of fact. Coming up first Sunday in June."

"You don't mean it," Macrae said. "I wouldn't thought we'd stretch to that kind of entertainment."

"What it is," Laidlaw said. "Exchange of skills and services. I'm trading off for a couple loads of hay I"ll get delivered when they cut."

"What, Punkinhead and his crew?" Macrae spat into the gravel by the roadside. "You'd need to get it in advance, and it's gonna be too early."

"You know my dog ain't in that fight," Laidlaw said. "Besides, good hay is hard to come by round here lately."

"Well, it's your business," Macrae said.

232

"Good party, anyhow," Laidlaw said. "We'll be practicing this evening, you want to walk up. Sit in if you want to. There'll be something to drink."

"Hadn't got any instrument," Macrae said. "I couldn't keep up with your crowd nohow."

"Well, come on up," Laidlaw said. "We'll loan you something."

"Thanks, then," Macrae said, ducking his head. "Thanks for the smoke."

He walked down the road to his own place, the sun warming his bare back. Now he saw more clearly how it must have been a dry spring here. The grass lay in withered mats beside the track. One of his father's miscegenated donkeys brayed at him from the woods as he went by. God only knew what other creatures lived half-wild up in there too. Macrae went by the van and climbed into the little pickup truck. The key was in the ignition but the starter gave out no more than a click.

Blind men didn't have much call to drive, he reckoned. There were jumper cables in the bed of the truck, so Macrae went back to the van and turned it on. The three dogs came gunning out from under the porch, barking wildly.

"Where were you when the lights were out?" Macrae muttered. He began driving the van into position, crossways across the ruts. With the first good lurch Charlie jerked up onto his knees, clutching a shotgun across his chest.

"What the hey—where you going?"

"Hardware store," Macrae said. "You're welcome to come."

"I pass." Charlie flopped down on his blanket, shoving the gun away from him.

It took Macrae a half hour of scraping the terminals and fussing with the cables before the truck would start. He disconnected the clips and drove off. When he came back, a long roll of tar paper slapping against the bucket of tar in the truck bed, Porter was awake and sitting on the porch steps. Sooner and the three home dogs were scuffling in the tall weeds in the yard, having reached some temporary truce among themselves.

"What's the plan," Porter said.

"See if we can stob up a few holes in this roof," Macrae said. "If you're willing. Pappy stirred out yet?"

"I didn't see him," Porter said. "You got a ladder somewhere?"

"We can just shinny up there by the kitchen," Macrae said.

He made a stirrup of linked hands and boosted Porter, then pushed up the tar-paper roll and clambered up after it, clinging to the drainpipe from the gutter, a paper sack of nails pinched in his teeth. The pitch of the roof was gentle and its whole surface was in patchwork layers of shingles and tar, like some huge swamp-colored crazy quilt.

"Careful where you set your weight," Macrae said. He twisted around and hauled the tar bucket aloft by the length of baling twine he'd tied to its handle.

"Found a starting place," Porter said. He lifted a corner of asphalt shingle and crumbled a large part of it between his fingers.

"There you go," Macrae said. "We'll roll a little fresh back over that."

Porter tapped flat-headed nails along a seam of the new roof roll. "Bad spot here," he called to Macrae, who was stopping fishmouths here and there with tar and a trowel. "Wood's so rotten, once you drive in a nail you can pull it right back out with your fingers." He demonstrated the technique.

"Just tar over it," Macrae said.

"Ought to get that bad wood out."

"Ought to tear the whole house down and build a new one," Macrae said.

A quarrel broke out among the dogs, signaled by the shrill rise of the fice's thin voice. The big black dog made a set at Sooner, who cowered and snapped from his crouch, then slunk away, his shoulders raised in a high pinch. The yellow dog stood aloof, watching cannily. The big black dog was stiff legged and snarling, then he relaxed and lowered his head to lick the fice's yapping face. Roused by the noise, Charlie put his head out of the van.

"Join the party," Macrae said.

Charlie ground a fist in his eye socket, yawned, and squinted up. "Looks like work to me," he said. "Anything to eat around here?"

Hanging from the rooftree, Macrae shrugged. "You could scout around the house."

"Ah . . . ," Charlie said. "What about your father?"

"Don't know," Macrae said. "He might be laying for you in there."

"Well then," Charlie said. "I believe I'll just go to town."

"Take the truck," Macrae said. "Key's still in it. I don't want you bringing the heat down here after that van."

A few minutes after the truck had bounced away onto the road, the door below them cried on its rusty hinge and Macrae heard the porch boards creaking. The old man came yawing out into the yard and straightaway crashed into the van. He cursed it, drew back, and began feeling its contours with his fingers splayed.

Macrae nudged Porter. "Blind man and the elephant," he hissed.

The old man's head whipped around, his neck craning toward the roof. "You there," he said. "You."

"Morning, Pappy," Macrae said. "You kick over my milk buckets yet?"

The old man rocked from foot to foot. The bib of his overalls was shrunken inward, hanging by a single strap. "All that scrabblen up there," he said. "Thought it was rats."

"I don't doubt you got a few of them too," Porter said.

The old man aimed one ear, rotated his neck, and presented the other. "You got that nigger up there with you, boy?"

"Man's got a name and his name is Porter," Macrae snapped. "You don't quit talking ugly to him he's apt to slit your ornery old throat."

"Well, I don't have anything against niggers," the old man said in a puzzled tone. "Known some mighty good niggers in my time."

Porter sat back on his heels and dropped his head back, shouting with laughter at the sky. He swayed from his waist, one way and the other, holding his belly and laughing.

"What's the matter," Macrae said uneasily.

"Just figured out I must be dreaming," Porter gasped. "I'd never sit still for talk like this if I was awake."

"I tell you," Macrae said. "It's practice in case you want to head on down for the Deep South, investigate your roots."

"What you think you're talking about?" Porter choked out.

"Told me you was an Alabama boy, didn't you?" Macrae said. "You and Joe Louis and all like that."

In the evening Charlie took the truck back out. Not in the mood for any jamboree, he told them. Macrae and Porter walked up to the Laidlaw place in the gloaming. The butt of Macrae's palm was blistered from swinging the hammer, and his shoulders ached, though not enough to be unpleasant, from the day of work. A shimmering layer of fireflies hung over Laidlaw's wide front field and the notes of the banjo came out clearly across it, louder and brighter than the guitar and mandolin playing behind. No light was showing at the house. When they reached the gate, Macrae groped around the post and lifted the chain from the nail by touch. A shadow thickened among the other shadows, startling him. He let the chain fall ringing against the metal tubing of the gate.

"Macrae," the shadow said, putting forth a hand. "Still keeping ahead of the MPs."

"By the hardest," Macrae said. The gate swung open of its own weight. "Didn't see you coming, Rod."

"You know how us all blend into the dark," Rodney said, his voice velvet smooth. "Who's that with you?"

"Porter," Macrae said. "And this is Rodney. Ran into Porter up in Baltimore."

"Army?" Rodney said.

"No, we're just business partners," Macrae said. "In a manner of speaking."

As they mounted the porch steps, Adrienne tossed back her hair and smiled at Macrae. Her hair had grown long since he'd last seen her. She was chunking chords on the mandolin, backing Martin's guitar solo. Laidlaw had wrapped himself around the banjo like a snake. The peg head and his crooked hand stuck up above the porch rail, outlined against a paling patch of sky.

The music stopped and Laidlaw undid himself a little. "Get you a drink," he said. By the doorjamb a half gallon of Jim Beam stood on the floor with a stack of plastic cups beside it. "There's beer in the kitchen if you'd rather. You know the way."

"This'll do me," Macrae said. He poured a good tot and passed it to Porter, then took another for himself, settling back against the porch rail. In the dark the music started up again. Macrae sipped, the smoked flavor of the bourbon warming the back of his throat. Laidlaw sang harmony to Adrienne's lead. She was facing the west, catching the last of the disappearing light. Macrae watched her long fingers moving rapid and sure on the double strings of the mandolin. She was nothing like Bea at all but he was still reminded. The creeping began all over his skin, but the music softened the misery into melancholy. Rodney and Porter sat in ladder-back chairs side by side, pursuing a whispered conversation. Macrae nursed his drink away and poured another, wondering what notes the two black men were comparing.

"Wait, now," Martin said. He stopped playing and cocked his head. A ghost of the remaining ambient light glowed on the lenses of his heavy glasses. Laidlaw deadened his strings with the edge of his left hand.

"If I do like . . ." Martin played a little trill and stroked back into the major chord. "Then you . . ."

Laidlaw touched the notes. "Like call-and-response."

"Try it from the start," Adrienne said.

The dark shouldered in, heavy and warm. No moon or star

broke the cloud cover that had closed across the sky at evening. The fireflies hung over the yard like a green galaxy. Macrae couldn't see the players anymore, though the music wrapped invisibly around him. He had memorized the position of the jug.

"Take a break," Adrienne said. Her face warmed into a halo of matchlight, then dissolved as the coal on her cigarette brightened. Laying aside the mandolin, she stood up and stretched, arching her back with her hands set on the waistband of her jeans. The spring of the screen door twanged as she went into the house. Martin put down his guitar and followed her inside.

"Pick it up, Macrae." Laidlaw fingered a pattern of muted notes with a pocking sound.

"Ahhh . . ." Macrae had drunk so much his hands were tingling.

"Go on," Laidlaw said. "He won't mind it."

Macrae pushed himself off from the porch rail, took a couple of numb steps, and fell into the chair where Martin had been sitting. The backs of his fingers grazed through the plush of the case as his hand closed around the neck. The guitar was undersized, small on his knee as a toy. He set his finger on the E string and zipped it to the twelfth fret. The note shimmered, sustained in the damp air.

"Oh my," Macrae said. The guitar had a generous voice for its size. His fingertips were tender, so long it had been since he played. That cheap guitar he'd bought for Christmas, leaning on the windowsill with its B string broken and still curling from the peg, beside the loose heap of drawings also abandoned there. Well, they'd have all been thrown out by this time. Maybe Rafael had got the guitar.

"Come on," Laidlaw said.

"I don't know," Macrae said.

"You know this," Laidlaw said. "I've heard you sing it."

Macrae consented, falling in with the tune. Key of C. He backed Laidlaw with an alternating bass.

"Well, sing it," Laidlaw said.

"Starts on the high part." Macrae waited for it to come around. His voice rasped, then trued to tenor.

"Some Continental soldiers round the bivouac
Played a game of cards in a mountain shack,
But everbody thowed down his hand
When the sergeant of the guard gave a loud command . . ."

Laidlaw joined him, harmonizing on the chorus.

"O Jimmy get the fiddle out and rosin up the bow,
Johnny tune the banjo up, we're gonna have a show,
Billy pass the jug around to Corporal McCoy,
We're gonna have a tune called 'Soldier's Joy,'
We're gonna have a tune called 'Soldier's Joy.' "

As the chorus ended Laidlaw pulled back and started vamping softly while Macrae swung into the simple lead line, just like he'd played it yesterday, the one Laidlaw had taught him only a few years before, when he was a kid dropping out of high school, the music drawing him up here through the fields. He finished it and raised his voice again.

"General Washington and Rochambeau,
Drinking their wine by the campfire's glow,
Big Dan Morgan come a-galloping in,
Said we got Cornwallis at the old Cowpens.

"O Jimmy get the fiddle out and rosin up the bow,
Johnny tune the banjo up, we're gonna have a show,
Billy pass the jug around to Corporal McCoy,
We're gonna have a tune called 'Soldier's Joy,'
We're gonna have a tune called 'Soldier's Joy.' "

At the end of the second chorus Macrae hit the C chord hard and clamped his hand across the strings. "Forgot the rest," he muttered.

"Not bad for out of practice," Laidlaw said.

"Better quit while I'm ahead." Macrae settled the guitar back into the case and slid the flat pick up under the nut.

"Didn't get no pleasure out of soldiering yourself, did you?"

239

Laidlaw balanced the banjo against the porch rail and crossed the floor to pour himself a drink.

"Not hardly," Macrae said, feeling for his cigarettes.

"What for you signed up, then?" Rodney's voice came out of the dark behind him to his left.

"Thought you knew," Macrae said, and with barely a beat of hesitation, "That or serve a five-year sentence."

Rodney laughed softly. "I know that deal. What they get you on?"

"Assault with this that and the other," Macrae said. "Intentions and deadly and I-don't-know-what. Cut somebody, was what it amounted to."

"Huh." Rodney lit a cigarette and stretched out the match to the one Macrae held unlit in his lips. In the flare Macrae saw Porter leaning forward with his elbows on his knees.

"He live?" Rodney said as he leaned back.

"He's fat and happy," Macrae said. "Fat, anyway."

"Could of pulled your time," Rodney said reflectively. "You do right, they'd turned you out in eighteen months, probably."

"Yeah," Macrae said. "I pulled some waiting for trial, though. Can't say it agreed with me."

"I hear it ain't any better in Leavenworth," Rodney said. "You might ought to've finished up your hitch."

"I meant to." Macrae picked at the blister on the base of his palm. "But it just didn't suit me."

Laidlaw snorted and rocked his chair back. "They'll write that on your tombstone, Macrae. 'It didn't suit me.'"

"Well," Macrae said. "Could do worse."

nineteen

"Country life," Charlie said. He sat on the porch in an ancient wooden rocker Macrae had repaired after a fashion by nailing a piece of blanket where the basketwork had rotted away.

"Hanh?" The old man rotated his head and shifted creakingly in another rocker, patched in a similar way. Bucket-seat rockers, they were now.

"Nothing." Charlie looked toward the barn, where Macrae came trudging with his shoulders bent to the weight of two milk buckets, squinting into the evening sun as it dropped red and circular into the pocket where the new school buildings lay hidden just beyond the western rise. He set down the buckets to adjust his grip and hefted them and went on around the back of the house. Charlie rocked gently. The nailheads securing the swag of blanket gouged into the small of his back. He took one of the shotguns onto his lap and thrust shells up the cylinder, one after another. The pipes slammed and squealed as Macrae turned on a kitchen tap. There was another bang as the water shut off, then Macrae's slow steps scraping over the floor. In these last few weeks Macrae had slowed down and also steadied in a way disturbingly strange to Charlie. He passed from one chore to another, conserving a tiny reservoir of momentum that was just enough to keep him going at the same nearly imperceptible rate all day long.

The screen door whanged open and Macrae paused just through it, his wet hair slicked tight on his head, a freshwater stain mingling with the sweat spots on his shirt. Cow manure on his shoes. Charlie wrinkled his nose. He was a town boy himself, always had been. His father had worked in a paper mill.

Macrae twisted his beer bottle open, looked at the cap in his palm for a second, and then put it in his pocket. Charlie hefted his own empty bottle and shook it feelingly, but Macrae ignored the gesture.

"Where's Porter?" Charlie said.

"Don't know." Macrae shrugged and wandered forward to the porch rail. "Out riding Rod's motorsickle, maybe. I guess."

Charlie set down the empty bottle and pumped the shells out of the shotgun again, bracing the butt against his knee and catching them in his free hand. The spring of the mechanism flipped each against his palm with a satisfactory thump. The other rocker squeaked as the old man twisted around, fingers working on his knees like the legs of a crippled spider, his voice high and querulous.

"Air ye just playen withat gun?"

"What?" Charlie said.

"Shoot if ye mean to shoot it. Else put it up."

Charlie clicked his tongue. Quietly he reloaded the gun, making the effort to do it quietly, in spite of himself. A squirrel strayed from the trees was picking at the edge of a bald area in the blasted grass. It sat up, holding something in its forepaws. Charlie took a quick aim and fired at the brick-hard bare spot, figuring the skip of the pellets would knock the squirrel over, which it did. In the echo of the blast, Sooner scooted out from under the porch and ran yelping toward the woods, while the squirrel lay on its side with a hindquarter spasmodically kicking. Charlie shot it again and the squirrel slid backward over the dirt, its movement stilled. He glanced toward the other rocker, but the old man was unmoved and serene.

"What you do that for?" Macrae said.

"Just a squirrel." Charlie pumped the second shell out and inhaled the burned-powder odor around the torn crimp. "Nothing but a rat with a furry tail."

"Skin him out and clean him and we'll drop him in the pot," Macrae said.

"Huh?" Charlie had never skinned a squirrel in his life nor even witnessed the operation. "Let the dogs have him."

"Pick him up and throw him out, then," Macrae said shortly. "Don't leave him laying there."

After supper Charlie invited Macrae to come drinking in town but he declined, as he always did these days. Not that he wasn't drinking, but he preferred to do it rocking on the porch. Porter wasn't back yet, still off with Rodney: Niggers running together, Charlie thought moodily as he drove. There was just enough light left in the sky to mark the lines of the ridges. As he traveled north the trees along the highway acquired more grooming and the pastures became lawns. He passed through the suburban belt and stopped at a bar in a shopping center on the outskirts of Nashville proper.

All that time, hours, years even, he'd spent staring himself down a barroom mirror, watching his hair go pale, creeping backward over his skull, lines cutting deeper into the loosening skin of his face. Years, certainly. The counter was a hoop shape jutting out toward a small dance floor ringed with tiny blue lights, where a few couples moved in slow time to country music on the juke. Charlie tracked them disinterestedly in the mirror, beyond his own rounded shoulders. He drank inexorably, the pile of small bills by his ashtray shrinking, and exhausted a pack of cigarettes. A man at the next stool over asked him for a match and tried to parlay the transaction into more talk, but Charlie stared him down until he shut up and faced the other way.

Reversed in the mirror, the hands on the clock's pale dial turned backward, erasing the time. The bar filled up, men and women in slightly self-conscious western wear. Uncommitted to particular couples, they shifted and recombined like boys and girls at a high school dance. Charlie let his feet drop to the floor and stood up, more than a little giddy. He crossed over to a gaggle of women and cut one he'd been watching out of the pack. Silver-blond hair, out of the bottle, her skin stretched tight at the corners of her eyes . . .

"Dance," Charlie said, not interrogative, and turned her onto the floor without pausing, fingers of his left hand laced through hers and the other tight to the small of her back. Her hips were angular under the denim that clung to them like a coat of paint. The inlaid snaps on her shirt pockets' tapered flaps made false points to her breasts. So near, she was older than she'd looked across the room, her face under the makeup as engrained as his own. A whiff of gin on her breath as she twisted her face away from him. He hardened his grip and gouged himself into her, feeling his anger quicken. Her fingers writhed on the back of his hand like a fistful of worms.

She gasped crossly as large hands forced them apart, and she stood away, brushing down her checkered sleeves and glaring. Charlie had forgotten her; he was facing a man a head taller than he, a dude cowboy with tight pants tucked in fancy boots. With a practiced turn he broke the grip on his upper arm and stepped out to the side.

"Out," the bartender said, strumming a weighted rubber billy across his left hand. "Both of you. Out right now."

A number of times he'd played this scene as well. The cars rowed on the asphalt were illuminated by big lights on poles. Charlie faced off again with the guy who'd grabbed him, a boy really, no older than Macrae but much slower and dumber. Easy enough. But another boy came out of the bar, a couple years older, with a military haircut, and held the dude cowboy by the back of his belt.

"Better let him alone," he said, and then to Charlie, "He ain't gonna bother you."

"Damn right." Half-disappointed, Charlie was.

The soldier, if he was a soldier, pulled the other guy farther back. He wasn't getting much resistance . . . Charlie climbed into the truck. The anger still circulated through him, trying to find its route. He was speeding, slopping the turns; he knew he'd blow a point-two if he got stopped but didn't care much about it. Somewhere around the county line he slowed, and by the time he turned in between the stone gateposts he was doing no better than a crawl.

Like sneaking in, or something. He sat in the truck, listening to the engine tick as it cooled, fading into the voices of the insects in the trees. They'd be asleep; the old man dropped like a rock right after supper, and Macrae too kept farmer's hours now, like he did every other farmer thing. Up at sunrise and rooting in the hay to find where the half-wild banty chickens laid their eggs. He milked, skimmed cream, made butter in an ancient churn, and sold lurid yellow balls of it up and down the road. A stint watching Laidlaw's sheep while the band was on the road also helped keep them in cigarettes and whiskey. There was a raggedy garden patch, planted by some invisible hand perhaps, bringing in cucumbers and some early squash and beans. Macrae tended all these things not so much like they mattered in particular but as if they came lockstep with breathing. It wouldn't last, though, not for Charlie anyway; he knew that. Something would happen. Sooner or later, someone would make it happen if it didn't on its own.

He got down from the trunk, belching, balled up his empty cigarette pack, and tossed it on the track. Across the yard the house bulged forward from the shadows of the trees behind it. The holes in the roof were all stopped now and there were beds, not too mildewed, but Macrae and Porter still slept in the barn. Charlie most often used the husk of the van, which sat on its axles partway up the rocky hillside, now they'd stripped it and sold off the parts they could. Easier tonight than waking the whole compound. The dogs slept through the back-and-forth of the truck but a foot on the porch boards would always set them off. He trudged up the hill toward the shell of the van. Twenty-five years since he used to come creeping in this way with his brother Dale, mouth thickened with cigarettes and beer, cursing and giggling a little maybe as they tried to shift the screen door on its rusty spring. Dale had been dead for almost as long, blown to bloody mush by a landmine in Vietnam. In fact, a great many of the people Charlie used to know had been dead for a very long time. He stopped, puffing a little, leaning on the side of the van, and looking back down the slope. Into his mind's eye came the picture of Macrae walking down the track at first light and stooping to collect the wadded cigarette pack he'd dropped there and walking on with his stride unbroken.

"Are you coming or not?" Macrae said.

"Is Rodney going?" Porter said.

"What's the difference," Macrae said. "It's us you're going with."

"Well ... a family thing," Porter said. "I'd be butting in, maybe." He saw that Macrae wasn't getting it.

"Hey, it's a party with a band," Macrae said. "There's gonna be people bringing their friends." He jerked his head. "But suit yourself."

Porter followed Macrae's glance to the old man, who sat at the kitchen table, dressed in vestigial church clothes, white dress shirt and shiny black pants from some suit. A loose necktie was threaded through the yellowed collar, ends dangling free.

"Been struggling with him too long to go through it all again with you." Macrae's lips closed on a line.

"All right," Porter said. "I'll tag along."

There was room on the truck's backseat for three but Porter and Charlie sat back in the bed together to keep each other company. Macrae drove a way south on the highway, then turned off on a narrower road that ran west. Glancing in the rear window, Porter saw there was no conversation passing between him and his father. The old man's head wobbled on his turkey neck. A pink freckled gap in the whirls of his white hair.

"What he put up such a fuss about?" Porter said. "Going to his own family party?"

246

Charlie shrugged, jangling his fingers over a scab of rust on the wheel case he sat wedged against. "If he just went blind this year . . ."

"Maybe he don't want'm to see him that way," Porter said. "Well, that could be."

The road was worsening, piebald with patches they watched whipping back beyond the flapping tailgate. In another mile the blacktop gave way entirely, to gravel, dirt, the unsheathed native rock. Porter clung tight to the splintery side rails, trying to keep his backbone from slamming so hard into the ribbed metal bed. The truck climbed a ridge of limestone sideways like a mythical mountain goat with shorter legs on one side than the other. The wheels found a new thread of macadam as they crested the hill. On the far side a fresh-mown pasture unfurled from the brow, full of parked cars and people milling. There were six folding tables laid with food, and a feather of smoke from a barbecue fire. The band was already playing under a wall-less tent on poles, against the snarling of a small gas generator that powered the sound system.

Macrae parked at the end of a row of other trucks and muddy-fendered cars. Charlie and Porter gingerly separated themselves from the truck bed. Macrae dismounted, swinging a milk bucket covered with a dampened cloth. A skirmish line of old ladies was advancing from where the tables were. One dug her horny talons into the pale underside of Macrae's arm.

"Miss Daisy," Macrae said in a reverential tone.

"What ye *got* there!" another old one cried. "What ye *bring!*"

"Butter." Macrae folded back the cloth. Down in the bucket the yellow cannonballs had partway softened and molded to each other. Daisy hauled him back around as he released the bucket.

"Ooooh, y'all still milking a cow, I see! Ooooh, just let me look at ye." She reared back, squinting from half his height. "Ain't ye grown! Still, I'd known ye anywhere. I'd known ye in a million."

"Good thing you don't work for the police," Macrae said.

"What's that ye say?" There were headphones clamped over Daisy's ears, mostly hidden in the cloud of her milk blue hair. She traced the cord into the bib pocket of her calico sundress and lifted out a small black box and fiddled with its dials.

"Donkey's ears." She grinned with scattered teeth. "What's that ye say?" But before Macrae could answer her eyes cut around him to the truck and the old man clambering out of the cab.

"Why, Walter, as I live and breathe." She scuttled to him, spry enough on her knobby knees. "How long since you come to see us on First Sunday?"

The other ladies closed in on him too, oooohing and ahhing, drowning his mutters in a wave of their talk. Wavelike they swept down the grass to where some folding chairs were ranked in a ragged circle.

Macrae dusted his hands together. His bucket too had been borne away, and a woman's voice was crying his name from higher on the hill. A long-lensed camera was perched on a tripod way up there, and down from it he saw Lacy running, arms windmilling, a smaller camera flopping around her neck. She wore a sleeveless one-piece mini, one of her thrift-shop specials, doubtless, covered with silly sunflower appliqués. Below the short skirt her long legs flicked like a stork's. As she reached Macrae she pushed aloft and hugged him with all her limbs together. It might have overbalanced him down the hill, but she was light, mostly hard edges, a surprising pocket of softness here and there. He held her off the ground and watched her shake her hair back from her face, a streaky gold mass of it, cut just anyhow.

"I never knew you were back around," Lacy said.

Macrae held her under her arms, faintly glazed with sweat, her natural smell. She clutched at him once more. He set her down.

"Me neither," Macrae said. "I mean, I thought you were off in Philadelphia at that school. Taking pictures."

"Nah," said Lacy. "I'm taking pictures here."

"Just visiting?"

She linked her arm through his and tossed her hair again against his shoulder. "Maybe not. I rented a little house out the Hollytree Gap. We'll see." With her other hand she reached across and squeezed his elbow. "It's good to see you."

"Hollytree Gap?" Macrae said. "My, my. Could walk that, just about."

"Walk it easy," Lacy said. "Don't be a stranger."

"You'll have to show me," Macrae said. "Hey now, Lace. This is Charlie and this is Porter."

Lacy's hand was long boned, slim fingered, cool against Porter's palm. She met his eyes easily and gladly. Hers were odd, particolored, the green of her left iris completing its lower round in gold. It was an accent on her beauty, for she was very beautiful, he saw, though she seemed hardly conscious of it and had done little or nothing to turn it up. It was just the way she came. Porter saw that Charlie, with his eyes narrowed, his face so carefully closed up, recognized that too. He let go Lacy's hand.

"Well now," Macrae said. "They've got a drink somewhere, I suppose."

"Down by the fire," Lacy said, and Porter thought he saw a shadow flick across her face. "They've been up all night with it, you know." She smiled then and guided Macrae down the grade. Porter and Charlie shambled after, passing the tables piled with food—ham, fried chicken, deviled eggs, cakes and pies to kingdom come. One bare space cleared and laid with long serving forks for when the barbecue was done.

The men around the smoking pits were tired and sooty, a processed bourbon smell leaking out of their pores along with the green hickory smoke. Two whole hogs, cloven from jowl to tail, lay blackening on wire screens across the pits. A fat man seemed more or less in charge. Sunburn ran all under his crew cut and down to the neck of his football jersey, a flashy acetate thing with a mesh net curling flirtatiously over his guts. He reached onto the rack and lifted a hind trotter, woggling the bone in the loosening meat. There was power under all his blubber. He rolled a bloodshot eye as Macrae stopped beside the coolers and the half-gallon jugs of whiskey.

"Well, I'll be dipped in—Macrae, who offered *you* a drink?"

"Punkinhead." It seemed a preface but Macrae didn't go on with it. His hunker by the bottles looked spring-loaded. The other men were straightening up from different positions around the fire, hands on their hips, a unanimous slitty-eyed expression on the fat faces and the thin alike. Punkinhead woggled the hog leg again and let it drop. Otherwise, nobody moved.

"Help yourself, Macrae," somebody finally said. "It's everbody's whiskey."

"Dry weather," Macrae said. He filled a paper cup and raised it to the group. "Obliged." He threw it down, then reached into the cooler. Porter's hand closed automatically around the beer he offered. Ballantine, damp and clammy in his fingers; the mild cool of it thrust straight up to his shoulder.

"Want a shot?" Macrae said.

"Beer's fine." Porter popped the ring and took a strangled sip, his throat swollen half-shut. With that, the stillness broke and the men stooped back to tear great dripping gouts of meat from the hog carcasses and shred them into jumbo aluminum pans. Scrabbling over the barbecue, they looked like a football huddle, hind ends poking out in all directions like petals on some flabby flower. Punkinhead worked something loose and tossed it over his shoulder to land in the scorched grass by Macrae's feet. A hog tail, bristle clinging to it, connected to a vertebra or two.

"Saved that for you," Punkinhead grunted. "Special cut."

"Shoo," Macrae said, kicking at the charred twist. "I wouldn't go and eat that, Punkinhead, might be some of your kinfolk."

Punkinhead made to lunge around but someone in the huddle caught his arm.

"Y'all cut that out," a voice rose. "Take it easy, both of you, why don't ye?"

Macrae poured himself another drink, got up, and turned his

back. They made a separate group of four, glacially drifting away from the fire, with a shuffle here, a shuffle there, all seeming unintended. Porter broke off entirely and walked across the hillside to where the band was playing.

Laidlaw cocked his head to recognize him, but the others were concentrated completely on the tune. Not Porter's kind of music, really. Rodney was nowhere in sight and it would be ridiculous to ask after him. Porter thought of inquiring if Rodney meant to go to such a party and saw him ducking his head to hide the alligator smile with his hand. *Huh, you think I'm stupid?*

Well. He sat down with his back to the band, safest way to turn it. Downhill the different clumps of people were swirling with a half-masked urgency, like schools of fish in a big tank where a bead of poison had just been introduced. Two beads, maybe. Porter watched the word diffuse. As it spread through the different groups everyone looked at him or Macrae or both of them, a quick glance and a turn away. Charlie was coming up the slope. He stopped and stood where Porter sat.

"Hungry?" Charlie said.

Porter stroked the sides of his beer can, already getting warm. "Not too." Behind, the banjo kept jangling annoyingly.

"Yeah," Charlie said, and lifted the flat of his hand to shade his eyes. "Been to a few like this before. Food'll be good, I expect. All homemade."

"Good party," Porter said. "Everybody eat'm a big lunch, show off the new babies, maybe have a speech or two . . ."

"That's it. Then once it gets late afternoon, the old folks and the church ladies gonna start going home."

"Young ones quit having to hide the whiskey . . ."

"Right," Charlie said. "Them boys down by the fire been up all night cooking and drinking. Hungover right now and just starting to get drunk again."

"Don't you know it," Porter said. "They're just about ripe."

"After dark, there'll be some fights start up," Charlie said.

"Over some of those little tighty-britches girls you see? Or whatever else. Anybody got a knife or a gun, we'll have a cutting or a shooting."

"Or a lynching," Porter said. "*God,* that sounds like fun."

"Yeah," Charlie said. "So what do you think?"

"Eat my dust."

Charlie nodded. "Might be best," he said, and frowned. "You want me to go with you?"

"What for?" Porter said. "*You* not going to have any trouble."

"I could leave," Charlie said. "I don't know nobody either."

"No," Porter said. "I'm feeling kind of antisocial."

"Whatever." Charlie put his hands in his pockets.

Porter sucked on his warming beer. "So what's the plan? I'm gonna sprout wings?"

"Get the truck keys off of Macrae," Charlie said. "We'll catch a ride with somebody—bet that girl probably got a car."

Macrae and Lacy had loaded up plates and were sitting among the chairs where the old people sat. She'd unslung her camera and slipped the strap over her chair back. Several conversations were going rapid-fire all around them but they all dribbled off when Porter walked into the horseshoe. One old lady's head kept wagging like a clock weight. Porter didn't know if that meant *Never thought I'd see the day* or if she just had palsy. He stooped and whispered in Macrae's ear.

"What the hell?" Macrae twitched in his seat. "We just got here."

Porter leaned down and whispered more urgently. Macrae slid his plate onto an empty seat beside him and sprang up onto his feet.

"You're here with me," he said in a carrying voice. "Anybody got a problem, let them take it up with me. Now or anytime." He looked all around but could meet no one's eyes.

"It's a mistake," Porter said, equally loud. "Just a mistake. I know your heart's in the right place, Macrae! Now just give me the goddamn car keys."

Macrae deflated, his shoulders caved in. "I'll walk you to it," he said quietly.

Charlie cruised the tables, piling a plate with barbecue and cornbread, dilly beans and deviled eggs. "All right," he said, taking a chair the other side of Lacy. "Somebody around here knows how to make sauce."

"It's an old recipe," Lacy said absently, her eyes wandering to where Macrae was coming back from the parked cars, head lowered, kicking his toes at tufts in the grass. He sat down again and reached for his plate. Two greenbottle flies hummed on his meat. He brushed them away, then set the plate down on the ground.

"Goddammit," he said. "Well, goddammit is what I say."

Lacy put a light hand on his knee. "They're not ready for it," she said gently. "You know they're just not."

"Well, screw'm then," Macrae said. "Just screw'm all." He stood up and smacked his hands against his thighs. "I'm gonna go down and get drunk is what."

Stiff legged, he walked over to where the younger men had taken their plates back to the fires to eat. Lacy waited a moment, then got up and followed him, a little distance behind. Chewing, Charlie turned his head, watching her lean haunches move under the yellow flowers on the dress. It was quiet now, except for the ripples of talk resuming; the band had stopped playing and come in to eat.

Macrae bent to pour himself a good one, drank, and coughed. He cleared his throat and poured again. Punkinhead was beached nearby on a bent-framed lounge chair, a plate of food rocking high on his belly. He turned his head and spoke across Macrae to Lacy, who'd paused a distance away from the group.

"Better watch out for Macrae, girl." A stain of sauce moved greasily at the corners of his mouth. "Macrae's running with niggers now. Got him a nigger girlfriend probably. Litter of nigger babies too."

"How many tits on a nigger?" somebody said. "How many babies can one feed?"

"Many's the welfare'll pay for," Punkinhead said. "You draw welfare on your nigger babies, Macrae?"

Macrae stood straight and rigid. Whiskey burned at the back of his throat like rage. "Well, Punkinhead," he began, "everbody knows how your mama got you. Down on her all fours in the slough, rutting with an old boar-hog. She'd of done it with dogs but the dogs wouldn't have her. Wouldn't let her crawl up under the porch. So it was down in the wallow for your mama, getting her jollies in that smelly old mud. And that's where you come by your fat hog belly and your stinging hog jowls and your slitty little mean hog eyes and them hog bristles on your head."

Macrae made a sweeping gesture, slicing his palm through the air, an invitation to the other men, Lacy, the world at large. "Get a good look at him, boys and girls, ain't he a beauty? He'd be a sight in a circus tent. The one where they don't let in the children."

Punkinhead had torn his arm loose from the man that was holding him. He flipped up his mesh shirttail and put a hand on the plastic grip of a sheath knife.

"Oh, you want to play nasty?" Macrae said. "You want to play nasty like we did before?"

"Back off, Macrae," somebody said. "You better back off this time, boy."

"I got the knife this time," Punkinhead said.

"It ain't gonna do you no good." Macrae stepped forward. Punkinhead whipped out the knife, a long blade filed thin from many sharpenings, a flexible silvery flash. Macrae sidestepped, reaching his long arm low, thumbing the wheel of his butane lighter. The whole front of Punkinhead's shirt blossomed into flame. He was yelling, anger and surprise with a note of fear too, and batting at himself with his fat hands. Someone knocked him to the ground and rolled him over to smother the flames. Another man threw water on him—there was a tub of water handy, to draw smoke from the coals. Punkinhead had dropped his knife and Macrae kicked it into the nearest fire pit. There was a smell of burning rubber and singed hair.

The fire on Punkinhead went out and he heaved himself onto his knees, bits of dirt and grass sticking all over his purple face. The burning mesh had melted into little strings that stuck all over the hair on his belly and back, among the angry blushing scars of the old knife wounds.

"Ought to gone on and killed you that time," Macrae said. "That old hog hide is tough to cut. But I ought to tried a little harder."

"You'd still be in the pen," somebody said. "No sweetheart signups with the army when the other feller's dead."

Macrae lashed his head around. *"Who asked you?"*

"Come *on*," Lacy said. "Drop it." She wrapped both hands around the back of his belt and pulled. There was strength in her lean arms. Macrae spun halfway around to save his balance. She caught him around the wrist and tugged him along.

"Ought to killed him the first time I tried it," Macrae snarled. "Should of just gone right ahead and got that job over with."

"Shut up," Lacy said. "You come with me."

Past the fire pits was a grove of cedar trees and a little way within it a three-strand barbwire fence, strands stapled trunk to trunk. Here Lacy let go of Macrae's arm, stooped, and fit herself between the middle strand and the highest one. Her long legs rucked up her dress as she swung them through. On the other side she yanked her skirt back down.

"What are you waiting for?" she said to Macrae.

"Watch that poison ivy," Macrae said. But Lacy had already turned her back and was darting away through the scrub cedars and shallow underbrush. Macrae ducked through the fence himself. A barb caught the back of his T-shirt and the wire thrummed as he pulled away.

Deeper in the thicket the trees were older, taller; it was much cooler there, and mostly dim, with an occasional yellow spangle of sunlight leaking down from a long way above. Macrae followed her over the soft mossy hummocks among the fluted cedar trunks. There wasn't so much poison ivy here, in fact. Lacy was moving fast and he didn't try to overtake her. The patchy light dappled on her back, and two butterflies, yellow and white, rose and fell in invisible waves around her flouncing hair. Away through the thicket they struck the trail, ribbed with rock and exposed roots, almost like a staircase. It ascended for some distance and then dropped down again. Macrae could smell the water now, and there was fern growing along the path.

A pace or two behind her he broke through the last line of scrub and came out on a bare rock ledge above the lake. It was ringed all around with cedars standing in a deep green silence. On the far side was a high wall of rock so sheer it looked like it had been quarried, dropping away on the right hand to a jumble of big boulders breaking up the water's edge. On a flat rock farther left on the opposite bank stood a flock of starlings rustling and chittering among themselves. The surface of the water was almost black and a light breeze had mussed it into little wavelets, as you might roughen a cat's fur with your thumb.

Lacy kicked off her stained white sneakers, dragging the heel off the second one with her long toes. She shucked out of the flowered dress, her small breasts lifting to points as her arms crooked over her head. Macrae saw pocks of gooseflesh on her skin, a hank of blond hair under her arm. She hung her purple panties on a tree branch by the dress, took a half step to the edge of the rock and dove. A narrow slash in the water broke the silence and immediately healed over again.

Macrae stripped and went in after her. A shallow dive into the water's first sun-warmed band. The surge carried him forward, rush of water pressing on the lids of his closed eyes. His arms dropped back to his sides and he surfaced, shook his head, and breathed. Lacy was breaststroking toward the far side of the lake, her head high in the water. Macrae pulled even with her in a sidestroke. She turned and smiled at him and swam forward again.

Macrae swam hard, outdistancing her, making it quickly to the center of the lake. He stopped there and rolled over on his back. There was a single small cloud overhead, crumpled and wispy as a tattered tissue. He closed his eyes and let the water rock him, but his legs wouldn't float and slowly he angled down, his heels sinking through the layers of temperature, declining into the cold. It seemed that he was floating only by his ears. When he came vertical he raised his arms to a point and let himself go under all the way, deep down where the sun never touched the water and the cold was ancient. He kept himself off the mucky bottom, though, where the big snapping turtles shuffled through the mud. There were snags down there too, and you might drown. Macrae opened his eyes onto the furry underwater dark. His rib cage was taut with his held breath and he could feel his heart sending a drumroll into the water. Above, the light was wavy and indistinct and very far away. It brightened as he floated toward it, shifting like the diamond meshes of a net that tried to hold the brightness of the sun. He saw Lacy's arms and legs stroking over the surface like the limbs of a water spider. As he swam under her, rising, he reached to grab her ankle, then let go and broke the water a few feet off, shaking his head in the shock of the full light. She turned her head and smiled to him again, completely unsurprised.

A curtain of shade closed over them. He turned and followed her, swimming along the quarried face of rock. There were water lilies growing here, a few just barely blooming, and a black dragonfly hovering over the thick green pads. Off behind him he could hear the chatter of the starlings very clearly. Together they swam around the corner of the rocky face and back into the sunlight. Lacy swam a few more strokes and hauled herself out of the water onto one of the big round stones coated with red-brown fallen cedar fronds. She blew out a long exhalation, puffing her cheeks, and roped her wet hair on the back of her neck. Macrae trod water a few yards away. He pulled a lily pad under by its drifting root and watched it pop back onto the surface when he let it go.

Lacy sat with her legs curled parallel under her on the rock, one hand propping her, her eyes closed and her face turned to catch the sun's reddening glow. The ends of her hair were brightening blond as they began to dry. Macrae stood waist deep in the water, watching her carefully. Her eyes came open into his.

"What do you have in mind?" Her tongue pushed lightly on her upper lip, exposing a pink triangle, a cat's lick.

Macrae clucked his tongue. "I could draw you," he said. "Like you are now."

"I know you could." She dropped her head back, collarbones tightening white under the tanned skin. "You ought to go to art school. You'd get in." She snapped her fingers. "Easy as that."

Macrae walked a little farther out of the water, balancing on the back of the submerged rock he'd found a footing on. "Oh, but I never was much for school," he mumbled.

"You've said that." Lacy's chin fell forward. There was a wrinkle at the corner of her mouth, from repetitions of that same downturned expression. Macrae ducked away from her, knee deep in the water now. He felt his shrinking nakedness, with an unfamiliar sting and wrench of shame.

twenty

The house Lacy had been living in was a brick box perched on a shelf a bulldozer had hastily dug into the hillside above the road. An apron in front had been cleared for a lawn, but the seeding didn't take and it filled in with weed, nettles and dandelion, some sumac and poke plants she let grow tall and bloom and berry. She had the place near free, for being a caretaker, but nobody was attending to what care she took. The owner, some junior corporate type, had got a sudden transfer and bailed out before he could sell. It was a model house for a failed development; the other houses had never been built, though there were several other driveways bulldozed off into the brush. From the road, you might not guess they ended nowhere.

A smallish place, with two cramped bedrooms and a larger cube that did for kitchen and living all together, but Lacy was loose in it like a dry seed shrunken in a pod. She spent most of the time she was awake down in the small square basement, where she'd built herself a darkroom, rerouting the pipes to the washing machine into a long, shallow utility sink. It leaked down there. Wet-weather springs were all over the hillside and after every hard rain there might be a couple of inches of water on the softening cement floor. She slopped through it, oblivious, barefoot or in rubber sandals. If she stayed down there long enough her feet would turn all white and wrinkly, while her fingers were steeped in an indelible chemical stink it was hardly worth the bother to try and scrub off afterward. Her flip-flops made hollow splashes like the echoes of an underwater cave, as she worked with practiced competence under the stain of the one red bulb.

The prints floated in the bath, images coming up softly in the bloodshot, wavering glow. She pulled them out of the fixative, clothespinned them to a line. When they had dried she logged the negatives and put everything away with barely a cursory glance. Eventually, she'd pin them to the new-painted wallboard in the big studio up at school, in Philly, look at them there, and figure out what she had. That would be later, when the cold had finally locked down here, the poke and sumac had turned red and ropy and collapsed under the frost, the standing water had frozen on the floor and cracked the slab, maybe.

She'd be long gone by that time, gone for good. If she didn't know when or how she'd made the decision, she knew it was decided now. After all, she'd always known she'd have a different kind of life. So she'd be just passing through after all, come back to see the place one more time, and see how much of it she might suck up a camera's snout. Nothing had surprised her but Macrae, and she didn't—why, hell, it would be sheer lunacy for her to have come back for him. She'd never really thought he'd be here, and he wasn't in her pictures. She'd taken plenty on that farm, the sagging barns, the dogs scrabbling under the porch, corn tasseling high above the fence posts, the strangely crossbred animals that roamed the place at will, the rag-eared stunted mules, a drove of half-wild hogs, and one enormous ewe, unshorn for a decade, dragging a whole thicket of brambles in her fleece. In some of these, when she watched them resolving redly in the wash, it looked like Macrae was nearby, about to step into the frame, or more likely had just left it. She'd asked him but he wouldn't let her, which struck her funny, somehow.

"I'll let you draw me," Lacy said.

Macrae switched away, lighting a cigarette with a sort of dodging motion she'd often seen. In jail, when she visited him there before the trial, and once again when he came back briefly with his head shaved by the army, eyes strange and ancient under that weird expanse of moonscape. He looked younger now, but same as then he wouldn't look her in the eye. He blew out smoke and stared at the camera swinging at her sternum.

"No go," he said, flaking the burned sulfur from the paper match. "I don't show up on film."

Macrae kept busy all that summer, busy enough he didn't hardly ever have to think. The cow was fresh, still a bucket twice a day, but probably needed breeding. He didn't quite know how that was being handled, and the old man didn't have a lot to say about it. No bull on the place, for sure, and yet there were some calves among the loose string of beef cattle due to be rounded up and trucked to market in the fall. A shot of cash money there would be in that, no need to question it too much. Maybe it was some broke-loose neighbor bull responsible.

There were a few spring lambs as well, roaming off in the woods with the ewes, and six shoats who'd fatten better if he ever could catch them and shut them up. As it stood he figured they'd just have a wild-boar hunt, come killing time. Plenty else to occupy him now. He hardly went in the garden but to pick; still, it never seemed too weedy and a lot was coming in, green beans and black-eyed peas and several rows of corn. His father didn't bother much about it but if Macrae put a basket in his hands he'd shell the peas or shuck the corn by touch, his milky blue blind eyes shifting and probing out over the porch rail like they still strove to see. Food on the table, anyway, and surplus enough for Macrae to lay up in the ancient freezer that hulked in the kitchen, letting out strange moans and cries like a haunted coffin.

In the evening he sat on the porch with Porter, feet up on the rail, beer cans and a whiskey bottle between them. A sting came into the air now at the cool of the day. Up the slope across the track a few leaves were beginning to redden on the dogwoods scattered through the other trees.

"Where's Charlie?" Porter said.

Macrae peeped into the keyhole of his beer can. "Off," he said. "Bar hopping, maybe." The truck was gone.

"Ay," Porter said. "Where's he get the jack?"

"Don't ask," Macrae said. His own private guess was that Charlie might have struck on the dregs of the tourist trade around Lower Broad and Printer's Alley, but he really didn't want to know. No guns went out when Charlie did, and no stolen cars came back to the farm: those were the limits mutely set.

"Didn't plan to," Porter said. "Do you hear something?"

Macrae bent his head to listen. "That's a bike."

Lacy came coasting around the curve of the track on her old heavy-framed three-speed, flaking crusts of mud from the hardened ruts as she thumped over them. The sprockets ticked lightly as she rolled onto the grass, swinging her leg off to dismount without stopping the bike. She rolled it to the porch and leaned it there. The dogs stirred and scrambled under the porch; Sooner stuck his nose out and then drew it back. Lacy kicked a stick toward him with her red hightop. She wore black cigarette jeans and a T-shirt that didn't quite reach the waistband.

"Hey there," Macrae said, breaking a beer loose from the plastic loops of the pack by his chair. "Car out of whack?"

"I like to ride." Lacy came up the steps, one hand fishing in a belt pack molded to her left hip.

Porter clucked his tongue. "All those hills." It was only a mile or so from Lacy's house to the farm but the whole height of the ridge was between them.

"Some of it's up," Lacy said. "Some of it's down."

Macrae handed her the beer. "What else can we do for you?"

Lacy tasted the can and set it on the porch rail. She pulled a long pair of scissors and a garish plastic comb from the belt pack and fanned them in her fingers like a hand of cards. "I need a haircut."

Macrae caught a laugh in his cupped hand. "This ain't no beauty shop."

"Come on." Lacy shook the implements at him. "I don't want to go spend forty dollars . . ."

"Hey," Macrae said. "I'd mess it up. Looks just fine to me anyhow, the way it is."

"Oh, hell." She shook her hair across her back, shadows rippling in the gold. "It's all split ends, all ratty . . . Just knock off an inch or so is all it needs." She turned to Porter, her double-colored eye catching the last of the daylight. "Don't you think he can handle that?"

Porter stood up and closed his hands over the spools of his chair back. "You have nice hair," he said. "I believe I'll go see what might be happening in the kitchen."

The old man sat at the kitchen table, his hands palm up under the glare of the overhead bulb. The frame of each hand was edged with callus, as if he went on swinging a hoe in his sleep, or something, Porter thought as he strolled around him to the stove. The old man's blind head tracked him like a magnet drew it.

"You there, Po'ta?" he said.

"Nose like a bloodhound," Porter said. The lid of a pot of black-eyed peas was rising on a cushion of steam. He took it off and turned down the burner and pushed a hunk of fatback down in the peas with a fork.

"I hear that Lacy girl out there, anh-hanh . . . ," the old man said.

Porter stirred the peas and salted them. He could hear the tones of Lacy and Macrae arguing out on the porch without being able to make out what they said. A string of red peppers hung from a nail above the stove. He plucked one off and diced it into the simmering pot.

"Her gray-gramma and his'n was sisters," the old man said. "My gray-aunt Allie . . . That makes close kin but not too close."

"If you say so," Porter said.

"Ah-hanh," the old man said. "You ever do around with white girls, Po'ta?"

"Jesus Christ," Porter said.

"I never known such a touchy feller," the old man said. "What time we gone eat?"

A green hose pipe snarled around an outdoor spigot Porter had dug out and repaired. Lacy knelt alongside it, the hose in one hand and the other sweeping her hair forward over her bowed head, in front of her feet. The T-shirt rode up over five or six pale knobs of her backbone. Under the stream from the hose her hair darkened and went lank. She shut off the tap and got up and shook herself.

"I been drinking," Macrae said, "and here you come ask me to take edged tools around your head."

"Wet cut," Lacy said. "Nothing easier. Come on, I know you can cut a straight line."

Macrae examined the scissors and comb he held like they were objects fallen strangely from the moon. He rocked forward and rose up from the chair. "All right, already," he said. "You don't like it, don't blame me."

He combed the wet hair at a slow mesmeric rate, straight down from the crown and all around her head. The damp made it hang together in little points he carefully snipped off. She sat one step below him, framed in his knees. He cut carefully, combing again and again to even up the wet ends. The light was dropping like a rocket now, and the doves were crying good-night to each other from the trees that ringed the yard. The wet hair had soaked her T-shirt around her clavicle and shoulders and he could feel the warmth of her coming up through the chilled cloth.

"You got gooseflesh," Macrae said.

"I'm all right." Lacy shivered.

"Hold still, then . . . almost done." He laid the scissors down and brushed some clots of wet hair off her back. Lacy leaned against his knees. He wiped his fingers hairless and lit a cigarette.

"Let me get some of that," Lacy said.

Macrae reached around her head and held the filter to her mouth, the taut touch of her lips just fluttering on the inside of his fingers. Lacy let the rest of her slight weight go against him, let her head roll back as she blew out the smoke.

"All set," Macrae said, rattling the scissors with the hand he disengaged. "So, ah, you want to eat?"

"Why not?" she said, and rocked forward from him as he stood up, dusting his knees. She twisted herself around and raised her hand and held it there until he thought to help her up.

Around the kitchen table it was quiet but for the click of spoon or snapping of a beer tab. The old man ate his hopping-john with subtle attention, a chunk of white cornbread in his left hand to trap the rice and peas at the edge of the bowl. Each insertion of the spoon into his mouth was careful and complete, though his jaw slightly overhung the bowl, in case of failure. The spoon raised and lowered and went searchingly around the borders of the dish.

"They ain't no meat?" the old man said. No one answered him. "They ain't no *meat,*" he said.

Macrae rolled his eyes. "You must of forgot to kill hogs this year."

"They's hams in the smokehouse," the old man said.

"Skippers got'm," Macrae said, "which you must of not been paying attention."

The old man let go his pone and flattened his hands on the table's metal top. His neck swelled a little, like a rooster's might. The blue-fogged eyes pressed out. Lacy stroked her thumb over a black chip mark in the enamel at the edge of the table, shaped something like a crushed cowboy hat. She was sitting where she'd always sat before, a good many nights all up from her childhood, and often enough she'd seen Macrae take a cursing just this way, bowing his mute head over some failure in his chores or messing up in school (though usually it was the old man who kept him out of school in the first place).

"What happened to Charlie tonight?" she said, meaning to change the subject.

Macrae cut his eyes past her and shrugged. "Gone to town I guess," he said.

"Out carrying on," the old man snapped. "Drunk ever night and Sunday too. Carrying beer to the supper table. Yore mama was alive, she'd tell ye."

Macrae raised his head and grinned. "She'd tell me not to waste my time looking after a mean old man like you."

The old man's jaw relaxed into half a goofy smile. Lacy would have liked a picture of that. It had all evolved into a game, she saw. Or if Macrae had the upper hand now, he used it a little more lightly.

"You better pipe down and eat your supper," Macrae said. "Before you hurt Porter's feelings, talking ugly about his cooking that way."

The old man turned his head searchingly, a hand poised in midair. "I don't say Po'ta can't cook all right," he said. He cleared his throat and picked up his spoon. "Ain't got no quarrel with Po'ta."

It was late enough when she made it home, standing up on the pedals to grind the bike up the last long grade. Easier to go than come back, for sure. At the foot of her driveway she dismounted and rolled it in, the generator-powered headlamp dwindling to a yellow dot, dying altogether when she leaned the bike against the wall behind the house. All the doors were locked, to protect the cameras, and she had to go back around front to get in.

A musty silence greeted her indoors. She turned on a light and the radio and went to the bathroom mirror. Macrae had done a nice job on her hair. She lifted a fistful away from her ear and let it fall back. With the raggedy ends lopped off, it looked thicker, swinging down in a smooth curve from her earlobe just to her shoulders in back. She nodded and went back into the living room, where the boom box broadcast a tinny squawk, and shut it off.

In the glossy black panes of sliding glass doors that let onto the hillside in back of the house, she stood before her reflection again, shaking her hair to see how it moved. She was not the least bit tired, never mind the exercise, the meal, and the beer. In its recesses the house made some aimless ticks and creaks. She took off all her clothes and rolled them up and tossed the bundle on the sofa bed. Her figure was a silhouette in the dark glass, a profile as she turned, stooping, tossing her head back, watching the mass of her hair fracture and reform as she came upright. From anywhere on the hillside, with the light behind her, she'd seem a marionette of shadow. To whatever deer or fox or bears might be watching . . .

In fact it had been a long time since she'd felt so singularly unregarded. It bothered her, though, that she couldn't see out. She crossed back to the lamp, now feeling her exposure in the bare knobs of her back, and turned it off. The glass was rendered transparent when she returned to the door, but still she pushed it open. The light of a waxing moon flowed over the slope. At the edges of the weedy yard the thistles had grown high and the breeze was strong enough to set their feathery heads dancing. She stepped over the metal runners of the door and stood with her legs set apart, her toes gripping the corner of the cool concrete sill. The wind licked over and over the yard, lifting the fine hairs on her body and leaving them standing with every pass. She stood there till she was broken out in gooseflesh, the nights were growing cold.

Another day, another morning, she loaded up the car with cameras and set out nowhere in particular. Whatever she had in mind, she wasn't finding it. A couple of times she pulled onto the shoulder for a slower look, trying to frame the scenes in her mind, but she never even got out of the car. A good many hours got wasted, though. It was past noon when she came jouncing through

267

the cattle gap and around the bend to park in front of Macrae's father's house.

Her back had sweated and stuck to the car seat. She peeled herself loose and climbed out. Charlie sat propped on the porch rail, turned three-quarters away from her, shirtless and barefoot. He wore a khaki-colored pair of pants with white bleach spots scattered on the legs, and he seemed to be studying something wrapped in his hands. She clicked the car door shut and stood with a hand on the hot metal roof. Charlie turned his expressionless head toward the sound. His hands dropped to the inside of his leg, almost as though he were hiding a weapon.

"Looking for Macrae?"

Lacy shrugged. "Is he around?"

Charlie looked down the length of the porch. "Probably. Somewhere, I imagine. Out there somewhere, being a farmer . . ."

"And you, you hadn't got any chores to do?" She was surprised to hear herself say it, though on her own ear her tone was more snippy than flirtatious.

"No more'n you do, I don't suppose." His lips bent back to show the tips of his teeth, a snaky smile. His eyes stayed on her, full of neutral concentration.

Lacy turned and reached through the open window into the backseat and snagged the straps of a couple of cameras. She had his full attention, that was sure; it felt like she was being tracked by a gun sight. He hadn't moved when she straightened up.

"Got time for me to take your picture?"

Charlie swung his other leg over the porch rail to sit upright facing her, raising his two hands, which after all were empty. "Right now, like this?" he said. The railing bowed slightly under the small tense weight of him.

"Any way you want," she said.

"Any way?" His left eye pinched, not quite a wink. "Sure," he said. "Sure, I got nothing but time." He swiveled and hopped down from the rail. From the arm of a chair he picked up a crumpled shirt and came down the steps, trailing it in one hand. It was hard to say how old he was, she thought. There were deep lines in his face and the fur on his arms and chest had whitened, but he was in top condition otherwise, not a spare ounce of fat on him anywhere. The muscle moved rather stiffly, stringy under his freckled redhead's skin. Sweat pooled around his collarbones and trickled toward his navel. It was a hot day. Lacy, a little humid herself, wiped her wrist across her forehead.

He passed her and walked toward the black oak tree, twirling around once to see that she was watching, then going on. His shoulders sloped a little forward. He reached his free hand to the back of his waistband and hitched up his pants by an empty belt loop. As if on a thread of invisible fishline, he spooled away from her. At the tree he stopped and turned back.

"Like this?"

She didn't answer him, but raised a camera and studied him through the lens. His questioning expression washed away as he searched out the pocket in the folds of his shirt and fished himself out a cigarette. Deep in the background, beyond the fence in the upper right-hand corner of her frame, cornstalks were stirring in the garden. Macrae appeared from between two corn rows, his back to them, chopping rhythmically with a hoe.

Charlie's head swung around, responding to the clink of the hoe's blade on a buried rock. For a moment she had his profile, the unlit cigarette askew on his lower lip, but she didn't take it. Macrae turned at the end of the row and hoed his way back out of sight as she let the camera down.

"Something's eating on that old boy," Charlie said. "But he won't never tell you what . . ."

"That's for sure," Lacy said, still fidgeting with her shutter release. Charlie looked at her, alert; she was surprised to hear her voice go on.

"He can't talk about what's bothering him, the kind he is, because he doesn't know. It's a loop. He'll have to find his own way out of it."

"You know a good deal, don't you." The cigarette dipped in

the corner of his mouth. "What's bothering him, then, do you know that?"

"Me," Lacy said, her voice flat.

"Is that a fact?" Charlie looked as if he'd move toward her, but didn't. "I wonder, now, what's bothering you?"

Again she covered her face with the camera. In the viewfinder his image was doubled across two semicircles of ground glass; she turned the focus ring until they merged. He lit the cigarette, puffed away the match smoke, licked tobacco flecks from his front teeth. His smile had no false promises, she could see that much. She'd said a good deal more than she'd intended. Oh God, she thought, as the shutter clicked, and I don't think I even like this guy.

twenty-one

At first light Macrae walked into the dew-spangled lower field, through grass tall enough to brush along his rib cage. He tramped about halfway across to the road fence and stopped, glaring across the way to where the rising sun drew back a curtain of shade from the new school buildings over there. A few paces behind him Porter stopped too and waited; he plucked a stalk of grass and set the round end between his teeth. The heavy seed head dipped and rotated as he chewed; a faint green tang spread over his tongue.

Macrae slapped his hands on his thighs and muttered something to himself. He reversed in his tracks and went past Porter, who followed him back along the furrow of grass they'd beaten down.

"What's the matter?" Porter said.

"Ah . . ." Macrae flipped a hand over his shoulder and kept trudging toward the trees that lined the inner fence row. "Need to figure out how to cut this hay."

By the trees stood an old manure spreader with its floorboards on the way to rotting out and its tongue plunged deeply into the dirt, and near it a bush hog mostly overgrown, rust overtaking its chipped coat of dull red paint. The machines looked as queer and useless as meteorites that might have fallen there to be slowly absorbed into the earth. Macrae exhaled and hauled a wrench and a screwdriver from his back pocket and knelt on the bush hog's flat carapace. The clanging echoed off the hill behind.

Porter watched from a cautious distance. He had taught Macrae a thing or two about carpentry, and more about plumbing, as they patched up things around the place. Meanwhile he'd learned some things himself, how to fence, to work a come-along, to manage an animal so it wouldn't spook. He'd discovered also that Macrae's patience with any living thing didn't extend itself to machinery. Yards off, he watched him sweat and pound and curse. At last Macrae sat back on his heels, displaying some inscrutable piece of mangled metal in his fist.

"Well, the goddamn thing was broke when I last left out of here," he announced. "And the goddamn thing is just as broke today." He slung the part, whatever it was, into the bed of the manure spreader, where the sodden wood muted its thump.

Porter walked with him back to the house, hardly listening to the grumble that continued half under Macrae's breath. They found Charlie sitting at the kitchen table, delicately massaging his eye sockets and breathing in steam from a fresh cup of coffee. Porter got himself a cup. Morning birdsong streamed in along the shafts of sunlight from the open kitchen door. Macrae rustled the leaves of the phone book, yanked the receiver from the wall, and irritably spun a number. Porter watched him doing the deal, holding the phone a yard from him and speaking to it out of the side of his mouth. At the end he made to slam the phone down, but relaxed at the last minute and let it glide gently onto the hook.

"Hate to deal with that son of a bitch."

"Don't do it then." Charlie raised a bloodshot eye. "What son of a bitch is that you mean?"

Macrae waved a dismissive hand. "Only one I know's got the gear to cut that field."

"Why not let it stand there, then?" Charlie said. "If it bothers you so much."

"It just got to be done and that's all there is to it."

"Well, you can't tell me there's any money in it, can you?" Charlie said.

"Forget it, then," Macrae said, crashing gloomily into a chair. "Don't let me interrupt your hangover."

———

272

Next Monday morning, Porter was roused by Punkinhead's crew hauling machinery through the gateposts with a great hue and cry. When he came out he found Macrae already standing on the porch, looking toward where the noise came from, with a headachey expression. So far no one had yet come into view.

"We gonna help?" Porter said.

"No," Macrae said. "No we ain't." From around the bend of the track came the grinding of a motor and voices calling out angry directions.

"What's the plan, then?" Porter said.

Macrae stood up. "I'm taking a walk," he said, wiping a loose hand at Porter and Charlie, parked in the rag-bottom rockers on the porch. "You all can do whatever you please." He stepped down from the porch and clapped his hands and whistled once; the dogs came scrambling from under the porch and went after him toward the barn. Porter got up and followed too.

Macrae went up the hill through clots of knee-length grass and the sparse cedars around the barn, the dogs ranging around him in crazy loops, sniffing and clawing the earth. The woods thickened around him as he proceeded, taller trees, some walnuts, elms, a sweetgum tree. Everywhere huge spiderwebs laced the branches tree to tree and Macrae got a stick to slash them down as he went along. The yellow dog started a rabbit from a windrow of last year's leaves and the others went yelping after it, Sooner bringing up the rear, going at an inefficient, prancing gait, his tail arched high. The dogs out of sight, Macrae stalked along at a gently rising angle round the hill's curve, with Porter trailing him at a little distance. When he stopped on a brow of limestone, Porter caught up.

It was a clear view down to the field and across to the new school, the highway, and the hills beyond. Mouse-sized cars whizzed silently up and down the road. In the pasture immediately below, Punkinhead's crew moved doll-like among the machinery, their voices thin and distant as the cries of birds.

"You own this, don't you, Macrae," Porter said. "How much of it you own?"

"Hundred acres, hundred and twenty." Macrae shrugged and sat down on the pitted rock. "Can't farm most of it." He beat the edge of his palm on the stone. "It's all this here."

"Could build on it, I bet," Porter said, pointing at the school. "Look how everybody's going to be moving out this way. You never told me you were rich."

"Who, me?" Macrae hawked and spat past the edge of the rock. "What they told my daddy, twenty years back. Developers come in his kitchen there with a suitcase full of money. He kept telling'm no and they kept upping it. Finally one of'm says, *Mister, you got to take this, you never saw such money as this here.*" He stopped and cut his eyes toward Porter, who'd lowered himself to sit nearby.

"So then?" Porter said.

"I wasn't but about two years old at that time," Macrae said. "I feel like I remember it but maybe I was just told. So then he says back, *Well, but I'd just have money, then. Wouldn't have no home place.*" He glared down at the men in the field. Someone had got the mower going and the others were hitching the baler to a second tractor's PTO.

"Huh," Porter said. "You got brothers and sisters?"

"Got a sister about eighteen years older than me," Macrae said. "Married to some navy feller over in Virginia. I was a late baby, I told you that." He frowned down at the diminished figure of Punkinhead rummaging in the baler's guts. "That thing'll snap his hand off for him, he don't watch out. You noticed how many of this crowd's short a few fingers?"

Behind them the dogs were crashing through the buckbushes. Sooner stuck his head out and stared at them and went prancing away.

"He's the one you cut," Porter said. "That fat white boy. Right?"

Macrae slitted his eyes. "You called it."

"What about?"

"What's it usually about?"

"Money or women," Porter said. "Or nothing, sometimes."

"You know it," Macrae said. "He was talking ugly about a girl. What him and her did and all like that. Lacy."

"Ay." Porter shook his head, squinting down the hill. "They don't seem like much of a match."

"There wasn't no truth in it," Macrae said. "He was just trying to get my goat."

"Sounds like he succeeded."

"We never did like each other much," Macrae said. "I wouldn't have him on the place, but there wasn't nobody else I know can cut this hay."

"That Lacy is a beautiful woman," Porter said.

Macrae looked at him. His face was so calm and slack that his eyes appeared to hover in his head.

"You could be paying her more attention," Porter said.

Macrae turned away, plucked a straw from beside the stone, and set it between his teeth. "She don't want to worry about me."

"Don't you see that look in her eye?"

"She's got education." Macrae peeled some lichen out of a pit in the rock and rubbed it between finger and thumb. "She's got her own way to go."

"You're making a mistake," Porter said.

Macrae blew the lichen crumbs out of his hand. "What if I am?" He stood up and dusted the seat of his pants. "It wouldn't be the first time."

Macrae parked his daddy's truck on the dead end of one of the nowhere driveways there in the development that never developed near Lacy's house, swinging the truck's nose around the circle to point back down the hill. He rolled the window partway down and took a joint from his shirt pocket and struck a light to it. The dope came from Porter's bag, which he had got from Rodney, who had got it who-knows-where. So-so quality, probably home grown, it brought more heaviness than enlightenment. Macrae sucked the jay and held his breath and exhaled, finally, the faintest discolored ghost of smoke. In between hits, he drank from a quart of beer wrinkled in a paper sack on the seat beside him. His tongue was thick; small veins pulsed in the whites of his eyes. The sun was going down behind the hill.

Done with the joint, he got out and shut the truck door, leaving the half-empty quart where it was. The scrape of metal over metal as the door closed was oddly loud and protracted to his stoned ear. The dead-end circle of the drive was surfaced by a hard-packed whitish grit; most of the actual gravel had washed down the embankment in the years since Macrae used to come up here, often on his way home from school before he quit, to do himself a number out of the way.

It was a little chilly. He wriggled his shoulders in the thin cloth of his shirt as he eased down the embankment into the woods. Crossing a fifty- or sixty-yard band of trees, he dropped down into the yard behind Lacy's house from above. Not a yard really so much as a clearing; the lawn grass had died and weeds and bramble had taken it back. Macrae kicked through thistles and ironweed, approaching the sliding glass door that let into the living room from the backyard. On other side of the glass the sofa bed was flipped out with a muddle of sheets and blanket on its thin mattress. Lacy had taken the house partly furnished and this was where she slept. The room was empty, the sliding door a half inch ajar. Several strands of Virginia creeper lipped over the metal frame and among them Macrae saw a twitch of movement: a little gray-blue skink, flicking its head out and then reversing so that only its tail hung exposed from under the warped wooden sill. A pool of sunset light reddened the area around it.

"Thought you'd be hibernating, sucker," Macrae said aloud. The skink drew itself completely out of sight, leaving Macrae ill at ease at the sound of his own voice. Spied on, like someone was listening that ought not to be. He looked behind him at the quiet treeline, then pushed the door farther open with a minor squeak, turned, and slid it to after him. Tiptoe. Nobody in the kitchen either, though through the window he could see Lacy's car parked out front, with the bike propped on its rear bumper too. There was a noise in the pipes—water going off and on in the basement.

Lacy had blacked out the door at the head of the basement stairs and hung a velvet curtain at the bottom of the stairwell. Most money she spent moving into the place. No light showed back around the door when Macrae softly closed it behind him. He tipped down the steps with a creak or two, with the same dope-fogged sense of foreboding as before. The curtain passed softly over his cheek and shoulder as he slipped through. The small cube of the basement was washed in a red glow. Lacy was taking eight-by-ten prints out of the sink and clipping them to a wire above. She froze when she saw him, then went back to what she was doing with a shake of her head.

"Slip up on me," she said, and turned her back. "You'll take years off my life."

"Ah, you can handle it," Macrae said.

Lacy hung another print. "You let light in here, you'd ruin my film."

"It's all right," Macrae said. "I checked the door before I came through the curtain." He took a step nearer the prints on the line. There was a figure in some of them, in nearly all. A leathery-looking man with close-cropped curly hair, of middle height and middle years, who rocked on a porch or was leaning out a car window or lighting a cigarette or playing with a gun. In some pictures he was shirtless, scratching at his small, tight stomach, stretched-out jeans slipping on the pointed bones of his hips. It was Charlie looking back at Macrae out of the prints, his eyes shaded and his expression hard to read in the uneasy red light. Macrae touched the corner of one print and watched the others shiver on the line.

"Where'd all these come from?" he said.

Lacy switched away from him toward the water faucet. "I wanted portraits."

"He's not even from around here," Macrae said.

"He's willing to pose," Lacy said. She stood over the sink, washing her hands with tense hatching movements, then laying

277

aside the soap and the rag. "Come on," she said. "I'm done down here."

Macrae followed her up the steps, his legs dope-torpid and leaden. He turned back once with the feeling somebody was behind him, but only the prints hung on the line. Just Charlie, that was all. The red light died as Lacy hit the switch at the head of the stairs. In the living room, Macrae stood looking slackly at the jumble of sheets on the sofa bed. Lacy moved around him and quickly folded the whole thing away, laying sofa cushions hastily over the seat.

"There," she said, straightening up from her stoop. "What's the plan?"

"Hungry?" Macrae said. Dumb, like a high school date. Lacy shook her head. A tail of hair caught on the corner of her mouth and she brushed it back and then rubbed her hands, still damp from the sink, over the lean thighs of her black cigarette jeans.

"Nice haircut," Macrae said. "You want to get high?"

"Later, maybe," Lacy said. She smiled distantly, a twist of her lips, a pinch at the corner of her mouth and eye, from weariness or working too long in dim light. The evening sky glow caught in her double-colored eye for an instant as she swung away from the glass door. "I know what, let's go swimming."

"What, now?" Macrae said. "A little cold for it, don't you think?"

"Scaredy-cat." Lacy brushed her blunt nails across his hanging arm. "Come on, I'll drive."

A fat red globe of harvest moon was balanced on the horizon's edge, against the darkening sky. It flickered in and out of the car windows, briefly eclipsed by the trees and phone poles shooting back down the road behind them.

"Red moon rising," Macrae muttered, not expecting a response. It was full dark by the time Lacy pulled the car off the road into a clump of trees in an unfenced, unmowed field. The moon had paled, climbing higher up the sky. A brace of motorcycles and an ancient red Malibu were also parked in the area.

"Company," Macrae said.

"They just come out to drink and neck," Lacy whispered back across the car roof. "Nobody goes as far as the pond at night."

"Yeah?" Macrae said. "Who owns this now?"

"When did you start to care who owned what?" Lacy bundled some bath towels under her arm and started up the slope of the field through the high grass. Macrae followed her from grove to grove of trees, toward the line where the woods grew thick. The breeze had picked up and a marbled cloud bank was hurrying toward the moon. Under the trees they lost the moon entirely. Macrae could barely even see her in the dark clothes she wore, but the wad of towels bobbed ahead of him like a lure. She seemed sure of the way, as if she'd been on this path yesterday. For Macrae it had been long enough to make him feel old. This trail was shorter, though, than the one they'd taken from the barbecue, and brought them out on the opposite side of the pond, high on the quarried wall.

"Wouldn't have thought this little bit of water would make a fog," Macrae said, whispering still without knowing why. Twenty feet down, a fat caterpillar of mist clung so tight to the pond he couldn't see its surface.

"It's foggy all over," Lacy said. "It just likes the water." She dropped the towels, brushed her fingers once more over his arm, and stepped away, flipping up the hem of her shirt. Macrae turned aside from her, kicking his shoes off, undoing his pants. When he glanced over his shoulder she was standing with her bare toes wrapped over the lip of stone. In the filtered moonlight her body looked poured in molten silver, itself a fluid. She bent her knees slightly and rose in the air like a torch, jackknifed, and drove down the wedge of her joined hands.

"Christ," Macrae said, scooting over to the cliff edge. "The rocks—" The roll of fog was undisturbed above the water and he wasn't sure if he had even heard a splash through the stoned cottony feeling in his ears. He went over without allowing himself time to think. In his mind's eye was the image of the rocks that jutted up just a foot or two below the water, the way they'd look in the daylight, with the narrow slit of deep safety between them. Even gravity wasn't working right tonight, nor time: his fall was so endlessly slow he could feel the cool mist beading on his skin as he sliced through it. When he struck the water the warmth of it surprised him.

He pulled the dive up as shallow as he could, driving out toward what he hoped, imagined was the center of the lake, and came up breathless, lungs stretching the wall of his chest. He gasped. Through a gap in the fog he briefly saw the moon. He hadn't felt such a surge, it occurred to him, since the botched stickup of the liquor store. Lacy was nowhere in sight, but he could hear the cupping sound of her strokes somewhere in the fog to his right.

He turned on his side and swam in that direction, reaching her faster than he'd thought to. She giggled as the fingers of his forward hand splintered against her rib cage. Rolling away from him, she went under, then her head came up a few yards away in a halo of mist. Her hair was smoothed to the curve of her neck like the fur of a seal. When he swam near she splashed at him and lowered herself flat on the water, kicking away. Macrae went down with his eyes closed, deep, passing under the turbulence her legs stirred above him. He came up vertically like a missile off a submarine, gathering water in his palms. A wave turned up glittering in the shimmer of the mist and broke toward her. She spluttered and splashed him in return. Macrae flipped onto his back and she washed up partway over him, pushing him under. He sank until he could disentangle, twisted, and swam clear and straight in the cooler darker layer of water, until his shoulder brushed rock.

There was a gap in the fog alongside the sheer wall where he surfaced. The moon shone down, catching his black movements, lighting the droplets he cast backward as he swam. Lacy came alongside him, breaststroking, her raised chin cutting a V in the smooth water. Together they swam past the edge of the rock face and on out toward the open center of the pond, where the fog was densest. The fog turned the moonlight particular, a suspension shining all around, gathered by the air. Macrae sloughed over onto his back and floated, kicking his legs lazily to keep them up. Near him he heard Lacy turn similarly in a warm trough of water. He stretched out his arm and their fingers linked and they were floating in balance. The breeze came up, catching a seam of the fog and lifting it.

Above, the silver-gilt mist swirled smokily as it thinned. In its place came the whole-moon light, surrounded by dark sky. The fresh wind was rolling fog back in quilted layers along the pond. Macrae laid his cheek against the water and watched the fog bundling under the rows of cedars lining the narrow shore. A few tendrils flattened and dispersed along the water's surface. Lacy breathed or sighed beside him, as if she were stirring in sleep. They lay quietly, barely joined, beneath the high full circle of the moon. Macrae was tingling all over with cleanliness. Half-in, half-out of his mind was a memory that they'd played this way as children. He knew for sure that Porter had been wrong.

By his request she dropped him by the roadside, not pulling in through the gate. Half-smiling, he watched her dusty taillights turn the corner, then walked in across the cattle gap. The moon was near setting but he could see well enough. He heard the sound before he came in sight of the garden: the *chop-chop-scrape* of a grubbing hoe in the hands of a familiar user. There was sure enough somebody in there, working the row of tomatoes with their wild vines tangling from one stake to the next. Macrae saw the X of overall straps on his back as he stooped to the work. The hoe's wide blade traveled neatly around the last plant in the row, breaking clods and raking the loosened dirt up in a mound around the stem. Done, the gardener raised his head and looked right at Macrae standing at the far garden fence. He raised his hand partway and then aborted the gesture, if it had been one.

It was his father doing all this. Macrae was quite sure he had been seen too. The old man turned away, propped the hoe against a post, left the garden, and walked up toward the house with a rapid sure step.

Macrae gaped and stared. The dope had worn off hours ago. He couldn't be hallucinating.

"What do you know," a voice said softly at his rear.

Macrae wheeled, scraping his back on the top strand of barbwire as he slipped along the fence, and caught his balance. Laidlaw stood a few feet back from him, still in the ghostly light.

"Jesus Christ on a cracker," Macrae said. "You about killed me there." He blew out a stiff blast of air and dropped his head. "I been thinking there was somebody behind me all day."

Laidlaw nodded. "I've had that feeling myself sometimes."

"Is that right?" Macrae said. "What are you doing roaming around in the dark?"

Laidlaw stooped and plucked a stem of tall grass and stepped over to where he could lean against a fence post. "Exercise." He stripped seeds off the stem between his fingers and set the bare stalk in between his teeth.

"Really," Macrae said. "Why don't you get your exercise in the daytime?"

"Don't you know it's hot in the daytime?" Laidlaw rolled around and looked into the garden. "Looks like your daddy's got that figured, out hoeing by moonlight."

"You saw him too," Macrae said. "That's a load off my mind, anyway."

"Why wouldn't I?" Laidlaw said. "I might try it myself one of these nights."

"No reason why not," Macrae said. He patted himself for cigarettes. Maybe he'd lost his pack out by the lake. "Nothing wrong with *your* eyes, but he can't see daylight. Ought not to be able to find the garden, much less hoe it. He walks around bumping into things usually."

"Huh," Laidlaw said. The grass stalk wagged in his mouth as his teeth slipped over it.

"Boy, I thought that garden was keeping itself up awful well," Macrae said. "He looked right up and saw me too. I'd swear it. He saw me right out of his eyes."

"Cataracts," Laidlaw said.

"What?"

"Could be he's got cataracts." Laidlaw took the straw out of his mouth. "It's a growth or some such right on the lens of your eye. It gets dark, your eyes dilate, you might can see around it some."

"You don't mean it," Macrae said.

Laidlaw broke the chewed end from the stalk and put it back in his mouth. "I've heard it to happen. Temporary deal, though. After while they grow so much it don't make any difference if it's light or dark."

"Well," Macrae said. "That don't leave much to look forward to."

"They got an operation for it," Laidlaw said. "Take the lens right off and give you glasses."

Macrae sniffed. "That'd cost some real money, I expect."

"Ain't he old enough for Medicare?"

"And then some," Macrae said. "You want to try to get him to take anything he thinks is welfare, you better do it in the daylight, though. When he can't see to shoot you."

"He's a mean old man," Laidlaw said respectfully.

"Can't move him any better than a mule," Macrae said. "This is going to need some thinking about."

Laidlaw didn't answer, standing with his elbows bowing down the wire between the rusted barbs, head cocked to listen to a screech owl calling from the nearest clump of trees. High on the ridge where the moon was sinking, a distant partner answered back. Macrae squinted inwardly, picturing medical machinery, bills, and hospital paperwork. That was a skin-crawling idea to him, trying to peer around something that was stuck right to your eyeball and wouldn't come off. Around the curve of the hill the milk cow lowed a time or two and then let up. Macrae scratched the back of his neck. There was an idea half-formed in his head but he didn't much like the look of it.

twenty-two

Porter started a pot of rice, waited for steam to leak under the lid, and cut the stove eye back to simmer. He opened himself a can of beer and headed for the porch. In the front room the old man was stroked out on a sagging couch, with a small black-and-white TV flicking shadows over the corners of his folded body. He was snoring but not loud enough to drown out the racket of the five o'clock movie, turned all the way up. Porter reached over and snapped the television off but the old man broke off in midsnore and raised his head, grumbling. With a slight sigh Porter turned the set on again, not quite so loud.

He opened the door and went onto the porch. A cold breeze cut across his face and neck and he turned his back to it, reaching to fasten a couple of top buttons on the flannel shirt he wore. Propped in a rocker, Charlie craned his neck to look at him.

"Hello, stranger," Porter said. "Where you been hiding yourself these days?"

Charlie swiveled forward, facing the dogs that circled each other in the bleached yard. "Here and there," he said.

"I been seeing the truck left here more often," Porter said. "But I don't see you."

"I been taking more walks," Charlie said. "Enjoying nature. The call of the wild."

Porter sat down in a rocker himself, bracing his feet when he heard the blanket seat start to rip along one of its nails, but it caught and held and he relaxed. Between his chair and Charlie's a strip of grubby sheet was spread on the porch floor, with an oil can and some other rags and a selection of their hot handguns scattered over it.

"What's all this?" Porter said.

Charlie squinted and reached for his beer. There were a couple of empties lined on the porch rail beside the full can. "Weapons maintenance time, must be," he said, and flipped his hand up the hill.

At the edge of the clearing, red leaves danced on the maple trees. Macrae was coming down the hillside from the shell of the van, carrying a load of shotguns across the rack of his two arms. The dogs pressed into his legs, whining and snuffling, as he crossed the yard. A bit roughly, he kneed them away. There was a yip and Sooner backed off with a resentful expression. The others came as far as the porch steps and stopped. Macrae laid the shotguns rattling on the piece of sheet and squatted down over them.

"What gives?" Porter said. "We gonna have a party?"

Macrae picked up one of the magnum revolvers, robbed the cylinder with an oily rag, and turned it over to peer at the strip of metal on the underside of the grip. "Never did file the numbers off these things," he muttered.

"Never got caught with any of'm either," Charlie snapped back.

Macrae stood up and took a box of shells from his pocket. The weight of the big gun heeled his wrist over. He thumbed shells into the cylinder and snapped it shut. Inside the house, a voice on the TV was uttering frantic praises of a used-car lot. Macrae strolled to the end of the porch and raised the huge pistol two handed. A pair of squirrels were chasing each other through the tossing branches of a maple and among the red dying leaves. Macrae tracked them with the gun barrel, then shifted to a leaf that had detached itself and was falling in little flirts into the yard. When it landed he let the gun swing against his thigh and turned and looked toward the other two, maybe fifteen yards away, in the opposite corner of the porch, not paying him any mind. The gun was heavier than ever when he raised it again and swept the barrel horizontally right to left. When the forward sight crossed Charlie's string of empties he stopped it and squeezed the trigger.

The nearest can burst into a cloud of beer droplets and aluminum shrapnel; another, unshattered can flew up and rang against the underside of the porch roof. The dogs all howled in a single voice and scrambled up under the floor as far as they could retreat. Charlie had flipped his rocker over backward and was coming up on all fours beside it. His mouth was open but speechless. Inside the house the old man rose up and cursed them in detail and finally subsided. The couch springs shrieked as he sat back down, and the TV crackled louder.

Charlie stood up and dusted his knees and stretched out his shirtfront to look at the beer stains. "If you plan on doing that again," he said, "you better make sure you kill me."

"What's the problem?" Macrae shifted the gun to his left hand and sniffed at the cordite pocks on the web between his thumb and forefinger. His ears were ringing. "It was just an empty can."

Charlie snorted and picked a shard of aluminum out of the fabric of his shirt. He bent over and set the spilled chair upright on its rockers.

"Hey, come on, Macrae," Porter said. "Put the gun down, you're making everybody nervous."

"Just test firing . . ." Macrae opened the cylinder and shook the shells out into his palm. "See? All done with." He snapped the empty gun shut and balanced it on the porch rail, isolated the spent shell and tossed it away before he dropped the others back into his pocket. For a moment he stood watching the high branches of the maple, but the squirrels were long gone.

"What's the matter with you?" Charlie said. He rocked the empty chair with one hand.

Macrae narrowed his eyes at him, wiping his hair back from his brow. The wind was blowing up the back of his neck. "Maybe I'm just restless," he said.

"Didn't know you had that problem," Charlie said. "Can't you go shanghai a cow or something?" He turned the rocker in the direction of the porch rail and sat down in it.

Macrae paced to the far end of the porch and turned and came better than halfway back. The floorboards were creaking under his feet and they could all hear the dogs shifting and scrabbling underneath. Macrae stepped on a loose plank and rolled from foot to foot, making the wood cry against the nail.

"Quit that," Porter said.

"I remember when you used to get jumpy," Macrae said, staring at the back of Charlie's head. "Usually about every two weeks it used to be."

"And look at me now," Charlie said, tilting his beer can, not bothering to turn around. "I'm a satisfied man."

Macrae rolled his weight back over the shrieking plank and walked to the far end of the porch. His left hand wrapped around his head and scrambled in his snaky hair. He came back and stood on the same plank again and pumped it till it cried. "What if you wanted to make some money?" he said. "What if you wanted to make a *lot* of money right quick?"

Charlie turned his head now and looked at him appraisingly. "I can get money in return for goods or services," he said.

"Is that a fact," said Macrae. "That's what you learned by you being a college boy?"

"Let's say I got no goods all that valuable," Charlie continued in the same bland tone. "Butter and eggs, a hot gun here and a hot gun there, and that's about all. I have to put my mind to services, what services I got to offer the world, you know?" He rotated the beer can between splayed fingers, looking into its keyhole. "Now, a service might be something I do, or something I could do but I don't."

Unconsciously Porter raised his thumb to his mouth and began to gnaw on the edge of the nail. Charlie raised his head from the beer can to look at Macrae more closely. "Like if I *could* blow your head off, but I don't," he said. "That is a highly valuable service right there."

288

"Somehow I thought you'd come to that," Macrae said.

"That's the way I see it," Charlie said. "Who are we talking about, you or me? I thought you'd lost your ambition, Macrae."

Macrae shifted his feet over the board. "I'd like to make some money, Charlie. I'd like that soon."

Porter hissed, jerked his thumb from his mouth, and examined the blood beading along the torn cuticle.

"Real money and all in one shot," Macrae said. "Not those little dribs and drabs."

"Hey, all right," Charlie said. "How can you keep'm down on the farm once they've seen . . ." He trailed off. Macrae didn't have much idea what sights he might have had in mind.

"Yeah," Charlie said, rocking the chair in a sort of nodding motion. "It can be done. There's always a way." He arched his eyebrows. "Have to get up early, though."

"What of it," Macrae said. "I'm getting up early enough as it is."

Down the windshield of the truck, frost patterns were breaking up and running in small rivulets melted by the sun, which was just showing itself over the spine of hills that ringed the town. Erratically, Macrae would flip on the wipers, sweeping the drizzle away in streaks. In the fingers of his other hand he rolled an unlit cigarette. The truck was parked in front of a Krispy Kreme on a short leg of a three-sided shopping center. The longest side was entirely occupied by a department store, but it hadn't opened, and the big central parking lot was mostly empty, just a few cars scattered over the employee section. In fact, nothing was open yet except the Krispy Kreme. The tavern on the far side of it was shuttered down and so were the card shop, barbershop, and pet shop that connected it to the department store's corner. On the opposite leg were a bookstore, a shoe shop, some sort of boutique, and at the end of the row, nearest the highway, a small branch of the First National Bank, not yet open for business either, though

Macrae could see a couple of tellers setting up at the counter, beyond the glass wall . . .

. . . if he turned his head that way. But he was facing forward, watching Porter paying at the register of the doughnut shop. Porter punched his way outside, knocking the door open with his shoulder, jingling the small brass bell that hung from the pressure hinge by a string. In one hand he balanced a cardboard tray of coffees and in the other he held a box of plain doughnuts.

"Move over, will you," Porter said, shoving the truck's passenger door wider open with a knee. Charlie slid sideways on the bench seat and drew up his legs. Porter squeezed in and pulled the door to. He handed out the coffee cups and opened the doughnut box across his lap, with a crackle of the plastic window on the green-and-white top. The warm-sugar smell flowed into the cab. Charlie hooked a pair of doughnuts on his forefinger and passed one to Macrae, who ate it in a bite, a brief explosion of sweetness and warmth. His stomach fluttered. Porter stretched the box toward him again, reaching across Charlie's lap.

"Go down easy when they're hot," he said. "Take yourself a couple more."

Macrae shook his head moodily, popped the lid of his coffee cup, and took a sip, then wedged the cup at a tilt between the windshield and the dash. A plume of fog spread over the glass. Macrae lit his cigarette and blew the match smoke toward the vent window.

"Ouch, dammit," Charlie shouted suddenly. "You jackass." Porter had clipped his cup in withdrawing the doughnut box and spilled hot coffee across the thighs of his khaki pants. Charlie swore at him again and kicked at his ankle.

"Will you knock it off?" Macrae inquired.

"Gimme air." Charlie drove his elbows out sharply to either side of him. The other two flinched away toward the doors.

"All right, all right," Porter said. "We're gonna need a better car, we really try to do this."

"Hey, shut up a minute." Charlie twisted to look out the back glass, then switched to the rearview mirror. "Here they come."

Macrae rolled his window down and adjusted the big rectangular side mirror. In the reflection he saw a little blood red Wells Fargo truck drawing up to the front of the bank.

"Looks like a toy," Macrae muttered.

"Looks like a paddy wagon," Porter said, his eye on the small barred window in the armored truck's rear door.

Two men got out of the cab and walked to the rear of the truck. One of them unlocked the door and opened it and they both reached in to gather several gray-stained canvas bags. The door relocked, they carried the load with no special haste or urgency toward the entrance of the bank.

Charlie wriggled in his seat. "You see?" he said. "You see how easy? Don't even have to go inside."

"I see they got sidearms is what I see," Porter said.

In the mirror, Macrae watched the two guards coming back out of the bank. It was true they both wore heavy cop-type gun belts, swagging low around potbellies. They looked small. One was gray haired, partly balding. The other wore a cop-style cap.

Charlie snorted. "They're little old men. They're not gonna hurt you."

"They look like guys with guns to me," Porter said, watching sourly in the mirror on his side of the truck as the guards clambered back up into their cab.

"You can't be afraid of a Rent-a-Cop," Charlie said. "Look at it the way they do. There you go on your regular morning—you raise up your head and you're staring down a shotgun barrel. Are you gonna grab for your weapon, or are you gonna hand over your little sacks of money that don't even belong to you no-way? Hell, those guys are just a couple years off retirement."

"Sounds good the way you *say* it," Porter said.

"Listen to me," Charlie said. "We came with our equipment this morning, we'd already have it done."

Macrae took his eyes off the mirror for a second. A pair of gloved hands was lowering a cage full of unhappy-looking Lab puppies into the pet shop's show window. Macrae sniffed and scrubbed the back of his wrist across his nose. In the cage, the puppies clambered over each other, scraping their backs on the wire. The mirror showed the Wells Fargo truck reversing, then bucking forward as the driver shifted to pull onto the highway.

"You tell me they're regular?" Macrae said.

"Every Monday, same time, same place," Charlie said. "They might come once in the middle of the week too, but they're always right here Monday morning."

"How you come to know so much?" Porter said.

"Huh." Macrae mashed his cigarette out on the outside of the truck door and let it drop to the asphalt. "Sleeping it off in the parking lot, I bet. Bet they probably woke him up." He glanced over at the tavern, drumming his fingers over the strip of broken chrome.

"I'm telling you, boys," Charlie said. "This one's a gift. Besides, this time we did our homework. Right?"

Macrae sat high and alone in the truck, parked in the derelict driveway in the woods behind Lacy's house, smoking one of Porter's joints and watching a last rim of sunset red die on the line of the western hills. When the roach burned down too small to hold he put it out and minced it fine in his fingernails and loaded the shreds into the tip of cigarette, Rafael's way, to get the last blast of the resin. Puffing lazily on the tobacco part, he drank from the sacked quart and wondered about Rafael, what he was doing now. If he was still alive, for that matter. You had to wonder that about people too . . .

Carrying the beer, he got down from the truck and wandered in a sloppy circle around the ring of the drive, kicking at the few chunks of gravel that hadn't washed out, at cans and bottles scattered there by other parkers. It was Sunday night; he might have been here just the same at fifteen, sixteen, stoned, his work for the next day undone, ready to stand hangdog in some classroom, under whatever teacher's question, not knowing the answer, whatever it was. Sunday night. The moon had risen, lopsided and pale. Macrae sat on the truck's front bumper, his legs braced out in front of him. He lit a second joint he had in his shirt pocket, sucking smoke across his puffy tongue, shivering some as it grew colder in the dark. He would have liked to get further away from himself than the homegrown weed was likely to take him.

He sat for a long, dope-torpid time, looking at his scuffed-raw boot toes in the weak moonlight. The high had sealed him deeper into his body, so that he was unpleasantly aware of the hiss of his breathing, swish of his heart . . . Finally he got up and wandered off into the trees, which stood moonlit, apart from one another and black as snakes.

There was a yellow glow at the glass door of Lacy's house. The light seemed to flicker with the tree trunks crossing it as Macrae moved undecidedly closer, but when he came into the clearing of the backyard he saw that really it was steady. He went nearer, his shins brushing through the overgrown weeds, stiffened now with frost. The light inside the door was soft because the table lamp had been set on the floor, on the far side of the sofa bed, which was folded out. On top of it, in the rumple of sheets, a double-backed creature moved, one head grunting, the other moaning. It kicked a slim leg toward the ceiling, pointed toes and bent its knee. With a peculiar urgency, it whetted itself along its inmost edges.

Macrae stood with his fingers splayed on the freezing glass, like a tree frog. The creature cried out loudly and fretted harder against itself, within the borders of his own transparent silhouette. A blink took him back to the peep-show booth where he'd sat jammed next to that woman who'd clawed his face and the other one with the hurt knee. He wondered how long they might have stayed there when he left, pumping quarters into the projector, if they were sitting there yet, nailed to the bench by what they saw. There was no shutter going to close across the scene before him now.

He was startled by the shock of his elbow crashing hard into the door. The big pane cracked in star lines, top to bottom, though he hadn't broken it through. On the other side of it, Charlie rolled away from Lacy, his body hair visible, yellow-gray, his muscles moving ropily under the slackened skin. He dropped to a crouch behind the bed, groping for a weapon, for clothes. A lock of recognition when his eyes found Macrae. Immediately he disengaged, stood up, and left the room.

Lacy's skinny nakedness was jerking on the far side of the glass. Her face was pinched and twisting, her mouth kept framing a word, *No, no.* Macrae couldn't hear her, actually. His fingers dragged over the ridged cracks in the glass. On the other side, her image fractured, splintering. She was stooped and struggling with the door latch; he didn't know if she was trying to get it open or hold it shut. He turned his back and then, after a moment, slid down the glass to sit on the sill. Behind him the light went off. The tall ironweed was spectral under the moon, and his breath came out in hazy clouds, it was that cold. He might have heard the front door banging. After a while the light came on again, brighter now; there was a squeak and the glass door slipped open. His head dropped back, deprived of its support. He pushed up on the knuckles of one hand and stood.

Lacy had on a flannel shirt whose tails broke on her thighs. Apparently she'd also brushed her hair. "So," she said. "You want to come in?"

Macrae stepped across the sill. The heat was on in here, his face flushed in it. "Why," he said. "Why'd you do it?"

"Why not?" Lacy walked away from him, toward the sofa bed. She'd placed the lamp back on the table; that was why the room was now more brightly lit. Macrae advanced a step or two.

"But Charlie," he said. "Of all the people in the world. Charlie . . ."

Lacy wheeled on him. Her split eye flashed. "*All* the people in the world weren't interested," she snapped. "And anyway, what's wrong with Charlie? You introduced us, right? He's *your* friend."

"He's a murderer," Macrae said, not knowing where it came from. "Kill you soon as look at you."

"Oh, and what about you?" Lacy said. "Just your dumb luck you didn't kill Punkinhead back that time, and if you had you'd be in jail forever."

"I never meant to do it," Macrae said. "It just happened. And if you never messed with him, it might not have."

"Oh, God." Lacy dropped onto the edge of the bed. She pushed back her hair and looked up at him, eyes liquid and sad. "They never touched me. Nobody did. They never really touched me."

Macrae was whispering. "So what did you do it for, then?"

"So what am I supposed to do?" Lacy said. "You're stupid, Macrae. You don't even see what's right under your nose. You could have—" She fell back on the bed as if shot, the tails of the long shirt splitting over her legs. "For the love of God," she said. "Give me a cigarette."

Macrae took one, lit it himself, and stooped to place it in her lips.

"And would you close the door?" she said. "It's cold."

The door stuck on the track as Macrae dragged at it. He wondered if he'd bent the frame. Lacy was lying on her back, blowing smoke rings. Macrae crossed over and sat down on the opposite edge of the bed.

"Signs of a misspent childhood," he said.

With a crooked smile, she rolled her head toward him. "Spent it with you, boy."

"That you did," Macrae said. "Let me get a hit." He took the cigarette from her and dragged and gave it back. Lacy was inspecting the ceiling again.

"You better give it some thought," she said. "Things don't just happen for no reason. You don't have to be this way. You don't have to be like you are. You could do something. Be somebody."

"I am somebody," Macrae said.

Lacy sat up. "Okay, all right." She grabbed an ashtray onto her bare knee and stubbed out the cigarette and leaned over to put the ashtray on the floor. "Then just you tell me who you are."

"I'm the fruit of my actions," Macrae said without a pause.

"God." She dropped back full length on the thin sofa bed mattress. "How do you come up with that stuff?"

"Tell me I'm wrong?" Macrae said.

"I wish I could."

Macrae looked toward the glass door, a cracked sheet of black, tears run through their shadowy reflections.

"So what are you going to do?" Lacy said.

"Next?" Macrae said. "Rob a bank."

"I know," Lacy said. "That much I know."

Macrae whipped his head toward her. "Charlie told you that?"

"Yeah, don't you think it's sexy?" she said. "Don't you just feel longer and stronger when you go strutting around with a gun?"

"Come to think," Macrae said, "not really." He pushed up from the bed and wandered in a figure-eight on the threadbare wall-to-wall.

"God, I think it's a nifty idea," Lacy told the ceiling. "I sure hope nobody gets arrested or killed."

Macrae felt like a dog looking for a place to lie down. He made another loop and stopped in front of her.

"Well, old girl," he said, "I'm sorry about all this."

"I know." Lacy sat up and looked at him, almost meek, hands folded in her lap. "Me too."

twenty-three

Macrae looked for Charlie, first off in places he didn't have much chance to find him: the shell of the van, the barn. But since the hard frost they'd all been sleeping in the house, someone on the couch and the other two in blankets on the floor around the big barrel-shaped cast-iron stove that was their only heat. The old man, meanwhile, slept upstairs in an unheated room. He was used to sleeping cold, thought it was healthier.

The cow had stayed in her stall after milking, standing head to tail with her spring calf, now a good-sized blocky heifer. Macrae went and stood against them, sharing their warmth and sweet milky odor. Then he went slowly down to the house in the dark.

Porter was slumped on the couch, bathed in the bluish light of the little TV, whose volume was turned down so low Macrae could barely hear it from the door. Charlie sat near the fire, close enough he could feed it from a washtub of stove wood near the legs of his chair without having to get up. It was suffocatingly hot, in fact. Macrae's father had already gone upstairs, to sleep, or maybe to read the newspaper in the dark up there, for all Macrae knew.

Charlie's hands flexed on the chair arms, his legs shifted as if he would stand, but he didn't. He turned his head to look at Macrae briefly and then looked back at the stove. The red-burning firelight masked his face more than anything, while Porter, lit starkly with TV, looked stony and too ashy pale. Macrae was still fairly high, so that the queer looks of their faces in this light got to him. He nudged the door shut with his shoulder and walked toward the stove.

Charlie prized open the stove's front hatch with a screwdriver. Flame leapt up and out toward his face. He leaned forward and got a piece of elm from the tub and threw it in and pressed the door shut with his shoe sole. There was a second thump as a big chunk of fire dislodged and dropped inside, squeezing out a shower of sparks through the chinks along the stove's base. Macrae watched them die on the blackened sheet of tin beneath it.

"You'll crack the metal," Macrae said. He circled behind Charlie's chair. There was a smell of marination coming off him, a ripe strong musky smell, if it wasn't another dope delusion.

"Didn't you take a shower?" Macrae said.

Charlie, still facing the fire, shook his head. Macrae was behind him, to the left, leaning slightly forward on his toes.

"You ought to of taken a shower, at least," Macrae said.

Charlie rustled in his seat. "We hadn't got any shower here," he said. "Just a bathtub and the drain's fouled up on that."

"All I know is what my nose tells me." Macrae paced from the stove to the wall, turned, and looked back at Porter, who was watching some cop show, must have been. The tiny gunfire from the set was like the sound of pencils breaking.

"Listen." Charlie closed his hands on the arms of his chair and looked at Macrae out of his strange green depthless eyes. "How would I know if she was supposed to be off limits? You didn't have any DON'T TOUCH sign hanging off of her that I ever saw."

"True," Macrae said. "You're right about that."

"How would I know?" Charlie repeated.

Macrae strolled a half circle between the stove and Charlie's chair. "We better not talk about it," he said.

"Fine." Charlie lowered his eyes and fidgeted with the small shiny scars on the backs of his fingers. "But. Tomorrow?"

"What about it?" Macrae said. A click and the room darkened and reddened as Porter turned off the TV.

"Are we good to go?" Charlie's eyes were flat as coins.

"What," Macrae said. "You got some reason to feel uneasy about me standing behind you with a firearm?"

Charlie said nothing to that. Porter was sitting with his arms folded over his chest, head bent forward toward the two of them, his eyes invisible.

"All right." Macrae arrested his pacing. "We're good to go."

"If you say so," Charlie said. "It's all I need to hear."

"Just a goddamn minute," Porter said. He unwrapped his arms and put his hands on his knees as he leaned forward. "What exactly are we talking about here?"

"Nothing," Macrae said.

"If it's about tomorrow," Porter said, "you got to let me in on it."

"We might have had a problem which we just now settled it," Macrae said. "Anything else you'd like to know?"

"Plenty," Porter said.

"Sorry," Macrae said. "I think you're out of luck."

The old patchy brown Camaro Charlie had stolen grumbled in the cold, idling in a parking space one rank away from the doughnut shop. Macrae's breath steamed out a crack in the passenger's window. His throat was too tight to eat or drink, and it was hard to talk.

"They're late," he croaked, drumming his fingers on the cracked vinyl of the dash. He twisted around, eyes passing over Porter, who sat behind the wheel, staring wooden headed across the empty parking spaces. In the backseat Charlie sat with his knees apart, a shotgun jammed between his thigh and the car door, happily slurping coffee. He winked at Macrae and offered the doughnut box.

Macrae pushed it away. "Where are they?" he said. He turned forward. The colon on the bank clock was blinking off the seconds. Macrae stroked his thumb up and down the blued sight groove of the twenty-gauge he held across his lap.

"Take it easy," Charlie said, the words muffled by pastry. He waved a section of doughnut toward the windshield. "We're on schedule."

On the far side of the windshield glass, the Wells Fargo truck rolled silently toward the bank. It was going so slow Macrae thought he could have counted the ribs on the hubcaps as they turned.

"Now?" Porter looked at Macrae, rolling his under lip up into the pinch of his top teeth.

"Go," Macrae breathed.

"Not too fast," Charlie said, and drained his coffee cup.

Porter clutched and shifted gears. The Camaro snarled, went thundering forward, crawling out of the northern exit of the parking lot, turning right onto the highway. A gout of Macrae's untouched coffee slopped from the cup wedged on the dashboard.

"God, where'd you find this car," Macrae muttered. "Sounds like a fifty-caliber machine gun."

"Hole in the muffler," Charlie said. "Don't worry, it won't slow it down."

From the corner of his eyes, Macrae watched the guards clamber creakily down from the cab, same pair as before, one with the hat and the other without. They ticked along like windup toys toward the rear doors of the armored truck. Porter turned again into the lower entrance of the parking lot, into the lane behind them. The two guards had turned their backs, stooping through the open doors to lift. The shadowed cavity of the truck's interior swam up to fill the Camaro's windshield. Porter stopped, almost touching the guard's legs. There was a ripping sound as he pulled the parking brake.

Macrae's feet were on the pavement, grinding. He swung the shotgun across his hip. The guard nearest him made a half turn his way, pistol in hand, held idly, loosely; he looked like a teacher before a blackboard, holding a pointer or a piece of chalk. It was the one without a hat. Macrae could see the color of his eyes, a streaky brown and ringed with unbelieving zeros of white.

"*You jackass!*" Charlie lunged around the front end of the Camaro, thrusting his shotgun ahead. "*Drop it now!*"

The pair of brown eyes flexed in their sockets. Macrae's finger was sweat slimy on the trigger. He saw the guard's hand come open and the gun detach and clatter on the asphalt. With the side of his foot Macrae pushed it up under the Camaro, which trembled queasily alongside him.

"Okay." Charlie sighed. He took a step and plucked the pistol from the second guard's holster, fumbling for a second with the safety strap. Police .38, but with a long barrel, like a Wild West six-shooter or something of the sort. Charlie took a cursory glance at it and jammed it into the waistband of his jeans. His left hand came back to the shotgun's tooled pump.

"Hands on your heads," he said. "You know the way."

The guards' hands came up slowly, like levitation in a magic act on stage. Macrae could see breath steaming from their mouths in abbreviated compact clouds. Charlie leaned around the truck's back bumper to check on Porter, who stood with the magnum revolver aimed into the driver's window, right hand braced over left wrist. Porter cut his eyes toward Charlie and nodded once.

"Fine." Charlie straightened up and turned back to the guards. "Just fine. All right, gentlemen, let's you lie down. On your belly like a reptile. Watch those hands, now."

Macrae's heart fluttered. He swallowed at the thick foamy taste in his mouth. The guards were lowering themselves knee by knee, stiff and awkward, clutching their heads with their hands. He saw where hair oil had soaked into the crown of the one's hat, a dark stain on the navy cloth, roughly the shape of Australia. The two guards lay face down on the pavement between the Camaro and the armored truck. It was going to be all right, Macrae thought.

The grubby gray cash sacks slumped on the wide back bumper of the truck. Not waiting for Charlie to prompt him, Macrae shifted the shotgun to his right hand, balancing it by the trigger guard, and leaned forward to pick up the nearest one. He was standing on one leg when he heard a voice just at his right and turned his head to see the policeman leaning out of the driver's seat of the squad car, eyebrows arched as if he had just meant to ask directions or the time. He had sandy hair and several days' growth on his upper lip, as if he were starting a mustache. A ring of white T-shirt showed at the open throat of his uniform. His partner was just a shadow on the other side of the seat. Macrae thought, These guys just rolled in here for a doughnut and they don't even know what's happening.

He was holding the shotgun low, as if he thought they maybe couldn't see it. Maybe they really didn't see it. The one cop looked about to repeat his question, whatever it was, when his face tore apart into bloody rags and he slammed into his seat back, then bounced forward against the wheel. A hot shell casing looped over Macrae's shoulders as he dropped to the ground. Worming his way backward under the shivering Camaro, he heard Charlie fire twice more.

The touch of the guard's dumped pistol startled him and he raised up suddenly. The hot exhaust pipe scorched his back, and he flattened himself, hissing in pain. A horrible sound of a blaring horn seemed to be coming from everywhere. The two guards were facing his way, under the Camaro's front end. One was looking at Macrae and the other had an eye on the stray pistol. With a forefinger Macrae twirled it farther out of their reach. He scooted out from under the car and came up on his knees in time to see Charlie pluck the other pistol from his waistband, stoop down, and shoot the nearest guard in the back of his skull, just below the sweat line of his hatband. His face slapped on the pavement like a spatula. The other guard pushed up onto his forearms and Charlie shot him from ten inches' distance, between his widened eyes.

Macrae came up crouching, peering across the Bondo streaks of the Camaro's roof. The first cop still lay against the wheel, the weight of his body blowing the horn in an interminable blast all over the parking lot. Macrae's ears were echoing from that. The second cop was hanging over the half-open passenger door, a shoulder cocked up and blood on his collar. Macrae couldn't see his head, if he still had one. He was wishing the horn to stop, but instead a siren joined it, from the bank.

"Let's load up those sacks," Charlie said. He slung the pistol away by its butt and it cartwheeled over the first cop's body and thunked onto the cushions of the patrol car's backseat. An accident, maybe. Macrae watched Charlie licking at the sugar glaze crusted to the corner of his mouth.

"Time to go," Charlie said. He had gathered a sack or two.

Numbly, Macrae grabbed some cash bags. Porter was backing away from the cab of the truck, the outsized revolver still held high and braced in his two hands. Then they were all in the car somehow, Macrae jamming the gears. The Camaro reared like a horse on its hind legs, with a screaming sound and a smell of burning metal.

"Take off the goddamn brake!" Charlie yelled, reaching across Macrae's lap to do it himself. Released, the car fired toward the highway like a shell from a cannon.

"What happened," Porter said. "What the hell happened?" He'd been on the far side of the armored truck, which was why he hadn't seen the patrol car coming in. Macrae wondered fleetingly why he and Charlie hadn't either. He caught Porter's eye for a second in the rearview mirror. Porter wiped his fingers over his lower lip, then looked at them, startled, as they came away bloody.

"Damn," he said. "Bit right through."

"Nerves," Charlie said. He leaned back, resting his arm across the seat back. "You didn't kill the driver."

"I damn well did not," Porter said. "This was gonna be a cash transaction, not a quad cop killing."

"Well, he's apt to know you again," Charlie said.

"Jesus Christ, Charlie," Macrae said. "You forgot to take care of the bank tellers and whoever was in the doughnut shop." His hands went rigid, seized up on the wheel. There was a stink of blood and burned gunpowder all through the car.

Charlie flicked his shoulder with his fingers. "Keep the speed down. Nobody's after us. We're all right."

It was true. Traffic was stacking up in the opposite lane, but they were headed out from town, so rush hour wasn't hurting them. The siren on the bank was already out of earshot and there'd been no new ones taking its place, though Macrae's ears still rang from the sound of that trumpeting horn. The sun had never come up that morning, and the iron gray sky had lowered almost to the tops of the trees that lined the road ahead.

"We're all right," Charlie repeated in the same calm reasonable tone.

Macrae looked at Charlie's curled fingers where they still almost touched his jacket's shoulder seam. "Got blood on you," he said.

Charlie retracted his hand and examined it. There was a fine spatter of blood there and on his forearm, blow-back from the shooting of the guards. He rooted on the floorboards and found some loose paper towels to wipe over the stains, but they had already set and begun to brown.

"Macrae," Charlie said in a low voice.

Macrae's head was locked on the road in front him. He didn't twitch.

"Don't go home," Charlie said.

"All right," Macrae said. "I can pick up the interstate between here and Franklin. Where you got in mind to go?"

"East," Charlie said. "I-Forty." He peered over the seat back. "No time to stop for no dogs this trip either."

Porter turned his face away, looking slackly out the window at the trees and phone poles snapping by. Even the Nashville-bound traffic had thinned out now. A bubble of blood was drying to a black knot on Porter's lower lip. Charlie's eye dropped away from him to the several gray cash bags jumbled on the seat by Porter's knee, half masking a brace of extra shotguns. A couple had the Wells Fargo emblem stenciled on the faded fabric, he noticed.

"Look there," he said. "Looks like we done pretty good, actually.

Porter bolted upright and vibrating in the seat. "Pretty good?"

he said. "Why you bloodthirsty little son of a bitch. We'll be running from this one the rest of our lives. With *luck*."

"Watch how you call me a son of a bitch," Charlie said. He dipped into his shirt pocket and lit himself a cigarette.

"Yeah, I know," Porter said. "You've blown people's heads off for less than that."

Charlie fumed out a gust of smoke. "You'd of shot that driver, we'd be better off," he said.

"You think?" Porter said. "Hey, I can do some jail if I have to. I been in jail, it didn't kill me. But I don't want the gas chamber or the chair or whatever it is they got around here—which is it, Macrae?"

Macrae watched the white hyphens of the center line sucking up under the Camaro's Bondo-splotched hood. The engine kept coughing out a sound of angry strangulation. "We need to swap out this car," he said. "I'd give that a high priority."

"Let it ride a little while," Charlie said. "First let's make a little time."

"They do have the death penalty in Tennessee, don't they?" Porter said.

"I guess they might," Macrae said. "I never had call to think much about it."

"Till now," Porter said.

"Knock it off, Porter," Charlie said.

Macrae took one hand off the wheel and wiped a slick of sweat on his pants knee. "Somebody light me a cigarette," he said.

"No rush," Porter said. "They always let you have one right before the execution."

"Porter," Charlie said. He shot him a look as he passed Macrae his smoke, but Porter was staring out the window. His tongue touched the scab on his lower lip, then sucked back in.

"I heard this story," Porter said. "Back when the gas chamber was new, you know? Go back forty years or whatever. First dude they threw in there, one of the first. Somewhere down South, I guess it was. Anyway, they wanted to see how it would go, so they had some kind of a window they could look at him through, and they put a microphone in there with him. To see what he might say, you know, when he saw the gas come rolling in. Last words or whatever."

"Come on, Porter," Charlie said. "Give us a break."

Porter kept watching out the window, eye on the road's shoulder, or just beyond, where a white picket fence went flickering by. A dog was straying, on and off the pavement. A little old lady was creeping toward a newspaper pitched to the corner of her drive.

"You won't guess what he said." Porter's voice was dry, half choking. He forced a swallow. In the rearview mirror, Macrae saw his Adam's apple catch and jerk.

"I don't plan to try," Charlie said.

"Save me, Joe Louis," Porter said. "That's all they got. Over and over, just like that. *Save me, Joe Louis. Save me, Joe Louis.*"

Charlie fisted his blood-speckled hand and drove it into the car roof over his head, two or three times, fast and hard. "Goddammit Porter, will you just *shut up!*"

Stiff with silence, Macrae drew smoke across the back of his aching throat. A cold draft snatched his exhalation out the vent. Charlie, breathless, hung his head into his hand.

"Save me, Joe Louis," Porter said.

swamp

It was dark and rainy, midnight-plus, when they crossed the causeway onto the island. One of the windshield wipers was broken, completing only half its arc on the glass of the passenger side. Macrae stared out through bubbles of rain at the pools of wet headlight staining the road. Through the crack in his window he could smell the salt marsh they'd just crossed over, and behind it a deeper, stronger stench.

"Stinks," he said shortly, and wound the window tight into its rubber seal.

Charlie turned from the steering wheel. "Paper mill," he said. "Land breeze'll bring it over, sometimes." He faced the road again, tight to its curves, the swamp immediately beyond the thin shoulder. "Smells a lot worse when you're right up on it. I grew up a block away from the thing. It's where my old man worked." His tone as if he'd named some place a man had died.

The car wheezed under them, almost stalled. Charlie pedaled the gas and it revived, lunging on the slick wet pavement. It was the third car since they left that morning. The second, a newish Buick, Charlie had commandeered at gunpoint from a single driver in a rest stop short of Knoxville.

"Great," Macrae had said. "Terrific, Charlie. They'll be up our tailpipe in fifteen minutes now."

So they had stopped again, at a mall on the east of town, where Charlie hot-wired an old Corolla, a junker with the body rusting out. The cash bags and most of the guns were in the trunk of it.

Ten or fifteen hours on the road, but they still hadn't counted the money.

The broken wiper ticked on the windshield, a spidery sound. Macrae let his head sag on the molded rest. He wondered if his father had really missed them yet. Would the old man try to milk by moonlight? Anyway, the cow was almost dry.

"Nobody showing a light," Porter said, looking out the left-hand window, where the short drives to the beach houses cut in between the live oaks and the dunes.

"Nobody around," Charlie said. "They roll this place right up once the season's over."

A great gray building swam into the headlights' cone. From its second story a large signboard hung from a four-by-four, weathered silver, faded white paint streaks faintly tracing an outline of some potbellied bird. Charlie turned in. He gunned the car, its engine coughing, over the border of the shelled parking area and around the rear corner of the building. With a whir, the rear wheels spun themselves hub deep in the soft sand. He let the engine die, but left the headlights burning.

"So much for that." Macrae cracked his door and squinted at the sunken tires.

"Don't worry about it," Charlie said. He reached down to pull the lever that popped the trunk. "We'll dig it out when the time comes. Main thing's to get it out of sight." He got out and walked to the rear of the car and leaned into the trunk, rooting under the bags and guns.

Macrae climbed out after him, knees stiff, his whole body shaky. The loose sand was insecure under his boots. He propped himself on the frame of the car. Opposite the building they'd parked behind was an enormous dune, high as a three-story house. A boardwalk led from the back door to stairs that climbed to the top of it. Live oaks overarching everything sealed off the intermediate space as tightly as a cave, lit by the ghostly headlight glare. The live oaks didn't let much rain through, though Macrae could still hear it pattering on the small round waxen leaves overhead.

Charlie clambered up onto the boardwalk, a tire tool swinging from his arm. He went to one of the big rear windows and pried the shutter that closed it off of its nails. A tap from the tire tool's elbow sent a glass pane tinkling inside. Charlie reached in to raise the sash and swung through into the dark. Some ratlike sounds came from behind the door and then it opened outward. Charlie stood beckoning in the frame.

Inside, the dark was a dusty velvet, sightlessly dense. Macrae felt his way along what must have been a hallway wall until he stumbled through some door and was walking through an unnerving vacant, invisible space. He took cautious steps, his arms outstretched. Something brushed across his face, a string. He pulled it and light blossomed from a yellow insect bulb above. It was a kitchen, long and large, and would have been open on two sides, but now the shutters sealed the spiders and their webs behind the screens.

"Electric's on," Charlie noted. "We're in luck." He went along a row of cabinets, opening them. Some were empty, some held dishes, and there were several stocked with canned goods. The white of their trim turned cream in the yellow light. Charlie took down a jumbo can of chili and rolled it in his hand.

"What is this place?" Porter leaned into the kitchen doorway.

"Summer hotel." Charlie threw the can to him. "You hungry?"

Porter walked to the black range and turned a dial. A blue flame leapt.

"Gas too," Charlie said. "Things are looking up."

Porter took an iron skillet down from a hook above the stove and ran his finger over a gritty rime on its inside edge. "Any onions?" he said.

"Ahhh . . ." Charlie snorted and stopped in front of a lower cabinet that was shut with a small padlock. The blade of the tire tool slid under the hasp and broke it free. Charlie sighed with a whistling sound. "Well, but we do have whiskey."

They ate canned chili from speckled bowls and washed it down with bourbon cut with the soft tasteless water from the tap, warm because there was no ice. Done, Macrae slid his dish into the sink and walked to the back door. It sounded like the rain had stopped outside. Leaning on the doorjamb, he pulled off his boots and set them just inside the lintel with his socks hanging in the tops of them. Barefoot, he crossed the damp plank walk and began mounting the stairs that climbed the dune.

At the head of the stairs the live oaks gave out and were replaced by sea oats. Climbing toward the waving fronds, Macrae began to hear the surf, hushing against the packed sand a long way below. When he crested the dune he saw that the tide was completely out, the water obsidian calm and still except for the measured movement of the waves into the shore. The rain had stopped entirely, and the wind had turned around. It came off the ocean now, hurrying clouds away from the low-riding sickle moon.

There was a creak on the steps behind him and he turned to see Porter and Charlie coming up, indistinct in the dark under the trees. The bobbing coals of their cigarettes marked where they were. The wind sliced lower, and the heavy seed heads of the sea oats clashed together on their tall stalks. Macrae stepped down from the boardwalk, spreading his toes over a patch of wet sand, pocked and stippled by the rain. Porter stopped on the planks above and stood, looking both ways along the horizon, the cigarette's red tip rising and falling from his lips. Macrae raised his eyes.

"You ever kill anybody before?" he said.

"Huh." Porter shook his head. "You?"

"Not that I know of," Macrae said. "Not that I ever planned on." He looked at Charlie. Porter did too.

"What do you want?" Charlie stroked the backs of his fingers, hands passing cyclically one over the other. "I'll tell you, boys . . . Only if it seemed like a good idea at the time."

It was Charlie's idea that they leave the hotel mostly boarded up, especially on the road side, so no lights would show at night. They took down most of the shutters in back, though, and Macrae unsealed a door that let him onto a third-floor gallery overlooking the road and the marsh. If the weather was fair, he would often sit there in the evening, cradling a glass of whiskey, watching the sun go down over the mazy channels that worked their interlocked ways through the plane of saw grass.

As often, he would sit on the beach side, where on the height of the dune beside the boardwalk there was a small octagonal gazebo, all screened in, a rusted tin weathervane whining on its roof's peak. Here was a bench where Macrae could sit sheltered if it happened to be raining, watching the gray water roll in and foam and shatter on the sand, letting his mind wash clean and lighten and fade to the palest blank.

The nights were often cold. They could find only one space heater, but still they fought shy of each other, sleeping in separate rooms. Porter made himself a nest in a corner of the kitchen, which the stove would partly heat. Most usually, Macrae would sleep in a roll of army blankets out on the third-floor porch, above the swamp.

The car was dug out, parked on a lattice of scrap lumber, so they were free to come or go. But the only one who ever went was Charlie, who made late-night runs up the coast to twenty-four-hour supermarkets near Murrell's Inlet or Myrtle Beach, re-stocking the canned goods and cigarettes and booze. He paid with money from the bank sacks, still uncounted, undivided. These lay in a scatter along with the guns, jumbled up with the damp puzzles and board games and mildewed ancient paperbacks and magazines that coated the rickety wicker furniture filling the hotel's musty common room. But Macrae had dipped into a sack at one point, taking a couple of bundles of bills, hundreds, stiff and new. This currency seemed to have lost all connection with getting and spending, so far as he was concerned. He carried bundles in his pocket like worry stones, and sometimes, if he was sick of smoking, he'd take them out and fan their brittle edges with his thumb.

———

The big common room was still shuttered and stale; a few low-wattage lamps barely cut holes in the dim of it. Porter sat at a moldy card table, pushing puzzle pieces around with one finger. Macrae was sunk in a fanback chair of tattered rattan, turning the leaves of a comic book. Outside, the wind whined along the boarded sills. Charlie stuck his head in from the porch and studied them for a moment.

"This ain't going nowhere," he said. "Who wants to go crabbing?"

"I pass," Porter said. "Raining."

"Fixing to quit," Charlie said. "It's going to break up and blow over."

"Don't you need gear?" Macrae said.

"Got the gear." Charlie hooked his hand. "Bait too. Come on."

They got down a dented old aluminum canoe from the rafters under the building, crossed the road with it, and lowered it into the still swamp water beside the hotel's dock. Macrae fastened the painter to the railing and followed Charlie back under the building, where he discovered some lines rolled on sticks, a bushel basket, a long-handled net, and a soggy paper sack he thrust toward Macrae's nose.

"Yiii," Macrae said, twisting his face away.

"No good till it's ripe," Charlie said. "Let's hit it."

The rainclouds were unraveling in streaks on the pale sky; in one spot a white ring of sun was trying to burn through. Macrae sat in the bow of the canoe, facing ahead, a paddle resting across his knees. In the stern, Charlie put them forward, paddling and sometimes poling. His paddle made a booming sound whenever it struck the gunwale. The wind came across from the ocean side in stiff little punches, lifting Macrae's hair and letting it drop.

The canoe slid across a dark smooth surface of water and entered a channel barely wider than itself, twisting among mud banks thick with saw grass. Macrae stretched out and grazed a blade with his palm.

"Cut you," Charlie said redundantly, as Macrae licked blood

from a thin slice like a paper cut. The grasses all stood parallel, straight up and down like swords stuck in the mud. Everywhere the same sour salty smell. The narrow channel broke into a wider one and Charlie paddled to the right. On one side a naked mud bank was drilled with thumb-sized holes like a sieve. As they drew alongside, a host of bone-colored fiddler crabs raised their claws to ward off the shadow of the boat, then scuttled for the cover of the holes.

"There's crabs," Macrae said, rolling his neck as they went by. "Ain't they?"

"Fiddlers," Charlie said. "No eating on them." He aimed the canoe into another narrow, twisting stream. Macrae looked back. Past the jigsaws of saw grass and mud stood the line of houses facing the beach, ramshackle docks reaching out from them like fingers into the swamp, their rooflines low on the horizon and a great empty sky above them reflecting the ocean beyond.

"You got any system for getting us back?" Macrae said.

Charlie shrugged, booming the paddle against the side of the canoe. "Just keep winding around," he said. "They all got to come out somewhere."

Then the canoe emerged into a channel almost river wide. Charlie shipped his paddle and waited. Carried by the current, the canoe was drifting north, toward the low mound of the causeway there. A couple of fishermen were silhouetted tiny on the bridge.

"Tide's coming in," Charlie decided. "Old blues'll be getting an appetite."

Macrae rocked the canoe slightly, turning toward him. "There's tides in here?"

"Sure," Charlie said. "We're in the main channel now. But anyway, the whole swamp fills up and drains out twice a day." He drove his paddle back into the water. The canoe's prow cut a rippling V. A few yards out ahead of it, a cloud of something insect size rose hovering and then pattered back into the water like light rain.

"What's that?" Macrae said.

"Shrimp." Charlie turned his shoulder into his stroke. "Creek shrimp."

"I could eat a shrimp."

"No bigger'n a fingernail once you shell them out," Charlie said. "They're sweet . . . But you need a net to get them."

Now the sky was streaking blue and the sun had yellowed enough to shed a little warmth. Macrae wriggled his shoulders inside his threadbare sweater. Charlie nosed the canoe out of the main channel and began following zigzags toward the mainland shore.

"Where we headed?" Macrae said.

"Where nobody don't go," Charlie said. "Where we'll be the first to try it."

Three white egrets were stilting along the shore, before the dark line of cypresses and live oaks, legs deep in the water. As the canoe passed one of them pushed aloft and flew, long wings flogging slowly, its white body still as a letter printed on the air. Then the others followed, wheeling over the marsh.

"This is it," Charlie said. "Tie up."

Macrae raised the painter and knotted it to an overhanging branch. He swung his legs over the bow seat, reversing to face Charlie, who had dipped into the sack and was typing club-shaped weights to the deliquescent chunks of meat. The rot smell freshened and ballooned. Macrae smothered a gag.

"What was that when it was alive?" he said.

"Old turkey neck." Charlie tossed a tethered lump out over the water; it met its own reflection with a plop. He looped the stick and string around a strut of the canoe and passed a second line to Macrae.

"What do I do with this here?" Macrae said.

"Keep a feel on it," Charlie said.

Macrae rolled the string in his hand. "Like a pull?"

"Like a pick-pick-pick." Charlie rattled his fingers unevenly on the metal strut. "Irregular. When he starts grabbing at that meat."

Macrae lifted the string over his tense inverted forefinger. "I think I got one, then."

Charlie leaned forward on his knees. "Bring it in slow. Slow. That's the way."

In half-inch increments, Macrae reeled the string back around the stick, paying it slowly over his thumb. The offbeat twitching in the string would stop and he stopped too till it resumed. Occasionally an outright jerk throbbed through line into his hand.

"Don't rush him," Charlie chanted. "Don't scare him. Bring him up where we can see him." Quietly, craftily, he raised the net from the hull of the canoe.

Macrae lifted the line and leaned just slightly out. He could see the edges of the meat feathering in the water, a foot down, and definitely something working at the fringe, a flash of white, a flash of red.

"Good enough," Charlie whispered. He stabbed the net into the water and scooped it up. The crab hanging in the mesh had a carapace as large as his hand. Charlie flipped the net and shook it loose into the basket, where it rattled its armored legs on the staves and raised its fighting claws angrily. Charlie turned the net's handle over to Macrae and lifted his own line.

The same procedure, but this time there were two. One came up inside the net when Macrae dipped; another larger one clung to the outside by one claw. Charlie had to smack it with his paddle's blade to make it drop off in the basket. Immediately it lunged to attack the first one they had caught.

"Go, suckers." Charlie's eyes snapped green. Macrae watched him watch the crabs. For several days he had been trying to recall exactly what it was he'd ever liked about Charlie, and now here it was. Of course, it was the thing he disliked too.

He was thinking that for the next hour. Never seen Charlie so happy, he thought. The crabs kept coming, fast and hard. The basket was three-quarters full before they had slacked off.

"Done all right," Charlie said, giving the basket a loving glance. He sat back and began to wind in his line.

"Can't we cut those loose?" Macrae said. "I don't much want to ride back with that stink."

"The weights," Charlie said.

"What they set you back, about fifty cents?" Macrae said. "I think we can afford it."

Charlie shrugged and cut his line. Macrae watched the bait sink out of sight.

"Don't know how they can stand to be in the same water with that," he said. "Much less eat on it."

"It's nature," Charlie said.

"It ain't my nature." Macrae reached overhead and untied the painter and coiled it at his feet.

"What do you do but go after what you want?" Charlie picked up the paddle and pushed off from the bank. Macrae sat still facing him. In the top layer of the basket, the crabs last caught kept on clawing at each other, angling for position on the backs of the ones below.

"You know your way around this place," Macrae said. "I'm surprised you ever would have left."

"This is a rich-people place," Charlie said. "By and large." He pushed his paddle into the water and dug. "Not for the like of me. My old man killed himself working in that paper mill you smelled over there in town. Didn't have no beach house, I'll tell you that."

"Still," Macrae said.

"Still, what?" Charlie said. "What about you, what did you leave home for?"

"I don't know," Macrae said. "Land's about played out, I guess. I'm not much farmer anyway. Ain't nobody living like that anymore, besides. You saw what it was like yourself." He tilted his head and looked at their two reflections traveling on the inky surface of the water. "Well, I just don't know, I guess."

Charlie shipped his paddle, letting the canoe drift while the water beaded off the blade.

"Yeah," he said. "I been a long time gone. There was a time I thought I'd set the world on fire, but I got to eat that." He grinned one-sidedly, showing a dog tooth. "Course there was some made a worse meal of it than I did."

Macrae stared into the crab basket. The ones they'd had in Baltimore, he recalled, had come already cooked. That seemed way back in a time of ancient innocence, before he'd become accessory to four murders. Charlie poked the paddle into the basket.

"Stir it up, fellas," he said. "Let's mix it up."

The crabs lashed at each other, burbled, and rattled.

"They're all against each other, aren't they?" Macrae said. The crabs had settled into new locks, clutching each other at every point. Macrae thought he saw one that had closed a death grip on itself.

"Oh yes," Charlie said, returning the paddle to the water. "That's nature too."

twenty-five

Macrae walked to the line of the surf and dumped a basket full of fractured crab shell in at the water's edge. Foam came sucking around his ankles. The undertow of the third or fourth wave swept the last broken claw clean away from the sand. He turned and went back to set the basket down at the foot of the stairs that rose on the dune's ocean side, meaning to come back and collect it later, when he returned. At the height of the dune, a changeable wind beat down the sea oats and tore at the screens of the little gazebo. The weathervane whined on the roof peak as it switched direction.

He put his hands in his pants pockets and headed south along the beach. Though it was cold he was going barefoot, for better traction on the sand. The wind was blowing on his back, splitting his hair over the back of his head and sweeping it forward into his face. He turned up the collar of his coat, the same pea coat he'd bought about this time last year with some of the first money he and Charlie made together.

Black groins built of phone poles and railroad ties chopped up the beach in seventy-yard sections, jutting through the breakers and into deeper water. Macrae zigzagged, going high on the beach to cross each groin, then cutting back down to where the wet packed sand made easier footing. The tide was going out. To his left, the close row of boarded houses mutely divided the beach from the road and the marsh beyond it. The wind had whipped the water into stiff peaks, each with a steely gleam in the cold sunlight.

In a mile or maybe a mile and a half he came to the last house and crossed over the last ground. A small area of the long sand spit beyond had been corralled off for public parking by a stone-and-asphalt breakwater. A jacked-up truck and a rusting red van were parked there, probably belonging to the clutch of fishermen who had set up poles and folding chairs over on the creek side. Macrae kept walking alongside the ocean, just clear of the waves rushing in on the shore. A flock of sandpipers whirled out just ahead of him, windblown; they landed and scurried over the sand and took flight again when he came nearer. The light seemed warmer now. It split prismatically on the sand, dividing into spectral colors.

In the water past the point the channel's current met the surf line in a foaming, rippling wedge. Good drowning spot, as Charlie had explained. On the far side was wild beach, with no construction, only bare sand and dunes and some stray pickets from an old sand fence—just that as far as the eye could see. Macrae moved a little farther around the channel's curve. A pelican came in flying low over his shoulder and dumped itself in the middle of the creek. Macrae stopped to look at it. Charlie had pointed out flights of pelicans passing over the ocean but Macrae hadn't been so near to one before. Another flopped down where the first one had, and then, behind it, a third. The tidal current carried them in a sedate file of three back toward the silver-gray of the ocean. They seemed unusually buoyant, floating comically high on the water. When the tide had brought the first pelican to the turbulence where the creek channel ran into the waves, it hauled itself into the air and made a long slow banking glide in a semicircle over Macrae's shoulder and fell onto the surface of the creek awkwardly as a bucket of slops dumped from the sky. The second and third pelicans repeated these same movements. Macrae watched as the last one folded its wings and drew in its dippered beak, composing itself in line with the others, floating back to the ocean as if they were all on a track.

The first bird lifted and again flew back. Maybe it was a game to them, Macrae thought, maybe something they didn't choose. He was fixed to the sight of them, though, wrapped up in their cycle.

His fingers crawled unconsciously in his pockets, turning back corners of the bills he carried there, as if for luck. With the same unbreakable fascination he'd stood rooted before the Port Authority ball machine, in the primeval time before Charlie. Now his feet were sinking in the sand and he didn't know what would ever move him from the spot, but after innumerable repetitions, the pelicans changed their minds and flew away for good.

Macrae turned and walked along the ocean the way he had come. A thought was forming in his head but he couldn't complete it. He could make the outlines but not the center. It was like trying to peer around a hair or some encrustation on the surface of his eye. The wind kept beating full in his face, making him squint and drop his head, and he had to lean over into it to proceed. He changed direction, cutting diagonally across the sand spit toward the fishermen. A couple of brown wharf rats looked at him from behind the rocks of the breakwater. He scrambled over it and crossed the pitted parking area toward the road.

As soon as he had come behind the line of houses, the wind dropped sharply off. The edges of his face felt as if they had been planed smooth or sanded by the wind. He walked along the row of power-line poles dividing the road's edge from the creek, one eye on the ground ahead of him, alert for sandspurs or broken bottle glass. Ahead, in the swamp, were the first banks of saw grass, where the creek lost its direction and became a maze. It was curiously quiet along the road, except for cries of gulls straying overhead, because the houses cut off the surf sound along with the wind. In this half silence he heard a familiar corkscrew sound some distance away, building and receding and rising again. Behind came a couple of low *crumps* that might be distant gunfire. It was these that made him want to find a hole to hide in, but somehow he kept walking in the open at the same pace he had set before.

At the dogleg where the island widened was a slick spot that looked almost like a road-surface mirage, but when the speeding car struck it, sheets of real water curved up from both sides. It was the beat Corolla, screaming to a halt at Macrae's knees. Charlie popped the passenger door and took off again with Macrae still scrambling half-aboard.

"Where's Porter?" Macrae said. There was no one in the back-seat, just a couple of shotguns clattering together, not half their arsenal. Through the back glass he saw a police car appear at the dogleg, red lights swirling on the roof. The siren sound whipped louder around his ears.

"The hell you going?" Macrae said. "It's a dead end down here, if you don't know."

"Looking for a place to turn around." The words squeezed out between Charlie's teeth.

"You're about out of choices," Macrae said.

Charlie beat the butt of his fist on the steering wheel. Macrae watched the cracked plastic flexing under the strikes. He looked over his shoulder again. The police car was coming up fast into the rear windshield.

"Gaining on you," Macrae said.

"That's all right," Charlie gritted out. "Let him get a little closer."

Macrae's chest was breathlessly tight. They were streaking along past the last few houses. Charlie lifted his foot from the gas pedal and then jammed it again, aiming for the low hump of the breakwater that ringed the public parking. Right foot still flattening the accelerator, he locked the brakes with his left and wrenched the wheel around. The Corolla cut a tight fishtail, throwing up a wave of smoke and sand. The rear fender slapped carelessly into one of the big granite boulders of the breakwater. Macrae made brief contact with a pair of astonished eyes in the patrol car as it overshot them. Then Charlie was barreling north on the empty road.

"Wouldn't of thought this old car had a move like that in it," Macrae said.

"You never know," Charlie said. He had relaxed just slightly, the points of his shoulder blades brushing the seat back. "You never know."

Macrae looked behind. The patrol car had hung its front end on the rocks of the breakwater; its back wheels were spinning up sand and gravel. One of the officers had got out and was trying to push it loose. The fishermen had thrown down their poles and were lumbering across the soft sand to assist.

The breakwater dropped out of sight as Charlie swished through the puddle again and negotiated the dogleg. As Macrae shifted forward, his hand knocked two of the big pistols together. He picked one up and looked at it. The barrel was warm, with a gunpowder tang when he sniffed the rim.

"Where's Porter?" Macrae said. Charlie didn't answer him.

"Thought I heard some shooting," Macrae said.

"Yeah," Charlie said. "You might of, at that."

On the left side of the car the trees fell away. The wide expanse of marsh was just beyond the shoulder there. Charlie held the car grooved to the center line, straightening out the snake-bend curves of the road. The weight of the pistol dragged at Macrae's wrist. He laid it on the seat and wiped his hands on his pants legs.

"Sweet of you to pick *me* up anyhow," he muttered. "Otherwise I might just sorta missed out on this whole thing."

"I didn't have no choice in the matter," Charlie said. "I got myself headed off down this way."

"Ah." Macrae cocked his head toward the sound of a siren cranking up again behind them. "Well, I guess they got themselves unstuck."

"It don't matter," Charlie said. "We got a good lead."

"Glad to hear it," Macrae said. He raised a finger toward the windshield. "What about that?"

The low line of the causeway was visible now across the swamp, though still maybe half a mile distant. Across it came another local police car, followed by two from the highway patrol. A paddy-wagon type of police van brought up the rear. Charlie exhaled with a whistling sound, but he didn't even begin to slacken speed.

"Hell," Macrae said. "Look at the Smokies. Not just the local yokels now . . ."

"We'll just have to beat them to the punch," Charlie said. "Tell me about it."

Charlie laid the car into another curve. Briefly the causeway was blocked from their view; then it reappeared, naked of traffic. Macrae knew the police would all be somewhere on the road ahead. There was only the one road. Charlie swept through a curve to the left. At its extremity, Macrae looked back and got a glimpse of the first police car ripping along a few hairpin twists behind them. The Corolla slammed down into a short straightaway that passed a small white church, no bigger than a boxcar, built on stilts out on the swamp. Twenty or thirty yards farther on, two patrol cars and the van were set up in a roadblock: Macrae saw a couple of Smoky hats sticking up from behind the dome lights.

"Will you shoot those sonsabitches?" Charlie cried.

"*No.*" Macrae barely breathed the word. Charlie was pumping the gas like a treadle, hunched so far forward his nose flattened on the glass. Macrae knew he'd never stop. But they were already past the church and rifling head-on for the roadblock before he was able to break the spell of stillness. With both hands he grabbed the wheel and whirled it toward the swamp.

A power pole ripped into the car's front end and for a split second Macrae saw everything quick-frozen. He had just time to bend his head away, so it was his shoulder that broke the windshield. High above the swamp, he levitated. Big chunks of glass were showering around him, their blunt beveled edges catching the sun, flashing like diamonds in his eye. Macrae's heart stopped at their beauty. He kept revolving slowly in midair. The whirling shards of glass illuminated him like stars in the galaxy of death he'd somehow come to inhabit. One of the pistols was orbiting him; the dark hollow of its muzzle covered him and then rotated past. He saw things that couldn't be there: Lacy's eyes ruefully on him again, her sleek pale body shimmering underwater at the pond. He saw Porter dragging himself with his arms alone up a flight of stairs in the hotel, his thigh shattered by a gunshot, bleeding heavily from the wound. His father was crossing from the barn to the house when he slapped a hand across his rib cage and dropped doubled over to the ground. Macrae saw himself stooping to raise the old man by a shoulder, saw the blue-blind eyes combing over his face.

I'll tell you what, boy, you don't think. Never knew what you meant to do before you done it. Never had a thought until you said it. Trouble is, you don't even talk that much.

Macrae cannonballed into the swamp, throwing up a spume of foul black water. "Charlie's gonna kill me," he said through a mouthful of mud, amazed at the sound of his own voice. He was bleeding in a couple of places, but all his arms and legs seemed to be operational as he floundered across the stagnant open water toward the nearest ridge of mud. A bullhorn was squawking something after him and a couple of bullets spat into the water—warning shots, Macrae figured, or else just badly aimed.

By saw-grass stems he hauled himself onto the bank and rolled across it clear into the shallow stream on the other side. Under the moving water the mud was packed enough to take his weight and he ran, stooped low, along the winding of it. The bullhorn kept on going; he gathered from the words he could make out they hadn't yet got hold of Charlie either.

The stream petered out and left him staggering across an open mud flat before he'd recognized what it was. Instantly he was sucked thigh deep in black fluff mud, soft and cloudy as jelly. He was pinned out in the open, in clear view of the new police cars now coming across the causeway. His legs flailed uselessly. Oyster shells down in the deep mud cut his calves and slashed the soles of his bare feet. From the causeway bridge another bullhorn called on him to surrender. He threw himself forward onto his chest and half swam over the mud toward the closest bank. Some shots struck the mud flat near him, with a spattering sound. Again he clutched the saw grass, slicing the heels of his hands, and flipped himself over into the next channel, where he landed belly down, nose to nose with an eight-foot alligator. The alligator snorted, reared back, and reversed itself, climbing the next mud bank. Macrae hadn't had the time to scream or wet his pants. The alligator had flattened a trail through the saw grass and Macrae wormed his way along this.

This time it was the main channel on the other side. The alligator was already drifting several yards downstream—at this distance it could have passed for driftwood. The tide was coming in and Macrae was startled to find himself footless in the water. The current was stronger, too, than he'd expected. He got a mouthful of water and spat it out and swam diagonally across the current till he reached the opposite bank.

When he stuck his head up cautiously out of the saw grass he saw he'd made it halfway to the mainland shore. The bullhorns were still keeping it up but they seemed fainter now, and farther away. He dropped into the next narrow winding stream and ran bent low along its route, making good time till something tripped him and he fell headlong, struggling to thrash himself clear. The biggest convention of crabs he ever might imagine. Two or three had clamped onto his pants leg; with a wild kick, he shook them loose. The crabs rejoined the others, burbling and swarming over whatever it was half-sunk in the mud. There was an awful stench to the thing. Macrae covered his mouth with his ripped sleeve. The rising tide was shifting the corpse; its rotting limbs stirred in the water, and this, along with the crabs scuttling all over it, gave it a misleading look of animation. A purple drowned-man bloat was on the few areas of flesh that were yet unpicked. One skeletal hand raised in an ambiguous gesture. Crabs tugging at the arm made the fingers seem to shiver.

Macrae flung himself onto a mud bank, dropped on his hands and knees, and retched himself dry. Crabwise, he backed away from the pool of vomit, down in the water on the other side. Dull and distant he could hear the sound of a motorboat coming up the channel and on it a bullhorn still calling for him to give himself up. He was trembling now, and his strength was gone. Wallowing, he dug himself shallowly into the mud alongside the bank, slathering his head with it, sinking down all the way to his eyelids like an alligator himself.

The searchers circled him for most of the day. Sometimes they were very near. Macrae heard them gasping and shouting when they fell upon the body of the drowned man. By then he didn't much care if they got him or not but he didn't have the resolution to call out to them.

Part of the time he might have even slept. Maybe it was dream and not hallucination when he thought the carcass that he'd stumbled on was Charlie. Though he knew it couldn't be . . . He'd seen an eyehole under the mask of crabs, exchanged a look of recognition.

The tide lifted him, then as it receded it lowered him back into the mud. Round sunset the searchers went away, but Macrae didn't stick his head up. A pair of egrets stalked solemnly past him, watching him from the sides of their heads. One walked stiltlike on long orange legs up into the saw grass, kicked itself into the air, and flew. The other waited, curving the long bend of its undulant neck this way and that, as though it would admire its reflection on the black water. The white feathers on its back and head were mussed by the wind. Of a sudden the egret drove its narrow head into the water and jerked back with a fish glimmering in its beak. The fish sparkled, shook a drop from its tail going down, then it was gone.

Macrae waited out the sunset. On every exposed part of him the mud dried and cracked. Against the red round of the sun he thought he saw a heron flying. He stayed put until it was solid night. When finally he felt willing to move he couldn't at first, so stiff with cold his joints were. But at last he could pry himself up from the mud. There was moon enough to see by. He found his way to the mainland shore and went stumbling over the hummocky land, under the oaks and cypresses, darkness of a cave. Once he crossed too near the yard of some isolated house, where a chained dog barked at him hysterically, hurling itself to the limit of its tether.

There seemed to be no other houses backing on the swamp. At last he got out of the low-lying thicket, emerging into a forest of pines. More widely spaced, these trees let in more moonlight, and the needle carpet was sweet smelling and grateful to his lacerated feet. There were a couple of deer moving a safe distance ahead of him, stopping when he stopped, revolving their long mule ears as they looked back. He saw them for the first time clearly as they crossed the highway, two does and a juvenile buck, filing silently into the pines on the other side.

The highway ran up and down, string straight, the moonlight pooling on it like more water. Macrae had come out by an abandoned filling station, a cinderblock pillbox with a cracked concrete pad in front. He rested there, propped on a rusting pump. A pair of headlights came boring down the road. Macrae didn't have the heart to hide himself. He waited, in plain view. The car pulled up and cracked a door. Charlie, in some other unfamiliar stolen car. Macrae hesitated, then climbed in.

twenty-six

There was a weird oppressive silence in the room. Macrae blinked his eyes stickily, turned his head against a pillow that lumped under a quilted coverlet. He saw a second double bed across the room and along the wall a few cheaply veneered pieces of furniture, bureau, desk, night stand. The window was shrouded in heavy dull green drapery. Above the curtain rod, the patterned paper peeled around a water stain.

The silence was the absence of the surf. Macrae sat painfully up. Every so often he could hear a car pass, tugging air down the road outside. Odd that he didn't remember coming here at all. He had been sleeping on top of the coverlet it seemed, and he still had on his swamp-stained pants, which had dried cakily along his legs. There was a rank marshy smell in the room, but maybe he had brought that with him.

He stood up and shucked the pants off of him, flaking a silt of dried mud onto the balding shag carpet. The fixtures in the bathroom were yellow stained and there was mildew on the shower curtain but the towels looked newish and freshly laundered. Macrae soaked his feet in the tub for a while, then turned on the shower. The soles of his feet were frayed along every edge and he had long shallow cuts wrapping his legs to the knee. His palms and forearms were chewed up too, and his right shoulder ached particularly. The cuts were bloodless, though, their edges whitened pale. Salt in the water accounted for that, Macrae supposed.

He stayed in the shower till the hot water flogged most of the ague out of his joints, then got out and walked drizzling into the main room, a towel furled around his hips. Now he saw on the other shabby bed a pile of clothing new from the store, a sweatshirt and a pair of blue twill pants and thick white socks and red hightop tennis shoes. Tags were strung to them on plastic thongs. Macrae clipped the tags off with his teeth, put on the pants and then the sweatshirt. The shoes were a loose fit but would do. He picked up the ragged pants he'd dragged through the swamp and dug out the bundles of cash and his pocketknife. The money was still damp and he could feel it pressing soggily against his thigh through the pockets of the new pants. He rinsed the knife in fresh water, working grit out of the hinge, under the stream from the cold tap, and dried it off as best he could with a washrag.

The rank smell persisted in the room. Macrae crammed his old pants into a small plastic wastebasket and opened the door and stepped outside. The highway was the fourth boundary of the three-sided box of the one-story motel. Metal-spring rockers, all painted pink and rusting patchily, were placed to the left of every room door. Behind him the door sucked shut on an air hinge. Macrae tried the knob, locked automatically. Maybe Charlie was somewhere with the key. On the other hand, there was nothing left inside he cared to keep.

Near the road was the motel office, and attached to it a little restaurant. Macrae made for that. Inside, a dial clock showed quarter to ten. A single waitress was on duty, Charlie her only customer. He sat near the plate-glass window that overlooked the road, eating pigs in blankets and squinting at the funny pages folded on the table next to the room key, which was wired to a big plastic disc. The waitress came bearing a coffee pot as Macrae drew back a chair and sat down.

"Just coffee is fine," Macrae said, waving away a shrink-wrapped menu card. The waitress poured and went back to the kitchen.

"I'd say you were entitled to an appetite," Charlie said, his eyes locked on *Peanuts*. "Been a day and a night since you last ate."

"Where are we?" Macrae said.

"Manning," Charlie said. "I think that's it."

"Where's that?"

"Oh, around fifty, sixty miles I guess," Charlie said. He didn't mention to or from what.

Shakily Macrae peeled open a plastic pot of creamer and dumped it into his coffee cup. "So," he said. "You bought me clothes."

"Had to be done," Charlie said. He snickered and turned the paper over to look at Ann Landers. "Yours was pretty well past it, I'd say."

"How'd you know my shoe size?" Macrae said.

"Eyeballed it." Charlie cut a section of pancake and sausage with the edge of his fork. Macrae stretched his leg out and inspected the shoe flaming on his foot.

"They didn't have nothing but this red?" he said.

"Red was on sale," Charlie mumbled through his mouthful.

Macrae raised the cup to his mouth. His throat was sore when he swallowed. No wonder if he took cold from laying up in the cold swamp water all that day before. The smell of seasoned meat and syrup dizzied him but he couldn't think of actually eating himself. He was beyond hungry and it had been a long time since he felt that way, almost a year if he reckoned it back.

"We make the paper?" he said reluctantly.

Charlie glanced neutrally over and pushed the folded front section across the table. Macrae picked it up and leafed to the interior. For a while he read, his stomach knotting tighter. Then he put the paper down and reached for the pack of cigarettes near Charlie's plate.

"Hell, wouldn't you know it," Macrae said. "They weren't even looking for us, not especially. Just checking out a break-in."

"They sure to God found us, though, didn't they?" Charlie said.

Macrae rolled the cigarette through his fingers. "Porter's dead," he said.

"Keep your voice down."

"He made it to the hospital," Macrae said. "But he didn't make it through the night."

"I can read the same as you," Charlie said, watching what he was doing on his plate. "Anyhow, we're better off."

Macrae stared at him as he raised his fork. A white circlet of sausage was furled in a flap of pancake pinned to it by the tines. On its underside a lucid drop of syrup and grease was swelling.

"What did I say?" Charlie asked him. He waited a moment, then closed his front teeth on the morsel. The fork came back naked in his hand.

"I'll give you the credit, Charlie," Macrae said. "You might of saved my life a time or two."

"If it seemed like the right thing to do at the time," Charlie said. He chewed. His pale eyes strayed to the window.

"But that don't mean you own it," Macrae said. "That don't make it yours to take."

"What are you talking about?" Charlie was still looking out the window, tracking the odd car that ran up and down the road under the overcast sky. Once in a while, with the clouds shifting, there came a fitful brightening of the light. Macrae stretched his hand across the table and picked up the key and got up and left the restaurant.

Inside the room he released the lever that locked the door and went to lie down on the bed. He was still carrying the unlit cigarette from Charlie's pack and now he found a pack of matches in the ashtray on the nightstand and struck fire to it. He lay there, exhaling smoke toward the ceiling. There was another water stain fanning out from the molding where it joined the wall, with a crack running through it, zigzagging about halfway across the room, stopping just short of the bowl light fixture. Macrae had been closer to a ceiling before, on the top bunk of a jail cell or on his rack at different army posts. The cigarette burned out on the filter and he felt for the ashtray and let the nub drop. The door creaked and Charlie came in and stood to one side as the air hinge sucked it shut.

Macrae swung his feet to the floor and got up. He dug out a

bundle of bills from his left-hand pocket and held it out to Charlie. "For the clothes and whatever," he said.

Feeling the money, Charlie clicked his tongue against his teeth. "That's a shot in the arm," he said. "That should cover it and then some. Well, and I was getting a little light on cash."

"It's your split. I guess you earned it," Macrae said. "You know, it's time to part company."

"Okay," Charlie said. "All right." He stooped and opened the top bureau drawer and took out two of the big magnum revolvers, holding them by the barrels. "Here, then, take your pick. A little damp, but they ought to do. They're loaded but there ain't no extra ammo."

"What do you think I want with one?" Macrae said. "I never planned on killing anybody."

"It might be a meal ticket . . ." Charlie shrugged. "Never know when one might come in handy. Besides, you gave me money, didn't you?"

Macrae took the pistol in Charlie's left hand and stuck it down the back of the new pants. He pulled the sweatshirt's hem out to cover the grip. "How'd you manage to hang on to these, anyhow?" he said.

"Had them buttoned in my shirt," Charlie said.

"Well," Macrae said. "It's a wonder they didn't drown you." He stepped around Charlie and opened the door.

"Luck," Charlie said.

Macrae didn't look back. He headed toward town along the highway's shoulder, the stiff new cloth of the twill pants rustling. His ears were still reaching for the sound of the surf. Every step scraped the gun barrel over his coccyx. The town was small enough to actually have an edge but it looked big enough to probably have a bus station.

It was late when he crawled off the bus at the Nashville Greyhound station, lightheaded and half-sick to his stomach from living on Coke and candy bars all the day and a half of inefficient travel. He walked over to Broad just to shake out his legs. Nothing was open but the bars and porno movies, and it was cold enough to have flushed all the vagrants off the street. A mean little wind sucked around the crew neck of his sweatshirt. He couldn't remember if he'd ditched his pea coat in the Manning motel room or if perhaps he'd shed it while he was still in the swamp.

An hour wait, and he caught a local bus and transferred to another that brought him into the southern suburbs. From there he walked, on the highway's shoulder. At long rare intervals headlights of a car came boring past him but he didn't even bother to stick out his thumb. As soon as he could he turned off and went the rest of the way roundabout on the back roads; it was longer but he didn't like being exposed on the long dark reaches of the blacktop. By that time he had ceased to feel the cold. There was a moon about half-full, whirling spectrally among the branches of some trees gone prematurely bare. Macrae was singing as he walked, scraps of old ballads, bits of things he recalled, maybe from Laidlaw's porch, unable to finish a one of them.

Near dawn he crossed the cattle gap and went staggering around the bend of the track toward the house. No light showed at the windows, but at this time that was no surprise. The moon had gone down and the black of the sky was washing out to gray. He checked first up and down the path that ran between the house and the barn but his father's body was not where he had envisioned it. Instead he found him on the floor of the porch, fallen between two of the crotchety rockers. He lay more or less on his side with one arm raised and partly covering his face. His white hair stuck out in all directions like a pattern of frost.

Macrae knelt a little way from him, reached a finger toward his wrist. The whole body rocked stiffly at the touch. He heard a dog snoring, up under the floorboards. There was no smell from the old man's body, which was dry and brittle as kindling wood. Well, Macrae was thinking, he never was anything else but himself. He lifted the body, scarcely a weight, shouldered his way through the unlocked door, and laid it on the sofa inside. A fire was already built in the stove and he had only to strike a match to it. The old man's eyes had set half-open and they caught the firelight as it rose. Macrae thumbed the eyelids shut, but they would not stay. There were no coins in his pockets. He went out to the yard and searched on hands and knees until he found two flattish pebbles. Head on his paws, Sooner studied him silently, from under the porch.

Inside, Macrae adjusted his father's body to a position that resembled comfort and put the little stones in place. He sat by the fire, whose light was dancing red and high, but the warmth of it didn't seem to reach him. After a while he went back outdoors. The key was hanging still in the truck's ignition and there was enough kick in the battery to turn it over. He drove to the highway and turned south, waiting for the heater to start working. In about a mile he came to a little roadside store, which to his surprise looked open.

He parked, got down, slapped the door shut. Under the overhang of the store's eaves was a large ice chest, padlocked, and beside it a mesh cage with something in it. Macrae stooped, hands on his knees. A small gray fox backed away from him as far as it could, its brindled fur bristling through the small squares of the wire. The cage was not quite high enough for it to stand.

Macrae pushed himself up and went into the store. A man in a polyester jumpsuit sat on a stool behind the cash register, watching a video on a tiny color television. Macrae circled the coolers on the wall, taking eggs, bacon, a stick of butter. He got a can of coffee from a shelf and carried it all back to the front. The cashier had black hair marcelled in sticky little waves around the borders of his baldness. He rang up Macrae's purchases without comment and put them in a paper sack. Macrae paid with a fifty from the bundle in his pocket and crammed the change back in his pants without looking at it.

"Where'd you come by that fox?" he said.

The cashier looked up from the TV with a half smile. "Trapped him," he said. "Out back there." He gestured with a limp hand through the back wall of the store, where the ridge rose still wooded and half-wild.

"That cage is too small for him," Macrae said. "Ought not to keep a fox caged nohow."

"Yeah?" the cashier said, his voice a tinny whine. "You plan on doing something about it?"

Macrae dragged the heavy pistol out of the back of his waistband and clicked back the hammer with his thumb. "I could kill you," he said.

"Hey," the cashier said. His mouth stayed open, but he didn't continue. From the TV came a breathy sound of sex. Macrae couldn't see the picture.

"Get on the floor," Macrae said wearily. He had forgotten cigarettes, and when the cashier had lowered himself behind the counter he took a pack from the wire rack by the register and dropped it in the bag. The cashier must have made some nervous movement; the stool fell over with a clatter on the floor. Macrae picked up the bag in his left hand and backed out the door. The fox made a stooping circle in the cage, looking at him with yellow eyes. Macrae groped the truck door open and put his groceries on the seat. He hooked his fingers through the cage roof and swung it up. The fox scrabbled for balance on the wire floor but quieted when Macrae set the cage in the bed of the truck. With one foot in the cab, he steadied the pistol and shot out the plate-glass window of the store. The kick slammed his arm against the frame; he'd been holding the gun too loose. But he figured it would be enough to keep the cashier's head down till he was down the road and out of sight.

Gray daylight filled the yard when he got back, though the sun had not yet risen above the line of the ridge. Macrae got out and carried his grocery sack to the kitchen and walked back into the front room to feed the fire. His father's body was clearly visible in the freshening daylight but he had no better idea what to do about it than he'd had before. Outside, the dogs had surrounded the truck and were all barking crazily at the fox. Macrae went out and lowered the tailgate. The fox stirred uneasily, squirting a musk smell from its glands, looking from one dog to another with its yellow eyes hot. Sooner jumped up, front paws on the tailgate, and Macrae batted the dog back down. He undid the catches to the cage and turned back the top. The fox shrank low, but when Macrae reached in to touch it, it lunged and bit through the ball of his thumb. As Macrae jumped back, wringing his hand, the fox sprang over the far rim of the truck bed and streaked for the woods, a gray blur low to the ground, with all the dogs after it, uselessly yapping.

Macrae sucked the blood from his thumb and examined the neat pattern of punctures. The idea of rabies crossed his mind, but really the fox had done no more than any sane fox would probably do. The dogs' barking was getting fainter up on the hill. Macrae went back to the kitchen and rooted under the sink for the bottles of peroxide and Betadine. Standing over the sink, he did his best to sterilize the wound. Charlie's way. He sat at the kitchen table under the swinging bulb, watching the brown splatter of iodine dry on his skin. The grocery sack slumped on the drainboard. Macrae didn't even have the concentration to get up and light himself a cigarette.

Finally, however, he scooted his chair toward the wall phone and dialed. On the fourth ring, Laidlaw answered sleepily.

"Hello," he said. Then, after a pause, "Who's there?"

"Macrae." The name was a croak.

"Macrae?" Laidlaw yawned. "Where you at?"

Macrae couldn't seem to answer. The receiver hummed in his ear like a conch shell.

"Macrae," Laidlaw said, "you need some help, or what?"

"I guess I do," Macrae said. "Yeah. In the worst way."

twenty-seven

High on the hillside, the blunt green cedars mingled with a few dogwoods, whose leaves had gone the color of a dried bloodstain. Amid them stood a single sweetgum tree, with broad wedgy leaves turning the warm shades of a ripening peach. Left of the sweetgum was an oblong of limestone set in the ground, roughly the size of a double mattress. They'd tried digging on two sides of it and run into the solid bedrock. On the third edge a hole had sunk some four feet deep, enough that it was awkward now for two to work together. Rodney was in it, turning up dirt, while Macrae and Laidlaw stood by, Macrae leaning on the idle shovel. The blade of Rodney's shovel rang on stone and he flinched and took his stung hands away from the haft.

"This thing is an iceberg," Rodney said. He rolled his eyes and glared at the rock. "I swear."

Laidlaw stepped forward and peered in the hole. "You're still on the edge, looks like," he said. "Just dig around it. No law says it has to be dead straight, is there?"

"There's no law says anything about it," Macrae said.

Rodney bent his head and drove the shovel down. He turned up a few more bladefuls of dirt, adding them to the mound on the far side of the hole, then stopped again and wiped his brow with his left forearm. "There's people do this for a living," he said. "There's graveyards. I mean . . ." He looked around. "You don't plan to keep drawing welfare on him, I don't think."

"Ain't nobody in this crowd drawing welfare," Laidlaw said. "Have a little respect for the dead."

"Well, shut my mouth," Rodney said.

"I'll spell you awhile." Laidlaw got down in the hole and took the shovel. Rodney set his hands on the rock rim and vaulted up and out, landing in a crouch, then straightening to stand by Macrae.

"Why by this rock?" he said, kicking at the pits of it with the torn leather toe of his brogan. "Be easier digging down on the flat."

"It's a good place here," Macrae said. He looked at the peach-colored leaves of the sweetgum, rising in the breeze. "Rock'll make a marker."

"That's true," Rodney said. "You could carve it, even."

Macrae shrugged. "Might do." He watched the dirt coming up from the hole, shaking off the shovel blade. An earthworm twisted its banded self, half-in and half-out of a clod.

"Who's gonna bury Porter?" Rodney said.

"Don't know," Macrae said. "I guess the government'll have to."

"I liked Porter," Rodney said.

"So did I," Macrae said. "I'd be willing to handle the job myself but I guess it just ain't convenient."

"No," Rodney said. He put his hand on Macrae's shoulder, curving his fingers into the pit behind his collarbone. Laidlaw straightened up, blowing. Macrae slipped out from under Rodney's hand and jumped down in the hole with his shovel held across his chest.

"Take a break," Macrae said.

Laidlaw climbed out and Macrae started digging. The shaft was twisting some, away from the stone, following the curve of the stone as it entered the earth—or emerged from it, more like. It wasn't such hard digging so long as he could manage to keep off the rock. Evidently it had been a rainy fall so far. He dug until he struck a vein of hard yellow clay, then paused.

"What do you think?" he said.

"Your head's sticking out yet," Rodney said. "How tall are you?"

"Tall enough," Laidlaw said. "No law says it has to be just so deep, is there?"

"No law," Macrae said. He levered himself out and stuck the shovel deep enough to hold itself in the mound of loosened dirt.

"Well, now," Laidlaw said.

The body lay beside the trunk of the sweetgum tree, sewn loosely in a sheet, then wrapped in a blanket, as for a burial at sea. Macrae had punched holes in the blanket and laced it up with baling twine. With baling twine he'd secured the arm that had stiffened above the old man's head, lowering it to the waist and fastening it, but loosely, so it might be disengaged.

Rodney and Laidlaw lifted the body, head and foot, though one man might easily have done it. Macrae looked on, his empty hands awkward, as they raised the body hovering over the grave.

"All right?" Rodney said.

"Wait a minute." Macrae spread two lengths of braided rope from the stone across the opening to the mounded earth where he stood himself. He held both rope ends, stooping slightly, heels of the red hightops sinking in the dirt. The bundled body was hammocked on the cords. Laidlaw and Rodney, with a rope's end apiece, helped lower. On the ropes the body slipped around the contour of the rock and into an underground pocket against the vein of clay. The other two released their ropes and Macrae drew them free. Across the shaft they faced each other.

"Somebody better say something," Rodney said.

Macrae swung his head away. He felt like something might be watching him, from where the woods thickened farther up the slope. The fox, maybe. He heard Laidlaw clear his throat and start to sing.

> "Oh, I went down in the valley to pray,
> studying about that good old way
> and who shall wear the starry crown.
> O Lord, show me the way.

> *"Oh, brothers, let's go down,*
> *come on down, don't you want to go down.*
> *Oh, brothers, let's go down,*
> *Down in the valley to pray . . ."*

Rodney joined in, and on the chorus Macrae followed. After all, it was an easy song.

> *"Oh, I went down in the valley to pray,*
> *studying about that good old way*
> *and who shall wear the starry crown.*
> *O Lord, show me the way.*
>
> *"Oh, fathers, let's go down,*
> *come on down, don't you want to go down.*
> *Oh, fathers, let's go down,*
> *Down in the valley to pray . . .*

They broke off. Silence, but for wind turning back the leaves and a woodpecker drilling a tree farther up the hill with a hollow tattoo. Macrae took hold of the shovel and began sweeping in dirt to cover the grave.

A clear day and a cloudless sky. The air was fresh from the cold, just short of freezing. In a ragged line they returned down the hill, carrying the muddy shovels and the lengths of rope. Rodney was the first to speak.

"You didn't think to invite Lacy to the funeral," he said.

"What?" Macrae said. "She went back to Philadelphia."

"Uh-unh," Rodney said. "She's still here."

Macrae glanced at Laidlaw, who walked with a shovel bouncing off his shoulder.

"That's right," Laidlaw said. "Saw her riding her bike around, not more than a day or so back."

"What's the matter?" Rodney said.

"Nothing," Macrae said. "Don't worry about me, boys. I'm just fine."

———

The cow was dry, so no milking to be done. There were other chores, repairs, the fences, but Macrae had no mind to work. Through the remains of the morning he sat rocking on the porch in the cold and in the afternoon went walking in the woods toward the ridge and beyond it. He had an idea he'd like to see the fox again but then you hardly ever saw a fox unless it was dead or in a trap, and this one was due to be shy for a good while. Besides, he had the dog pack with him.

Clouds were blowing in from the east, blue gray and swollen with rain. The wind felt damp whenever it blew, and the cloud cover brought a premature evening gloom. The other dogs had ranged far away from him; only Sooner kept near. Together they scared up a deer on the far slope of the ridge, a fat doe, lazy and almost unafraid. Sooner was the more alarmed, backing into Macrae's shanks and trembling with excitement, while the doe watched them from higher on the hill, her dun hide almost invisible against the dry leaves browning on the ground. Finally Sooner broke and charged with crazy barking and the doe broke too, to spring crashing around the curve of the hill and out of sight.

Macrae went back over the ridge and came down above the spot where they'd done the burial. The scar on the torn earth somehow troubled him now. He got down on his hands and knees and scooped leaves dropped from the sweetgum and some maples and a pin oak, sweeping them till the grave was covered over. His bitten thumb hurt, dragging over the rough ground. Macrae inspected it, squeezing the edges. Have to soak it in Epsom salts. He hoped it wouldn't need a doctor. Then Sooner came slamming out of the woods, breathless, tongue lolling, from chasing the deer. He ran to where Macrae was on his knees and tried to lick him in the face.

"Heart of a whore," Macrae said, and slapped the dog away. Sooner backed off and looked at him woundedly.

"All right," Macrae said. "Guess you're my dog now." He reached out a hand and Sooner reapproached, allowing his ears to be pulled and rubbed. There was a pattering on the limbs above as the wind climbed, and Macrae thought the rain had caught him, but when he came out into the open he saw that the sound was just leaves loosened by the wind, rattling down through the branches.

It was close enough to dark he broke a bale of hay and scattered it for the cows as he passed by the barn. The black bicycle was propped against the porch. He saw that first, before he saw her sitting in a rocker, hugging herself, her lips thin and blue.

"Hey there," he said, mounting the steps. "Don't you look cold, though. Hadn't got enough on for this weather."

Lacy stood up. She wore just a jean jacket over a T-shirt. "I heat up riding the bike," she said. "It's sitting still that gets you."

"You could have gone inside," Macrae said. "The door's unlocked."

"I was waiting for you," she said, with her teeth clicking slightly.

Macrae wrapped an arm over her shoulders and drew her through the doorway. There were live coals in the stove still. He added wood and poked it up and adjusted the dampers top and bottom. From the sofa's arm he lifted a plaid blanket and swirled it around her. "Something hot," he said. "You want coffee?"

Lacy's back bowed under the blanket. She adjusted the hem of it round her throat. "Got any tea?"

In the kitchen, Macrae put water on to boil, then ransacked the cabinets. In one he found a dusty box of Lipton tea bags, stale no doubt, but good enough to stain the water when he poured it in the cup. He strengthened the brew with a splash of bourbon and poured a straight shot for himself before he went back in the other room.

"You spiked it," she said, sipping and watching the fire flash at the chinks of the stove.

"Medicinal," Macrae said, and sat beside her on the sofa. Through the windows there was just hardly enough light for him to make out a few bare branches entangling the fading sky. "Thought you'd be gone by now," he said.

"Timing," Lacy said. "I changed my mind."

"Everybody's got a right to," Macrae said. He sucked at the rim of the jelly jar that he'd half filled with whiskey. The firelight was blushing on her face.

"What happened at the bank?" she said, not looking at him.

"It didn't go well," Macrae said.

"In a manner of speaking," she said. "I could figure that out from watching the news."

"There you have it," Macrae said.

"But did you kill those people," she said. "You?"

"Nope," Macrae said. "Not one. I never even fired my weapon." He could feel her eyes raking the side of his face and he made himself turn to face her. "It's the truth," he said. "I wouldn't keep it from you."

Lacy let her eyes float toward the fire.

"It was all Charlie," Macrae said. "Charlie shot the lot of them. Never stopped to ask us our opinion."

"And why," Lacy asked the stove. "What did he need to do it for?"

"Witnesses," Macrae said. "It's how he thinks. You should have gone ahead and went to Philadelphia."

Lacy set her empty cup down on the floor, tucked up her knees, and hugged them. "I wanted to be somewhere you could find me."

"That's nice," Macrae said. "But if I can find you, he can too."

"So what?" Lacy said. "I told you, I never cared so much about him anyway."

"Porter's dead," Macrae said. "There's nobody knows who went to the bank but you and me and Charlie."

"Well, goddammit, then." Lacy reached across his lap and took the jelly jar and had a drink. "You could always come with me."

"What, to Philly?" Macrae said. "What would I do there?"

"That's what you always say."

"Ain't nobody running me off of this place," Macrae said. "I'll go when I get good and ready."

345

"And that's your final say." Lacy shrugged off the blanket and her jacket in the same motion. "All right." She stood up, her back to the fire, and tore the T-shirt off over her head. It was very warm in the room by this time. Macrae pinched his lips dully between his front teeth. His bitten thumb had begun to throb.

"You plan on going in swimming somewhere?" he said.

"What do you think?" She kicked her khaki pants away. "Look at me," she said. "Do you want to draw my picture or what?"

Macrae looked.

"You can run but you can't hide," Lacy said.

Macrae reached out and put his hands on her bare legs, just above the knee. "It was somebody famous said that," he said.

"Maybe so," Lacy told him. "But I'm the one saying it now."

A long time later he woke up to the ends of her hair grazing over his face. She was kneeling over him, dressed again, her hair shrouding his head from the daylight.

"I've got to go get some things," she said. "But I'll be back."

"What?" Macrae tried to sit up, start thinking. His tongue was thick in his head.

"I'll be back sometime this afternoon," she said, standing up and way from him. The light struck full into his face. It was mid-morning. He'd slept in.

The kitchen showed signs she'd been up long before. Coffee was brewed in the pot; a skillet and plate had been used and washed and set to dry. Macrae poured coffee into a tin cup and went onto the porch, where the cold could help rouse him. It was sunny out. He had a smile stuck on his face and a general mood of careless happiness he knew was ill secured.

Once he felt decently alert he went upstairs and entered the room where his father had lived. An old-man musk still hung in the heavy air. The bed was unmade and clothes were scattered all over the place. One chair was overturned, lying on its side. Aptly enough, it looked as though a blind man lived there. Macrae picked his way around the bed and opened a top bureau drawer. Beneath the scrambled socks and ragged handkerchiefs were a couple of shoe boxes holding things of real or sentimental value. Macrae had been in trouble once for playing with them as a boy. He opened one now and found it mostly full of paper, some real estate documents and a couple of insurance policies. He closed the lid, figuring he'd have to get in touch with his sister now, though not today. An old woman, he'd think her, and God knows what she'd think of him . . . In the other box were trinkets: a couple of old pocketknives, broken cuff links, ornamental key chains with keys to which the locks were lost, his mother's wedding rings, a dented brass watch on a tarnished chain, and a tattered box half-full of twelve-gauge shotgun shells.

Macrae dropped a couple in his palm. They were ancient, the old paper kind. No call to do much bird hunting when you were blind, he reckoned. Anyway, these were buckshot loads, bought for varmints probably, heavy enough to knock down a dog that might have been plaguing the livestock. A deer, even, if you were the kind to hunt deer with a shotgun.

The shotgun hung on pegs above the bed's headboard. Macrae reached across the twisted blankets to take it down. Dust had thickened the oil on the action but it all worked smoothly enough after a couple of repetitions. He pushed three shells into the breech and put the rest of them in his pocket. The room cramped down on him. He had to lower his head under the ceiling, almost make a formal bow to get out under the lintel of the door.

He went downstairs and looked around. Another mess of blankets on the floor where he and Lacy had lain, occasionally sleeping. He picked these up and folded them, then put a stick on the fire. The heavyweight pistol Charlie had let him have lay on a table next to the TV, and he thought of taking it out with him but decided against it. He'd set the shotgun just beside the door and now he picked it up and shot the pump back for an extra safety and propped it back where it had been.

It was warmer out than the day before, didn't even fog his

breath. He might let the fire go out, he thought, clean the stove, and get a fresh start. Afterward, he would do that. He lifted yesterday's shovel from where it leaned against the porch rail and carried it out beyond the barn.

Rodney was right, it was easier digging down here, considerably so. The spot he'd chosen was behind the barn, a place where brown dead weeds stuck up through traces of old rotten straw. Maybe there'd been a manure pile here, though he couldn't say for sure. The earth was soft, black, and loamy, and light on the shovel's blade. Nothing particular nearby to mark the spot, but then this time he wouldn't want to mark it.

The hole was better than waist deep by the time he had to finally break for food. He washed up, made a fried-egg sandwich, and ate it standing over the stove. His urgency puzzled him a little, but he wanted the job finished, that was all. He cleaned the skillet, since Lacy had left it clean, before he went back out.

The hole dropped deeper, easily enough. There were some rocks around four feet, a few thick roots to cut with the shovel's blade. The dogs came out and circled him awhile, sniffing and rooting at the fresh dirt mound, before they lost interest and wandered off. He dug on, his arms and shoulders warming and stretching with the work. Standing on the matted strands of yesterday's hay, a couple of black cows regarded him, chewing their cuds.

At the bottom of the hole he struck into the swamp again. A dark malodorous liquid seeped over the mud and fouled his shoes. The mud was gluey, harder digging, and catching at the back of his throat was the smell of marsh and rotten meat, though surely he must have been imagining it. Anyway it was too soupy to keep digging, and the hole was shoulder deep. The edge crumbled on him as he tried to haul himself out, but finally he come worming over the lip.

He pushed himself up and sat cross-legged in the weeds. It was later than he'd realized, the hour before sunset, with the light already beginning to yellow and slant. Barn swallows wheeled crying around the eaves, their long tails forking the sky. Lacy would surely have been back by now, he thought, but she probably hadn't known where to find him. Macrae's face melted back into the smile of the morning. He shouldered the shovel and walked toward the house.

The shadows of the trees were stretching long and dark across the yard, and Macrae had his eye on the house, so he didn't see Charlie right away, leaning on the fender of the parked truck. He must have been there a little while, though, or the dogs would have been barking. Or else they never barked at all because they'd got to know him. Charlie pushed himself off the truck's hood and took a few steps toward Macrae, who brought the shovel down from his shoulder and held it across his chest. Several shovel lengths away he stopped, still within easy range for the big pistol he dangled at knee level, swinging stiffly over the ground like the stub of an amputated third leg.

"Ruint those new shoes I got you," Charlie said.

Macrae looked down. Both his feet were clubs of mud, and cold as death, he noticed now.

"What you been doing?" Charlie said.

"Digging a hole," Macrae said.

"Huh," Charlie said. "Where at?"

Macrae took one hand off the shovel and jerked his arm. "Back of the barn there."

"Oh," Charlie said, considering. "Expecting me, were you?"

Macrae nodded. "You're early, though." It occurred to him that Charlie might very well have stopped by Lacy's house before coming here.

"Well," Charlie said. "I guess that's the breaks."

Macrae thought of the mate to the pistol Charlie held, lying on the TV table inside the house. He began to move in a slow circle, not closing the distance, just trying to get the lowered sun at his back. In his pocket the lump of shotgun shells rubbed on the front of his thigh. Charlie was squinting.

"Don't," he said.

Macrae stopped still. Charlie kept squinting, the reddish light of the sun on his face. Otherwise his expression was thoughtful and remote.

"Back of the barn, you say?" he said. "I don't know. Maybe we better just go in the house."

Macrae balanced the shovel vertically on its blade, let go the handle, let it drop. He turned his back on Charlie and headed for the porch. A nail in the first step squealed under his weight. As that sound died, he just heard the slight ticking of a bicycle's sprockets back on the track, but he kept himself from turning around. The putrid marsh smell climbed in his head. He trudged up the steps one slow foot at a time and stopped and looked back with one hand holding a post.

Charlie was standing well back of the steps, keeping a comfortable distance. Some way in back of him the black bicycle lay dumped on its side with the front wheel spinning silently. Lacy moved away from it in a crouch, gathering handfuls of stones from the track.

"I guess you better go on in," Charlie said.

The pistol was pointed right at him now, Macrae saw. He had thought Charlie would follow him into the house so the shots would be muffled, but now it seemed more likely he would shoot him in the back just as he crossed the threshold. Reluctantly he turned and approached the door. The latch had not caught when he had gone out before, and a touch of his fingers was enough to send the door drifting into the dim interior. He hesitated and looked back again.

"It's nothing personal, Macrae, you know," Charlie said. "Don't make it hard."

Macrae slid his left palm across the inside of the door frame just as a rock slammed down on the tin porch roof with an explosion like a hand grenade. His hand was on the grooves of the pump, swinging the gun up, struggling with the breech—the last shell was stuck half out of the chamber but a poke of his finger sent it back in line and the breech locked shut behind it. Charlie was twisted around in his tracks, the nose of the pistol sniffing for Lacy.

"Yo!" Macrae called to him. "You got a quarter?"

Charlie unwound back his way, eyes brightening, trace of a smile on his face, a touch of the old excitement. A plume of orange fire bloomed from the pistol's muzzle. Macrae's whole hand convulsed in the trigger guard. Roaring, the pellets left the gun barrel, expanding and diffusing like a flashlight's beam, illuminating Charlie head to toe. A pellet creased the top of his arm like a beesting, another socked into his collarbone like a fist. As the whole buckshot load spread across his chest with a snare-drum roll, Charlie bent backward from the knees, and his hands, surprisingly empty now, clapped together before him. A spent paper shell twirled out of the breech and hovered in midair as Macrae closed the pump. Charlie's life was leaving him, projected all at once: women, drugs, and prisons, the deaths of other men; Macrae saw it all flaring out of Charlie's pale green eyes and entering his own and with complete deliberation he pulled the trigger again.

Charlie exhaled a spume of blood; his hands clapped one more time. He dropped onto his knees and then over sideways, completely prone, his face against the dead grass of the yard. Macrae threw the shotgun away from him. For the moment he didn't care if he never picked it up again. He stumbled down the steps, dizzy and stunned from the roaring noise, his shoulder throbbing from the kicks of the gun butt, and walked a loop around Charlie's corpse. Nonsense, but once he had passed the body Macrae could believe it had already entered the earth, easily as an acorn or a winged maple seed.

Lacy was standing a pace or two from the spilled bicycle, whose wheel still hummed a ghostly revolution. She was there, whole and entire. Macrae realized she must have always been there. A couple of grubby rocks still dangled in her hands. Macrae stepped not quite close enough to touch; she dropped the stones and raised her head his way. They looked as if they were seeing each other for the first time in their lives.